Since the Sirens:

Sirens of the Zombie Apocalypse, Book 1

E.E. ISHERWOOD

Introduction to the *Sirens of the Zombie Apocalypse* series.

I have plans to write nine books, or more, in this series. Come with my "everyday family" as they escape zombies, endure losses, share their strengths, and look for hope in a crumbling universe that refuses to let the lights go out.

The *Sirens of the Zombie Apocalypse* series is designed to start with the quiet dignity of a solitary woman in her kitchen and end with the ferocity of a planet-wide nuclear war. That's just a figure of speech, by the way, not a spoiler!

Each book forces that rotten door open a little wider, but this first one is very personal. It's dedicated to my grandmother. She was 104 when she passed away, and she's the basis for Marty Peters—the woman you'll meet in a few pages. Zombies don't discriminate based on age, but lucky for Marty she has a secret weapon. His name is Liam!

Welcome to *Since the Sirens.*

E.E. Isherwood

ISBN: 1522774831
ISBN-13: 978-1522774839

Fiction / Science Fiction / Apocalyptic & Post-Apocalyptic

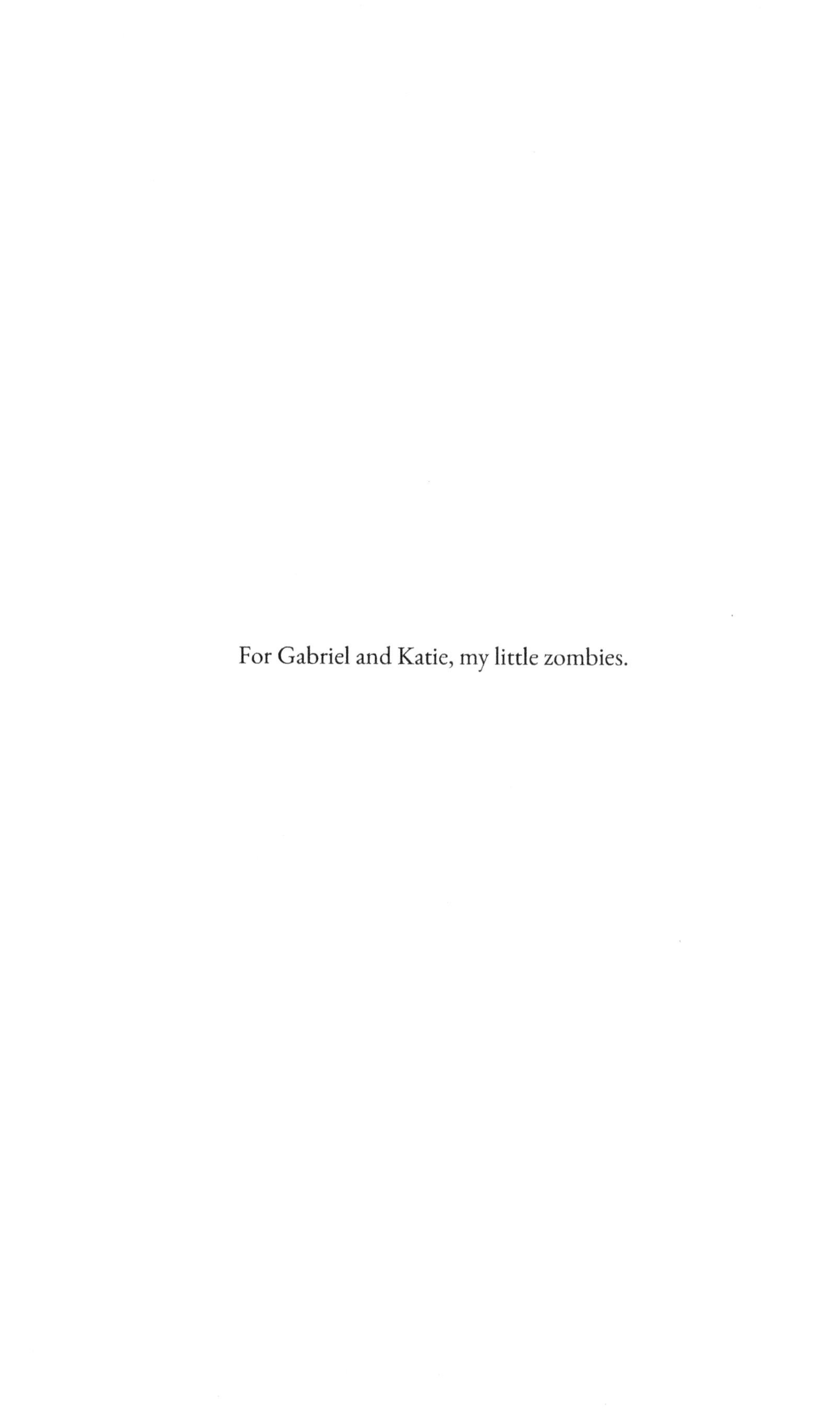

For Gabriel and Katie, my little zombies.

When the end came, those left alive found their own religion.
The dead, however, became militant atheists.

PROLOGUE: WORLD OF ZOMBIES

At fifteen, a young man with Liam's average size and weight wouldn't attempt to double-wield shotguns. Most men twice his age, even those in the military, wouldn't try it in battle. But they weren't the hero. He was. A wild-haired, lanky, scholar-athlete wannabe who just happened to be good at this one thing.

"Lock and load. I'm going in."

"Wait up," JT cried out as he fiddled with his sniper rifle. "I can't take this thing in there. They'll be on top of me before I can use it."

"I'd use the fifty-cal if I were you." Liam couldn't heft such a large weapon, but JT was built like a college linebacker, even if he acted more like the fifteen-year-old wimp he'd been before the world went to Hell.

"Nah. Not enough ammo. Used it all on the bridge. I'm going with *these.*"

Liam chuckled at his friend. The young man wore a get-up more commonly found in a biker bar—all black leather pants and jacket adorned with silver studs. His white t-shirt was as clean as when his mom set it out for him—Liam wasn't going to tell him how he knew that. Somehow, it all worked. The young man also dual-wielded his choice of weapons but with much more practical .357 Colt Pythons.

"I wish some of the other guys were here," JT huffed as he broke down the rifle and prepped the revolvers.

Liam felt the same way, but Charlie and Jacob both fell in the fight to get them to the end of their mission. He had a few extra seconds to ponder their mistakes, so he could avoid ending up like them. He looked to the sky.

They're dead. Just lousy spectators, now, he thought.

JT finally gave him the go ahead. "I'm ready."

Liam pulled at the door of the secret government base they'd been searching for, though he stopped to consider his fortune. The cure to the plague was inside, as were the men and women responsible for creating the mess in the first place. With a little luck, they could take care of them both in one glorious battle. He briefly imagined the cheering crowds of survivors. The young women anxious to thank him. Fifteen or not, he'd be heralded for this.

"I said I'm ready," JT repeated.

"I'm going!"

The expected white lab coats were there, but the people wearing them had already been infected with the Six-Sigma Virus—so named because it killed with ruthless efficiency. He didn't dwell on the tantalizing beakers and vats of bubbling green liquid. The cure—if it existed—was useless in the moment. If they had it, why didn't the scientists use it? The answer was both grim and obvious, and now those ruined people had to die, just like all the others. The New World demanded blood, not a fabled cure.

"Let 'em have it," he shouted.

He selected his first target for the automatic combat shotguns. She was a brunette in the stereotypical white ensemble which reminded him more of a mad scientist than a CDC employee. He avoided looking directly at the smiling face on her ID badge affixed to her chest.

"Die, zombie scum!"

The trigger pulled easily on both his weapons. Together they more or less removed the woman's rotting head from her shoulders, precisely the way he was supposed to do it. Of all the different types of zombies he'd read about and seen in movies, it was the one consistent piece of knowledge applicable to all of them. Remove the head, and you eliminate the threat.

JT's .357's began to sing just as something cut the power, throwing everything into total darkness. The flashes of the guns became the only source of illumination. The strobe effect led them both deeper into the dark vault. A fitting effect for the final challenge of their long quest.

"Switching to FLIR," he said with absolute calm. Despite the sick researchers shambling around—all with sickly gray skin and glowing red eyes—he didn't lose his cool. He was proud he'd been able to push the fear away and stay glued to his objective. He imagined it was how proper military men might handle the same situation.

"Got it," JT replied.

The infrared headset worked miracles for him. "Wow. That's the ticket. I can see 'em all!"

They fired at will. He and JT stuck together until the middle of the room. The tables of vats and beakers on the far side required them to split up so they could clear the room properly. He marveled at the amazing fidelity of the scene as he watched a shotgun shell forced from the breech of the weapon along with a puff of gas. The infrared mode didn't strip out any of the detail.

"This is awesome," he screamed into his headset.

He brought down several more zombies in quick order before reaching the back wall. JT came running up from his side of the room, bragging as usual.

"How many did you get? I killed ten."

Liam doubted his friend's count, but he hadn't been keeping score just then.

"What do we do now?"

JT smiled from under his IR headgear and pointed to an alcove on the back wall. "We've made it to the end, my friend. We just have to push that button, and this place will self-destruct."

"And all this will be over? This whole adventure? That doesn't seem right ... "

"Yep. We win." JT clapped him on the shoulder.

"This is all too easy," Liam responded. Easier than the bridge where they'd lost their two friends, no question there.

"Who cares. Just push it, and we can get out of here."

It probably ran on batteries because it had a little blinking red light under it. Just as you might expect of something designed to blow up the place.

He finally relented and pushed the three-inch button into the wall with a quiet click. A moment later the building began to shake. A massive door along the back wall slowly slid open and revealed hundreds—maybe thousands—more zombies in the next chamber. All of them moved toward them with the same slow zombie shuffle, shouting the word "brains" while holding their arms in front of them. They greatly desired the fresh meat in their midst. Liam had seen it before, though never with this many.

He began to reload his shotguns when a female voice broke his concentration.

"Help me, please!"

JT shared his concerned look.

"Under here," he yelled while pointing both shotguns at the cabinet door beneath the lab table.

"After you," JT said dramatically while training his Pythons on the same spot.

Liam lowered the shotguns, ignoring the groans of the horde drawing close. He unlatched the door to see a young blonde-haired woman coiled up inside. She held out her hand, and the boys helped her to her feet.

Moans and groans momentarily forgotten, Liam couldn't help looking her over.

Blonde. Tight-fitting jeans. Nothing above but a stars-and-stripes bikini top.

"We're here to rescue you," Liam declared with his best attempt at bravado.

"No, we're all going to die," she replied. "There's too many."

Liam was dumbfounded. "Then why did you get out of your hiding spot?"

He watched her blue eyes tear up, and he instantly regretted the words. Her eye sockets were messy puddles of smeared eye liner from previous tears.

"I—I didn't want to die alone."

"Oh, hell," JT droned from behind him.

"We'll do our best," he said to cheer her up.

Her smile was weak, but it was there. She had faith.

We can do this.

Zombies came in from the entryway, fell from ceiling tiles, and swarmed from the back until they converged on the trio. Each doomed warrior expended a good chunk of ammo before the zombies trapped them for good.

He had to shout over the noise. "JT, you lied. You said all we had to do was push the button. That's how we win!"

The horde pressed up against them. The two boys stood with their weapons forward and their backs against the helpless damsel in distress. Thinking it over, it was pretty near to one of the screenshots he remembered from the game's download page.

His friend sounded beaten. "I've never made it this far before. I was just making things up."

"Well, that figures."

Liam could do no more than watch as his avatar was brought down in a zombie chomp-fest. The pain was amplified because JT's character died a full second later. That would be one more point against him in their brother-like rivalry in video games.

The girl they were protecting died last.

A female computer voice filled his headphones. "Match ended. Hunter team efficiency 37%. Hunter team losses equal 100%. Player 'Meat Me in Yonkers' has maintained the rank of Rookie."

"Dang it!"

He yanked off his headphones and tossed them onto a pile of books on his desk next to the PC tower. The computer game after action screen glared at him as if to mock his purported expertise. He'd let two of his friends die early on in the simulation and failed to lead the rest of the team to victory. They'd been in a position to rescue one of the valuable non-player characters, but she died in that room same as them. JT even got more kills than him, in addition to capturing that all-important braggy extra second of life.

The distant voices of his friends came out of his discarded headphones. His volume remained turned up well beyond what Mom and Dad would find appropriate. Even great-grandma Marty would probably think it was too loud.

He snickered as he put them back on. The headphone and microphone combination was necessary so he could talk to his three friends. The wintry conditions on the county roads made it impossible for them to meet in person as they all preferred but playing online while chatting was the next best thing.

"Guys, *World of Zombies* is kinda lame. It's not nearly as cool as *World of Undead Soldiers*, which you all know also has zombies."

Left unsaid was that he'd played the other game for years. He was, in fact, a master at killing all manner of undead. Vampires. Yetis. Even zombies. But a game with only zombies was a different beast entirely, and not one he found very challenging. It took brains to fight those other beasts, as each required a particular kind of weapon or magical talisman to defeat. Zombies just stood there and died with simple bullets. The game designers made no effort to make them interesting or different.

Jacob laughed. "At least you didn't die in the middle of the game. I slipped off that bridge like a newb lord."

Liam pushed back in his chair and crossed his arms. If his friends wanted to play again he might indulge them once more, but there was no reason to stop playing his preferred game. Sure the video quality was better, and it was the "latest and greatest" from Saratov Systems—his favorite game company—but new wasn't always better.

A loud bang rattled the floor beneath his chair. The sound defeated his amplified headphones still blaring the end game credits.

He rolled his eyes.

Dad had been shopping again. He'd watched him unload the car earlier that evening after pulling it into the garage and closing the garage door. Dad proudly called himself a gun nut, and he often proved it. Not even icy streets could stop him from buying guns at auction.

It sounded as if he'd dropped some while taking them to the basement.

Internally he debated helping. He knew he should. His game was a total loss, and nothing required his butt be in his chair, but he was kind of Dadded-out at that particular moment. It rubbed him the wrong way his father would go to any length to get those stupid guns, but he wouldn't budge when Liam asked him to drive through those same road conditions to get him to JT's house for the night.

While he debated that point, his friends started up the next game. A screen asked if he wanted to join.

Sorry, Dad. I'm reeeeal busy.

He clicked the screen. "All right, guys. I'll give this one more shot. Let's go find some zombies."

In six months, the zombies would be looking for him.

CIV

Martinette Peters leaned against her oven and thought about hunger. She guessed she'd cooked tens of thousands of meals during more than a century of living, but this morning was different. She was off the script.

These days her breakfast was prepared by Angie, the nurse who lived in the upstairs flat of Marty's two-family red brick home. Bacon. Eggs. Toast. The same things she'd made for her the past two years. Every day. Without fail. But today Angie hadn't come down at her regular time and hadn't answered the intercom or her telephone. Marty waited as long as possible for her chef but soon thought about how to cook those things for herself. What was once second nature now required proper planning.

She studied the cabinets, the pantry, and her cooking dishes. Everything she needed was far above. Either she was getting shorter, or Angie had intentionally placed everything on shelves out of reach.

She walked from the kitchen, leaning on her cane. A bag of bread hung from her free hand. That, mercifully, had been within her grasp on the counter. The phone rang as she guided herself into her comfy chair. Her cane remained nearby.

"This is the Metropolitan Police Department, City of St. Louis, with an emergency alert. Violent disturbances have been reported in multiple locations within St. Louis city limits. There is a risk of injury or death to any participants or bystanders. If you hear this message, we urge immediate evacuation to safer areas. Follow instructions from city or police officials in your neighborhood. Be alert for additional emergency messages. ... This is the Metropolitan ... "

Shifting in her seat, she listened as the robocall repeated through the answering machine. She screened everything these days, responding at her leisure, if at all. Despite having many friends and relatives, she seldom had energy for chit-chatting. At 104 years of age, she assured herself it was okay to be picky.

The announcement finally ended with a beep, leaving her to her thoughts.

Well, I'm not going to run for the hills!

She glanced at the two-wheeled walker in the corner, tennis ball-swathed feet fresh and yellow—she hated using that big device. If she were going to chance an escape, which she certainly was not, she'd use the smaller, quad-footed cane sitting by her side. She despised that thing too, but grudgingly admitted it helped her get around more effectively than grasping at walls and furniture while patrolling the cozy single-level flat.

Ignoring the robocall's instructions, she resumed cross-stitching under the timeless rhythm of the wall clock. Angie would call sooner or later, and then the day would start properly.

It wasn't long after the phone alert when she heard a great banging sound from the front of the apartment. To her hearing-amplified ears, it sounded like someone had fallen down the stairs leading to the upstairs flat. Over the years, she'd heard many things dropped down those stairs, including many by her grandchildren who just loved playing on them despite her stern warnings. She had also come to know the sound of someone tripping up the stairs or falling down the steep flight. This was a case of the latter.

"Angie, is that you?" she asked, though she knew her raised voice was still too weak to be heard in the front of the house, through a wooden door.

Getting up, she patiently grasped her cane, pushing up on the armchair with her free hand. Normally it was Angie who would come down to help her when she had trouble getting out of her chair after being comfortable for too long. A quick buzz on the intercom was all it took. This time, she was able to make the transition from sit to stand unaided.

She lamented that if someone up front was counting on her to help them quickly, they were in trouble. With her hunched back and sub-five-foot stature her gait was a slow shuffle at best—foot, foot, cane. It was, however, very steady most of the time. That, at least, would give the desperately injured some modicum of hope of eventual rescue.

She hurried—in her own way—to the potential fall victim. At a snail's pace, she passed her curio cabinet and shelves of fine china in her dining room and emerged in her front living room. She steadied herself on a big armchair, then pushed off to the last stop, the interior door in the front foyer of her home.

Lord help me move.

Soft moans and scratching indicated this was indeed an emergency. She steeled herself to see the fallen victim as she opened the door inward.

"Oh my, Angie. Are you all right?"

Angie had bounced down the stairs sure enough, but a mere fall was the least of her problems. Her skin was ashen, and her eyes were bloodshot—or bloody, it was hard to tell—and her usual perfectly manicured hair was sitting in greasy knots. Her light-colored nightgown was soaked with sweat and stained with many red streaks and blotches from top to bottom. The fifty-something nurse looked almost skeletal, and her emotional state wasn't the expected embarrassment or agony from the crash, but instead...anger? Her right foot was unquestionably broken—it was pointing in the wrong direction.

Why isn't she screaming?

While Marty had scoffed at the warning on the phone, she was aware of the panic sweeping the nation and was certainly aware of the mystery Ebola-like sickness which so troubled many of her family members. They were at her flat just last night urging her to stay with them until it all blew over. She demurred, declaring she felt perfectly safe for the time being. She assured them if things got *really bad* she'd oblige them on their offer. Secretly she felt it couldn't possibly get rotten enough for her to leave. For someone who had lived through the Great Depression, World War II, Vietnam, and the War on Terror, she did not panic or scare easily.

She wasn't panicking now, but she was hasty about shutting the door.

"I'm sorry, Angie. You aren't looking right. I'll call 911 and get you some help."

Before she could get the door fully closed, Angie stuck her arm and shoulder into the void to reach for her, preventing a good seal.

"My lands!" It was as close as she came to cussing.

2

A woman of 104 wasn't going to kick or shove a person lying on the floor hard enough to get them back through an open door. It would be difficult for someone half her age, so she released the door and did the only sensible thing she could at that moment—she walked away.

Perhaps it was habit, or maybe just a little bit of panic creeping in, but she went back into her flat rather than step out the front door to the relative safety of her front porch. After several seconds, she realized her mistake and partially turned around to see if she could still slip out —and saw Angie slithering into her flat, blocking escape in that direction. Angie had an evil look she had never seen on her friend's face before, and she was struggling to get off the floor.

"Angie, you're hurt badly and aren't yourself. Please wait where you are, and I'll call a doctor."

She considered her options as she pushed herself through her home, understanding that she was likely in mortal danger. Angie was probably infected with heaven-knows-what, though it was beyond her reckoning how anyone sick or healthy could lay there with a broken ankle and not make a peep. Working her cane with her left hand, her free hand was in her pocket holding her rosary. At her age, death was never far away, and the rosary was an important reminder of the faith she always kept close, but this was not how she wanted her story to end. She needed a plan.

She could easily lock herself in any room of the house—a bathroom would be the best choice for now—but she didn't know how strong Angie might be. If she could survive a broken ankle and not complain, what if she could put her head through the thin wooden doors? The growling sounds of the sick woman behind her spurred her to continue without stopping to consider potential side routes.

"I'll just be a moment, Angie."

She walked into the kitchen at the back of the house, looking around frantically for something to help her. Her heart was beating hard at the effort to simply walk at such a brisk pace. She scanned the kitchen table, the oven area, and the open door to the basement—her great-grandson Liam lived down there, but he was gone for the day to the library. She would never be able to get down all those steps. Her eyes finally fell on her impressive collection of kitchen cutlery, and she chuckled to herself at a funny thought.

Maybe I could fight her with a knife? Ha!

Her painfully slow progress brought her near the back door, the only real alternative left. Going into the backyard was a definite option, but that would put her outside her house for who-knows-how-long. What about food, water, her pain medications, the telephone? Could she survive until Liam returned? The shuffling noises entering the kitchen made up her mind.

She slid out the stout back door, pulling it shut behind her. The exterior screen door slowly followed suit. The concrete porch was a flat, open space with a small awning overhead, providing limited shade for a few chairs and one large freestanding porch swing she kept around mainly for the grandchildren. She liked this flat for a lot of reasons, but the biggest was how few stairs she had to use. The bright-eyed Marty who moved in all those years ago never imagined she'd still be here at 104 with a disdain for steps.

She hobbled, her back starting to flare up in pain, to the closed window near the back door so she could get a look inside at her friend. She had to put her face up against the glass to see through the glare of the morning sunshine. Her cane, with its four small feet, waited patiently at her side.

Angie was right up in the window looking back at her.

Oh, my. Poor Angie.

She could see Angie had to be standing on her broken foot, banging herself against the window quite forcefully. The interior screen frame was already ripped and bent, but her greatest concern was how much pain the woman must be suffering from that injury.

She moved away from the window to consider what to do next. She ran through a Hail Mary prayer, not for herself but for the more endangered soul inside. She sat down in the sturdy armchair. She knew she'd have trouble getting back up, but there was no choice but to take a quick rest. And think.

A hedge separated her immaculate yard and well-tended flower beds from her less tidy neighbors on both sides. She saw none of them outside, which wasn't terribly unusual. Most of the kids and many of the young adults were probably inside playing with their video games or whatever newfangled technology was out these days. Or they could all be inside suffering like Angie. That image hung on the air.

"Those police called a few hours too late. I let Liam go out today without a care in the world. I need to get back inside, so he has a safe place when he returns."

It was time to save her own bacon and prevent her from becoming someone else's problem. She hated asking for help for tasks she could do for herself. Even worse was depending on others for things she *had* done herself but was physically incapable of doing now. A rescue, for instance.

I'm starting to feel old. Finally.

The tiny yard offered nothing regarding weapons—not that she had any desire to hurt Angie. If she could still hold one, a gun might be a useful deterrent. The concept of a cowgirl granny lifting a shotgun, heroically reentering the house, and chasing off the bad guy would have given her a laughing fit on any other day. Today it just made her mad.

If she were ten years younger she might be able to sneak to the front door, open it, and lure Angie out—then move around the house and through the back door. Today, just walking to the front would probably give her a heart attack and running from the angry nurse on the return trip would kill her, one way or the other.

Her eyes fell on the garage.

Can I get there?

3

She had mild difficulty getting out of her chair, but the banging on the window kept her motivated. At the far end of her small yard was her one-car garage. A small wooden structure she seldom visited these days. It had been painted a tidy white, had a sloping black asphalt shingle roof, a tiny window on the rear wall, as well as small portals on each of the sides. The walkway led down the center of the yard but snaked to the right side of the garage. When she reached the service door she made a horrible realization—the key was hanging on a wall inside her house! She had never cussed her whole life; it just wasn't her style. Instead of cursing, she prayed.

She looked into the garage through the tiny window of the door and saw sunlight. The main bay door was already open. As she made her way into the alley and through the front of the garage, she noticed almost all the garages on her block had their fronts open, many with detritus tossed on the ground as if sneezed out. She and many of her neighbors had been robbed.

Looking in, she saw the previously pristine space was a tornadic blast of her belongings. She hadn't driven in twenty-five years and didn't own a car, but Angie's should have been sitting in front of her—it had been taken. So had anything else of value. The boxes of power tools. A couple of the grandkids' fancy bikes. The snowblower.

It's June, for heaven's sake.

Looking at what was left, she had to find something which would help her get back in her house. Trash cans. Old lumber scraps. Bags of soil. All manner of car-cleaning products, lawn-care accessories, and pre–World War II shovels, spades, and other old equipment she was unable to categorize. Her late husband never gave up on a good tool.

At that moment, the emergency tornado sirens began to howl their deep and unmistakable wail. It couldn't be weather—it was a clear day. They were supposed to warn of a tornado, but mostly the trumpets sounded only during their monthly readiness tests. Even with bad hearing, the eardrum-splitting decibels from the siren tower located just around the corner were painful as they continued to wail like the devil's version of Gabriel's trumpet.

Her eye came across something the thieves had overlooked or hadn't wanted that gave her hope. Thirty feet of her past lay coiled on the floor, in the guise of a stout, braided rope with one end tied in a loop with the famous Honda Knot cowboys used to make their lariats. It was a souvenir from her honeymoon at Marvel Cave—eons ago. She and Al got the lariat from the aged proprietor of the small river cabin they rented. He liked to pretend he was a cowboy and talked about his time roping steer over in Kansas City. He wanted to give it to "youngin's" like them.

She used a rake to hook it, so she didn't have to bend down to pick it up. The braids felt good in her hands, and she savored the memories of its origin. She drew strength in the notion her husband was helping her from above. She leaned against the wall of the garage, considering how to advance her cause.

"I'll only have one chance. I'm already pooped," she said to herself. Sweat beaded profusely under her snow-white hair.

She looked around for the one other tool she thought she might need and found the long handle of a broom without the brush attached. Easily done.

Slowly, she started making her way to the back porch again. The infernal siren continued to blare, adding anxiety to her already desperate plan. At the halfway point, she paused for a rest and wondered whether she shouldn't just go out the front gate, down the narrow path between her flat and the neighboring home, and just keep walking until she found help. Forget about Angie for now and just find assistance. Lots of risks either way.

"Lord give me strength to make the right choice," she said to anyone listening. She seldom prayed for herself, but now she allowed herself to ask for help. After a minute's pause, she decided her best chance to see this day to the end was to take charge of her own problems and recapture her home. Even if she didn't live through the night, she wasn't about to spend her final hours on earth sitting on a deck chair listening to Angie claw away at her kitchen window.

"And, please, Lord, turn off those trumpets!"

4

She closed the distance to the back of her house, the rope heavy across her thin shoulders; the broom handle held tightly under the arm not working the cane. She saw herself reflected in the glass of her back window, stooped over and hobbling up the path like some elderly, deranged Calamity Jane.

She admitted she did not look very intimidating, but she was a survivor in the truest sense. She lost her first daughter in a freak car accident. A son lost to war in Korea. Financial ruin after Al died. And the *coup de grace* was breaking her hip when she was 99. This, she told herself, was a minor speed bump in comparison.

So, on she went, pulling up to the door and window. She tied off her rope and took a seat in the same chair she'd used a few minutes before. She was winded now, and her back was fast becoming a major distraction. She almost never consumed pain meds but using them after such exertion would be justified.

The plan was simple, as it had to be for a woman of her rapidly declining abilities. She would tap the window with her broom handle to get Angie's attention and draw her over there one more time. She hoped that would give her an opportunity to open the screen door long enough to push the main door, so it would open wide. From there, things would get interesting.

As with most major events in her life, this one began with a prayer.

"Yea, though I walk through the valley of the shadow of death, I will fear no evil: for thou art with me; thy rod and thy staff they comfort me."

She tried to stand up and realized her back was nearing its limits. With great effort, she did manage to stand, but this would likely be her last unassisted "up" of the day.

"As if I don't have enough problems."

Standing and wobbling a bit, she righted herself and made for the small segment of brickwork between the door and the rear window. She had the rope looped over her head, the broomstick in her left hand, and the cane in her right. Her best guess was she could just reach the window with the stick and still be close enough to the door to open it. She considered whether Angie would even hear her banging on the window over the din of the emergency klaxons.

I'll have to trust God on this one.

She let go of her cane and stood unassisted as best she could. With all her strength, she swung the broom handle with both hands. She had feeble arm strength, and her whole body was already taxed to its breaking point—but she did manage to make a satisfying bang on the window glass before the stick slipped out of her hands and rolled into the grass just off the concrete porch. It was now or never. Was it enough?

She maneuvered herself to the screen door and was dismayed to see how far open she needed it, so she could gain enough leverage to push the heavier inside door. It was taking too much time! She gave the door a push and was relieved to see it slowly swing open into the kitchen. Now all she had to do was move out of the screen door's path and close it before Angie returned from her attack on the window. It disturbed her deeply to hear such anger and pain, but it also scared her half to death, knowing she didn't have anything between her and the inside of the house but a slowly closing, flimsy aluminum screen door.

It latched shut with a satisfying click, but she felt the panic rising as Angie appeared in her blood-stained nightclothes and began flailing at the door.

My stars!

She nearly forgot what she was supposed to be doing but regained her wits enough to pull the rope from around her neck and get it into position. She had no idea what to expect of this plan, as she had absolutely no experience breaking screen doors. Would the whole thing collapse outward? Would Angie kick it open or accidentally hit the latch to open the door like a normal person? So many variables ran through her head as she stood inches away from danger.

The lining abruptly ripped near the top, and Angie leaned through the broken screen. As Angie's head poked out, Marty—city slicker or not—pulled a simple rope trick that the old proprietor would applaud unabashedly. She circled the lasso over Angie's head and pulled the loop, so it cinched around her neck. If Angie noticed it, she gave no indication as she continued trying to push through the door. She grabbed her cane and started walking as fast as her orthopedic shoes would carry her, knowing Angie was going to make it outside—if her plan continued to work.

The other end of the rope was tied to the only thing of any weight close enough to her back door—her porch swing. It was an awkwardly shaped freestanding model, and she'd seen it moved enough times over the years to know it took pretty good effort on the part of a couple of people to drag it around. If she were really lucky, it would hold Angie long enough, so she could walk around front and backtrack through her house to shut the rear door again.

Lots of ifs.

5

Angie came screaming and flailing out the door. She nearly grabbed her before being pulled up short by the rope. Angie stumbled, stood up, and lunged at her again, but Marty was silently lifting and pushing her cane, trundling forward just out of reach. She risked a glance back over her shoulder and was dismayed to see the plague-driven nurse was dragging the swing behind her, a few inches with every lunge. Angie was slightly above average height and weight for a woman her age, but the sickness seemed to give her some added oomph even as it took away some of her mass.

She made it through the front gate and started making her way along the forty-foot corridor between her house and her neighbor's. The effort made her very dizzy, and she had to lean against the brick wall while she regained her bearings and settled her vision. She wasn't very far up the path, and Angie had made it through the gate—*Forgot to close it behind me!*—dragging the swing behind her. She could hear it slide off the concrete into the grass.

The fog lifted just enough, and she was able to take one step at a time, constantly leaning against the wall to steady herself. The relentless fury of the sirens was clashing with the angry screams from Angie, making her ears ring. She was definitely panicking now, aware of the danger of falling over and knowing if she did it would be for the last time.

Angie had made more progress down the narrow corridor, with twenty feet of rope behind her linked to the swing. She realized she was going to lose this slow-motion race and fall prey to whatever it was Angie intended to do to her.

A "thunk" sound accompanied a wild scream from Angie.

The porch swing ran up against the gateposts. It wouldn't fit through. Not even close.

Marty couldn't manage even a little smile at her good luck. She could only focus on her feet below her and her hand on the wall to her right. One foot. Other foot. One hand. Repeat. She seemed to be walking through molasses.

"Lord, I don't mind if you call me to you today, but please let me make it inside, so Liam doesn't go outside again to look for me," she said softly, half to herself, half to her Redeemer.

With enormous effort, she reached the front corner of her house. She leaned to her right to view the yard, also positioning herself so that over her shoulder she could see Angie furiously thrashing against the rope and the jammed swing. No time to delay. She turned her head back to the front and began her final push to the front entrance, up the small ramp her grandson had built for her, so she could avoid the two steps up to her front porch and entryway.

The ramp had been constructed with sturdy hand railings, which provided a solid purchase on the incline, but even so, she saw stars when she finally had the door handle in her grasp. She swayed dangerously. The handle was on the left side of the door. This was it. She grabbed the latch and pushed.

It was locked!

Of course. Angie did most of the door-locking these days. The keys were inside....

Maybe I could sit a spell?

No, you old fool.

Steeling herself for one more task, she grabbed her cane—no, her cane had fallen somewhere during her escape. She looked down. She was holding her rosary with her free hand, rather than the cane.

"Now when did that happen?"

When she thought she was going to die back there, she must have made the switch from the worldly cane to the spiritual talisman to prepare to meet her Maker. She now assumed her time had not yet come and, though she devoutly depended on her faith, she depended on that cane, too.

"Looks like I'll have to do it the hard way."

She propped herself up, then dragged her body leftward along a few feet of the brick facade, leaning hard the whole way. Then she was in front of Angie's place. The entry doors for the upstairs and downstairs flats were next to one another. The handle for the upper flat was on the right side of the door. If Angie's place was unlocked, she knew the interior door was open, and she could reach her own flat. If...

She pushed the latch and pushed.

Locked.

Have mercy!

She considered sitting down and letting the end come. It wasn't suicide—forbidden by her faith—rather an honest end to a hard day.

Looking at her hands, she saw she'd scraped them good and hard in the last few minutes though she hadn't felt anything. She was really out of it. Teetering between sitting and standing, she remembered something through the dizzying haze. Angie had often complained about her front door sticking when she tried to push it open. Several handymen had been through over the years trying to fix it, but none of them seemed willing to replace the whole doorframe. They were confident each time they had loosened it for good. Later, it would stick again. Sometimes you had to push really hard on the door and depress the latch at the same time to get it to dislodge. It was no problem for the relatively young Angie, but for her... If Angie's door was unlocked, she would still have to find strength to get in.

She looked to her right—no sound was coming from the corridor. Was that good or bad? She tried the latch, giving it a half-spirited second attempt and a little shove. It would not budge. The stars were swimming dreamily in her eyes. She took a moment to lean her head directly against the wooden door and rest.

Her vision came into focus just in time to see Angie standing at the corner of the house; the rope looped around her neck, the other end hidden somewhere around the bend. The swing chair could not have fit through the gate; Angie was free of it. The sick nurse reoriented on her quarry and began closing in.

Marty had no time for a prayer. Pure instinct and perseverance drove her at that moment. She knew in her heart that door was unlocked—Angie was a trusting soul, unafraid of the outside world, going in and out with great frequency to do her chores. She grasped the latch with both her tiny, wrinkled hands while pushing with everything she had against the door. It would only work if the door was really unlocked. If if if ...

She spilled through the entryway as the sound of rage from Angie grew louder, even eclipsing the incessant scream of the sirens. Only by the grace of God did she manage to hang on to the handle, so the heavy door didn't throw her to the wood floor as it opened. Now all she had to do was close it again, but this time, physics was on her side. The door was heavy enough that as she pushed it, it also forced back the blood-stained hands that had arrived a second too late to affect its trajectory. Angie was unable to make the sharp right turn at the door jamb to put her hand into the diminishing gap. The heavy thing slammed, and she quickly double-locked it.

She didn't remember the stumbling walk from the front of her house to the rear. Couldn't remember if Angie stayed in the front or moved to the back, observing her through the side windows. She had no recollection of closing the back door and pulling the curtains shut on the kitchen window. She didn't know how she reached her bed and fell in fully clothed, shoes and all. Rosary in hand, she would barely recall the little prayer she said before finally losing consciousness.

Dear Lord. Please help Liam find his way home safely.

She fell asleep to the sound of trumpets.

THE LIBRARY

"Where's Liam? Where's Liam?"

That was the sound of his worst nightmare the past few months. Mom and Dad and their incessant, demanding, infuriating repetition of that question. It was almost like they were afraid to let him out of their sight. As if he were still a five-year-old. In a mad stroke of irony, it was the one thing that made staying at his great-grandma Marty's house bearable. She didn't ask stupid questions.

He'd run out of her house this morning as soon as possible, just as he'd done most of the previous three weeks, to find refuge among his kind online and do important things, like slaying the undead and e-chatting with his friends back in civilization. His home away from home away from home was the public library.

"I'm going to the *lye-bury,* Grandma. See ya tonight!" He reveled in mispronouncing the word library, though not to antagonize his sweet old great-grandmother. He butchered it on purpose because his dad said his mispronunciation was a special broken word that was "more obnoxious than bloody fingernails on a chalkboard."

Shouldn't tell me your weakness, Dad!

He knew his father's second most-hated word was nu-cue-lar power —but it was harder to fit into everyday conversation. So, as a sarcastic homage to his father, he continued the tradition. Today, Grandma only answered him with an affirmative nod as he walked out the door to relative freedom.

Though it broke the unwritten teenage rule of time management—awake all night and sleep all day, like vampires—today he reached the library just as it opened at eight o' clock. He wasn't interested in small talk, or chatting up strangers, so he didn't care to know the name of the well-dressed, somewhat older woman who unlocked the doors and sat behind the counter every day, but she at least recognized him with a wave. He figured it was the blue jeans and soft-drink-logo shirts he liked to wear.

"Good morning and welcome back. I didn't expect anyone today."

He didn't think to ask her why. He was anxious to avoid her and get to the computer area, so he could set up shop. He passed by with a hurried wave in her direction.

When he arrived in the technology area, the computers were still off. He turned on the PC where he had taken a seat. While he waited for it to spin up, the woman came along and turned on the half-dozen or so other computers. He could see she had a frown on her face, but he kept his nose in his phone, trying to begin text conversations with his other friends who should be coming online. Normally there would be three or four of his friends from school—a cabal that would meet in one of their homes during the summer. He was now the outsider since he was staying with his grandma in the city.

"Where is everyone?" he wrote to the lone avatar sitting on his screen. It belonged to Terrance, who had for some reason named his character "Share the Spirit" and used skins in-game with Olympic themes. Funny because Terrance never lifted a muscle to exercise a day in his life, though he was overly competitive inside the game world.

"Dunno. You have the game loaded yet?"

He wasn't in a rush to get things started since he knew he'd be at the library all day. As the computer came online, he logged into the server for *World of Undead Soldiers*, and leisurely prepared his units while he waited. His friends should be crawling out of bed and joining up soon.

He sat there fiddling with things for another fifteen minutes. He and Terrance wanted to give the other guys a chance to link up before they headed into the wilderness. It was always harder to jump in on the run.

At last, they made the call. The other guys weren't going to make it.

He thought it was highly unusual *all three* were missing, but it was no reason to cancel the engagement. He'd go out by himself—lone hero style—rather than sit back at Grandma's.

All thoughts turned to the battlefield as he and "Share the Spirit" were immediately "in it," fighting for their lives with their reduced group of soldiers.

His sense of time melted away as the game consumed him.

An hour went by when he got some texts from JT, one of his AWOL buddies.

***

"I got the guns. Where u want them?"

"Dad?"

"Oh srry Liam. That was 4 dad. Hope you guys are running 2. Like a real adventure!"

"cya"

***

Is this a joke?

The texts showed up on his phone in one blast, as if they were delayed.

He tried to reply but got a "network busy" message.

He thought about asking Terrance for his opinion of those messages, but the computer game screen was frozen. Forced to observe the real world, he felt a sudden and powerful vibration. Some of the computer monitors rattled and a couple flashed off and back on. But the important thing was the connection...

Losing the link to the internet rarely happened with modern technology and infrastructure, but when it did, it always happened at the worst possible time. A host of undead and supernaturals were arriving on his screen and the game world would continue running while his character stood there and died.

"Crap!"

He knew he'd said it too loudly in the library but looking around he saw no one he might have offended. There were no other patrons besides himself.

Even the woman behind the desk was out of view.

Suddenly, to his great delight, the screen unfroze. His character was still alive! He re-joined the battle, to the relief of "Spirit" who was getting his butt handed to him in the storm of creatures. Together, they stood a chance.

His attention was once again focused on the screen, the outage already a distant memory.

2

Another hour went by before he came back into awareness of what was happening in the real world. The lights began flashing as if the library was closing.

Not how things were supposed to go.

Without haste, he messaged Terrance in-game to let him know he had to drop out. The library was apparently shutting down early today. An expletive-laden tirade came back at him, suggesting he tell the library to stick something illicit in a dark orifice.

With a chuckle, he stood up and stretched.

Then the power went off, killing the dull fluorescents on the ceiling of the entire building along with everything else.

His primary concern was that he was glad he exited the match cleanly. His character was safe in his stronghold until he returned to the game world tomorrow, next week, or next year. If the power went out while he was in battle, he would have lost all his loot and would have returned to his stronghold with nothing. It was a major downer to have to start from scratch.

Instead of moving toward the exit, he texted Terrance an extended analysis of a portion of the adventure they'd just experienced. He looked forward to getting back together so he could check out some new weapons he'd picked up while they were fighting the beasts.

When he hit send, he got another "network busy" message. He slammed his phone on the laminate table a bit harder than he wanted.

This totally blows.

Frustrated at the intrusions of the real world upon his game time, he stood up, grabbed his backpack containing the extra laptop he kept for those times when the library computers were filled with other patrons, and headed for the exit.

When he arrived at the glass doors, he found the librarian on her feet, looking outward in silence.

"Ma'am, what happened to the power? Is the libary—I mean li-*brary* going to be open tomorrow?" he said with a chuckle.

Turning around, she looked at him like he was crazy. Liam could see she'd been crying, an unmistakable puffiness combined with smeared makeup.

"Don't you know what's going on?"

"Yeah, the power went out," he said matter-of-factly.

"Not that. I mean with the city. With Ebola. With *zombies.*"

He looked past her and her drama. Everything appeared normal; he really couldn't identify anything unusual in his field of view. He noticed nothing out of the ordinary when he walked in this morning, so he had no help there. And zombies? That was the craziest thing he'd ever heard. What would some random librarian know about zombies?

"I don't see anything unusual."

"Don't you listen to the news? NPR? Anything?"

"My dad says NPR is run by the government, so you can't trust anything they say." He was content to believe his father on this point because the few times he did listen to NPR, he was bored to tears. His conclusion was anything that mind-numbing had to be propaganda.

"Does your dad think the cable news, nightly news, and radio news is also propaganda?"

"Well, actually—"

"It doesn't matter. Do you have anyone taking care of you? Where are your parents? Can you get home from here?"

He considered the many possible answers to those questions. He decided to keep his response as simple as he could.

"I live with my grandma about thirty minutes from here." He pointed in the direction he was going to walk.

"You should take care of your grandma. Keep her from getting sick."

He looked again out the window and saw nothing to support the woman's claims. He saw the crazy look in her eyes, the smeared makeup, and her position in front of the door and absently wondered if *she* presented a threat to him.

"My grandma is 104. She's probably sitting in her comfy chair right now knitting or crocheting or whatever it is old ladies do. I'm sure she's safe and sound—"

And then to reassure his strange captor, "—but I'll go check on her to be sure, thanks for the advice."

He stepped back as if waiting for her to let him out.

She took the invitation, unlocked the door, and held it open. Once he was through, she stepped out as well, locked it, and then raced to the lone car on the lot. He heard her complain to herself about how she wasn't supposed to come into work at all today. In moments, she jumped in her car and went speeding down the street, opposite of where he was heading.

He was left scratching his head.

In no particular hurry, he began his walk. Even with the freakishly distraught woman egging him home, he didn't see anything out of the ordinary in the neighborhood; as his dad would say, she was a plain nut. He put in his ear buds and was comforted by a rock song almost as old as his father—Supertramp's "Take The Long Way Home."

Too bad I can't go to my real home.

He thought of Grandma. He had told the librarian the truth. He was absolutely certain he knew what she was doing. The same thing she was always doing. The same thing she'd probably be doing until the day she died. Sitting in that stupid chair knitting, quilting, or whatever the heck she called it.

Even though he loved the old woman, she was the most boring person he'd ever met.

3

Walking back to Grandma's was a downer. He knew it meant the day would be spent in his dreary basement living quarters playing solo games on his laptop, reading, or listening to music. By no means would he spend the day on the same floor as Grandma and risk having to come up with things to say the whole time. Too much energy required. Just because he was on loan to her this summer didn't mean he had to be in her pocket the whole time.

Ha! On loan. That's what his father called it. More like a prison sentence. A fifteen-year-old boy and his 104-year-old great-grandma had nothing in common as far as he could tell. Computers. The internet. Wi-Fi. Texting. He tried to explain all this to his technology-challenged grandma—he dispensed with the "great" in casual conversation—but she never seemed interested. Even showing her videos of fuzzy bunnies and cute little kittens evoked a "That's nice" but not much else in the way of conversation. He'd run out of ideas.

He returned again to "Where's Liam?" She was a breath of fresh air compared to the inquisitions of his mom and dad. Where are you going? Who are you meeting there? Will there be girls? Drinking? Drugs? And on and on and on. The constant nagging was part of what drove him insane and helped contribute to the massive fights he'd been having with them. No doubt it helped expedite his banishment to Grandma's. A cooling off period for everyone involved. It had already been a few weeks, and he still hadn't communicated with the 'rents. It was fine with him. His biggest worry was that he'd have to see them both on his birthday in a few weeks.

One day at a time.

His parents stopped paying for his monthly cell phone service as punishment for one of his exploits—he couldn't remember which—and they wouldn't even turn it back on as he left for Grandma's. Talk about cruel and unusual. But once there, his grandma insisted his phone be turned back on, so she could communicate with him using her standard telephone. He had to grudgingly thank her for helping him regain such an important piece of his technological repertoire. It linked him with Grandma, but more importantly, it linked him back up with his friends.

When they weren't discussing their games, he and his friends were constantly talking about horror movies, TV series about zombies and similar supernatural thrillers. They all read the same kind of books too. He was interested in lots of genres of horror but capitalized most of his non-game time by reading the classics on the end of the world: *The Stand, Earth Abides, Alas Babylon*, and countless zombie stories. Of course, he and his friends visualized themselves as the heroes who saved the world. They even played video games where they could be those heroes. When they talked theoretically about what would happen if the world did end, most of his friends believed they would meet the fall of civilization standing up, facing the harsh new realm with a cool and detached form of heroism. They would be the guys taking out the zeds, zacks, or whatever. Chasing away the corrupt government. Exterminating the barbarian cannibals. And they'd naturally be coveted by buxom women.

He was filled with bravado in front of his friends but privately wasn't so sure he was ever destined to be more than an extra when the movie version of the demise of society was filmed. Most books packed-in characters who defied all the odds to survive. Some had quirky skills that just happened to be what was needed at that particular moment—sort of like the old gardener who had used a spade for fifty years and could miraculously detach zombies from their heads with it. He knew that just didn't happen.

He accepted he would probably be an infected loser when the end came. Books only show the heroes. Everyone else gets sketched into the background as mindless extras, though each one has a story as rich and detailed as the hero. As humans succumb to infection, either by malfeasance, poor clothing choices, or just dumb luck, they instantly transferred from the "important" column to the "afterthought" column in book after book.

The guy who thinks he can shoot a crowd of infected at point-blank range.

The girl who tries to run away only to stereotypically trip and fall.

The unsupervised child who innocently lets the undead into the house. *Those* guys.

I don't want to be those guys*!*

At that moment, he heard gunshots from somewhere to his right. He yanked off his ear buds. He knew the sound from his time at the gun range with his mom and dad. You can't mistake the sound of someone banging out round after round from a gun. Then a second and third chain of rat-tat-tats started to hammer. Like it was a bank robbery or something.

At least I'd recognize the zombie uprising before some librarian.

Then a tornado siren began to howl—coming from the direction of Grandma's street. He could also hear another one starting up somewhere behind him. Clear skies were overhead. The morning kept getting weirder.

Unperturbed, he decided to drop into the little corner market for his daily infusion of whatever energy drink was on sale. It helped him survive the tedium of living at Grandma's. He'd need an extra or three if he'd have to hole up until tomorrow.

Walking in, he could see a few patrons up near the checkout counter. They were all huddled around a small radio. He immediately recognized the grating voice of the President of the United States.

"—you must stay in your homes to survive this crisis. I have authorized all governors to deploy the National Guard to their home states for the duration of this event. Local officials will follow this broadcast with instructions specific to your area..."

He wasn't entirely listening. He tended to ignore politics and political "stuff," such as messages from the president. His takeaway was that some disaster was happening somewhere and that *those* people should be doing something.

He walked to the refrigerated section to grab the drinks he needed. The display lights were off—all power was off in the store—but the large front windows helped him see into the cooler well enough. As he was staring at the selection of beverages, he heard two people arguing in the next aisle, a man and a woman.

"I told you the president was going to ruin this country! But did you listen? Noooooo."

In response, the woman made a sound with her mouth very much like she was throwing up. She then said, "You never did like him. Everyone hates the Socialists; that's why he can't get anything done for this country. You'd probably like to see this nation in ruins if it meant he got the blame for it."

He heard the words, amused at the couple's tone, but had no interest otherwise. More political nonsense he didn't need to absorb. Of more importance at the moment—what flavor energy drinks to grab. He pulled out what he needed and headed for the register.

The attendant would not peel herself away from the radio. He held up a five to cover the two cans in his other hand and slapped it on the counter, then walked away. It wasn't something he'd do any other time, but he was getting frustrated at people acting so abnormal this morning.

I don't have time for all this BS.

When he returned to the light of the day, he stood near the front door as his eyes adjusted. He watched a man sitting in the passenger seat of a car parked almost in front of the store, drinking out of some kind of hard liquor bottle. He turned and looked at Liam with sleep-filled half-closed eyes, then faced forward again as if he were on a long drive. He felt embarrassed for the dreamer but had no desire to engage or even acknowledge him. He began walking toward home.

He hadn't gone a hundred feet when he heard, and then saw, an orange sports car—a Barracuda he guessed—roaring down the narrow two-lane street from behind him as if it were on the open highway. The vehicle thundered by with enough force he was buffeted by the strong turbulence.

What the hell?

It was going the same direction he was walking, so he jumped into the street to see where it went. Several blocks down it hit its breaks hard, squealing maniacally, then banked left down a side street out of sight.

As he stood there, he felt the hair begin standing up on the back of his neck. He had a strange feeling the car was running from something evil, and the "something" was close behind him that very second...

He turned around expecting to see something horrific but was pleasantly surprised to see nothing out of the ordinary, not even other moving cars—as long as he ignored the tornado sirens. And the drunk man in the front seat of the car at ten-something in the morning. His momentary feeling of panic faded, but he quickened his step as he made for home. He downed one of his drinks almost without taking a breath and considered going back to the shop and getting one to replace it, but he had a sudden desire to get back to Grandma's. Something *was* different this morning.

THE LONG WAY

During his twenty-minute walk to the block where Grandma lived several other cars passed him, though none were going as fast as that orange one. A few times, he saw people running out of their houses to jump in cars or load junk into vehicles parked on the street. Clearly, something big was going on, but was it a tornado—thus the sirens—or what. He'd get it all sorted at Grandma's. Sure, she didn't have the internet or even a cell phone, but she seemed pretty well-informed most of the time. He imagined her sitting in her sewing chair listening to a radio right now, probably with Angie close by.

In fact, he had this image so firmly in his mind's eye it took him several moments to digest what was going on when he finally saw his grandma's house. There on the front porch was Grandma Marty. She didn't have her cane or anything—just looked like she was dragging herself along the wall near the front doors.

First, she fiddled around with her door and then slowly moved to Angie's.

He stood on the sidewalk a couple of houses away, on the opposite side of the tree-lined avenue. Several cars were parked along the curb, making it difficult to get an unobstructed view. He began moving with haste—not quite a run yet as he wasn't sure what was happening—but, he was going to help if she needed it.

Grandma stood at Angie's door, leaning her head against the wood. Was she trying to get into the wrong residence? He had never known her to have even an ounce of dementia, but this certainly seemed like a start.

He almost tried shouting over the sirens to get her attention but then Angie groped her way out from between the two houses. She had a rope or something trailing behind her, and the nurse screamed demonically when she saw Grandma.

Then things happened so fast it forced him to stop in his tracks. Grandma looked over, saw her pursuit, and then threw herself hard against that door. Somehow it opened for her, and she seemed to tumble out of view. Angie lunged for his grandma, but inertia took her wide of the target. The door slammed just in time.

He stopped and pulled up behind one of the large trees.

OK. This is Twilight Zone material.

He leaned out to look at Angie, making a positive identification that the crazed person was the same gentle woman he knew as Grandma's nurse. She was slamming her fists on the heavy wooden door, making no attempt to use her keys to get in or use the door's handle. What the hell was she doing in her bathrobe? He'd never seen her come down from her apartment less than fully dressed, with makeup to boot.

The tornado sirens made it difficult to hear distinct sounds, but he knew Angie was not throwing out words. She wasn't cussing or yelling insults; she was merely pumping out a guttural scream, something horrible and inhuman.

In a flash, she seemed to tone it down. Instead of beating the door, she appeared to sniff the air and move sideways along the front of the house—heading back the way she'd come. It looked like she was trying to peer inside, but the drapes were drawn over the windows. In a few minutes, she went back around the side of the house out of his view.

He was armed with one empty and one full beverage can, a laptop, and a cell phone. He tried to call Grandma to find out what just happened, but the number he dialed rang and rang, then the tone changed to a raw squeak. Either the network was down again, or she couldn't get to her phone. Or both. He'd have to go in to find out.

He wasn't a weakling, despite being just fifteen years old, but he knew he could never subdue such an angry person as the odd nurse who almost snagged his grandma. Up and down the street he could see people running, walking, or scrambling into cars to speed away, and the truth hit him: the president had been describing *this* disaster, not one far away. For once in his life, he wished he'd paid attention to the news.

The librarian—she mentioned Ebola. Did Ebola make people go crazy?

He took stock in his surroundings, trying to put things together. Gunshots had been a curious anomaly twenty minutes ago but were now constant as they mixed with the blare of the sirens. The specific threat wasn't clear, but he knew he needed to hunker down. Like Grandma minutes before, he had to figure out how to get into her house.

2

He was fairly confident he could outrun the nurse in a foot race, but he ruled out going right to the front door. Angie could be on the side of the house waiting to pounce, and he suspected both doors were now firmly locked. He wasn't sure why, but he felt an almost primal fear of Angie, based on her erratic behavior. She was ill, that much was clear, and he wasn't going to get anywhere near her and risk getting infected. He needed to find another way in that didn't involve Grandma opening those heavy doors again. He didn't want her infected by Angie either.

On the backside of her house, there was a small cellar door that led to the lower level, his living area. If he could reach the backyard, evade Angie, and have enough time to use his cellar key, he could get in and help Grandma do...whatever it is she's doing.

He had just stepped into the street when another car approached at high speed. He didn't know the make or model, but it was a modern-looking and sleek reddish sports car going much too fast for the small street. The driver spotted him but made no effort to slow down. He veered dangerously close as Liam lunged between two parked cars. Without thinking, he raised his middle finger, an act of defiance he knew the driver witnessed.

That's for trying to kill me!

The car sped down the street, broke hard, and turned crisply to the left at the first cross street.

He spent several long seconds checking both directions to ensure no more moving cars were heading his way. It was becoming deadly to spend any time at all out on the roads. He moved across and down the street, using the parked cars as cover to shield him from Angie. It was only a minute or so before he heard squealing tires once more. Another car was coming from behind him.

No, the same car. It was the same red sports car making another pass.

He panicked. He knew why the driver had come back.

He threw himself between two parked cars, though he figured he'd already been spotted. He had about ten seconds to think up a plan. Hiding was the best he could do; he moved off the pavement, so he was shielded from the street side. He wanted some steel between himself and the road-raging driver.

The rumbling vehicle approached and decelerated with the telltale sound of disc brakes grinding and tire rubber grabbing the asphalt.

"Where you at, boy? I've got something to show you." The man's deep voice was clear even with the siren noise.

The tone was obviously malicious. He had to know how near the car had stopped in case anyone got out and he needed to run.

He popped up slowly and tried to look through the lightly-tinted window of a four-door foreign car. He knew right away he'd made another mistake. It would have made more sense to look underneath the car. Too late. He was spotted. The car was directly on the other side. And the passenger-side door was opening.

He went instantly from squatting fright to explosive flight. He ran on the grass up the row of cars, behind the stalking red menace.

The passenger door slammed shut, and the car squealed as it backed up the street. There were at least two men inside, both cackling like hyenas.

"You can't run, boy!"

Gunshots followed. The passenger shot a handgun in his direction, sometimes hitting and breaking glass on nearby cars. Laughter followed each shot.

He ran as fast as he could but couldn't outrun a car. He was unwilling to run toward any houses, or he'd become an easy target out in the open front yards. Instead, he let the car reverse on by, and then crossed the street in front of it.

The maneuver had the intended effect of surprising the driver and shooter. The car had to stop before it could move forward again. The angry driver popped the transmission into drive, the wheels spinning forward even as the car continued moving backward. It gave him enough time to cross the street and run in the other direction. This put the shooter on the wrong side ... as long as he didn't move to the back seat.

The car readjusted, moved forward again, and caught up to him in seconds. However, the driver merely yelled obscenities at him and then accelerated down the street. The passenger continued to fire his gun randomly out his window. They'd evidently gotten bored of the game. A relief, too, as he had sprinted himself to exhaustion.

I could have been killed. On my own street!

He crouched between two cars for a few moments, recovering his wits and breath. He peeked out from behind a small truck to see if more vehicles were coming, or if the two lunatics were trying to trick him by returning on foot. But all looked safe. He moved fast to the far side of the street, watching for Angie, but she must have gone into the back again. She was not in the narrow corridor between the two buildings. He ran farther down the street, his brain in overdrive, processing the broken pieces of his day.

Internet shutting down was unfortunate, but probably not unheard of. Library shutting down in the early morning was definitely abnormal, though. President giving a speech wasn't weird, or even interesting, but taken together with everything else his speech was clearly a piece of it. Finally, his boring old street had gone bonkers with speeding cars, dangerous gunmen, and a nurse in a nightgown trying to claw at Grandma. And what was the deal with those sirens?

The tornado sirens were on a tall pole at the end of his block. He would have to walk practically underneath them to go around the corner and then back up the alleyway to the rear of Grandma's flat. He could cut between one of the many houses and save himself the longer trip around them all, but he wasn't sure if they each held hidden hazards. Now was not the time to anger a neighbor. He was freaking himself out just thinking about the possibilities. He paused by one of the large trees and took a look around.

He saw people moving as he peered through the windows of several homes on the other side of the street. They didn't appear to be sick or crazy like Angie, but he really couldn't say with certainty.

One of the big brick flats did have someone that wasn't right. The front screen door was closed, but the inner door was open. A small woman, with a pale face, cropped hair, and a light blue t-shirt was standing in the doorway behind the thin screen. From his vantage point, he couldn't hear her over the sirens, but she appeared to be howling or yelling or something of that nature.

He had to take his chance in the open and keep moving.

As soon as he stepped from behind the tree, the woman animated and began clawing and banging at the screen door. He stopped again, his mind screaming, "*Go! Go!*" but he couldn't look away. The woman viciously tore away the screen and pummeled her way through the wooden frame as the door's tiny latch tore off. In moments, she cleared the debris and was walking quickly, directly at him. A small grassy yard and twenty-four feet of roadway separated them. His brain was still screaming for him to run, but he felt like he had detached himself from his body and could only watch.

The woman, barefoot and with black stretch pants—had she just come from a yoga class?—entered the street. No cars blew through to run her over.

That would have been nice.

Her shirt was sweat-drenched and stained with large blotches of red. Blood had exploded all over one side of her head and shoulders from an ugly wound on her neck. And yet she was up and moving.

She was well across the street when he finally had enough control of his body to take a step sideways, preparing to begin running for real—

A gunshot rang out with a thunderous clap, and the woman's chest exploded outward. It didn't even slow her down.

I can see right through her! He froze again, staring. A second shot ravaged the uninjured side of her head, but she was dangerously close. Reaching for him. Another couple of steps . . .

Yoga lady tripped on the curb and slammed into the large maple tree beside him. She collapsed into a bloody pile of flesh and bones at its base.

He could only stand there, staring, completely locked up.

Another shot. Bits of wood and bark sprayed from the tree several feet above his head. That finally woke him up.

The shooter was in a house across the street. Rather than aiming at him again, the man waved out of an open window, motioning Liam to keep moving.

Are these things in every house?

He waved his thanks to the good Samaritan, then—pretending he wasn't already exhausted—ran as fast as he could.

3

He finally reached the corner of the street. He crossed to the other side and paused to look back in the direction he had come, half expecting to see a wave of crazies pouring out of the houses. Even the people fleeing to their cars had diminished for the moment. As before, if he didn't know anything was wrong, the block would look pretty much normal.

His ears throbbed from the shrill screaming of the emergency sirens above. He walked down the street with his hands over his ears, until he realized he could pop his ear buds back in. That brought it down to a constant—though still overwhelming—hum in his head.

He arrived at the alleyway. Like most streets in this part of town, the flats lined the main streets, and each block was cut lengthwise down the middle with a small, paved alley where each house had a detached garage and homeowners parked one of their vehicles. He would go up the alley to a point behind Grandma's house, see what he could see of Angie, and plan from there.

But before he could even step into the alleyway, he noticed Angie's car parked at an odd angle in the middle of the street, fifty or so feet beyond the alley. The car might be necessary for any kind of escape. It would also simplify the Angie problem. It would be nice just to run her over and be done with it.

Wow. Seriously, dude? Murder?

As he walked toward the car, he wondered if it *was* murder? Did the gunman who saved his life murder that crazed woman? Was she a person? He had read so many zombie books he thought he knew the difference between a living, breathing person, and the walking, infected zombies—but had he just seen one? Was that woman already dead when she attacked? Or just really sick? Either way, she meant to harm him. The gunman killing her had saved him. But what of Angie? Was she sick or *dead*? It wasn't so simple in real life.

The car looked abandoned, parked as it was in the middle of the street with both front doors open wide. The passenger side was closest. He approached carefully and was shocked to see the seat on that side was covered with more blood than he'd ever seen in his life. Lots of blood. Something nasty was in the space in front of the seat, but he couldn't get himself to look at it directly.

That is not *a foot.*

He looked over to the driver's side; it was mercifully clear of most of the blood. However, there were no keys in the ignition. He scanned around the outside of the car but saw no clues as to what went down there. He backed away, turned around, and slowly jogged back toward the alley.

Not a foot. Not a foot. Not a ...

4

He imagined the discussion he'd have when he finally saw Grandma. Rather than their usual rehash of the weather, he'd be able to tell her about being shot at, being assaulted by a yoga student, almost getting run over by a speeding car, seeing something disgusting in Angie's disturbingly abandoned car, and he could even toss in the bit about the librarian's freakout. Oh yeah, and he could share how he saw his 104-year-old grandma escaping the clutches of an insane nurse on the front porch of his house. "And how was your day Grandma?" he'd say with a cheery grin.

It only took the collapse of civilization to give us something interesting to discuss.

Soon he'd have that conversation. Right now, he needed to focus on how to get past Angie. He didn't have any weapons, but he would need something creative. She didn't seem to be in the mood for talking.

If it came to it, he wondered if he could kill her, or anyone. As much as he detested the idea of being forcibly assigned to Grandma for the summer, he had to admit he liked the friendly nurse from upstairs. She had a knack for talking to him—she said she had a granddaughter about his age, so that gave them a shared frame of teen reference. While they never sat down over coffee and chit-chatted, he didn't mind running into her at the house. That made it all the harder to contemplate harming her.

Glad I don't have to put Grandma down.

That thought heaved his stomach and made him light-headed for a few seconds. He had to stop walking and lean against a nearby fence pole. He forced those feelings aside; there were more pressing matters at hand. He was coming up to the correct house. The sirens made it impossible for him to hear if Angie was rooting around out back, but for once, he thanked the sirens for covering his approach as he tried to get a look into the backyard of Grandma's house. He couldn't see Angie, so he passed Grandma's garage and went to the next house, hoping to catch a glimpse of her from that angle.

Before he could get his bearings, he noticed a couple of men at the far end of the alleyway come out of a garage carrying some yellow power tools. A third man riding an ATV pulled out of the same garage. It was piled with stuff. None of them looked like they lived in the area. None of them appeared happy to see him. They dropped what they were carrying and swung rifles, so he could see them. They weren't pointing them at him, but their message was clear—beat it!

He rushed into the neighbor's yard, forgetting for a second they might not appreciate his intrusion. The men might come searching for him, but he doubted it. They appeared to be cleaning out garages, not looking for young boys to murder. The thought—and its normalcy in this situation—blew him away.

This isn't at all how I thought the world would end.

5

He spotted movement ahead. Angie was randomly walking around in Grandma's backyard, not thirty feet away. She was hidden from the alley because she was almost directly in front of the garage. Fortunately, Grandma had fences lined with many flowers and bushes, making it nearly impossible for anyone to see through without effort. It was unlikely Angie would notice him sneaking around the yard next to her. But he didn't know what to do next.

There were probably many kinds of weapons in the garages behind any number of the houses, but the thieves in the alleyway put the fear of God in him. He'd rather face Angie bare-handed than face three men with guns and an angry look in their eyes.

His only real option was to get her attention somehow, then get her to follow him out of her yard, giving him time to swoop in, unlock the cellar door, and then seal the door to keep her out. He formed a plan quickly, not wanting to delay to the point new elements wander in—such as the men in the alley, the zombies in the houses, or just trigger-happy neighbors who might think he was infected. A common scenario in the stories ...

Each corridor between the flats met the backyards at a gate. He opened the neighbors' gate on the far side of the house, intending to guide Angie around the home, down the corridor, and lock her in the wrong back yard.

But Angie had her own plans. She'd gotten over the fence somehow and was now in the yard with him. She must have noticed him after all. The noise of the sirens covered her approach as he was looking around the far side of the house, waiting to begin his great plan.

His heart bungeed into his stomach as fear gripped him. She was ten feet away before his brain kicked in—much faster than the yoga girl incident—and he began to run up the corridor toward the front of the neighbor's house. Angie was fast, not running, but sauntering at a good clip on long legs.

How did Grandma outrun her?

He rounded the corner of the front of the house, not bothering to look behind him. He knew she was coming.

Liam dashed across the neighboring front yard. If he slipped and twisted an ankle now, he would likely die twenty seconds later. Even a minor mistake would be unforgiving. He didn't want to turn down the first corridor toward the open gate of Grandma's back yard, so he ran across her front yard toward the corridor on the far side of her house. When he was safely at the corner, he finally chanced a look back to see Angie plowing across the yards with that rope around her neck.

He plunged into the final corridor, pushing his hand into his front pocket to retrieve the key he would need to open the back door. He made good time to the back fence blocking this side of the house and took a leap, hoping to clear it in one bound like a stunt man. He grazed the top and fell into the yard, dropping the key in the process—it squirted backward onto the walkway. It was now on the wrong side.

Unbelievable, he thought. He was *that guy* from every horror movie ever made. The idiot who gets killed because he couldn't handle himself well enough to make good on his easy escape.

He stood up just as Angie was rounding the front corner. She paused ever so slightly as if she had to reacquire him now that he'd been out of sight for a few seconds. Then she came for him.

His brain was finally, thankfully, firing on all cylinders. He jumped the fence in one clean bound, stooped down to pick up the key, dropped it in his pocket, and turned around to repeat the process. His feet felt like they were one-hundred-pound weights, but he managed to get off the ground. As he leaped, a hand on his back shoved him hard into the fence's top bar. His strength and momentum carried the day, and he made it across, though he had some serious scrapes on his thighs and bruised his shoulder on his second landing.

He was on his feet, not trusting Angie couldn't climb, and ran for his back door. He noticed Grandma's porch swing lying against the gate on the other side of the yard. It provided a ladder-like way to get over the neighbor's fence.

Was Angie a sly zombie?

The key opened the basement door. Without a second glance, he shut it behind him and locked it quickly. For the first time since he moved in, he was glad to be greeted by the aroma of mold mixed with mothballs. He unplugged the clothes dryer, yanked off the venting, and pushed the whole appliance, walking it across the floor until it was directly in front of the small door.

He collapsed in front of the dryer to collect his thoughts. He was scared to death outside, but now, strangely, he felt nothing. No fear. No sadness. Nothing. It was just a series of episodes culminating in him sitting here on this basement floor, alive. For now, that was all that mattered. He assumed his feelings would catch up eventually.

It wasn't long before the sirens spun down. He estimated they'd been going for an hour.

About the time it takes a dumb teenager to figure out his world is broken.

As the shock morphed into quiet exhaustion, he drifted off into thoughts of what he'd just survived. He played the morning over and over in his head as if to confirm it actually happened. In time he returned to the present and stood on his shaky legs. He had to get upstairs to check on Grandma. He angled his forearm to see his watch; it had already been twenty minutes since the sirens stopped ...

QUANTUM DECISIONS

Marty found herself in her backyard, barefoot.

It was summer. It was sunrise. It was breathtaking.

A bluebird had landed in the birdbath not five feet in front of her and was busy primping as if it didn't have a care in the world. Certainly, an old lady presented no threat. Soon other birds joined the pool party, and she just stood there like a giddy schoolgirl watching the magic of Mother Nature within those tiny creatures.

"Welcome aboard, Marty."

A man's voice. Standing right there beside her was Al—short for Aloysius, a name he hated. Her deceased husband was with her once again—or she was with him. It didn't matter which it was. It felt as if he had always been there, just like the old days. In a sense, that never changed, even after he was gone. To be with him again was wonderful, she thought.

And Al was young again! She drank in his blond hair, the deep blue eyes, and the smile that charmed her from the moment they met. He looked no older than the young man she met seventy-five years ago. He was dressed smartly in his Army uniform—just like the day he packed off to war. He knew how much she loved a man in uniform. And he was standing right next to her again.

"Pinch me, Al. I think I'm in Heaven."

"Hiya, Marty. How ya doin'?" The Jersey drawl was exaggerated as he did when he was trying to impress her. And he called her by her nickname too. She really hated her full name just as much as Al hated his.

"You aren't in Heaven, but I know how you feel. It's great to see you again."

She looked around. Everything was so perfect; it *had* to be Heaven. But if it wasn't—she had a sudden fear that if this wasn't Heaven, it might be ... somewhere else.

"You aren't anywhere bad. We're merely taking a stroll in your mind. Your recent trauma has...opened new doorways. This is a way to reunite and look ahead. Are you ready for what comes next?"

"What in Heaven's name are you going on about?"

"The plague. The infected dead. The chaos. Are you ready to help your family survive this thing or not?"

"Al, my love, you might not have noticed, but I'm 104. My days of doing much of anything important are well behind me."

"Said the lady who single-handedly fought off a horrifically infected woman who was once her nurse. Not many people would have been able to survive that. You're a fighter. Have been since the day we met. That was amazing how you remembered that old rope."

"I felt your presence helping me figure it out."

"My dear, you figured that out all by yourself."

Her mind had to be playing tricks on her. Her religious beliefs were very strong, and she didn't believe in ghosts or spirits or anything supernatural walking the earth. But she desperately wanted to believe this was real. That *he* was real.

"What of poor Angie? Is she still alive?"

"I don't think so. I think her soul has moved on. Her, and many like her, are succumbing to this sickness."

They prayed together. She and Al. Just like the old days. Somehow, she was on her knees, and they both prayed to the Creator for guidance. When they were finished, Al took her hand and helped her back up, and they walked over to the patio to sit together as if it were just an average day. It could have been any day from among the 70-plus years they shared together. If it wasn't Heaven, it sure felt like it to her. But it also made her sad to sit there with him, knowing he couldn't be real.

"But I'm real enough, my dear. I'm here to help you face this challenge. People out there are going to need you. Liam is out there right now. He's young and reckless, but you know, deep in his heart, he would stop at nothing to protect you. He's probably riding a fire truck on his way here right now."

They laughed together.

"But why would anyone risk their life for an old woman? It doesn't make any sense."

Al had a twinkle in his eye when he looked at her but said nothing else on the matter.

They sat there for a long time, chair next to chair, hand in hand. She didn't want it ever to end but knew it would.

"I have to go, and so do you, my sweet Marty. I wish I could tell you everything is going to be all right and that everyone you love is going to survive this catastrophe. But you've seen outside your window. Things will get worse. Then they will get *much* worse. The sick will get sicker, and the survivors will become more and more desperate as their reality crashes. You have to look deep in your heart to help your family get through this. You're very special—that I'm here talking to you tells me that. You can help them. You can help everyone."

"I'm an unlikely hero. I can barely stand up on my own anymore. Someone is going to be saddled with taking care of me ... "

"You don't give yourself enough credit. In another universe, you passed away peacefully in your sleep today. The opportunities for you in this one are still endless. You could live to be 120!"

She was full of questions, but at that moment, a wounded raven dropped out of the sky and landed hard right in the birdbath, chasing the songbirds away. Its head was covered in blood as if it had been digging inside something ... fresh. The dripping blood turned the pristine water red.

"That's curious. I'm so sorry you must endure this filth."

"What caused this disease?" She asked him, as he got up and pulled her out of her chair.

"My love, you were always whip-smart. That was one of the things I adored about you, and still do. That's the right question but the wrong time. The really important question right now is how can you *survive* the disease?"

"OK, how do we—"

2

"Grandma!" Liam was not quite shouting, but loudly whispering, if such a thing was possible.

He ran up next to her bed and was comforted to see she was alive. She had been mumbling in her sleep as he approached. He tried not to think again of the possibility she might have been dead. Being alone scared him more than the plague right now.

"I'm so glad you're safe, Grandma. Things aren't right outside."

He briefly considered mentioning he saw her out front struggling to get away from Angie, but something made him avoid the subject and instead focus on his tense encounter with the impaired nurse.

"I ran into Angie, and she chased me around the house, but I managed to jump the fence and get inside the cellar door before she could touch me. She has some kind of sickness."

She gave him a clear-eyed look but continued to lay on her bed in silence. She was still fully clothed, shoes and all. She was holding her prized rosary, which wasn't unusual, but both her hands were on her chest grasping the string of beads and its crucifix as if she had lain down and never expected to wake up. It was very disconcerting.

He watched her for a moment, expecting some sort of reaction, but she remained silent.

He didn't push the issue.

"Well, I walked back from the library, and it's just as crazy everywhere else as it is in your yard. There are speeding cars, people shooting guns"—he left out the bit where they were shooting at him —"and sick people running through the neighborhood. Oh, and there are thieves rifling through garages in the alleyway."

No response.

"Grandma, do you know what's going on?"

She had dozed off again.

He removed her shoes, considered trying to get her under the covers, but instead found a comforter and threw it over her. *She must be really bushed to nap when so much was going on outside*, he thought, but understood her advanced age gave her the right to sleep whenever she dang well pleased.

I'll just wait until she wakes up, and then we'll figure this out together.

The hours ticked away.

He listened at the windows. The city outside was in full-on collapse the whole time.

3

He spent much of the afternoon resting from his ordeal getting home. If he wasn't checking in on Grandma, he was fidgeting with the radio, trying to get news about what was happening. Other than the emergency alert message—playing on all stations—there was no useful information forthcoming anywhere on the dial, other than "Find safety."

As the sun set over the city, he checked the rechargeable flashlight he found in Grandma's cupboard. His father was a bit of a type-A and had insisted she had a fully stocked larder at all times, as well as a stash of survival gear such as flashlights, sewing kits, fishing kits, and all manner of camping supplies. He also made sure she had a high-quality toolbox with an appropriate quantity of quality hand tools. He told Liam he knew Grandma would never use any of them, but anyone who was watching over her or helping her out would have everything necessary. Dad often dug into the tools while fixing things up in the house.

As he was looking things over with his bright flashlight, he wondered if he himself was a piece of equipment in Dad's toolbox for Grandma? Did he send him here to protect her? Was he that smart, or just lucky? He always seemed to have a way about him that said he was looking ahead to what may come. Like buying insane amounts of ammo when it went on sale. Mom always said he was crazy but never made a serious effort to dissuade him from purchasing his "life insurance," as he called it. It felt unnatural to ascribe any positive qualities to his father, given their recent falling out, but he knew Dad did right by Grandma at least, giving her these supplies. Now he had a fighting chance to help her.

So, what was he going to do? Hunker down with Grandma inside her house? It seemed the most obvious solution, given her advanced age, and the hostility he'd found on a simple neighborhood walk. He heard the gunfire outside, and the men ransacking garages didn't inspire much hope in things staying friendly on the block. No wonder that man who shot yoga lady was perched in his window with a hunting rifle. Staying home and riding things out was a plan, but probably not a good one.

The other option was getting Grandma out of the city or at least somewhere safer than this house. Where could they go? He was just a kid during Hurricane Katrina, but he had a vivid recollection of the people stuck in the New Orleans Superdome. Were St. Louisans lining up downtown at their football stadium this very minute? It didn't seem like a good idea to have so many people in one place with a disease going around.

Unless the radio broadcasts started passing along useful instructions, the window for timely help was closing quickly.

He glared at the radio. "Enough with the 'waiting for instructions.' Just tell us what to do," he muttered.

He considered getting her out to Mom and Dad's house. Would they be pissed he took Grandma on an underage car ride? She hadn't driven since the 1980s, and probably couldn't even reach the pedals anymore. If they did drive out of the city, it would have to be him behind the wheel. On the other hand, maybe Dad would drive into the city. That would solve his problems by handing the responsibility to his father, but something about that notion didn't sit well.

Was there somewhere better to drive her? Maybe over to Illinois? It was a shorter distance in terms of time spent in the crowded city compared to driving south toward home. Once over the Mississippi River, it was open country. At least they could avoid the plague victims over there. The big problem was Grandma couldn't just live in a car or tent somewhere eating baked beans until things got back to normal. Of course, he could—

He hesitated to finish his thought but knew he had to look at all options.

I could just leave her.

It sounded harsh as he thought it. Could he leave Grandma on her own? What if he told himself he was going to get help and then come back to rescue her? Even as the thought entered his mind, he knew he would probably never come back once he was out, especially if things were worse out in the wider world. Maybe if the military settled things down ...

Leaving Grandma would free him to travel light and fast, but the idea of ditching her simply for expediency was disgusting.

Oddly, he thought of his father at that moment. He knew his dad would do everything in his power to save the woman, and he knew it would let his dad down tremendously if Liam walked in the door saying he left Grandma to fend for herself because "she was inconvenient."

Oh, great. I'm now my father.

But, he had to admit that sometimes—just sometimes—Dad got things right.

He was startled from his reverie by a presence in the doorway. She was awake at last.

4

"Grandma!" He ran over and gave her a hug before he knew he was doing it.

"I'm happy to see you too, Liam. I think we're in a bit of a pickle together."

He filed that away as the understatement of the year. Gunshots nearby accentuated the issue.

"Help me over to my chair, if you would. I'm still a bit wobbly from my—" she hesitated as if deciding to expand her thought. "—fainting spell. Those tornado sirens nearly made me jump out of my shoes."

He helped her, then sat down nearby and began speaking in the nervous cadence of someone who has been waiting a long time to talk. He told her about the walk home, in all its detail.

"Whoa! Take a breath. Are you saying someone shot at you? Are you OK?"

He forgot to edit that part out.

"How long have I been sleeping? It's dark outside. Is this still the same day?"

"You slept through the afternoon. I've been getting a bunch of stuff together in a backpack, so we can escape. I've just not figured out how to travel or where to go."

She was thoughtful for a few moments.

"OK, Liam. I want you to get out of the city. You can escape before it gets too bad."

Here it was. He recognized she was giving him his out. He could walk away with her blessing, and it would be a logical story when he reached Mom and Dad's. "She ordered me to go!" He turned it over in his head. Looked at it from multiple angles. But always, he saw his father shaking his head. Would Dad leave her at the most desperate hour like this? Would any man?

Hell, no!

"I'm sorry, but I can't leave you. We have to get out together or stick it out here until it's safe again."

"You know that doesn't make any sense. I'm an old woman. I'll probably be dead before you know it, and then you'll be stuck here after things have gotten so bad you can't think of leaving. You have to get out while you still can."

"Grandma, I'm not leaving you. My dad would never leave you. My grandpa would never have left you. Great-Grandpa sure as heck wouldn't have thought of abandoning you. I'm staying."

Grandma nodded, giving him a grim look.

He wondered if she was proud of him for making his decision. Or was she disappointed he was putting himself in danger at her expense? She offered no clues.

"Well, then," she said, "we have to decide what we're going to do to survive. I'm afraid staying here could be a problem. If there are robbers about, we won't have much hope of stopping them from coming in, and the sick people like Angie aren't going to make getting out of the house very easy either. The police said we have to evacuate to safer places but didn't say where to go that was any safer than here. The most obvious is somewhere out in the country where there aren't as many people. Maybe your mom and dad's place?"

He was proud he had come up with virtually the same ideas. Getting to his house outside the city did seem the most sensible plan, even if he did have a little fear of showing up after illegally driving across town. Many of the miles he'd logged in pursuit of his learner's permit had been driving Dad to Grandma's, so he knew at least one route home fairly well.

"Can we take Angie's car? I don't think she'll need it. It was parked on the next street over. Not sure why she put it there, but it was covered in lots of blood and had a—" he grimaced—"a foot on the floor. I think someone stole it from the garage—the car, not the foot. Or maybe she was sick while driving home."

He paused as they both sat in thought, then continued, "Also, there are no keys inside it. I checked because I thought about driving it back here."

They looked at each other with sudden realization.

"We have to go up into her flat and find a spare set of car keys," Grandma said without enthusiasm. He guessed she was worse off than she admitted about losing her friend.

5

They agreed to spend the night in the flat. For Grandma, this gave her time to recuperate after her "scare" with the sirens. For Liam, it was a chance to pack up everything he would need to help get them out of the city, such as her bottle of ibuprofen, some water, her walker, and a few bites of food. Just enough for a long drive through the inevitable traffic.

After packing the essentials, they sat down to eat a heaping dinner of spaghetti and meatballs—his favorite. If they were leaving, it made sense to try to use some of the remaining food. The electric was out, but the gas for her old stove still worked.

Preparing his backpack was initially exciting—a "real adventure" his friend had texted him earlier in the day—but as he realized they were in a true emergency, with real bullets, his enthusiasm withered. Now he wasn't relishing going outside one bit. He was quietly moving the long strands of pasta on his plate, hardly eating them. That seemed to get Grandma's attention.

"Eat, Liam. You'll need your strength."

He looked up and resumed eating with a little more zest.

She began talking again, her tone more somber. "Liam, I want to talk to you about something important. I know you and your family get set in your ways, but I'm afraid for your soul. You need to think about going back to church."

Inwardly, he groaned. He knew she lamented the choices of his family to stop going to church every Sunday—his mom and dad often talked about it—but he saw that as extra free time he didn't want to give up. Sunday services were a bore that he dreaded each time he went. He was unwilling to make promises to her based solely on the mysterious disruptions outside. Surely the government would get things fixed, and everything would soon be back to normal. What then? And was it right to profess faith in God only because you need something? How wrong would it be to tell her he found God, but not really mean it? He saw this as a massively complex question his brain was unable to process with spaghetti hanging off his lips. He felt the shadow of silence growing longer. Something needed to be said.

"I'll think about it, Grandma. Really. I will."

That should do it.

Shoveling the last of the noodles into his mouth, he focused on eating, hoping to indicate the conversation was over. He felt her hard stare, but she passed some toasted ravioli rather than push him on his vague response.

He was thankful she dropped it, though it made the rest of the evening a bit awkward.

Before she finally went off to bed, she summoned him to the living room. "I want you to go downstairs, way in the back in the farthest corner and look for a black plastic box up in the rafters. It's something your father put there for me."

As instructed, he made his way into the dark basement, struggling even with his flashlight to weave through the piles of old junk his grandma insisted be kept down there. Not one to let go of old stuff, she had quite a collection of aging rocking chairs, long-since-replaced light fixtures, and many pieces of furniture, tools, and equipment hoarded by her and great-grandpa Al.

And there in the corner, high above everything else, was the promised black box wedged up into the rafters. He had to use an old walking stick to poke it from its perch and make it fall into his waiting hands. The box was surprisingly heavy. He caught it one-handed, dropped the walking stick, and wrapped his other arm around the box as he balanced himself to keep from dropping it.

Pass completed, touchdown! And the crowd goes wild!

As he walked up the steps with the box, he had a pretty good idea what it was. For years, his father had taken him to the local shooting range to practice with a variety of weapons. First, it was BB guns, then airsoft guns, and finally the famous .22-caliber rifle. From the box's size and shape, this was clearly a container for handguns: roughly sixteen by sixteen inches and eight inches thick.

He set it up on the coffee table in Grandma's living room. Using a small light, she produced a key that undid the safety lock securing the container. It popped open and, just as he had suspected, there was a handgun inside. Two, in fact, packed with gray insulating foam inserts to keep the contents from shifting inside.

Picking up the first gun with both hands, Grandma placed it on the table.

"You probably didn't think your old grandma knew anything about guns, eh?" She was smiling as she said it.

"This is heavier than I remember. This is a Ruger Mark I Target .22. The other one is identical. Your great-grandpa bought both of these way back before you were born. There had been a break-in on our block, and Al told me he wanted me to be ready in case something like that ever happened again."

She sat back in her chair as she continued.

"Oh, those were the days. Simple times. We took these guns out to the country a few times, and I even shot one. Can you believe that? Got pretty good too. But, like so many things in life, it just became too much trouble to practice, to maintain them, to think about them. Someday I'll tell you about my lasso rope that fell into similar disuse." She chuckled a little at her own joke.

"Anyway, a few months ago your dad was here telling me I needed to be prepared for anything that might happen in the city—you probably don't remember all that rioting business last year? I told him I was fine and that I even had two handguns. Well, he was not impressed. He had me show him where they were, then he took them and said he was going to clean and service them to make sure they were working properly for me. The next week he had them both back in this case, with this box of 1,000 rounds to go with it. I'm sure he knew I would not be able to use these anymore, but he told me where he was going to put the box, and he said it would be there 'in case of emergency.' I guess he was pretty smart about that."

He eyed the shiny black objects sitting there. In the darkness, he could only see the harsh lines of the Mark I, but he knew it well. In fact, he was beginning to believe his father was smarter than he ever let on. How else could one explain that Liam had spent considerable time training on a Mark I with his dad? He never thought to ask him where it came from, but it sure seemed likely he got it from Great-Grandpa too. And now, at this critical moment, he would be carrying the same model. Did this make him the gardener with the deadly spade?

Dad always said the .22 was the best training round because it was so cheap and had very little recoil. He said Liam would eventually graduate to more powerful rounds, but if a person could master the . 22, all the others would fall in line. It was all about stance, awareness, and a steady arm. Plus, the consequences of breaking any of the cardinal rules of gun handling was minimized during the learning period with the tiny round. He assured Liam it was still quite deadly, of course; assassins had used the small and quiet caliber to good effect for many years.

He never pushed for bigger guns because he loved going out and "plinking" with the little one. At least, he used to enjoy it. Lately, his dad would drag him to the range whether he wanted to go or not. Looking back, he realized he was acting like a whiny baby each time he complained he didn't want to go shooting.

I didn't want to go with him.

Now he looked at them with a silent appreciation for the lessons he'd been taught.

"I hope we don't need these, Grandma."

"Me too."

"Why don't you hit the hay, and we'll get started at first light. I'll be sleeping right out here on the couch. I hope you don't mind that I don't sleep downstairs?"

"Not at all. Why don't you keep one of these by your side from now on?"

He picked up the gun. Felt the weight. There was no mystery to it. It was just another item in the toolbox pre-positioned by his father.

He couldn't help but feel a longing to see his dad.

A distant explosion faintly rocked the items in Grandma's china cabinet.

"I can't wait to see the sun rise again," he said, as much to himself as to her.

"I'll pray for us before I go to bed."

"Thanks Grandma." He was an agnostic—didn't know what he believed—but was respectful of Grandma's overwhelming faith. "And I meant what I said about considering going back to church."

She gave him a kindly smile, turned around, and was slowly off to her room.

The last thing he remembered of that night was the sound of a car speeding down the street at high speed, followed by the unmistakable sound of squealing tires under extreme braking. He held his breath waiting for the sound of an impact, but it never came. Thirty seconds later, he remembered to breathe again.

He didn't get any quality sleep, but it did serve as a deep breath before his upcoming journey. He wondered if it was destined to end in extreme braking? Would he and Grandma meet their demise as raw sounds in someone else's bedtime story?

He drifted to sleep while jumping fences—Angie close behind.

ANGIE

Liam woke up exhausted. When he did sleep, he'd had horrible dreams of zombies, lots of running, and pulling the trigger on a gun that would never fire as he was overwhelmed by plague victims.

The actual gunfire, speeding cars, and screams from nearby houses insured his slumber was sporadic all through the night. He also heard a big explosion nearby but was unable to pull himself out of his comfy sofa cushions to check it out. He was glad to get things moving at the first sign of light outside.

He went to Grandma's door and found her already up and sitting in a comfortable chair.

"I'm an early riser." She never complained. "Two houses behind us blew up last night and burned to the ground. I watched to make sure the fire didn't spread."

"Did you get any sleep?" he asked while peeking out her window.

"Oh, I got enough. I slept most of yesterday." It was true enough, but not really a straight answer. Nothing could be done now. "I made you some eggs and bacon. Have to get rid of it."

He wasn't a morning person or a breakfast person, but he took the time to shovel down the home-cooked meal.

"Sorry for eating so fast. I just want to get up there and get it over with."

"I understand. I can make you plenty more if you're still hungry."

"No, Grandma, but thanks. You stay here, and I'll be right back. Shouldn't be that hard to find Angie's keys up there."

She gave him a little salute and watched him walk away. She said she would conserve her energy and stay in her chair to wait for him. "Be careful," she added.

"The zombie from up there has already come down," he replied, then paused. He looked back and said, "Sorry, I meant no disrespect." He hurried to the front of her flat, through the access door to Angie's stairwell, and up the steep flight. The door at the top was already open, giving him access to the upstairs living area. He stepped around a puddle on the dim landing.

The room was shadowy because the drapes were thick and dark. He didn't have his flashlight with him. The floor was covered with debris, so he had trouble moving to a window to let in some light. When he finally did pull back the curtains, he was stunned.

Blood. Lots of blood.

There were piles of clothes scattered on the floor, along with sofa pillows, a tablecloth, and smatterings of shoes, purses, and other accessories. It appeared as if Angie's entire wardrobe had spilled out onto her floor and got drenched with blood.

He shuddered to think of Angie bleeding so bad, knowing she was still walking around somewhere outside. It didn't seem possible any disease process could produce such horrible results.

Is she really dead?

He'd read books with many different definitions of zombies. Some were back-from-the-dead "undead." Some were the recently deceased; they reanimated while still warm but remained clinically dead. Some were alive but infected with something that made them as good as dead. Would the people walking around his neighborhood fit into any of those neat boxes?

He still had a job to do in the apartment, and he began working his way around the edges of the room where the blood was absent, and some semblance of order remained. He could still detect some of the personality of the woman who, until recently, was someone he admired.

He found a picture of Angie with her granddaughter—a bubbly blonde with her arms slung around her grandma, giving her a big hug. He picked up the simple desk frame to get a better look in the low light, deliberately turning away from the central part of the room with all the gore on the floor. He wasn't without feelings, but true empathy didn't come naturally to him. However, the events of the last twenty-four hours had awakened something urgent inside him—he suddenly, desperately, wanted to know if the girl in the picture was safe.

After a deep breath, he resumed his circuit of the main living area. He tried to think where the normally organized woman would put her car keys in her home. His keys were always in his pocket or on his nightstand, so he thought to check the bedroom, but turned up nothing.

He walked back out the bedroom door and noticed Angie's cat was hiding amongst some of the clothing on the floor. Not in the middle of the room, but near the edge of the cyclone of destruction. The little guy was probably scared to death. He moved to kick off some of the clothes that were on top of it—and saw with horror that the cat was not only dead but lying in a pool of blood with most of its insides ripped out.

Liam threw up.

Standing there trying to recover, he noticed the keys hung on a hook right next to the doorframe on the way *out* of the apartment. If he'd thought to look when he came through the door, he could have avoided this whole mess.

He grabbed the keys from the hook and rushed out the door toward the stairs. Then ...

2

Marty heard the sound of someone falling down the stairs. It had been a scarce twenty-four hours since the last person fell down those stairs, so there was no mistaking the sound this time.

Liam had gone up into Angie's apartment to retrieve the car keys, but she hadn't considered whatever made Angie sick could have still been up there, waiting to pounce. Maybe it was something simply floating around in the air as a pathogen. What had she done? What kind of caretaker was she?

The front room's door was wide open to the stairwell. If Liam was now sick, he could come right through, and it would all be over for her. She felt paralyzed with indecision. Try to close the door? Do nothing? She hated that it was such a dumb mistake.

She knew she couldn't just sit and wait to die, so she repeated the previous day's motions—pushing herself out of her chair, grabbing her walker, and trundling through her house until she found herself once again near the door to her neighbor's home. She was certain Liam was lying just around the corner.

Putting on a brave face, she looked out; she wanted to see Liam before she shut the door on him forever.

She hadn't even considered the possibility he simply fell down the stairs by accident, but that appeared to be what happened. She could see the blood on the bottom of his sneakers. He was knocked out but breathing normally in the early morning light within the foyer.

With that realization, all the strength she felt drained out of her. It was a profound relief to be sure, but now she was an empty, weak shell, as all that nervous energy dissipated. She needed to sit down. She managed to make one quick detour to grab a comforter from her sofa, walk it back to Liam, and drape it as best she could over him. She didn't want him to catch a cold from a draft on the open floor.

She scraped her way to the sofa, turned around, and plopped onto the cushion. Her slight frame scarcely made a dent in the fabric. She let go of her walker, letting it stand by her feet.

I'm not even half the woman I used to be.

It was a common refrain in her mind lately. She knew her days were numbered. The years left to her were probably less than the fingers on one hand. She no longer played the denial games of her younger self—she only spoke the most brutal and honest truths to herself.

"Oh, Liam. I'm so sorry your mom and dad left you here with me. I'm sure they're thinking the same thing right about now. They thought they were doing me a favor by putting you in my care. Giving me someone extra to help around the house. Someone to talk to. Someone to care for. Everyone needs that." She sighed deeply with exhaustion in both body and spirit.

"If you were with your parents right now, I would probably just sit in my chair until the end."

Looking at the crucifix on her wall, she wondered seriously if that was the attitude she should take. Her Christian upbringing taught her to care for those less fortunate, stay strong in body and soul, and enter the Kingdom of Heaven after a life well-lived. Nothing could have prepared her for this situation. Plague. Chaos. Sick people. What does the Bible say about surviving the end of the world? Sure, Revelation was replete with end-of-world imagery, but it was no guidebook for how to endure it.

Was it suicide to knowingly stay put, acknowledging survival in the coming storm was impossible? Just cower in the disintegrating neighborhood until the food and water run out. Then the end would be quick.

Isn't it also certain death for a woman my age to go into *the storm?*

Even several minutes of prayer brought her no closer to an answer.

She weighed her chances of staying in the house by herself, sending Liam out without her. She could survive for a week or two under the best of conditions. She had plenty of food, thanks to her well-prepared grandson—Liam's father—but she knew it was only a matter of time before hungry and less prepared neighbors began scavenging. It wouldn't be hard to take from the oldest lady on the block. That says nothing about thieves or brigands from beyond the neighborhood. Sick people like Angie would also ensure she could never leave again. Staying or going, being on her own was certain death.

Thinking of Liam passed out on the floor in the next room also gave her more to worry about. If they went out into the city, she would be slowing him down to the point she would surely endanger him. She couldn't even manage him here in the house. What would she do when people, plague, and the sick made life difficult for them? There was absolutely nothing she could contribute.

I can't even shout anymore.

Tired, she stared off into space for an indeterminate amount of time before she heard Liam stirring.

That brought her back to the present and the question she still couldn't answer.

3

Liam was lying on the floor at the base of Angie's stairs when he came to. Grandma had tossed a little blanket on him, or at least he assumed it was her, though she was nowhere to be seen. From his position on the floor, he was looking up the stairs. His headache let him know the full story of his rapid descent.

Yep, I'm that guy.

He slowly sat up, anticipating a pounding headache. Fortunately, it wasn't as bad as he feared. He remotely considered everything that could have happened on his way down—broken bones, broken neck, even death—and felt pretty fortunate. He wondered if dialing 911 would reach a live person anymore.

He tried to make his way to the first riser, so he could sit in an upright position and take stock. Next, he stood to test his legs. He felt a little dizzy, a little achy in his noggin and along much of his right side, but overall, he was fit for duty.

I got the keys!

He moved back into Grandma's house to find her sitting on the big sofa. She looked very tired when he first saw her, but when she saw him, she flashed a big smile. The warmth returned to her demeanor.

"I'm so sorry, Liam, I shouldn't have sent you up there. I wasn't thinking about your safety."

"Don't worry, Grandma. It was my fault I slipped on ... something and tumbled down the stairs." He looked away from her as he remembered what he saw upstairs.

"Do you want to know what I found up in Angie's apartment? Besides the car keys?"

"Oh, I guess so, since you made the effort to go up."

"Well, there's a *lot* of blood. And tons of her clothes were in the middle of her living room. And her cat ... was no longer alive. But mainly ... blood. I couldn't tell if it was hers. It was kind of gross, which is why I ran out and fell."

She nodded solemnly, "Were there any clues as to how she got sick?"

"Dunno. How do people normally get this plague? Sneezing? Coughing? Sharing germs?" He hesitated for fear of voicing the one method he hoped would never prove true. The most common *fictional* method for people to become zombies—biting.

"Um, Grandma, did Angie look like she'd been bitten by anything? Maybe her cat?"

Or maybe a human ...

"I'm afraid Angie was so bloody; I really didn't see any one place where she might have been bitten. She was just covered all over."

He hadn't been looking for bite marks on his walk home. Now he couldn't even remember the color clothing the yoga girl was wearing, much less if she had bite marks on her. The adrenaline rush and confusion had clouded his memory. He remembered the bloody look of her eyes, and it matched the blood-drenched stare Angie gave him.

"Grandma, do you think we should leave? This disease seems real bad."

She told him about the message on her answering machine, "It said to seek safer areas. The message didn't say to hunker down and wait for authorities. It didn't say the army was coming to help. It didn't even suggest order would ever be restored. And then those tornado sirens blasted for an unusually long time as if to amplify the severity of the warning. The hour-long blast was a big shout to get out, Liam."

She paused to let that sink in.

"The phones are dead. Radio only loops the president's message. I don't think help is coming, and it's going to keep getting worse in the neighborhood if we stay here. Yesterday they were robbing garages. Tomorrow they're going to start robbing homes."

He knew she was right, even though he really wanted to stick things out in the safety of the house. Going back out into the growing chaos wasn't something he relished. But his embarrassment on the steps proved even his own home could become a deathtrap. He considered whether just breathing the same air up in Angie's apartment had exposed him to whatever made her sick.

"Grandma, I was packing last night, so most everything is ready. I was really hoping we'd wake up and things would be getting back to normal, and we wouldn't have to go anywhere, but it doesn't seem like that's going to happen."

The sounds of the neighborhood had begun picking up as the sun rose and hadn't slowed down once it was well in the air. First, it was just distant gunfire and squealing tires, the same as most of the night. Then it started to increase in frequency and volume as if it were getting closer. Some gunshots seemed very close. And the screams. Those were picking up as well. Just getting to Angie's car could be a challenge if things got much worse.

"OK, Grandma." He reassured himself. "We have to get our stuff and get out of here."

He grabbed the backpack he prepared and staged it by the front door. His most precious items were the two handguns. One he carried in a holster inside the belt and waistband of his pants. The other, along with the ammo, he stuffed into his pack. He would have to carry everything because Grandma wasn't able to lift anything but her walking cane.

He took a minute to consider his plan. First, he had to find Angie and make sure he wasn't going to accidentally let the sick nurse back into the flat. Then he would run out of the house, cut across several yards, and emerge on the street where her car was parked—avoiding other sick people or criminals as needed. A quick run to the front seat, shove the keys in the ignition, and then a high-speed return to pick up his fare.

Sounded easy. But he knew any dumb mistake would put him in the role of *that guy* again. It was something that made him double his efforts to think of everything that could go wrong with his plan.

I'm sure I'm missing something.

4

Liam looked out every window in Grandma's flat and Angie was nowhere to be found. He could think of several places she could be hiding, but he hoped she decided to move on to find other humans to attack. A twinge of guilt followed the thought.

Rather than overthink things, he let Grandma know he was going to run out the back door and that she should shut the door behind him. He would be running for the car.

"Good luck, Liam. I'll be praying for you."

He knew she would. "Thanks, Grandma. I'll take all the help I can get!"

And with that, he opened the door, walked out, and Grandma closed it. He was quickly over the fence into the next yard. And the next. And the next. In a couple of minutes, he was in the last yard, ready to jump the final fence before the run down the street toward the car. His brain started running a little slideshow in his head, showing all the ways he could fail. Tripping. Ambushes. Gunfire. Getting run over. His heartbeat was revving to keep pace with the images in his head. No matter what he did to settle himself, he couldn't push them away.

He knew he had self-doubts about his abilities, just like anyone would, but he was haunted by his recent mishaps as "the guy who blows it." More images spun up in his mind, fueled by every zombie book and movie he'd ever consumed. Would he get out onto the street and trip and break his ankle, to be easily hunted down by a sick person? Would he be the guy trying to start the car over and over, only to have a zombie pull him out through the window, or have one of the marauders in the area put a bullet in him just to get his working car?

And P.S., if I die, Grandma dies, too.

He had a vivid vision of Grandma standing in her kitchen where he last saw her. She was still there looking out the back, waiting. The vision faded, and he was glad because his next thought was that Angie was somehow in the house with her.

It was too much to digest, and he had to sit down in a bed of flowers to give himself some cover while he kept his heart rate from exploding, and his brain from panicking. Nothing like this had ever happened to him.

So many things can go wrong!

He could see the car, and it didn't look like anything was going on in the immediate area. Now was his chance, if he could settle himself. He tried thinking of something peaceful—the lake where he spent a lot of time as a child—but that only reminded him of another incident where he almost drowned. So, he focused on the moment and studied one of the yellow wildflowers nearby. He ignored everything else for several minutes until his heart rate was back to normal. When he was ready, he willed himself to stay in the moment.

He was up and over the final fence, and he felt strong as he topped it. He landed well and sprinted for the car. The hundred-yard dash took much longer than he remembered in grade school gym class, and his awareness was crystal clear as he sprinted. There were wisps of smoke drifting from the two burned-out houses behind Grandma's, and the air was foul with the smell of burnt wood and synthetic housing materials. There was a very slight breeze. The position of the sun indicated time was moving closer to late morning. The neighborhood was fairly quiet just then; gunshots and screams were ebbing low.

And then Angie was there. She must have been hanging around in the alleyway and had a good bead on him as he ran down the street. She stumbled around a corner and began another earnest pursuit.

It was a replay of yesterday, and all he could think about was falling down, twisting an ankle, tripping on his own feet, or some similarly stupid calamity. He slowed down a bit and became hyper-aware of the ground over which he was jogging, scanning for any sign of potholes that could end him.

He looked at the distance to the car and knew he could outrun the lumbering and broken-footed nurse, but he wasn't sure if he could close the door and start the car before she was upon him, possibly breaking windows to get inside. It was time to use the gun and remove all those hypotheticals.

He pulled the Ruger from his waistband, toggled the small safety on the grip, and aimed for the center of her mass. He had done the routine a thousand times before, though he had never shot anything living.

Is Angie alive?

He had mere moments to bobble that thought before he pulled the trigger.

Nothing happened.

He pulled back the slide, thinking he needed to chamber a round, but in doing so, he made the horrible realization that the gun was empty.

OH MY—

She caught up with him then, with his arms extended in front and her arms reaching toward him. The nurse was slightly taller and weighed a few pounds more even in her "condition." He did have the advantage in dexterity, though. As the blood-covered woman pushed into him, he dropped his useless gun, grabbed both her arms and used her momentum to pull her forward as he sidestepped and stuck out his foot to trip her.

Angie fell to the street, her face absorbing the brunt of the impact, though she let out only the smallest grunt. He regained his own balance, wiped the nasty blood off his hands onto his jeans, reached down to pick up his gun, and sprinted for the car.

In moments, he was in through the passenger side. He pulled the door closed behind him, pushing the lock down in one smooth motion. He tried to ignore the fact he was sitting in sticky congealed blood. He definitely ignored what was sitting on the floorboard in front of him.

I don't see the foot.

He shuffled over to the driver's seat.

As he put the key into the ignition, Angie stumbled up next to the passenger side window. The fall had scraped all the skin from her forehead, and the exposed bone and blood gave her an even more unholy expression. She was looking directly at him through the very thin glass of the car door.

The car engine turned over, but it took him a few seconds to orient himself with the gear lever on the console, so he could slap it into drive and get moving.

Angie was banging and screaming obnoxiously outside the window. A million thoughts clouded his mind at that moment, but the one that stood out most was how glad he was Angie seemed oblivious to tools. One strong rock would be enough to break the door's glass and end this whole affair.

He solved the shifter question, put the car in gear, and smashed the gas pedal. The car lurched ahead, requiring a quick steering adjustment to keep him on the pavement, and he pulled away from the scene.

He turned around at the next intersection, so he could backtrack to the front of Grandma's house. He sped by Angie who had been loping along the street in pursuit. He briefly thought about swerving to "take her out" but he couldn't quite convince himself it was necessary. He wanted to pick up Grandma and just leave the nurse safely behind.

I did tell her to meet me in the front, didn't I?

As he turned left around the corner, he was more than a little worried he forgot to mention that part of his plan to Grandma. When he got close, he didn't see her at the front door.

He pulled up to her house, avoiding the few cars still parked on the street, pushed the emergency brake, then jumped out of the still-running car and ran for the front door, hoping against hope she would appear at the entry.

Please! Please! Please!

5

He wasted no time at the front door. If she wasn't there already, she wasn't going to get there in a hurry. He moved to the back of the house on the run.

He slammed the rear door after coming through, quite out of breath.

Grandma was indeed still camped out in the kitchen, right where he left her. He decided now wasn't the time to chastise himself.

"OK, Grandma, let's move up to the front door and we'll jump in the car. I parked it out front."

She was very understanding, or maybe just didn't notice the oversight.

The trek to the front of the house felt like it took ten minutes. The entire time, he could think of nothing else but someone walking along the street, seeing the open car door, jumping in and driving off. He also imagined zombies seeing the open door, stumbling in, and hiding in the back seat like in a bad movie. He did everything he could to push these thoughts away, but it only added to his anxiety. He worried he was on the verge of having another panic attack caused by—worry.

Out of habit, he patted his pocket to ensure his phone was there. Each time he left the house he repeated the ritual, even under such pressure. Content he had it, he hung on to Grandma's arm as they both moved slowly forward. She used her cane, so moved fine for her age, but he had to resist the urge to physically pull her.

He opened the front door and held it wide while he helped her out onto her front stoop. He reached down to grab his backpack and slung it over one of his shoulders.

He took an opportunity to look around but saw no one in the immediate vicinity.

They both inched down Grandma's ramp and then along the walkway to the street curb. He reached over to open the door to gain access to the back seat. He was careful not to push her in, though his brain was begging him to do just that.

Once she was inside, he threw his backpack in the space next to her, slammed her door, and jumped into the driver's seat.

He dropped it into gear, stomped the gas pedal, and they were accelerating up the street, away from Grandma's house. He realized why every car that went through here seemed to be speeding. He eased up to allow himself to catch his breath.

I did pretty good.

"Liam, I left my cane on the curb."

Oh sh—

He slammed on the brakes and looked over his shoulder.

"Do we *need* to go back for it?"

He wasn't about to admit it, but he was scared to return. He wasn't sure why given that her home was the one place in the entire world he knew was safe at that moment.

"I think I'll be in a lot of trouble if I don't have something to help me walk. I don't think either of us wants me to have to hold onto you for the rest of my life."

He couldn't argue with that. A better driver could probably have turned around in the narrow street, but he decided to proceed forward until he came to an intersection where he'd have plenty of room to reverse course. When he found the right spot, he needed every bit of that wide space.

After turning around, he kept the speed low enough to be safe. They arrived in front of her house without incident. Both could see the four-legged cane out the right side, sitting on the grass next to the curb, right where she had left it. He pulled up next to it, got out, ran around the car, grabbed the cane, then ran around the car again and hopped back inside. He tossed it into the front passenger seat and saw it promptly tilt off, so its base sat on top of the bloody foot.

He had no time to consider that horrible image. He pulled away from the curb heading in the wrong direction. Up ahead, he saw a lone figure standing in the street and knew who it was.

He slammed on the brakes.

"Grandma, Angie's up ahead. What should I do?"

He secretly hoped she would let him plow her over and just be done with it, but he knew that wasn't Grandma's style.

"I'm so sorry, Angie." She hesitated for a few moments, though he never doubted for a second what her recommendation would be.

"Let's carefully go around her, and we can leave her forever."

He drove the car slowly toward Angie, who gravitated to the side of the car to try to gain access to the people she could see inside. Once she moved away from the front of the car, he hit the gas. She bounced lightly on the side mirror.

Blood had poured from the wound on her forehead to cover her eyes and cheeks, and totally drench the front side of her already blood-stained nightgown. Where she was getting so much blood was beyond his reckoning, but he and Grandma both gasped when they saw her up close.

Grandma said a short prayer for her friend.

He couldn't even muster the requisite "Amen" when she was done. He couldn't help but feel their problems were only getting started.

His free-associating brain summoned a line from an old Rolling Stones song named, appropriately enough, *Angie.*

In his rearview mirror, the nurse shrank as he sped away.

Goodbye, Angie.

COAGULATION

After avoiding Angie in the road and leaving her behind them, Liam and Marty were dismayed to see several other sick people wandering the formerly peaceful neighborhoods of south St. Louis. He still wasn't ready to run anyone over, as long as he had a choice. He would use other means if he had to dispatch one of them.

"Oh crap!" he blurted, remembering something critical.

He looked in the mirror at Grandma, afraid she would chastise his language, but she said nothing.

"I need to pull over and load my gun. I pulled it out when Angie attacked me—did I mention that?—on my way to her car, but, of all the stupid things, I forgot to put rounds in the magazine before I walked out the door. I'm such an idiot."

He pulled over into a parking lot for a large supermarket. He let the car run while he grabbed his backpack, pulled out the box of ammo, loaded nine small rounds into the thin metal magazine, then slid the assembly into the bottom of the pistol grip. He chambered a round, and after some consideration put the safety on so he couldn't accidentally fire the gun while sticking it in his holster. That was one accident he was determined not to suffer.

He reloaded the other pistol as well. If he ended up needing it, he was fairly sure he wouldn't have time to load it at that point. Then, to be complete, he loaded the two spare magazines. Be prepared! That's what years of Boy Scouts taught him. He returned the backpack to the rear seat next to Grandma, so she could grab water or snacks.

He knew there was only one highway that ran directly from downtown to the south, Interstate 55; that made things easy for someone new to driving.

As they approached the on-ramp for the highway, he discovered the direct route also made things simple for everyone else. A massive traffic entanglement greeted them at the bridge interchange where the surface road went under the highway. Cars up-top and cars going up the access ramp were all stopped, and people everywhere were out of their cars, standing around. A few seemingly sick citizens lingered in the grass next to the highway or stood behind chain link fences.

Some cars made it off the highway and they drove into the network of side streets. Everyone pointed south. Without the use of the highway he needed an alternative, so he pulled over to consider his options.

The radio. He turned it on while mentally slapping himself for not doing it sooner.

Only one station on the AM dial was live as far as he could tell. Every other station, AM or FM, was repeating the same emergency response warning along with the president's radio message. Apparently, the stations were ordered to play that nonsense rather than something that could actually help people on the ground. Or maybe the radio people were on the run too?

They'd be some of the first to see the big picture.

The one station still live was headquartered in downtown St. Louis and apparently had a reporter on a high-rise roof somewhere because they were describing traffic in the downtown area:

"And we're looking at southbound 55 and can tell you it's snarled as badly as all the other highways we can see from our vantage point. Southbound is *completely* stopped. Northbound is also a mess coming into St. Louis, but everyone should be aware once you reach downtown, there is nowhere to go. The bridges to Illinois are all blocked now by the state police and what appears to be National Guard units. They are turning people back to the Missouri side of the bridges. As we've said before, you should try to get out of St. Louis while you still can. Just don't try to escape through downtown."

The reporter began talking about the north side of the city, and he said, as much to himself as to Grandma, "I bet the entire interstate is a parking lot from here all the way out to Mom and Dad's."

Grandma didn't respond. She was alert but casually looking out the window.

The radio continued, "We have reports from some people talking to our roving reporter that there is a Red Cross station down by the Arch. From here we can't confirm that, but there could be medical help. If you can't make it out of the city, that might be a good place to rest. And we've heard a rumor there is a big FEMA camp at the Gateway Speedway just over the river in Illinois. If you are in the Illinois listening area, you might find help there."

The two announcers then began some banter between themselves about troubles in their respective neighborhoods, which he found annoying. He needed something that would help him *right now.*

He was beginning to understand the sickness was a regional problem.

The chaos had spread everywhere in the bi-state area. He had hoped —with the same sense of futility he felt upon reaching Grandma's— that once he reached home-home, he'd find safety.

What if it's everywhere in the world?

2

He drew a mental map of the city. The most famous edge of the metropolis was the Mississippi River as it passed downtown St. Louis and its crown jewel, the Gateway Arch. That was roughly the eastern border. To the north, he was less clear of the geography but was pretty sure the Missouri River was up that way. The south was his neighborhood. He knew that to get out of the urban and suburban sprawl, they'd have to cross the Meramec River—a relatively small waterway compared to the giant Mississippi below it. Rivers bracketed three sides of St. Louis. He aimed for the southern one.

Grandma's home was a couple of miles south of downtown St. Louis; even so, they'd found the highway south was already choked to death going outbound from the city's center. Was every car in the city already out and parked on this stretch of road? Or was it the same going north or west? If so, it meant almost no one had actually escaped from the city. Everyone was on the road, but still within the gravity well of the collapsing star.

What's keeping everyone bottled up?

The radio had no answers. He decided to push through some of the comparatively empty side streets and see if Interstate 55 was more accessible farther south. He knew it was a long shot, and the farther south he went, the more cars he found on the roads with him. He'd sat in enough traffic jams as a passenger to know that when traffic stopped, drivers would try just about anything to find alternate routes. At every exit and entrance for I-55 that he approached he saw many more cars use the exit ramps and drive into side streets. Always south.

Without working electricity and streetlights, gridlock increased with every block. There were just too many cars. He had to keep rolling over to smaller and smaller streets. He was considering using one-lane alleys if he had to.

While driving on a side street through one of the old neighborhoods, he noticed the flashing lights of a police car behind him. He panicked; this was *not* the time to get in trouble with the law.

"Oh, no! Grandma, I got pulled over by a cop."

"Were you speeding?"

"I don't think so. I was just kind of driving around looking for clear streets."

"Mmm huh." She seemed to understand, but she said nothing further. She rolled down her window, directly behind his seat. Liam assumed it was so she could talk to the officer herself.

Let her deal with it.

Always respectful of law and order, he pulled over as quickly as he could. He had his seatbelt on, so he felt confident he had covered all his bases. He looked in the back seat to see if anything was out of the ordinary. The guns might cause trouble. He took his out of his waistband and stuffed it next to the seat by the middle console. The other was safely hidden in his backpack next to Grandma.

A doubt nagged at him—a lesson from his books—but he admitted that feeling always seemed to be in his head now. He'd never been pulled over, so he had no frame of reference of how it should go.

He didn't expect the gun in his face, followed by a calm voice asking for his money.

"I'll take your wallet, thank you very much."

The dark man wasn't a police officer—the gold chains and multiple watches were big clues, if the gun in the face wasn't hint enough.

Liam held his hands up to signify compliance. He said his wallet was in his right front pocket.

"Well *get it*, I don't have all day." The man gave a little giggle at his statement; then he seemed to notice the blood on the passenger seat and the foot sitting prominently on the floorboard.

Why did I leave that there?

"Looks like you had a passenger. What happened to him?"

"I don't know, sir. It was there before we jumped in the car."

"We?" The man noticed the small woman sitting quietly in the back seat. He moved a step closer to the back, so he could see directly into the interior.

"Well, well. I'll take that fancy necklace, Miss Daisy. And that backpack looks quite juicy." It was lying open at that moment, the snacks and drinks clearly visible. Liam silently cursed himself again for being so dumb.

"No, Grandma needs her meds. Please don't take it."

"When I need your opinion I'll ask for it, *boy*." He slapped Liam's head by reaching inside the back window.

Liam knew it was stupid to think it, but he didn't want to be taken advantage of like this. Instead of being scared, it made him angry.

Grandma, meanwhile, was gathering the pack by forcing in all the contents that had spilled out.

"Sir, please leave her medications. You can have the rest." He thought he was being smart. She didn't take any irreplaceable prescription meds, but maybe the guy would feel sympathy.

The man moved back to the front, directly outside Liam's window.

"You don't get it. I'm taking it *all*! If you say another word ... " He jiggled the pistol menacingly.

Grandma piped up, "I'm getting it all together for you."

Liam sat stewing in his impotence. *Can I start the car and speed off without getting shot? Probably not. But maybe if I push him back first … I've been lucky so far.*

He shoved the door open to push the guy backward. It didn't surprise the thief at all. The man was so agile that he helped pull the door open, side-stepped, knocked Liam dizzy with a stiff punch, then dragged him out of the car onto the street.

Liam heard the soft murmur of Grandma's voice saying, "I have your backpack ready, sir." Then he blacked out.

3

Liam woke up lying face down on warm asphalt. One side of his face was in excruciating pain, but he could move his jaw and didn't feel anything crunchy in his mouth.

Still dazed, he staggered to his feet and saw Grandma sitting in the back seat, her head lolling to one side. She'd put on a flowery head scarf, but it had come undone and sat flatly over her head.

Oh, God, don't let her be dead!

He ran to her window and heard a soft, nasal sound coming from her. She was asleep.

Relieved, he leaned against her door. His head was throbbing, and the flashing blue lights from the police car parked behind them made it worse.

Then everything came rushing back. He looked around for the man with the gun, sending another wave of pain through his aching head, but he steadied himself against the car and noticed the backpack was still resting beside Grandma on the car seat.

Then, he saw feet sticking out from behind the car.

Carefully, he moved back toward the rear. The thief was lying on his back between both vehicles; his eye was a bloody mess, but otherwise his face and the rest of his body looked normal. He wasn't infected or anything. But he was very dead.

How did I miss seeing him before? Too scared about Grandma, I guess.

He looked around for a Good Samaritan in a high window but didn't see anyone who might have saved them by killing their assailant. Cars moved on distant streets, but no one seemed interested in him. He thought about saying a prayer of thanks for his good fortune, but like so many false starts in his recent past, he didn't know if he believed his prayer would be heard by anyone. He secretly hoped there was someone listening. Perhaps even the same God Grandma believed in.

For now, he said a quick "thank you" to anyone who would listen and jumped back into Angie's car to start it up.

He thought about going back to check out the cop car but didn't like the idea of stealing from anyone. Plus, if he was caught ransacking a police car ...

Instead, he put his ride in gear and drove quickly away from the scene. It had all happened so fast he hadn't had time to be afraid. He saw himself in the rearview mirror as he drove and realized ... he was looking at a survivor. He just survived an encounter with a hardened criminal. He survived multiple encounters with Angie, the plague victim. He even survived falling down a flight of stairs.

But it all seemed so random. He knew any of those incidents could have ended his life, making this whole survival *schtick* the mockery he knew it to be. He saw the survivors of this thing as big, hulking men carrying large guns, sharp swords, and wearing full police riot gear. How else could anyone truly survive such crazy times?

He wore jeans and a lime-green Mountain Dew t-shirt, and his 104-year-old partner in survival was dressed in a light blue pantsuit, complemented by a plain metal cane. Hardly the stuff of legend.

Whoop de do. We've survived the twenty-four hours since the sirens.

He tried to get back into the important task of driving. He found the highway again and was disappointed to see the traffic remained stopped. The memory of the gun barrel between his eyes buzzed as he observed cars continuing to pour off the exit ramp, into the streets of this part of the city. Streets that were nearly clogged. It wouldn't be long before everything was in total gridlock. Before he was trapped.

He turned the car around to give himself some open space because he needed a chance to think through his next move. They weren't going to make it driving south on the highway or any of the side roads. He pulled over into an empty parking lot, far from anyone or anything that could harm them. He again remembered the gun in his face but ignored it. He aggressively scanned for threats as he tried to concentrate.

Could they walk out of the city? He'd seen many people walking along the highway, but how far could Grandma go on foot? She could walk pretty well for her age, and he'd seen her walk for short distances without any cane at all. But those were rare instances when she was at 100% health and rest. Now, she could barely stay awake while sitting in his back seat.

He thought again about the gun in his face but pushed it back with a few calming breaths.

"How far could we both get on foot?" he whispered.

Not far.

As he sat there, he found himself unable to further ignore the incident with the thief. Of having the business end of a gun touch his nose. Of being punched. Of being yanked out of the car and tossed to the ground. His hands started shaking, so he gripped the wheel.

How close to death did I come?

He imagined himself being shot dead. Oddly, he thought of his parents, and how they'd never know how he died. He imagined Grandma getting pulled out next. He imagined ...

NO! I will not let that happen!

He silently wept. He couldn't help himself. He was slightly embarrassed Grandma might hear him, but once it started, he was unable to check it. His head collapsed on the steering wheel as he let the emotions of the past day consume him.

In the back, Grandma slept on.

For the first time in his life, he envied her.

MAPLE SYRUP

Liam sat, exhausted, in the front seat of the car. His tears had dried, and he found himself staring out the front window. It hadn't been long since he'd pulled over. Glancing back, Grandma was still asleep.

He attempted to move beyond the botched robbery. He needed to look forward. Time for the "big guy pants," as his dad would say.

He turned on the radio again.

Did they say all *the bridges to Illinois were closed? Surely not.*

All stations were now playing the emergency announcement loops, including the one previously broadcasting freely. They advised listeners to evacuate the city but were stingy with clues about how to do it or where to go. A week ago, he wouldn't have listened to a government broadcast to save his life. Now his life *did* depend on a government announcement, and he was dismayed to discover they had no answers.

Going south didn't seem possible, given the traffic situation. Going west might work in a pinch, but that would take him into the bulk of the population of the city—enough reason to avoid that way. North would take him directly away from his goal, so that made no sense at all. Finally, he figured his best bet was to drive east into Illinois, where it was less crowded, then turn south and try to return over a bridge into Missouri somewhere. It would require going through downtown, which made him anxious just thinking about it, but it was the only place to cross.

With no help from the radio, he had to make a choice soon. He gently woke up Grandma.

She opened her eyes, looked out her window, then into his backpack.

"He's gone, Grandma. He didn't get our stuff either, but I'm not sure what happened. I was lying on the ground, and when I woke up, the crook was already dead. He got shot. I jumped in the car and sped us out of there."

"I must have passed out from all the excitement. I'm so glad you're OK. I'm not doing a very good job taking care of you, am I?"

"We're both alive. That's all that matters now. Someone shot the yoga woman for me, too. I think I have a guardian angel. I've learned an important lesson; the rules are changing. I'm going to be smarter from now on, so I can protect you and me both."

Grandma leaned forward just enough to touch his shoulder with reassurance.

"We make a good team," she said.

"Well, teammate, we need a new plan now. Traffic on the highway to the south is completely stopped. All the main roads next to the interstate going that way are also filled with people trying to escape. It didn't look like any of those vehicles were going to be moving anytime soon, so I pulled into this parking lot to think. The radio has nothing useful on where to go. I figured we'd try to get across a bridge downtown and then drive south on the Illinois side of the river."

"Sounds like a good plan, Liam."

"Will you help me navigate? I'm afraid I don't know where to go." The extent of his driver's education with Dad ended at Grandma's house. The rest of the city was a blank space as far as roads went.

"I'll do what I can," she said from behind.

He pulled back onto the road, in the direction of downtown. Unlike the lanes going south, the northbound side of the road was virtually devoid of traffic. He wasn't willing to use the term "good luck" just yet. He knew how fast luck could go down the toilet.

He felt a trace of a smile on his face as he sped through the dying city heading for freedom.

Looking in the rearview, Grandma's face was far more stoic.

2

The street was a major thoroughfare in this part of the city. It had two lanes of traffic in each direction, with a breakdown lane in the middle. Very few cars were going either way. The massive backup of south-bound traffic hadn't reached this far north yet.

Several cars burned on the roadway in front of a row of apartments. Strangely, other cars were moving among the burned-out hulks, seemingly unconcerned with the danger.

He was gaining his sea legs on this terrible ocean. He immediately stopped the car and looked for alternate routes where he could turn down a side street and avoid even being close to such destruction. Grandma was in the back seat, watching ahead as well.

"Grandma, I'm turning. I don't think we should go anywhere near those burning cars."

"Watch those cars on fire," she yelled a little too loud at almost the same time, as she sometimes did when her hearing aids acted up.

He smiled as he made a left, then a quick right turn onto a narrow avenue running parallel to the main road. They entered a more residential area. A few cars lined both sides of the street, but there were also a lot of trash and debris blowing around, as if many of the houses had simply thrown their contents right out their doors.

More ominously, he saw odd characters walking aimlessly. Sick? Infected? Lost? Stealing?

He wasn't stopping to find out. He hit the gas, quickly pushing fifty miles per hour down the narrow street. Not bad for a fifteen-year-old with a learner's permit.

The passenger window shattered as several gunshots exploded from the houses lining the right side of the street. He instinctively jerked his head as low as he could even as his heartrate started to outpace his car.

"Grandma! Get down!"

The rear passenger-side window blew out next, followed by the one on his side. The shots were either coming from both sides or going completely through the interior.

The rear window blew out a second later, and the headrest on his seat crumpled.

That was close!

He glanced in the mirror. Grandma had fallen over sideways in the back, covered with tiny pieces of safety glass.

"Oh, my lands," she exclaimed.

He risked a sideways peek, but the shooters were well hidden. He was going much too fast. Shots continued behind them, and he could see in the side mirror a couple of men had run into the street to shoot, even as he drove away.

Only a few seconds more ...

He took a right turn too fast, scraped against a car on his side, but was just able to maintain control on the new street. The sedan lost some paint, but they escaped the flying bullets.

Rather than being scared, he was mad as hell again. People were using this disaster as an excuse to—do what exactly? Were these bad people showing their true colors or good people gone wrong due to the chaos? It had scarcely been one lousy day since law and order was put on hold. Things were going downhill fast if this was how it was going to be.

He slowed enough to take a left turn back onto the main street safely and was pleased to see they had traveled beyond the burned-out wrecks. Were the men on the previous street the same ones who burned the cars on this one? Why would anyone randomly destroy cars and shoot at people they didn't know? Were they trying to kill him? He had no explanation that fit the circumstances, and he sure wasn't going back to interview them.

Pardon me. Would you refrain from killing me while I ask you a few questions?

They quickly overtook another vehicle—a cramped, blue coupe—with a family inside who looked over at him as he matched their speed for a second before accelerating past them.

The open road was just as dangerous as everywhere else. Even a friendly-looking family couldn't be trusted. He could trust no one but himself and Grandma.

In the distance, he got his first glimpse of the Gateway Arch as it twinkled in the mid-day sun. He had many memories seeing it as a kid—how many times had his parents excitedly pointed it out as they were driving? It was a source of fascination and pride for locals like him. A snarl of traffic came into view on the street ahead, interrupting his pleasant memories.

Will anything be easy ever again?

3

The traffic wasn't as bad as it appeared at first glance. A major intersection in this part of the city was catching traffic from the nearby highway, as well as the growing procession heading downtown. Several other drivers must have gotten the same idea to head that way once they realized the highway out of town was toast.

After several minutes snaking through the busy intersection, they found open roads before once again coming upon a jammed cross street. It was much worse than the previous delay.

They were only a couple of miles from downtown. They could now see the big Anheuser-Busch brewery that was a cultural icon in this city. As they came through the big intersection, they could see the traffic ahead had stopped completely. As cars came up on the tail of the northbound traffic jam, they shut off engines, and passengers got out and joined the people ahead of them on foot. He could already see a few cars coming in behind him, which would make sure he never got out of this entanglement.

He turned the wheel hard to his right. Angie's severely damaged car jumped the curb and came to a stop in a tiny parking lot for a fast-food joint. He heard a loud pop. He backed his car sloppily into a spot up against the building, allowing himself a clear shot to drive in any direction he chose—except into the traffic jam itself—should he change his mind about joining the sea of walkers going downtown.

Several other cars took his lead. Soon the little parking lot was full, as were several other open spaces on this side of the road. He was silently impressed with himself for thinking of something that was so useful to his fellow travelers. It felt nice to lead, even if it was just a bit of luck on his part for thinking of it.

His pleasure faded once he exited the vehicle and saw its condition. Angie had some pride in her vehicle and took care to keep it washed and waxed at a local hands-on car wash. If she saw her car now, she would fall over dead.

Not funny, Liam!

Four windows were blown out. Several bullet holes peppered the passenger side, including a couple up near the engine. It was a miracle nothing got permanently damaged under the hood. He walked around and inspected as much as he dared. One bullet had mangled the locking assembly of the passenger-side rear door, making it impossible to open. He reached in through the broken glass and grabbed his backpack. As he pulled away, he noticed the front tire had gone all the way flat and it made the car look sad.

"So much for getting to Illinois." He said it out loud, but mostly to himself. They were now committed to the only place anywhere that seemed to offer some help—the area down by the Gateway Arch.

Grandma exited on the driver's side and shook herself free of the bits of glass. She reached back in to grab her cane and then casually leaned against the exterior to wait for Liam to gather his stuff.

She quipped, "I guess we don't have to worry about locking the doors," and let out a little giggle. He had to laugh too.

One of the people nearby gave a little whistle when he took in Liam's damaged ride.

"Whoa! You a stunt driver, kid?"

Liam wasn't really in the mood to deal with strangers but couldn't resist bragging about it.

"Not really. A couple of dip-wads a few miles back were shooting up cars. They got the drop on us, but I just put the hammer down and blew through their trap." He said it with the same emotion he would if he were talking about the weather.

He looked at Grandma to see if she would scold him, but she was looking the other way.

The man seemed unimpressed. "Yeah, we had to drive through someone's lawn to get around some fellas holding up cars about three miles to the south. I guess we're all lucky to make it here. Good luck wherever you end up," he said as he walked away.

So much for basking in the glory.

With his pack slung over his shoulders, he walked around to Grandma. She was looking at the crush of abandoned cars and beyond, toward the shining landmark.

"Do you think you can walk to the Arch from here?"

She was silent for many moments before responding.

"I don't see any other option at this point. I'm going to need your help, but I think I can do it."

She held up her cane, so she could bring it closer to her face.

"I'm going to need your help, too, Mr. Cane. Don't let me fall!"

She chuckled a little, then slammed the cane back to the ground and started walking—slowly—away from Angie's wrecked car.

An obscure quote from one of his dad's old movies hit him as he left the sad-looking car that had gotten them this far.

I'm not parking it; I'm abandoning it.

He had a feeling they'd never be back. The car would probably rust in that spot until it blew away on the wind.

Wow. I'm a real downer.

Or, everything would be back to normal tomorrow and he'd have to pay for all the damage. Even if it sapped all his savings, he much preferred that ending than the other one.

Finally, it fell too far behind to see, and he resolved to only look to the future. At that moment, the Arch towered into view miles down the street. The safety of the port was so close, yet so far away.

4

After the excitement at Grandma's house, the struggle to escape Angie, getting beaten up by a criminal, and the stress of driving the car in the chaos, the walk toward the Arch was anticlimactic.

A small girl behind them blurted out to no one in particular, "When we get downtown, I hope they're serving hot dogs and soda, like at a baseball game!"

He was holding Grandma's arm as he walked but turned partway around to look at the child's parents. They wore tight-lipped grins as they shared the good things she would find ahead. Anything to keep the children happy and unafraid.

Would there be any help at all downtown? After what he saw on the roads of the city, he was pretty sure of the answer to that, but still, he had hope and tried hard to listen to the conversations of his fellow travelers to see if they knew more than he did about what was ahead.

The friendly crowd of walkers continued to grow. It was a lot like heading to a baseball game. He and his father didn't make a habit of it, but whenever his dad got free tickets to a game, they would go for a father-son adventure at the ballpark. The only differences between that crowd and this one was the colors—not as much Cardinal red today—and what people carried. He saw lots of coolers and bags of food, as well as firearms. Open carrying of guns was something you would *never* see on any typical day within the city limits of St. Louis.

He looked carefully now and saw that more than a few men and women were carrying things slung over their shoulders, covered with fabric or trash bags. Some had their rifles right out in the open, which made it even more obvious that others were hiding theirs. He didn't understand what they were trying to prove, but he wasn't going to call attention to them.

A man standing off to the side of the crowd held a cardboard sign for the walkers to see, "God did this to you. Repent!" Liam wondered what Grandma would think about such an insensitive statement, but if she saw it, she said nothing. He wasn't willing to blame God for the plague; he saw God in context with boring Sunday sermons or with high praise from family members. Never did either suggest a benevolent being could inflict something like this on the human race.

The man's sign was getting other people talking about the root cause of the catastrophe. Liam tried to overhear conversations as they walked. The first person he could hear clearly was talking about some clues he received on his shortwave radio.

"... a frequency I don't get. The guy lived in Minnesota or Wisconsin; he wasn't very forthcoming about that. He sounded like he had watched too many movies. He called the sick people zombies as if they were something real. He then said you can only kill them by destroying the head. Ha! This isn't *Night of the Living Dead* or whatever that movie was called. So, we ignored him and went on to look for more operators, but the only other one we heard with new information was farther north in Canada, and all we got out of him was that people were chewing on his livestock. He said he had no weapons to get them to stop. Nothing we could do to help him, of course."

The guy was moving much faster than he and Grandma so he couldn't hear much more of his conversation, but he noted the man carried a big revolver in a holster on his left side.

As more people passed, he heard several of their theories. It was now on everyone's mind, it seemed.

"I heard it was a medical experiment gone wrong."

"A friend of a friend said she knew someone in the police department. This was a terrorist attack." And then, speaking so quiet Liam almost didn't catch it, the person said, "It was the same guys who did nine-eleven."

"It was our own government." A half-dozen people had different iterations of government conspiracies.

"It was the maple-syrup-lovin' Canadians." He heard several people talk about Canadians as if the threat was real, but he couldn't quite take them seriously. Normally he wouldn't dare insert himself, but he had to know. "Excuse me, why would the Canadians cause this plague?" The woman who spoke of it responded calmly and easily, "They want our stuff, of course."

He determined it was best to avoid laughing. Soon the woman and her entourage had moved far ahead.

He heard a host of other theories, just in the few minutes since he'd passed that sign. "It was the Republicans. They always wanted us city people to die." "It was the Liberals. They was foolin' around with science and unleashed this Ebola-thing on us by accident." "It was the Snowballers." "It was the Communists." "It was the anarchists. They want government to go away." And so on and so on. The crowd consumed each theory, readily adding more and more.

Several people toted large, hand-printed signs, with variations of the "Repent! The end is here!" motif. One said, "This is the tribulation!" He knew that had something to do with religion, but he was surprised to see the people carrying such signs appeared completely normal. Almost serene. There were no crazed-eye preachers anywhere in sight.

Holding onto Grandma, he realized they were both now floating along with the crowd, and everyone was equally clueless about why they were there. It made him feel small and helpless.

People power-walked by them, barely giving them a glance. He wondered, would he notice an old woman and a young boy if he was walking in this mess by himself? How many people in this procession were going to be dead soon? That made his stomach wobble.

Don't panic, Liam.

"Panic is the real killer in many emergencies," his dad's voice said with reassuring calmness from a memory.

He kept those words in mind as he steadied his breathing.

He craned his neck to look around the crowd, which over the last several minutes, had started to thin out. Everyone moved along the sidewalks on both sides of the street, as well as on the grass-covered median. He guessed they'd been walking along for an hour, which would put them about halfway there. Grandma was puttering along, but she was slowing down, stopping to rest more than he liked.

He knew she needed her rest, but an odd feeling had been growing in the pit of his stomach—a sense it wouldn't be wise to fall too far behind the main crowd. He was disturbed to see fewer people behind him than ahead. It wasn't empty, but things were thinning out.

"Grandma, I know you're tired, but we have to keep moving."

"I know, Liam. I'm so tired, though. I must sit down." She remained standing—there was no place to sit other than the curb of the street, and Grandma would have trouble getting down and back up.

Gunshots cracked from somewhere behind. Not close, but not as far as he'd like either.

He gave her a drink of water and a grain bar, hoping to give her a quick boost. He knew enough about the 104-year-old set to know there was no word for "boost" in their lexicon.

Liam didn't want to scare her, but he wasn't going to lollygag, either. Once she had taken a drink and pulled down a few bites, he practically pushed her.

"OK, we have to push on."

Grandma didn't fight him but didn't pick up the pace as he'd hoped. Even a fury of gunshots and some nearby screaming didn't get her moving.

I refuse to panic!

He looked over his shoulder, afraid of what he'd see.

5

While dragging her along, a middle-aged woman in a business suit, sans the jacket, came ambling along. She seemed distracted until she spotted Grandma.

Without prompting, she took Grandma's other arm, and together she and Liam were able to support her much better as they walked along. He gave her his thanks, but Grandma remained silent. That could only mean she was *super* worn out.

"I think she's bushed. Thank you so much for helping her."

"Anytime," was the woman's only response. She was looking ahead and into the traffic jam as if searching for someone. He assumed she had lost a friend.

After fifteen minutes or so the woman abruptly stopped and told him to wait against a bridge abutment just as they went underneath it.

This gave him a chance to look behind again; he was horrified to see almost no one. There were a few stragglers, mostly elderly walking without helpers. Some people had just stopped to sit or lie down, perhaps giving up. And, far down the street, he thought he could see a few of the *really* sick. Still, there had to be a whole city of people south of him. He couldn't imagine where they'd all gone.

He felt like the lone gazelle dropping behind the herd. Ahead of him, he could see the last of the main group walking away. They were very close now to the park that surrounds the Arch. Maybe a quarter of a mile. Gunfire was coming from that direction, though a few shots were echoing down side streets almost all the time now.

He didn't see the mystery lady. Not ahead. Not behind. Not even in the nearby cars, which were sprawled everywhere on the street and in every available parking area in sight.

Oh, crap! We're in for it now.

He looked at Grandma and considered his options once more. She appeared to be totally out of hit points. Could he force her to go faster? Should he try?

A deep, dark voice advised him to sit her down under this bridge and then just walk away.

Another voice argued she was his responsibility no matter how difficult things became.

Where did his obligation to save her outweigh his obligation to save himself? Wasn't his life—at fifteen years old—more valuable to save than hers?

Why would that thought even cross my mind?

"Grandma, I'm not going to leave you here. We have to keep moving. Can you walk a little farther?"

"Oh, Liam. I think I'm a goner. My head is spinning, and it's very hard to see." She hunched over even more than normal, holding herself up with a combination of her cane and the concrete bridge pylon. "I don't think I can go another step without falling over."

"Well, then, I'll carry you!"

Bent over and gasping for air, she cocked her head so she could look up at her tall grandson and give him a look he knew very well. It said, "Liam, you are one crazy boy, but I love you anyway. And no, we aren't doing that."

He debated pulling a stunt he saw in a movie—just grabbing the small woman, tossing her over his shoulder, and carrying her, no matter what her protests were. He knew he could lift her and carry her but couldn't assure himself that he wouldn't break her ribs.

As he argued with himself, the mystery woman returned, running around cars inside the traffic jam, as if she were trying to find a suitable path through the obstacles. She was pushing something.

A half minute later, she was close enough for him to see the huge wheelchair in front of her, and she brought it right up onto the sidewalk where Grandma was swaying.

"Did someone order a ride?"

He stood incredulous while the woman moved behind Grandma and helped her fall backward, gently, into the chair. The seat itself was immense, apparently designed for a client of considerable girth, and Grandma's pixie size made her look like a child sitting there.

But she *was* sitting.

"Where did you find this?"

"I've been looking for this since I first saw you. It was on one of those lifts that stick out the back of a trailer hitch. I work with nurses, and travel to hospitals, so this type of thing jumps out when I see it. You have to hurry. She looks like she needs some medical care."

The woman looked over her shoulder at the few people wandering about on the route they just traveled. Some were lying down, but some of those on the ground were being set upon by others who weren't ... *normal.*

"Anyone healthy behind us must have gone to other streets. Nothing but sick back there," she said.

"Will you come with us? We can make good time if we both push her."

"No. You'll be fine. I'm going that way," she said, pointing west. "Hurry," she repeated.

Without a further comment, she dove back into the traffic jam.

"Thank you!" he shouted as she was nearly across the street.

She lifted her hand but kept moving.

"Can you believe our luck?"

He tossed Grandma's cane across the arms of the chair, then began pushing her, nearly running when the sidewalk wasn't too bumpy, and never once looked back.

A blood-freezing scream told him every detail about the sharks in pursuit.

VICTORIA

The Gateway Arch grounds were chaos, thousands of people crammed into the greenspace under the 630-foot monument. The Gateway to the West was now the Gateway to the East for these people —a passage to safety over in Illinois. But there were so many people, and they didn't look like they were moving.

"Grandma, are you ready to dive into all this? That's where we need to go." He was glad to be off the streets, crowd or not.

"I'll go where you push me, Liam. I'm too tired to arm wrestle you over it."

They caught up with the many other new arrivals queuing up, and soon entered the perimeter of the park. A row of armed citizens and police officers watched from the outside rim of the greenspace, each holding their weapons toward the ground, at the low ready position. A handful of officers and civilians on horseback also wandered around. Where they found horses downtown was another of the mysteries of the day.

He remembered reading somewhere that the Arch's park is "a patch of greenery next to the concrete jungle of the urban center of St. Louis, about a mile long and a quarter of a mile across." Outside the park, dead bodies littered the streets. Any schoolchild could piece together what happened. People like Angie attacked the police and were put down like rabid dogs. Seeing that many corpses—and their blood—in the light of day was unsettling, but he gripped the wheelchair handles with determination and pushed through.

The police presence reassured him, but not because they had guns —lots of people he'd seen today had weapons, including him. These men and women represented authority, a hope that society was holding it together despite all the chaos. He gave the nearest officer a wave and got a nod in return. He felt as if he had returned to humanity with that little acknowledgment.

His faith didn't last long. Once inside the outer ring of armed order the interior of the park was anarchy. People huddled in small groups all along the path and well out into the grass on each side. Kids played in the reflecting ponds, something forbidden under normal conditions. He remembered being yanked out of one and scolded during one of his visits as a child.

They rolled up to a little parking lot filled with police cars and trucks, as well as several civilian vehicles. A large box truck sat almost directly in the path ahead. The back door was open, and a man stood back there, yelling at the crowd, "Guns! Ammo! On loan! We need you armed!"

It was perhaps the most unusual thing he had seen today, and that was saying a lot. The thought of police allowing this man to toss guns out the back of his truck—it just wasn't done. Ever. And yet—

"Grandma, let's check this out." She didn't reply, so he took that as an affirmative.

It carried the logo of a local sporting goods store. Lots of police and civilians congregated near the back, and the man worked with a partner to take down some information from each person and then hand them a rifle or shotgun. No money changed hands. There were stacks of ammo and a cornucopia of firearms in the cargo area. If he were in a cartoon, his eyes would be swirling with longing and desire. He moved the chair, so he could drift into the line.

It can't hurt to try.

In a few minutes, it was his turn with the man holding the guns.

"Can I get a rifle? I want to protect my Grandma." It was completely true, but boy, did he want a big gun.

The man wore a black button-down shirt from his store and he took a few seconds to size him up. Liam knew at that moment what he was going to say. His own eyes flashed behind the man, spotting a large —no, huge—tan rifle sitting on its end, up against the wall of the truck. He doubted he could even lift the thing ...

"Look, kid, I appreciate your situation, but we need *men* on this line. Police. Ex-military. You and your grandma don't belong anywhere near guns. You need to be inside the park staying safe."

And there it was. He was "just a kid."

His emotions welled up inside as the man moved to another customer. An older woman got a gun after giving her name and address. No other questions asked. So much for needing *men*, he thought.

He wanted to stay and argue but knew it was useless. He tried to move out of the line while avoiding the concerned looks of the men and women still there. Soon he was lost in the crowd, moving ever deeper into the park. Anonymity brought relief.

He tried to keep the wheelchair on the straight and narrow of the path but couldn't help looking from side to side at the many strange people who had washed up in this tidal basin of humanity. A large black family sat to one side; it looked like multiple generations made it here together. Old ladies. Several middle-aged men and women. A playground's worth of children. Many appeared very scared. He couldn't understand the fear here amongst all the armed police. To his left, among the hundreds of people, he spotted a young boy much like himself—only he was with his mother and father. Liam felt a little jealous because that youngster had found his family. He tried to be happy for him, but his heart wasn't really in it.

He rolled Grandma past an old cathedral, though it was clear the place was full and not taking in new tenants. Hundreds of people gathered around the front doors, hoping to get in. He kept moving toward the Arch itself.

Dozens of other vignettes emerged from the crowd. Wounded men. Coughing and hacking women—danger! Small children walking rudderless. The aged. The feeble. The mentally challenged. And pets of every stripe. No one wanted to leave without their pets. Dogs were the most visible, but small pet carriers were prolific as well—probably holding back the cats. There were even some big birds on people's shoulders. He couldn't identify many, though he did recognize a Macaw when he saw one.

"I wonder where all these pets go to the bathroom?"

Grandma might have heard the question, but if she did, she kept the answer to herself.

It wasn't far before the path revealed the larger scene beyond the park and well beyond the Arch. The Mississippi River, 2,000 feet across, was a disgusting brown that churned wildly as it flowed under the downtown bridges at high speed. Small boats flitted about in all directions like water bugs, their purpose unclear. Several aircraft buzzed above. Most were military, though some helicopters were probably reporting traffic—an easy job when no cars moved throughout the city.

The spectacle distracted him for a full minute until a weak voice pulled him back.

"I need to get in the shade, Liam."

He obliged and hastened back from the crest of the sunny hill toward one of the many tree-lined and shady paths through the park. All the benches were full, but some space remained on the concrete; most people chose to sit under trees in the grass off the walkway. He scanned the trees to find one best suited to Grandma's needs. Some had large groups of scary-looking men under them as if entire biker gangs agreed to meet there. Some had distinct family groups. One had a score of priests and nuns below it. He searched for one with enough free space, so Grandma could get the shade she needed without asking people to move. He knew it was a tall order given the size of the crowd, but he was patient.

He settled on an ash tree that shaded a couple of young families, one with a baby stroller, as well as a woman sprawled in the grass near the path. She appeared to be sleeping, which was just fine. She wouldn't give them any trouble.

"Here you go. Shade as promised!"

Grandma didn't say anything.

She has to be exhausted.

As he situated her under the tree, he couldn't help but notice the sleeping woman was closer to his age than he first thought. She wore an elegant black dress, completely out of place in the sweltering heat and humidity of this park-turned-refugee-camp. The knee-length skirt had hiked high up her thigh as she lay on the grass, revealing more than his grandma would consider appropriate for a fifteen-year-old boy to see, for sure. Embarrassed and feeling like a voyeur, he tried to focus on pushing the chair into position, but with the distraction, he drove the wheelchair off the pavement. He felt it drop off the small edge and immediately knew what he'd done wrong.

So did the girl.

2

"What. The. HELL?"

The girl sat up while waving her pinched hand wildly. She looked like she'd been sleeping for days. Her long, brown hair was a ratty mess, managed only by the grace of a black headband. Her face, as pretty as it might be, was covered on one side with misplaced locks of hair, dirt, and grass. Her makeup had been smeared, giving her the appearance of sunken cheeks. The green eyes were striking—he had to look away, a decision reinforced by her yelling.

"That was my hand! Who the he—" She broke off, noticing a little old lady in a wheelchair.

"Oh, sorry, ma'am. I meant no disrespect. This wasn't how I expected to wake up." Looking around, she continued, "Though seeing all these people now, I don't know *what* I was expecting."

Grandma waved tiredly in her direction. "Please, child, Liam just lost control of my chair—it was an accident. We've been on the road all morning, and we're just looking for some shade."

"I'm very sorry for running you over." He pretended to attend to Grandma as he apologized.

As the young woman stood up, he could see she was about his height, maybe a little less than his five-foot, eight inches, and she had an athletic look about her. Her calves had real definition—not that he was looking at them. Her profile reminded him of any number of girls on his high school track team. Something about how they carried themselves gave it away. It was an intangible quality, but he had seen it many times in runners. Was she short or long distance? He'd have to—

"Hey, Crash Cart. You finished?"

Just shoot me now.

"Yeah, I'm uh, just wondering why you're dressed up like that?"

Good save.

She gave him a disapproving scowl but asked a question rather than address his.

"Do you have spare water or anything? I've got nothing but what you see here." She held out her arms and swished them down and in front of her, as if presenting her clothes as her only possession.

"Grandma has the only water, and we're saving that."

"Nonsense. Here you go, dear—please take a little." She pulled a water bottle out of his backpack, which she kept next to her on the ample seat of the wheelchair.

He wasn't surprised. Grandma would try to help anyone she met. She couldn't help the thousands of other people in this park, but she could help this girl.

"Thank you. My name is Victoria."

"Victoria, huh?" Grandma paused, just for a couple of extra seconds. "My name is Marty, but you can call me Grandma like everyone else seems to do. I'm 104, by the way. You were going to ask. This is my rescuer and great-grandson, Liam."

He gave her a nod, trying to stay relaxed, but he was deathly afraid he'd say something stupid, or check out her minimal but sufficiently curvy chest—

Oh, crap!

He found it impossible not to look. The dress wasn't even low cut, but it was a dress, after all, and it complimented her figure. She adjusted a mobile phone inside her bra. It was too much. He sat down on the pavement next to the wheelchair, kept his eyes forward, and looked at people walking the wide path next to him. He gave his phone

one of his many quick glances to confirm it still wasn't connecting to the network, but he slid it back into his pocket and turned as she spoke again.

"Thanks for the water. Hope neither of us has the plague." She followed that with some nervous laughter. She used just a splash of water on her face, and made a half effort to untangle her hair, then took a seat opposite him on the far side of the wheelchair. It took everything he had to avoid looking at the legs now stretched on the grass.

3

"You asked about the dress."

She breathed a long sigh.

"I'm from Colorado; I came here a month ago. I just graduated from high school and got picked for a pre-med summer internship at a local medical school. I felt lucky they took me, you know, because things have been getting bad for the past several weeks. Fuel shortages. Food shortages. Stuff we all know."

"But when I arrived, they put me right to work. The hospitals are worse than you can imagine ... " She paused, as if seeing it in her memory. "They're just awful."

"Anyway, after weeks of things getting worse and worse I had to get away. So, two nights ago, when some of my new friends said they were going out to a place downtown, I invited myself along. I'm not twenty-one, but nobody cares anymore."

He noted she just graduated from high school, so she couldn't be *much* older than he was.

"We ended up in a place down here," she pointed north of the city center nearby, "and inside was wall-to-wall packed. I hung with my colleagues and spent a couple of hours dancing, talking, yelling—you know, stuff girls do out on the town. At least in normal times ... "

Her voice was clear but distant.

"There were tons of drugs and alcohol right out in the open, but that wasn't for me—I don't do either. But the fun and loud music took my mind off things for a while, and when I came up for air it was already two in the morning. I was done."

Victoria stood up and stepped a few paces away from the tree, then turned around to face them both. She conveyed a nervous energy and seemed to brace herself for the next part.

He got a better look at her, almost daring himself to gaze in her direction. He had next to no experience around girls in a social setting. He steered clear of them in school. There weren't many girl gamers who enjoyed the types of video games he played, and none of his friends had girlfriends, either. He had too many other things to keep himself occupied.

With Victoria, he willed himself to play it cool and actively listen and nod, wondering if his embarrassment showed. However, he was struck by her silver chain with a small cross hanging around her bare neck. He couldn't define the reaction to it, but he found himself less intimidated, and could look at her without most of the usual awkwardness. He tried to understand where the feeling had come from as she continued her story.

"So, several of us were preparing to leave when we heard a 'pop pop pop' over the blare of the music. We saw the front security guy stagger-step our way, his gun still in his hand. He was being chased by ... some very sick people. Then things got out of control."

Victoria seemed shaken as she recalled her tale, but it was already familiar to him after his morning. The plague victims had gone insane —become zombies, if you fancy that term—and had found a nice cache of fresh meat inside the noisy nightclub.

"I saw those sick people come in, so I ran the other way—out the back door. No way I was going to touch those bat-stuff-crazy infected; they had the double-Ebola already." She hesitated. Her voice was a broken whisper. "I didn't tell anyone. I just bolted. I left them."

She spoke with real sadness. "And outside was no better. A few people stood around smoking as the first of us tumbled into the alleyway. I got there just in time to see a couple of infected harass them, too. So, I kept on running."

She pointed to the north again, then motioned toward the central part of downtown. "I headed that way. I broke the kitten heels off these shoes, so I could run even faster." She looked down to her black shoes, now covered in scratches and road grime from her escape.

"Nearly all the lights were off here in downtown at two in the morning. It was eerie, to say the least. The lights of the Arch were still on, so I joined a small group also trying to get here. Along the way, plague victims continually seeped out of the darkness to attack us. Guys tried to fight them—to protect us girls, I suppose—but they always ended up getting brought down. Since we had no weapons, all we could do was run."

She got quiet once more. "God help me, I ran. I left all my friends behind. I kept running. I betrayed everything I believed about being a good Christian. A good person. I didn't try to save anyone but myself. How selfish am I?"

He didn't know how to respond. He wasn't religious, but he could respect the devout of any faith. She had taken her desperate running as a sign of weakness in her religion, while most people—including him—would see her actions as just the opposite. It wasn't like she could carry the slower people on her shoulders.

He looked up at Grandma, suddenly aware of the implications. Would he be forced to run and leave her behind? *Could* he leave her behind? The thought had crossed his mind a few times, but now Victoria's story made it all the more real.

"I'm not sure how long I kept going. It felt like a bad dream. I ran all the way to the river's edge before I stopped. I wanted to jump in and just float away, but after what I'd seen in the shadows, the black water scared me too much. I began to wish I would have made even a token effort to save someone else."

She shook her head, as if tossing out the bad thoughts.

"I was so amped up that first night, I was scared to be alone. I got away from the water and walked around aimlessly in the small crowds under the Arch until dawn. Eventually, I found myself staying close to the police officers near the edge of the city. At least I knew *they* had guns and could protect me. Several times they did."

"In the late morning, tornado sirens began to wail. The panic they caused down here was incredible. People scattered in all directions. I watched as some jumped in the river only to get washed away. Many people left the park; others came in. I was one of those who left. I tried to get back to my dorm, but it only took a few close encounters to realize I'd have to wait under the protection of the police down here, or I'd end up dead. By the time it got dark last night, I was safely back inside the park. I tried to find someone in charge, so I could ask what to do next—but that person doesn't exist, apparently."

A soft laugh.

"The last thing I remember was collapsing next to this tree, right here. I sat down to lean myself against the trunk and fell asleep instantly. I woke up when you ran me over." She pointed at him, but without much hostility this time. Maybe even a wisp of a smile.

"I'm sorry. I'm *unloading* on you. I just needed someone to talk to. A confession, I guess."

"That's OK, dear. Liam and I are good listeners."

Victoria looked around again, as if getting her bearings. "How did all these people get here? Where are they going? Is anyone helping the sick? Is anyone rescuing those still trapped in the buildings downtown? Where are the medical teams?"

Grandma answered, "Sweetie, I think you know more than we do."

Victoria crossed herself, "Then God help us all."

Grandma responded with a similarly solemn, "Amen."

4

They settled in after Victoria gave them a little more backstory. He also told her of their adventures, up to the point where they reached the Arch. She seemed impressed he was able to get his great-grandmother safely to this point, which made him feel proud, despite all the doubts he'd had along the way.

Grandma fell asleep as they traded details of their stories, and the afternoon crept on. He and Victoria sat in the grass, a bit away from Grandma so she could rest and recover in relative peace. The crowd was thick everywhere now but was very subdued, given the situation. From time to time, they heard gunshots on the periphery of the grounds. He assumed it was the police cordon being tested by the infected. He couldn't see anything nearby to suggest zombies were in the park ... yet.

"So, what are you guys going to do next? Are you going to try to get over to Illinois?"

He looked out through the line of trees and could barely make out the two bridges that bracketed the Gateway Arch grounds. He didn't see traffic moving in either direction. He was pretty sure they were closed. He hadn't mentioned that to Grandma as he didn't want to worry her with all the other problems they were wrangling.

"I don't think the bridges are open anymore. That could make getting to Illinois difficult, especially for her. I don't think she's ready to swim across." He laughed a bit at his joke, but the truth was he did wonder how they could sneak over there. He didn't want to admit he may have come downtown for nothing.

Victoria gave a wan smile. "I had hoped to get back to my dorm room to change these clothes, but then I want to go to the airport and see if there are flights to Colorado."

He hadn't even thought about airplanes since this whole disaster started, but he had a feeling getting a flight wouldn't be that easy. One recent news event broke through his gaming-fueled information isolation; the Ebola crisis from the previous summer. He remembered how they stopped all flights from the affected countries to prevent the disease from spreading to the United States. It worked, or so they were told. The disease never broke out in America, despite a few isolated cases. "No cordon is ever 100% effective," the news had said.

But was there some parallel with this new disease? He'd heard it described as both flu and "Ebola-like" by people over the last couple of days. Did it simmer somewhere overseas only to explode at some point because the proper protocols weren't in place? Something to chew on, though he knew it was unlikely he'd ever get the truth.

The talk of Colorado jogged a memory of another family member, his dad's mom. Liam's minor claim to fame—actually he was more embarrassed than anything—was being related to a politician. Grandma Rose ran for, and won, a seat in the US House of Representatives the year before. She wasn't around much—she lived in Colorado—so he knew very little about her other than she sent $100 bills for birthdays for as long as he could remember. His dad mentioned her once recently, while talking to Grandma Marty on the phone.

I wonder if she'll survive in the Rocky Mountains?

Liam imagined Colorado would be safer than most places, with its remote mountain ranges and sparse population. He doubted Grandma Rose—a rich politician—would be out in a tent in the mountains staying safe, but if Victoria ever made it home, he might at least ask her to look her up.

Although he had his doubts about Victoria's travel chances, he opted to say nothing to dampen her spirits. As with the boy earlier, he felt the pang of jealousy, because he didn't want her to find refuge while he labored in the chaos of this city. The ill-feeling passed faster this time. He knew he would be happy for anyone who escaped, especially this pretty girl conversing with him.

She continued to talk about the details of her life, but he found himself increasingly distracted with worry. His mind was in overdrive to answer the only question of consequence.

What are we going to do next?

5

He snapped back to the present as a priest hovered over Grandma, mumbled a prayer, and put ointment of some kind on the backs of her hands. Her head was slumped over.

With a bolt, he was back by her side. "Excuse me; my grandma's not dead."

I'm 99% sure.

The priest was an old black man, with white hair and sad eyes. He was in black pants with a black shirt, with only a white collar to give his profession away.

"Hello, my son. This is just a precaution. She doesn't have long with this plague going around."

There was an anger building inside Liam he didn't quite understand. No matter how well-intentioned, he didn't like the idea of this priest essentially giving up on Grandma.

He stood there and watched the ritual, not knowing what to say or do.

The commotion must have jostled Grandma awake, and she took things in stride. "Father, please. I'm not dying!"

Thank God!

The priest looked at her for a moment, finished his prayer, and departed with a final, "Go with God."

Grandma crossed herself. She looked at Liam and Victoria. "Don't let them bury me while I'm napping."

She winked at them and began rooting around in the backpack by her side.

"I wish I could go back to sleep," Victoria said.

He thought for a second before replying, "Well, it seems like you had a good night's sleep under this tree. At least until we found you and ruined it."

Both of them gave an honest laugh at that.

"I tell you what I really wish for today—my Bible. I know it probably seems silly and puritanical, but, you know, I like to feel the presence of God watching over me. It always helps me find peace to read through the challenges of all those men and women during ancient times, especially the Old Testament. It makes me feel part of something larger, and not just one woman alone in all this trouble."

His mind raced. He wondered if he should say something suave like, "You're not alone anymore," or if he should just play it chill and say something neutral along the lines of "I wish I could find comfort in a book."

Instead, he said, "I'll find a Bible for you."

"Oh, no, you really don't have to. I'll grab mine when I go back to my dorm."

“Of course.” He felt a little stupid for having made the comment. Anxious to move on, he asked her more about Colorado. He envisioned following her back to her dorm and teaming up with her to get to the airport. Grandma could come along, and they would all get out of the city by way of Colorado.

What am I thinking?

Many times over the last couple days he had incidents where his brain betrayed him, either making him too slow, too cocky, or too scared. Sitting here with Victoria, he explored new territory when it came to his mind going off the reservation. It wasn't just that he found her attractive—he found lots of girls attractive, though he was normally deathly scared of making that fact known to them—but with all the tension and stress of the last twenty-four hours, he saw this girl as someone worth his time, and possibly his life. He knew he would do almost anything to save Grandma—but he knew, and she knew, some things would just be the end of her. She wasn't going to magically get out of her chair and run away from a horde of zombies. In many ways, she lived on borrowed time. In contrast, Victoria represented a new-found willingness to lay down his life to ensure such a vivacious girl goes on living, no matter what the personal cost.

But I've only known her for a couple of hours!

He admitted that was all the time he needed.

LAST RITES

Liam and Victoria had both settled down next to Grandma, as he needed to catch a little shut-eye after his long day. Victoria seemed in no hurry to leave and even offered to watch over them while they slept, which made him very happy.

It felt like only minutes later when Victoria shook him awake.

"Liam. Check this out."

He opened his eyes to find another priest with Grandma. This time, she was awake and talking animatedly to the theologian. He listened as the man spoke in hushed tones.

"We must be very careful. The park is filling up too fast." He looked at Liam and Victoria crouching next to him, "Do either of you know where the Arch service dock is located?"

"I've jogged by there a couple of times," Victoria whispered back. "I know it."

A runner! I was right.

Whispering now, the priest gave them instructions to move to the dock after it got dark, and he would be there to meet them.

Liam heard his message but didn't really understand it until he had a chance to speak with Grandma.

"That was Father Cahill. I've known him since he was ordained—about the same time your father was born. He was administering last rites on me," she giggled. "I think he was the third one today! Look at all this oil on my hands. When he saw who I was and realized he knew me, we started talking. That's when he told me he has something he wants to show us. I'm not sure what this is all about, but I trust him with my life. I trust him with my soul."

"Did he say I could come too?" Victoria asked, with just a touch of anxiety.

"Of course, dear. As far as I'm concerned, you're welcome to stay with us as long as you need."

He kept quiet, though he felt a faint glow in his heart get just a bit brighter.

"OK, I'll stick with you guys until they get this all sorted out, and I can walk back to my dorm."

They settled back down as the evening wore on. Realizing the danger of showing food or drink in the nervous crowd, they snuck a little food and drank just enough to feel something in their stomachs. So many others clearly didn't even think far enough ahead to have one afternoon's worth of provisions. Many were walking around begging, or just shouting to whoever would listen that they needed this or that. The crowd had been calm for most of the day, at least the several hours since they arrived, but the atmosphere was slowly changing as the "pleasant afternoon" of waiting evolved into the "long night with no food or water." Or sanitation.

A crowd this big normally would have banks of port-o-potties and scores of support staff to keep them operational. This crowd had now ballooned to the tens of thousands, and there was nowhere for anyone to privately do their business. Naturally, this meant everyone just did it wherever they felt like it. Without any leadership to tell the crowd what to do, people just did whatever they wanted.

When Liam, Victoria, and Grandma got up in the fading light of dusk, they found the thirty-foot wide paved path filled with people who were sitting on every square inch of pavement, save one small channel of walkers right down the middle. It made it very difficult to move the huge wheelchair without begging sitting or sleeping people to move just a few feet farther out of her way.

It took half an hour to go the short distance to the dock. It sat in a depression that was hard to see from the main path, although there were a few people loitering about the area. There was simply no way to hide anything in the park with such a crowd.

They could see a small doorframe next to a closed garage door at the end of a small paved service lane on a downward ramp.

Once again, the trio pulled to a stop and began waiting.

Even if the doors opened, there would be no way to get in without being seen.

"Grandma, how are we going to get in?"

"The Lord will provide."

He and Victoria both said "Amen," although he had his doubts.

2

Their prayers were answered in short order—just as dusk fell.

"Hello, my friends."

Father Cahill had been waiting in the crowd and came to see the lady in the huge wheelchair. Liam noticed he had removed his white collar.

"All through the day, I've been collecting the aged and the infirm and bringing them through this door, but earlier there weren't as many people. Now you can see they've flooded all over, including right here at this dock. I can get you in, but this might be the last time we're able to get anyone inside without there being some trouble. I doubt we're going back out, either. Are you sure you guys want to ride this thing out inside the Arch museum? That's where I want to take you."

The three looked at each other and nodded their heads in the affirmative. Whatever was inside had to be better than sitting under a tree with an increasingly desperate crowd. Victoria said things were worse at night. Plus, Liam believed there might be someone in charge who knew the situation. He might be able to figure out how he could get Grandma to safety if he could get some time with that person. It was a long shot, but currently the *only* shot.

"All right. I have one other person I'm going to try to get inside. He's that older gentleman sitting near the door. My plan is to go help him up, tap on the door and hope they open it for me. When you hear me knock, move quickly over there. I'll try to get them to hold the door open for you. The closer you are to me, the better, if you catch my drift."

He scuttled off.

Liam and Victoria situated Grandma in her chair while all three faced the door fifty feet away. Father Cahill seemed to have trouble getting the old man to stand up, and some men and women sitting in the vicinity volunteered to help.

He could see what was going to happen now that several more people were paying attention.

"Let's make our way in that direction," he whispered. "Victoria, will you push the chair? I want you to push it inside, no matter what happens to me. Can you do that?"

"Yes. But let's all get inside."

That's the plan.

They changed positions while keeping one eye on Father Cahill and the old man, who was now up and standing, but the priest seemed hesitant to do what he needed to do next. He was holding the old man, the gentleman's arm slung around his neck. Father Cahill noticed Liam had moved his group closer, nodded to Liam, pivoted to the door and gave it a loud knock in an apparent secret cadence.

"Pick it up, guys, and don't stop."

The knock attracted the attention of several men near the door, already alerted by the commotion with the old guy. Some who were sitting were now standing, and some who had been standing were now moving toward the door. Everyone in earshot of the knocking was curious.

The door opened with a flourish, and two chiseled men with sleek black rifles popped out. They pushed past Father and his ill friend to let them in and held their guns in a menacing fashion for anyone who fancied a peek inside.

Victoria pushed Grandma right up to the closest man and yelled, "We're with Father Cahill!"

The man with the gun made no movement to open a path for the wheelchair. He stood his ground. His friend was looking in another direction, gun trained on some of the men who were closest.

One of those men yelled, "We're with Father Cahill!" Then it was a chorus.

How did this happen so quickly?

Victoria looked deflated at the turn of events. There was no way to prove who they were. No way to prove they were with the clergyman, unless he came back out.

The two gunmen began stepping backward as if to retreat into the small door. However, just as they were starting their motion, Father Cahill was there. He yelled in the ear of the nearest man and pointed to

Victoria and Liam. The two men once again moved out from the door and pointed to Liam's group.

Victoria plowed ahead. The wide chair was just able to fit into the door, though the wheels scraped as it went through.

Liam punched through too, though he felt the crowd surge behind him. He was glad he didn't have to sacrifice himself to get the three of them in; he wasn't even sure he would have been able to sacrifice himself. Not against two guys with that kind of hardware or a hundred scared civilians.

In the dark, it was hard to gauge numbers, but he guessed there were maybe thirty or forty people near the door by the time they got in, meaning there was a sizable crowd angrily looking at a closed door right about now. Would it take them long to figure out they could break it down?

Every disaster book he'd ever read was now screaming the answer to him. The death clock had started ticking—how long would it take for this stronghold to fall?

3

"Thank you, Father. You could have easily left us out there."

"No problem, my son. I'd do anything for your grandmother and anyone important to her. I'm just sorry I don't have more to offer you than a dark cavern for sanctuary."

"Are those people going to break through that door?"

The two security guys were moving some heavy equipment from the garage area over to the door they'd just come through. The biggest item was a riding lawn mower; apparently, this was an area where they stored equipment for maintaining the Arch grounds.

The five of them left the guards to their task and started walking up the hallway to the main museum.

Between the two legs of the monument was an underground area dedicated to ticket sales, two tram-loading areas to get up and down the legs of the Arch, a large museum devoted to frontier living, and a little gift shop and candy store. In the middle of it all was a large waiting area with plenty of seats around the walls, so people had a place to sit while waiting their turn to go up in the structure. It was now filled with sick people, along with lots of elderly folks, and even a few young parents with infant children. It was a group where Grandma would fit in perfectly. Victoria rolled her into the vaulted space, and they found an area along the outer wall where they could park the wheelchair and have a little room to sit next to it. The dull light of some dim bulbs hanging from the walls provided light in the subterranean refuge.

Father Cahill helped the older guy sit in the same area, though the man made no effort to talk to them, or even look at them. He merely slumped against the wall, clutching himself as if he was freezing. Liam didn't like the thoughts swirling in his head about all the sick people in his field of view. Did they all have the plague?

Do I? Would I know it?

Though he didn't voice the question, the priest seemed to sense the reticence of both Liam and Victoria as they looked around the room.

"I'm afraid we don't know who has the sickness if that's what you're thinking. It was the first thing I thought of when I started bringing people in here. Heck, when I saw the growing crowds up top, I was thinking it. How does the disease move around? Is it airborne? Passed by direct contact? By fluids? My best guess, based on hearsay, is people either get bitten by another infected person, or they seem to get a type of flu which leads eventually to the Extra-Ebola—a.k.a. E-Ebola. Without proper medical facilities, we aren't able to make even the most basic medical checks of these people. We can't even take someone's temperature. However, they wouldn't survive for very long up top in the heat of the day—so on balance, myself and the other clergy decided it was worth the risk. I guess if we all have it, we'll all die together down here."

Liam wasn't reassured.

"There's a preemie baby somewhere in this room that we had to get out of the heat, and that's why we brought in several very young children in addition to those who are clearly sick, or the infirm, like your grandma."

"Who are you calling infirm? I'm only 104."

He gave Grandma a big smile. She was returning to her feisty self again.

"Of course. I meant these *other* infirm people," the priest said in a very quiet voice. Everyone chuckled along.

Father Cahill then motioned to the far side of the room, near the entrance to the main museum. "Those folks over there are the families of the officers up top. The only condition given by the police who volunteered to protect the crowd was that their families be given refuge in a defensible position on the Arch grounds."

"Oh, man. You mean the police aren't actually on the job?" he replied.

"Technically no. The entire St. Louis police department is working today, but that's only on paper. The Archdiocese had contact with the brass over at City Hall as we tried to coordinate some kind of refuge here at the Arch, but they made it clear they couldn't order their officers to do anything as of the president's speech yesterday. City government has come undone. We were able to work out a compromise of sorts with some of the officers who were willing to bring their families here. The department supported the effort because they knew there wasn't much else they could do."

"But what about the rest of the city?"

"I'm not sure. You'd have to ask one of the officers."

He considered that as advice for later. He felt compelled to understand the wider world, as it could offer clues as to how they could escape the city, and where they could go.

Father Cahill was saying, "—and finally there are a few Red Cross and CDC folks in the candy shop. They're using the tables back there as a kind of command center, although they're just the managers and not the field personnel—so they have no medical supplies or trained medical people. I'm afraid their presence, and the rumors they brought medical help, are what attracted many people here."

"Well, that's just great." Liam wasn't in the mood to cut anyone any slack when it came to protecting his family from the plague. He saw the people in the shop standing around, talking.

"How can they fight the disease if they have no resources?"

"Liam, my young friend, I think it is safe to say no one here is fighting much of any disease."

Yep, that's just wonderful.

4

Since they carried very little, there wasn't much effort required to settle in for the night. Victoria was still very protective of Grandma's food and water but risked doling out more to her in the near-darkness of the interior. He was watching Victoria and appreciated she took none for herself.

He had a short nap sitting under the tree earlier in the day, so he wasn't yet ready to settle in for the night. He asked Victoria to keep an eye on Grandma while he went to look for answers.

He went right to the candy shop.

There was just enough light he could get around everyone sitting on the floor. There were many more people crowded in the vault-like room than he initially thought. Other than a few coughs and a baby crying, most people had chosen to remain silent as they waited for ... who knows. It was unnatural. He figured nothing like this had ever happened before, not even close, so no one really knew how to act or what to expect.

The medical folks were still standing where he'd seen them earlier. Others sat around a couple of small tables, but he was shocked to see what they were doing.

Drinking.

"Hey. Excuse me. Can I come in?"

A young-looking man with suit pants, a white shirt, and a horrible tie was among those standing at the door; he motioned him in.

"Come on in, friend." He saluted with a bottle of beer. Others in the group did the same.

"Umm. Thank you."

They pushed out a chair for him, and he sat. He felt very uncomfortable with all the eyes on him, and the room fell suddenly quiet. He decided to get it over with.

"I just arrived here with my grandma and a friend. I'm tired as hell, but I'm trying to find someone with answers."

"Grandma, huh? Was that the old lady you were pushing in that wheelchair? I saw you guys come in."

"Yeah, that's her. She's been through a lot, but we're safe for now."

"I don't know how safe we are." Tie-guy said with a slight chuckle, "How old is she? She looks to be about a hundred!"

"One hundred and four, to be exact." He was proud of the fact, though he really couldn't explain why once it had come out of his mouth. If she were a lot younger, their escape would probably have gone a lot smoother.

"I was wondering if you could tell me what's going on? I mean, with the plague."

Everyone at the tables looked around at each other as if deciding who would answer him. It was the man with the ugly tie who spoke up first, and Liam noticed he downed a good portion of his beer before starting.

"I'm Douglas Hayes from the CDC." He waited for a few seconds to let that sink in. "And you are?"

"Liam Peters."

"OK, Liam, I know what you're thinking right now, 'big-shot CDC guy who has all the answers,' but I'm sorry to disappoint you. I know very little about what's happening outside this room. I'm more of a middle manager," he waved his hand as if presenting his colleagues and said, "We're all more or less middle managers."

"The priest said you guys might at least know what's happening," Liam continued.

"We're not going to tell some random kid," Hayes replied with a stern face before laughing a second later. "I'm joking! But seriously, we don't know much," Hayes said with a laugh. He then pointed to a plain-looking, red-headed woman and said her role was to scout out locations for constructing tents and generators as part of the advanced team dedicated to St. Louis. Another person was responsible for shipping the equipment from Atlanta. Hayes went around the room, assigning roles to every fourth person or so—and as the Father said they were more logistical in nature than medical.

The only person even remotely connected to medical information turned out to be a middle-aged, Indian-looking "IT support person."

"You want to tell this kid anything?" Hayes asked her.

"Hello, Liam. Sure, what the hell. I've already told the police over there. I'm April." She had a British accent, which Liam found fascinating, "I'm afraid I know absolutely nothing for sure, as I've been telling my friends all day. The CDC isn't very tight with email or internal file security—I know that probably sounds crazy—and I've been able to glean some information by looking—accidentally—at some critical correspondence inside the agency."

She gave a nervous laugh as she drained the final portion of her beer before going on. "The main lesson I learned is that this plague has caught everyone off guard, including the CDC. I've hacked into the accounts for people all across the chain of command, and it's always the same—emails full of confusion, anger, and impotence."

Hayes continued, "Anyway, we were sent here as part of an advanced team that was supposed to get the jump on the plague in a city that hadn't already succumbed. Most of the East Coast is already gone. St. Louis was deemed far enough west that our bosses thought it would provide good intel on how the disease spreads and hopefully offer help in mitigating that spread. They were able to get us out here but, with the breakdown of transportation networks, they weren't able to get our gear here, and no one knows whether the medical teams ever departed Atlanta. The US military seems to have commandeered everything that flies."

Hayes tilted his bottle to drain it in his mouth.

"We got here late yesterday afternoon and have been waiting ever since. None of our cell phones work reliably anymore, but when they do we get no response from anyone in our chain of command. Glad you asked, huh?"

Hayes slammed his beer bottle on the table.

"So now we're sitting here drinking beer, spilling our guts to whoever asks, waiting for the double-E Doomsday Bug to roll through the city and make our jobs obsolete."

Victoria walked in the door just in time to hear Hayes' last sentence. Her response, standing next to Liam, was to make the sign of the cross.

Hayes, seeing this, went on, "That won't help, I'm afraid. You won't find god, religion, whatever, in the cities anymore. At least those on the East Coast. This is it, folks, the end of humanity."

Victoria was unperturbed. "Then we need prayer more than ever."

Hayes chortled, then seemed to recompose himself. "We'll see, won't we?"

In the face of such bad news, Liam didn't know what to say. He'd read enough to appreciate the moral dilemma of whether God was present when such evil was consuming the world, but that was only in books or in the movies. In the real world, it was a lot more ambiguous. He admitted to himself he couldn't visualize entire cities of zombies. All of it gone? Did the intoxicated people in this room really represent the final, best efforts of the government? His dad always mocked government ineptitude, but these guys were caricatures of the theme. Everyone might die because they did nothing.

"So, do you know anything about the plague itself? What caused it?"

"Dunno."

"Where it's from?"

"Dunno."

"Can anyone survive it?"

"Dunno. Hey, kid, don't you get it? We don't know *anything.*"

"But you said you had access to secret network files and all that. Surely there has to be something valuable in there?"

The IT woman spoke up, "That's just it. There *were* no files. Lots of emails looking for guidance, but very little actionable intelligence and almost no files relating to this outbreak anywhere in the system. Absolutely nothing about patient zero—the source of the whole thing."

"I don't get it. What are you saying?"

"I'm saying—we're saying—the CDC not only doesn't have any clues about the origin of this disease but as best we can tell, it didn't have any idea the bug existed until it had already scoured through most of the East Coast. We were caught totally and utterly flat-footed."

He felt mad more than anything else. He expected to glean some clues on how to save Grandma, and instead he was told that the one group in charge of solving this hadn't even deployed their researchers to start researching.

"So, you guys are pretty much useless now?" he said with more sarcasm than he intended.

Hayes' eyes went cold. He glared at Liam for just a second before laughing it off. "Whoa there, partner! We did the best we could. We made it here. We did our jobs. Everyone else dropped the ball."

He didn't want to let them off the hook but knew he was being unfair.

"Sorry. I meant did anyone get out to study the disease?"

"Oh yeah, lots of teams went to the East Coast. Some even went out the front door of the CDC headquarters into greater Atlanta as it succumbed. But everything happened so fast there was no time to make any headway against it."

"There are no reports in the system. I've looked. Teams go out and never report back in." April looked disappointed as if she had spent a lot of energy on this task.

He turned around to leave. Obviously, he wasn't going to learn anything from this group. But something occurred to him as he was saying goodbye.

"Oh, one more thing. This is my conspiracy-theory father talking, but is there any way someone could have deleted all the files in your system? Could that be why there's no data?" He laughed a little, indicating his belief it was a crazy thing to suggest.

The room became very quiet. He sensed the change in attitude.

Douglas stood up, pulled at his tie, and looked around at his colleagues.

"Congratulations, my smart-ass friend. It took us twenty-four hours to figure that out."

The implications were obvious and stunning.

"So, you're saying that not only is the CDC not fixing this disease, but it may have had a hand in causing it?

Hayes answered as he walked deeper into the room, away from Liam. "Maybe they didn't cause it, but if anyone there knew who did, it's been purged. Why do you think we're just sitting around drinking and chatting up the locals?"

Looking at Victoria, he saw her once again making the sign of the cross.

He thought about mimicking her, but the moment passed.

5

He and Victoria returned to Grandma and told her what they had learned in his discussion with the "experts" on the disease. Grandma was nearly asleep, so she didn't say much. Victoria shared her thoughts too. They both talked in whispers so as not to wake anyone else—or scare them.

"They said the *entire* East Coast was gone. Wow. Wouldn't we have heard something on the news about massive plagues in all those cities? Did they mention Denver before I came in?"

"I should have asked them about Denver. Sorry."

"It's OK," she replied in an upbeat manner.

"So. Would we have heard about all the sick people on the East Coast? I don't know. I don't watch the news, so I can't say whether there were clues about what was really going on or when this started.

Maybe they thought it was just the flu—not E-Ebola? A bad run of the generic flu wouldn't be big news, would it?"

"Probably not. But that reminds me of a story," Victoria said as she looked around. "I thought this was a tall tale when I heard it, but after what you just told me, it may hold some truth. Back at Washington University where I started my internship, we heard this rumor."

She again looked around, like it was going to sound crazy.

"One dark and stormy night," she said with a scary-sounding voice, followed by a laugh. "Isn't that how all horror tales start?"

"Just tell me!" he whisper-shouted.

"Eesh. Where's your sense of drama?" she stuck her tongue out at him. "Any-hoo, these two policemen were stationed outside the morgue of the research department at my school. They said no one was allowed to go in or *come out*. They supposedly got called in with a report of mischief inside the morgue. They figured it was students pranking the nurse on duty with the old 'he ain't really dead bit' but when they got there, they found several corpses really were 'alive' and there were no interns yanking the strings. They pulled back the sheets and found each of them thrashing around in their restraints, despite having the most grievous wounds you can imagine. The rumor said the cops ran out of the morgue, shut the door, and gave the order to seal it. Everyone else was pushed off the floor. The next day the morgue was completely vacant, but otherwise open for business. That's why nobody believed it could have been true."

Victoria finished her story, and the pair sat in the darkness of the cavernous chamber in silence.

"How long ago do you think that happened?" he eventually asked.

"I heard that well before the sirens. A week, maybe?"

"So, in that period, the plague must have exploded on the East Coast, it may have been starting here in Missouri, and it was all hidden from view. That doesn't seem possible to me."

"Me, either. But seeing infected people walking around has changed my perspective on a lot of things." Victoria laughed quietly. "I still don't believe the morgue story, though. Sick? yes. Look like they're dead? Maybe. Morgue dead? No way."

Despite her attempts at humor, her story scared him.

"Let's get some sleep and maybe tomorrow things will look a little better," he added.

Both settled uncomfortably onto the concrete floor, leaning against the hard wall. He offered his backpack to Victoria as a makeshift pillow. She accepted his gift readily and returned the favor by suggesting they lay near each other so they could each share the cushion—on opposite sides. It still wasn't much more comfortable, but it made him infinitely happier.

Thirty minutes later, as he was nearly asleep, a "crump" sound from outside jolted him awake. Several cops snoozing on the far side of the room jumped up, ran to the exit doors, and shot out into the main crowd under the Arch. He intended to stay awake and discover what they found out there, but the day caught up with him, and he drifted to sleep.

His final thought was of the CDC folks.

"Why do you think we're drinking?" Hayes had said. He thought he understood his meaning, but it jumped out at him in his half-sleep. Maybe they weren't drinking because they were afraid their bosses had scrubbed the records. Maybe they were drinking because they knew what was in the records that had been scrubbed?

He couldn't decide which scenario was worse.

TOURISTY STUFF

"ATTENTION PLEASE! ATTENTION!"

A police officer's booming voice cried out from the other side of the subterranean room, and it shocked Liam, Victoria, and Grandma awake. The man yelled a few more times and waited until he was sure everyone in the place was awake, with eyes on him.

Liam stole a glance back at the candy store and wasn't surprised to see it was pitch black inside, and none of the CDC people were stirring. He wasn't familiar with the concept of a hangover but did know that rough mornings followed late-night partying.

Or they just up and ran.

He tried to laugh that off, but it had struck a chord of truth.

The officer began his announcement.

"Thank you, everyone. Good morning. I'm Captain Osborne of the Missouri Highway Patrol. I'll get right to it. Last night, we almost lost the entire park. The cordon many of you saw coming in has been pulled back. We were able to stabilize the lines as we made them shorter, and we were also assisted by a few military units, including one tank and several Marine Corps Amphibious Assault Vehicles. As of this morning, the lines are holding. That's the good news."

Many voices shouted questions.

"I'm not done!"

That checked the anarchy. He paced as he continued.

"The bad news will take me much longer, I'm afraid. First, there are more infected than we ever imagined. Since we still don't know how this thing is spreading or why these infected citizens keep attacking the healthy, we can't take chances. We have *no choice* but to keep killing them. I'm sorry if that bothers some of you. It's our reality. That said, it's entirely possible we'll all run out of ammo before we can kill the whole city."

He inserted a laugh to soften the horror.

"Second, even though a few military units showed up, they came of their own volition and are probably classified as deserters from the main force sitting over in Illinois. They may have saved our bacon last night, but no one is coming to save theirs. Third, the military guys said they had orders to prevent anyone from crossing the river. They intend to keep the disease on *this* side and will use lethal force on anyone trying to cross to them—not even their own men can go back."

The small crowd started to pepper him with questions, but he took a deep breath, and bellowed, "So. Where does that leave us?"

The gallery quieted.

"I'm sure you know that my fellow law enforcement officers, my brothers and sisters you all passed as you came into the park, have been trying to keep this place secure from the infected victims, so we all have a chance of getting help and get the hell out of this mess. Our families are here, same as yours, and same as those people up top we're trying to protect. But now it looks as though no help will be coming."

Rather than noise, the captain got perfect silence.

"We lost many men and women last night. Even though we held them off, and improved our lines, the endgame is that unless we fight our way out of here we're going to be trapped."

Osborne paused a little too long, and the crowd finally exploded with questions, thinking he was done.

"Hold up! Let me finish. Our plan is to start organizing civilians for a breakout. We know there are plenty of men and women with weapons up top, and we think our only chance of escape with some sort of organization is to make those citizens aware of the impending collapse. To that end, I need some healthy volunteers. We are woefully short on manpower. You'd really be critical to helping the police, but you are ultimately helping yourself get clear of the infected assailants out there. We're gonna get out of here. Just give us time."

He and Victoria looked at each other, then at Grandma. She nodded.

They ran without looking back, wanting to make a difference.

2

They waited in a line of eight or nine others. There were a couple of young people besides themselves, but most volunteers were quite a bit older, and few looked overly athletic. Everyone could carry and use a radio, however, which was the only condition for volunteering. Some more people dropped in behind them as the captain gave assignments to those in front.

The volunteers ahead were given radios and moved off individually with officers waiting in the wings.

When it was their turn, he and Victoria stood shoulder-to-shoulder.

"Ah, finally someone who looks like they can handle some touristy stuff. I take it you two are together?"

"We aren't together-together, but we are together," Victoria said at the same time as he replied, "Oh, it's not like that." They looked at each other in a bemused fashion, to which the no-nonsense captain said, "Fair enough. I think it would be best to have you both go together for this task, though. Would that be OK?"

Both gave a too-quick affirmation.

"Step over to Officer Jenkins to my left," he said with humor, "and she'll get you squared away. Thanks in advance for doing a tough job."

As they stepped out of line, he overheard the captain say, "They're a cute couple. Reminds me of my daughter," to one of his aides. He wasn't about to ask if Victoria heard him.

He had no chance to think about what just happened because Jenkins took them deeper into the area dedicated to the police force and their families. She talked at an insane rate as if she were on caffeine or speed or something.

"Thank you both for doing this. I've got your radio. You'll need that to report back. I see you don't have the most comfortable shoes on. We'll try to find you a pair of sneakers. And ... "

She babbled on for a full minute and he didn't understand nine words out of ten. He caught some points about guns and tactical deployments and one or two lines about the failed power situation. He wanted to stop her for clarification, but one look at her eyes told him she probably didn't remember what she'd just said. They walked along next to her as she led them down a long hallway to a metal door that was propped open. She handed Victoria a radio, which she said was on the proper frequency. After a quick lesson on how to use it, she tossed a flashlight to him, saying they would definitely need it. She said goodbye and started running back up the hallway.

"But what are we supposed to be doing?" Victoria asked to her backside.

Jenkins stopped in her tracks but didn't come back. She paused and took a deep breath as if trying to steady herself in a whirlwind.

"Oh, yeah. Sorry, I thought I already told you. You have to climb the stairs of the Arch to the top, then look down into the park and report what you see. You two are our secret weapons. Go quick! Good luck."

She was off.

They cautiously entered the space behind the metal door, which was some kind of maintenance area. A stairwell led up. He held the flashlight, so he went first.

The long climb up the dark stairwell gave him plenty of time to wonder if the girl behind him was thinking about their mutually confusing interaction with the police captain. He knew his mind should be focused on survival, and getting Grandma to safety, and being smart about reporting from the top of the Arch—but he couldn't stop thinking of the big distraction behind him. They had both disavowed anything more serious between them. He didn't even realize something *could* be serious with her until he was saying there wasn't.

Why does she mean that much to me?

Behind him, the distraction gave no clues.

3

There are 1,076 stairs leading to the top of the Arch. A world-record holder could climb them in less than seven minutes. He had read that information on a metal plaque commemorating the event at the base of the stairs.

"I think we can beat seven minutes, don't you, Vicky?"

"Oh, don't call me Vicky. I *hate* that name. And yes, let's go for the record. I need a real challenge these days." She sounded drained, as if heading up the dark tower had crushed her spirit.

He wasn't sure how to interpret her tone or what she had said.

What am I doing wrong?

Silence followed him up the steps for the bulk of the climb.

To pass the time, he tried to visualize the arch-shaped building they were climbing. He'd been up in the Arch many times but had never gone up or down the metal-framed maintenance stairs. They were off limits to the public. Instead, the monument was designed to allow patrons to reach the apex using small trams—a sort of sideways subway with egg-shaped cars so small only five people could squeeze into each one. The builders installed a set of metal steps up each leg that could serve as an escape route if the trams broke down. It was closed to the public because it wasn't easy to climb all the steps, nor was it particularly safe—with steep ascents and harrowing descents going the other way. Today there was no power to run the trams, so the only way up was the lung-busting stairs.

As they neared the top, they found themselves frequently stopping to catch their breath. It became obvious why the captain chose the two most athletic youngsters. After minutes of silence, he delicately offered, "I'm sorry I called you Vicky."

"No... you're fine. I'm sorry. I had no right to get snarky." She paused while she took a few steps. "The way you said it brought back ugly memories for me. You can call me anything you want, really, as long as you don't call me by that particular nickname. Fair?"

"Totally. I'll just stick with Victoria. I really like your name."

Try not to sound like an apple polisher!

Finally, they came to a door with a small window centered about two-thirds of the way to the top. A low light filtered through the glass, indicating daylight ahead. He turned off his flashlight as he peered into the tram unloading zone near the topmost observation area.

He took so long that Victoria tapped him on his back.

"What's wrong?" she said in a soft voice.

He turned around and put his finger over his lips, pointed to the window, and sat down heavily on the topmost step. Victoria took her turn.

A zombie park ranger blocked their way.

She slumped down next to him.

He was fast becoming an emotional mess. The whole climb up he clung desperately to the flashlight, unusually afraid of the crush of pure blackness around them. He kept thinking about the gun in his face. His misstep with Victoria made him feel distinctly alone. He thought reaching the top would be a relief but instead he felt lower than ever. This new problem, along with his lack of weapon to dispatch it, weighed heavily on him. He felt a tear slide down his face and tried to wipe it away quickly. He didn't know if Victoria had been looking at his face, but the motion was unmistakable. The sniffle didn't help. She took his hand and they sat in silence for a few minutes. Her touch gave him strength, though he couldn't explain what exactly he felt at that moment. Protective of her? Was she protecting him? Were they helping each other cope?

"You want to know something funny? I left my gun downstairs. I put it in my backpack last night because I didn't want to sleep with it tucked into my pants. I figured it would keep waking me up as I rolled around on the hard floor. Everything happened so fast with the police request, I didn't think about grabbing my pistol again. I thought I was going to be the hero and protect you and Grandma, but I'm turning out to be anything but."

She squeezed his hand and let go.

"Do you want to know something funnier?" she asked. "I never got my replacement shoes from our fast-talking teacher. I was hoping she'd find sneakers to go with my cocktail dress!" She pointed down to her dress pumps with the heels broken off. "I tried walking the steps in bare feet, but the metal grating made it unbearable. I'm surprised you didn't hear me yelping while I was trying it out."

They both had a quiet laugh, breaking the tension.

"OK," she continued, "we can't go back down without trying to get in there. I don't think I could climb these stairs again. I say we think of a plan to deal with this guy, so we can do what we came here to do for the police."

"I agree, but what? Once that thing sees us, it's going to pursue us forever."

They discussed their limited options and settled on what appeared to be the only viable plan.

Liam took up a position next to the door while Victoria opened it and yelled loudly at the dead park ranger. The man kept his feet but stumbled down the steep stairs of the tram loading area. He came through the door moving fast; Victoria crouched behind the door and held it open. Liam, standing behind the door and above Victoria, saw the ranger arrive. It really didn't take much of a push to keep his momentum moving toward the steep staircase beyond. He tumbled face-first down the flight while he and Victoria continued through the door and slammed it shut. It took about thirty seconds for the ranger to regain his footing, climb back up the stairs, and wail at his missed meal through the small window.

"Well," Victoria said triumphantly, "we did it. We successfully switched places with a dead man." They laughed harder than the joke deserved, letting go of some of their pent-up anxiety.

"At least we aren't in his grave!" he added, to more snickers.

They could now see the apex of the Arch with all its windows for the observation ports. They could not see the companion tram-unloading area over the top and down toward the beginning of the other leg.

"I wonder if there are more undead on the other side?"

"All we can do is move forward and deal with things as they come. You ready to reach the top of this bitch?"

He mentally beat his head, realizing he probably shouldn't have used that word in front of a girl, but Victoria didn't seem to mind.

"I'm not one for cussing, but yes, let's climb this female dog!"

Together they went over the top.

4

There were no more zombies on the other side. They assumed the ranger had attacked someone in the observation area, and the injured party or parties dragged themselves to the steps going down the north leg, leaving the ranger to wander around in this confined space until fresh meat showed up.

"My god, there is a lot of blood up here," Victoria said while stepping around blotches of blood stained into the carpet.

His stomach turned at the sight; remembering Angie's cat didn't help. Or the foot. But he was able to, as his father would say, "keep his proverbial lunch down," for which he was very grateful while in the presence of Victoria.

"Let's stay away from that tram station for now; it could be slippery."

He agreed but added, "We have to go down one of the sides. We know at least one zombie is waiting for us in the south leg. I wonder if there are any in the north leg?"

"We'll save that as a delightful surprise for when we're done up here."

They moved to the topmost section of the monument; a marker informed them they were 630 feet above the ground.

The interior of the observation area is about the width of a typical subway car or municipal bus. The floor has the same curvature as the top section of the Arch as seen from outside, but the windows are slanted at about 45-degree angles away from the interior and sit on a low shelf, so when you look out the narrow portal, you're practically lying on your belly. Small children often lay down on the windows, usually with a concerned parent holding their legs as if the glass was about to blow out. He always found that a riot.

The slanted windows gave them a glorious view of the entire Arch grounds, as well as magnificent views in all directions with the exception of directly north or south, as those were blocked by the legs of the structure itself. To the west was the sprawl of downtown St. Louis. To the east were the river and numerous bridges linking Missouri with Illinois. One massive bridge to the north was new and modern-looking with twin piers rising high above, providing anchor points for hundreds of bundles of suspension cables. Always thinking of his books, he remembered a similar bridge from one of his zombie stories. The name Steubenville stuck out. Many heroes died blowing it up. He shuddered at having to do such a thing and wondered if he would ever have to resort to such desperation.

They got their bearings and focused their attention on the western half of the park, nearest the city. There were people on the riverfront side, but the captain had said the infected were coming almost entirely from the city side. Looking down, they both realized how hard it was to see individual people.

"Binoculars would have been helpful."

Victoria responded, "And a catered lunch would have really made this climb worthwhile."

She gave him a big smile as she pulled out the radio and called down. He was relieved when a man answered and not the fast-talking woman who sent them.

"This is Victoria and Liam. We're in position up in the Arch."

After ensuring she wasn't still on the air, she said to him, "I'm not sure what the protocol is, do I say 'over' when I'm done?"

He shrugged.

The radio crackled, "This is Arch base. We want you to report if you see large groups of ... crazies. Over."

Oh, I see plenty of those.

They looked out again. The muzzle flashes on the exterior lines of defense made it easy to see that outline. Everyone seemed to be holding the plague at bay. He was happy to see a lone tank moving back and forth along a frontage street, using its mass to crush the undead in front of it. Three Marine vehicles were parked between buildings. They sent round after round down the long streets whenever small threads of plague victims appeared, evaporating them.

"No, sir. We don't see any large groups. Over," she let go of the button to wait for a reply.

"Roger that. Please report in if anything changes. Out."

"So how long do wait up here?" she said while placing the radio on one of the window frames.

He had no answer. He wouldn't complain if he could spend all day up here with her—until he remembered Grandma was still downstairs, alone.

They settled in and waited. Each took turns moving to different windows to try to see if anything happened that would be of interest to the police below. It wasn't long before they made their first call.

"Hello, Arch base. This is Arch—" Victoria keyed off the mic. "What are we calling ourselves?"

"Arch summit?"

"This is Arch summit. There's a big mess of zombies to the north, pushing the line up that way. It looks pretty serious."

"Zombies? Good a term as any. Thank you, Arch summit. Understood. Out."

They watched a small group of men and women move through the crowd to a point on the northern line. Neither could see what happened in any great detail, but soon the line returned to where it had been and appeared stable.

"It's like white blood cells going to fight a virus," Victoria said. "We're in charge of sending the white blood cells where they're needed. They attack and push back the deadly virus."

He appreciated her analogy but looking down on the entire scene he thought she had it backward. Infected were stumbling down roadways as far as he could see. The little clump of cells below—mankind—was resisting the endless white blood cells being sent by the zombie host now controlling the rest of the city. It made him feel the futility of the thin ring of defense upon which they depended for their survival.

We should run.

He thought about it seriously. Blowing up a bridge wouldn't be so bad if it killed all of *them*. By comparison, all he could do was run for his life. For now, his job was to hold the line. Give the police the time needed to get them all out.

A little later, they noticed a single barge floating free in the river. They watched it collide with the pylons of several upstream bridges, pausing on each leg as it scraped by until it resumed meandering downriver. At the point closest to them on the water, they could see directly into the sunken hold. Even from such distance, the mass of infected inside was easily recognizable, all moving without purpose in their open-topped prison. The boat avoided the last two bridges out of downtown and was soon drawn away by the current.

"Well, that's one way to get rid of them," he said.

Hours went by without anything else of interest happening until Liam noticed movement on some of the streets.

"Victoria? Do you see this?" Liam's stomach was a fist of tension while she walked over to his window.

When she saw it, Victoria struggled to key the radio and make her call.

5

"Hello, Arch base. Come in. This is Arch summit." Victoria's voice was shaky and fast.

It required a few repeated calls, but someone finally answered. A woman—it wasn't clear if it was Jenkins—requested Victoria's report.

"We're seeing a huge mass of people on the north side moving toward the south. We think they're *living* people. They're shooting into our line. We can see flashes of guns, aimed at each other. I say again; these are people shooting other people—*not* zombies."

"Holy crap. Hold on a second. Over."

Looking down, the renegades had come in near the water of the riverfront, where the cordon was thin. They headed directly for the Arch. For them.

As if learning the fact at the same time, the radio crackled, "We see 'em. They're here. Looks like several gangs and other criminals. No Boy Scouts out there. You guys better come down. Out."

"That's it?" Liam didn't know what to expect of their mission. Did they give the police the information fast enough to make a difference?

They took a last look down. The cordon held firm most of the way around the park, but in the north, it took confusing twists and turns. It was destabilizing. He had read this scenario a hundred times in his books.

"OK, Victoria, which side are we going to go down? Do we choose door A and go back the way we came, with a raging sick ranger to deal with? Do we choose door B and go down the blood-filled stairwell with an unknown number of zombies below? Oh, and as a special bonus, we can come out at the base of the north side where even now a gun-toting crowd of criminals is closing in."

"Can I choose door C and jump out a window, please?"

"They gave me a parachute, so, yeah." He gave her a big smile.

She was also smiling. "It's good to see we both still have our sense of humor intact, despite the insanity down there."

"All that shooting has me scared sh—, uh, to death, but yeah, I just want to get back to Grandma now. I have to get her out."

"You think they'll make it into the Arch museum? What about all the police?"

"I think the police will fight hard to protect their families but look at the swarm of attackers. There's just too many. And if the northern line falls, we'll have bigger problems than armed gangs." He watched the buckling lines and imagined two white blood cells fighting each other as the deadly virus paced nearby with a menacing grin.

The host is committing suicide.

"Do you think we could open the door, let the ranger back up into the observation area, and give him the slip as we run back down and shut the door?" Victoria asked.

"It's worth a try. I like that better than exploring the north leg, waiting for a sick person or persons to jump us the whole way down."

They made their way to the south leg's unloading zone only to find their friend was no longer at the door. It had been several hours since they left him; he moved on. That meant he was somewhere on the 1,076 steps below.

"Want to change your answer now?"

He thought about it and decided he'd rather face the one zombie he knew was down these steps than an unknown number in the other leg.

"Let's go down this way and deal with him when we find him. We'll just have to move slow."

"Do you want a drink of water?"

"Do I ever! You found some?" he said excitedly.

"No, I was just asking," Victoria smiled as she joked. He couldn't help but laugh, too, although he made like he was going to punch her in the arm for saying something so mean.

He started down the dark staircase with the flashlight. Despite multiple layers of danger around him, he felt infinitely better than his walk up the steps earlier. He had his friend back.

Victoria, with the radio, trailed behind.

ANTIBODIES

Liam was stoked to be on good terms with Victoria again, but on the way down neither made a peep. The steep stairwell in the narrow space of the upper Arch was bad enough to do in the dark, but knowing a dead man was walking somewhere below sent his fear factor right out the window. If there were windows ...

Victoria tried to stay as close as possible; her quiet footfalls echoed his from the step behind. She kept a hand on his shoulder, so they would not get separated. His initial optimism as they started the descent had worn off, though he was overjoyed he wasn't doing it alone. He thought he might go insane if he had to try.

And if the light went out?

He looked down at the flashlight, as if to will it to stay on. It was bright and steady. The walk down was nearly as taxing on their legs as the climb up had been, though it was a different kind of pain. Adding to their suffering, they'd had no food or water since the start of the day's adventure.

The staircase wound itself around the machinery of the mechanical tram sharing the space. Rather than one continuous set of stairs, it was broken up with dozens and dozens of landings, so it could bend with the curvature of the structure. They expected to find the missing zombie on each landing as they went down. And each vacant landing heightened their anxiety. Was he on the next one? Was he still in the stairwell at all? Was he attacking Grandma at this very moment? Liam's imagination ran wild.

He tried to balance the prudence of a cautious descent with the pressure of escaping the Arch before the whole structure was overrun with the armed attackers swarming below. He wondered whether the mindless infected were worse than the men and women preying on their vulnerable peers.

About twenty minutes later, they reached the machine shop where they'd started. His stress level was off the charts because the ranger *had* to be somewhere close. They couldn't have missed him on the stairs. The same door was open that led up the hallway into the main waiting area. The zombie must have gone through there because it couldn't have been hiding anywhere else.

"How did that thing get past us? Do you think he was hiding?" He didn't figure that was a behavior of a normal zombie, but then, what was the normal behavior of a dead person? Seeing a real-life zombie made him realize "normal" and "zombie" could never be used together.

"No, he couldn't—"

They jumped when screaming began. *Someone* had found him.

But when they entered the main waiting area, they discovered it wasn't a zombie causing all the commotion; it was the criminals. They had already breached the north entrance by breaking all the glass doors and were now yelling and screaming back and forth with the police officers nearby.

He scanned the room and did see the ranger, after all, just making his way to some of the elderly and infirm people on the right side of the room, nearest the candy store. Well away from the police or the looters. Well away from help. While it was a matter of life or death for those closest to the crazed ranger, the zombie was a sideshow relative to the shouting battle in the rest of the cavernous room.

The looters wanted safety inside the Arch. The police replied that they would have to leave. Weapons of all kinds pointed at each other.

Liam and Victoria watched from the south hallway where it was very dark. He shut off the light and tried to establish some sense to what was happening.

The looters came in from the north, across the room from them, and controlled that entrance and the tunnel leading to the north leg of the Arch. The police were on their left, holed up in the museum. The large waiting area, filled with the elderly and the sick, was between them and both the police and criminals on the far side.

The sight of sick people lying on the floor, and the screams from those now being assaulted by the park ranger seemed to give the looters a reason to pause before they burst in with their greater numbers.

"There's Grandma. I have to get her out." He finally caught sight of her in the chaos. Grandma was right where they left her very early in the morning. He couldn't tell her condition, but she was still in her big wheelchair. She was maybe fifty feet from them, but only several feet away from the park ranger and his probing teeth.

"Wait here," he whispered.

"Be safe," she replied.

He ran out of the darkened hallway, straight for his guardian. A few senior citizens in the middle of the room were making for the south exit. He felt bad to use them as distractions, but they gave him the cover he needed from the criminals on the far side of the room.

Even so, while he was on the run, one of the invaders yelled, "These people are infected! Kill them all to save yourselves!"

Screams of fear erupted around him, overlaid with the intense sound of escalating gunfire.

He sprinted the remainder of the room while bullets whizzed by to reach Grandma. She was awake and clutching his backpack as a shield. He said nothing, just grabbed her chair, spun her in the right direction, and intended to push to save their lives.

The park ranger was nearby but wasn't the major threat. Not by a wide margin. But he was the *only* threat to the old man who had come in with them and Father Cahill. For a split second he locked eyes with the old guy as the ranger chewed on his neck.

"I'm so sorry," Liam said to the man, even as his dying eyes glassed over.

Liam took a deep breath and pushed off. He was already covered in sweat from mastering those stairs in both directions, but now his forehead dripped with beads of fear. Running into the field of fire only made sense compared to sitting in it.

With no hope of outrunning the bullets, many citizens on this side of the room stayed where they were and simply huddled in fear. He and Grandma sped by more than a few people doing nothing to save themselves, but the congestion made him an intolerably slow-moving target.

"Run!" he shouted at them. Mostly he screamed to keep his own feet moving.

He didn't dare try to go up the ramp to the south entrance because people who made it that far were being shot in the back as they neared that exit. Instead, he aimed for the same hallway he'd just left. Victoria would still be there—he hoped—and together they could get Grandma to the safety of the maintenance room.

As he pushed the wheelchair, he willed himself to be invisible. Despite the chaotic noise, a little prayer slipped out as he huffed.

"Please, God, help us."

Somehow Grandma heard him.

"Lord, let us fly."

Bullets sang "Amen" as they cut through the air.

2

While he rolled the chair back across the room, the police moved out of their space in the museum. Light came in through the north entranceway and it profiled the looters, giving targets to heavy shotgun slugs and bullets from service revolvers. That forced the bad guys to stop shooting the civilians and focus instead on the police.

With one final push around the corner, he was able to take a breath. They had escaped the carnage in the main room. Victoria dropped in behind him and together they ran to the relative safety of the machine shop down the hall. His ears rang after the loud exchanges of gunfire in the hollowed-out space.

At the final door to the maintenance room they had to help Grandma from the chair, so it could be folded to fit through the doorway then opened on the far side. They closed and locked the door, but he figured it wouldn't last long against bullets if they were discovered.

"I think I left my cane back in that room. Liam, would you mind fetching it?"

He was about to ask if she was out of her mind when he realized she was smiling innocently at him. *Who knew Grandma had such a dry sense of humor?* She had, in fact, left the cane behind, however. He was thankful they still had the chair.

Once they were safely in the room, he opened his backpack and drew out a water bottle and some grain bars for himself and Victoria.

After the climb and adrenaline bursts caused by gunfire, he was famished. His chest heaved up and down while he caught his breath.

Grandma waited for them to dig in. "Thank you, Liam. What in the world is going on?"

"You're welcome," he wheezed. "Victoria, let her hear what's on the police radio. That will make it clearer than if we tried to explain."

After some fiddling with the radio for better reception in its new location, they were shocked to hear a chaotic blast of yelling and cursing coming from it, unlike anything they expected on a police channel. Through the noise, they picked up some fragments:

"They have moved into the Arch's north entrance. My husband and the boys are trying to hold them off, but we're trapped."

"—the South team has managed to organize citizens, but we have very little cover. Trying to arrange transport to Carondelet."

"This is North Gate. We have a new situation here—" a man said, but the other callers soon squelched him.

He felt bad for the police but knew there was nothing he could do to help them. He was trapped in a stainless-steel room.

While the chatter continued, he grabbed his gun from the pack and put it back in his waistband holster.

"I'm never taking this off again."

He paused before looking at his companion. "Victoria, do you want my other gun?"

She peered at him in the harsh glare of the flashlight and seemed to think about it for a few seconds but shook her head.

"I appreciate the offer, but I'll be the plucky comic relief."

"The what?"

"I just don't think I want a gun, Liam, but thanks."

He tried to give the Mark I to Grandma.

"No, I'm too weak. I couldn't even pull the trigger." She chuckled.

Their appreciation of their chances of surviving this crisis underwhelmed him. He couldn't fathom ever being separated from his gun and didn't understand why anyone would choose to be unarmed. Grandma maybe if she couldn't hold it, but Victoria?

And perhaps the most important realization of the exchange was that he, Liam, was now wholly responsible for protecting them. One boy with a couple of pop guns against a world gone mad.

You said you wanted to be the hero.

3

They continued to listen to the radio for another half hour or so. The police in the museum had been able to survive against the infringing looters, but neither side could get the upper hand. The radio chatter was a little unclear, but it sounded like some of the sick and wounded lying in the middle of the waiting area had begun to show signs of reanimation—which caused havoc on both the police and the looters.

Up top, the battle had gotten very serious. The renegade urban gangs had lots of firepower and were able to push well into the park—up to and including the north leg of the Arch. But they couldn't go farther because the defenders on the rest of the cordon, organized by the captain and his police volunteers, had been able to hold their positions. The looters and gang members also had problems behind them, as the infected had followed them through the breech and were now nipping at their heels. Unable to get into the Arch and unable to get all their members safely inside the cordon, they now found themselves fighting enemies on multiple fronts. It made the ones inside the Arch desperate and nearly suicidal. The police admitted they were in serious trouble in the museum.

By late afternoon, another report from the radio operator called "North Gate" caught their attention.

"This is North Gate again. I'm in direct line-of-sight to thousands of infected pouring into the northern side of the park. As best I can tell, they're being attracted by all the gunfire. There are a few remaining civilians who are hiding in the parking garage or nearer to the river, but the swarm of dead are overwhelming anyone who stands in the way. The gangs pushed many civilians into the path of the zombies, which, in turn, has infected lots of people near your interior lines. You guys should be prepared for this."

The captain himself replied.

"Thank you, Ben. We owe you one. Hope to see you again so we can laugh about this over a beer. Over."

"Me too, Cap. I'm OK for right now. But I'm not sure how long I can hang under the bridge without being spotted. Maybe I'll fly away like a bat." He let out a nervous laugh, which was reciprocated by the captain as they signed off.

The trio listened to the radio for a while longer, expecting at any time to hear the whole park had been run through by the dead. They never heard from the north gate again, but several other stations kept reporting in. Things were not going well for the good guys.

Comms were cleared by a gruff new voice.

"Break, break. This is Raptor HQ actual."

The radio chatter from the police stopped cold.

"We are the blocking force located on the east bank of the Mississippi River. All bridges are under our control. No. I repeat N-O personnel will be allowed to cross the bridges, use boats, or otherwise transit across the water, by order of General Hodges, II Corps, United States Army. We've had several—Shall we call them volunteers?—disobey orders and cross the river to support you. Those men and women won't be allowed back, either. Be advised, I also have orders to terminate the infected now converging on your position. I'll give you all the time I can. Say sixty minutes. Out."

It appeared the Army could see what was happening too and took this delicate moment to remind everyone in St. Louis they still weren't allowed across the river.

The angry voice of the man who had called for volunteers from the group inside the Arch that morning blared from the radio.

"This is Captain Osborne with the Missouri Highway Patrol. On behalf of all of us laying down our lives to protect these citizens, let me just convey—" and went on to teach Liam a whole host of new curse words and make his ears burn with embarrassment because Grandma was right there listening, too. A glance at her showed no emotion on her face.

His world had been spinning out of control since the sirens turned off two days ago, but now he'd felt as if his rescue parachute was packed with bricks instead of silk.

"No help is coming," he said, as much to himself as to the others.

It can't get much worse.

4

"Well, what do we do now? We can't exactly step out of this room and make a run for it." Victoria was right, but no one had any better ideas. The stairs up the Arch were open, but going back to the top was pointless, and Grandma would never survive such a climb.

Looking around the room, they found various tools, workbenches, and maintenance equipment for servicing the top-to-bottom tramway. No weapons of any kind—not that anyone expected to find guns stashed away in a public piece of property like this.

He was probing the edges of the room when he said, "Hey, look at this grate on the wall. It seems to have a tunnel behind it. I can't see where it might go, though."

The thick metal grate, about three feet wide by three feet high, had a stout-looking lock on it. The wide latticework made it easy to see down the tunnel. A couple of keys hung on a small hook next to the opening. It wasn't rocket science from there.

He unlocked the grate, swung it sideways on hinges, and dropped the lock nearby. He started to follow the flashlight's beam into the darkness, but Victoria stopped him.

"I'll go," she said. "You need to stay here and protect your grandma." For a moment he feared Victoria was going to find an exit and run off and leave them. *That's crazy. But so is letting her go in there by herself.*

She cut off his protests quickly. "You're the one with the gun. You've got to protect your grandma." She took the small police flashlight from him and crawled down the concrete duct. After a few feet she disappeared around a turn, and he felt his heart drop. Grandma, as if reading his mind, reached over to squeeze his arm.

There was virtually no light in the room, except the illuminated EXIT sign over the door. He turned on his flashlight and started rooting around, looking for something that might help Grandma get down the tunnel if Victoria came back to tell them they could escape through it.

When she comes back. Not "if." When.

Grandma, in her chair near the door, said, "I think the shooting is getting closer."

"I have to find something to get you through this tunnel."

"Oh, no, I can't possibly go through there. Just leave me, Liam. Get yourself and Victoria to safety."

He knew she would say something like that, which is why he was determined to find just the right thing to get her to go with him. Absorbed in his search, he jumped like a scared cat when someone banged on the door. A disheveled man with a horrible tie peered in through the window: Mister Hayes from the group of CDC people.

"Do we let him in?" Grandma asked.

"If we don't, he's going to alert the whole place to this room."

He opened the door. As Hayes ran in, they heard a volley of gunshots. He pushed the door shut hurriedly but took care not to let it slam.

Hayes stood hunched over his knees, shaking.

"Shot ... us ... all," he wheezed.

Just then a small beam of light brightened the darkness in the room. Victoria crawled out of the tunnel. He had to fight down the urge to run and hug her.

"This tunnel leads out. It has another gate on the other end. Hopefully, one of these keys is for its lock. I think the exit is in a railroad tunnel. I could see the tracks with my light."

"Please help me find something to get Grandma through there." With Victoria's help he continued searching the room until he found the "something" he was looking for, hanging on a wall in a far corner. He grabbed it, adjusted it, and slapped it down in front of her wheelchair.

"It's your lucky day, Grandma. Just lay down on this mechanic's creeper, and I'll pull you to safety."

She looked at him, then at the creeper, and finally at the hole in the wall. Whether she was calculating her odds of making it through there or maybe just deciding if she really wanted to die in the Gateway to the West, he didn't care. He wasn't going to give her a choice. The building sound of gunfire seemed to make up her mind. She stood up, and with Liam and Victoria on each arm she was able to settle onto the creeper.

"Victoria, check the window. Mister Hayes, grab those other keys off the wall and hold Grandma here while I break down her chair."

Hayes had recovered control of himself, but his hands still shook as he got the keys, and his voice sounded ragged. "Thanks for letting me in. I never thought it would come to this. Why did those men start shooting us? Don't they know we're the government?"

Loud cracks of gunshots, seemingly outside the door, cut off the conversation. Everyone made for the tunnel.

He took charge. He finished breaking down the chair and ordered Hayes to go first with the keys and the chair.

"Victoria, do we need two flashlights down there?"

"It'll be fine, there are a few turns, but it's very flat and uniform all the way to the end. It isn't that far."

Hayes was already working his way into the darkness.

"OK," he said, "I guess you're going next, Grandma. You ready to roll?"

"I'm not getting any younger!" She loved that one.

As he began pushing her on the creeper, he heard banging on the door again and saw a shadow at the window. Victoria, closest to the entry, dashed for the tunnel just as a face exploded against the glass. Bullets tore through the upper part of the door and ricocheted off the metal of the machinery in the room. He hastened his pushing to give her room to jump in behind him.

"Turn off your light, Victoria," he called back over his shoulder. "Hurry! Let's go!"

Her light remained on. He looked back, shocked that she wasn't in the tunnel. She stood in front of the entrance, the grate in her hands and her watery eyes reflecting her light.

"It was nice meeting you, Marty. Take care of her, Liam."

She slammed the grate back into place, clicked the lock shut, and tossed the key into the tunnel. She gave him a determined look. "I have to do this," she said in a broken voice. Finally, she removed herself from his sight, the light from her flashlight bobbed toward the stairwell.

"Victoria!" He blurted it out without thinking who might hear. The echoes hurt his ears.

She had locked herself out and locked them in with no way for anyone to follow them.

He sat there, turning over options. In the end, he knew there was only one. He started to push the creeper again, to get as far down the tunnel as he could before anyone else came in the room. He was glad it was too dark for Grandma to see the tears on his face.

I wish I'd kissed her. He hated himself for thinking that selfish thought, but it was true. He wished he had gotten to kiss her before she left him like they do in the movies.

Heroes kiss the girl, then push them to safety. Not the other way around.

He looked back again, saw the merest hint of glow from her flashlight. It wasn't moving. She must have paused on the steps. Drawing the shooters away, at mortal risk to herself. *She* was the hero.

The shooting at the door continued for a minute or so. Apparently, the gunmen weren't very good at destroying door handles, or the steel was bulletproof. By the time he neared the end of the tunnel, men's voices echoed down the pipe behind him. They yelled to each other about a light going up the metal staircase.

He and Grandma found Hayes waiting for them in the strange sideways light of a hazy railroad tunnel.

The key had worked.

Thank you, Victoria.

HEROES

Liam and Grandma slid out the end of the service duct into a train tunnel with a double line of tracks running through it. Several people were already sitting inside. If they were surprised to see three people fall out of the dark hole in the wall, no one bothered to ask questions. They just went back to whatever they were doing.

That was fine with him. He wasn't in the mood to jaw-jack, as Grandma would say. He and Hayes helped her into her wheelchair. The loose rock under the railroad tracks made it difficult to roll her around, but they weren't going anywhere for now, so she was content to be parked and given time to relax. Lying on the creeper for the trip and getting back up had sapped her strength.

He slammed his backpack on the dirty rocks and took a seat next to it. He was getting more and more upset at the turn of events leading to the sudden loss of his new friend. He recognized the muffled sounds of gunfire coming from outside the rail tunnel but wasn't ready to think about what was going on out there. For now, it was more important to rest and formulate some kind of plan. Maybe a plan to save Victoria.

He was just turning to thoughts of going back in when Hayes sat down and began rambling.

"I can't believe those hoodlums shot us. We tried to tell them we were with the CDC and we were there to help, but that seemed to enrage them. The hell of it is, we aren't even really *with* the CDC, more like glorified roadies who move the gear for the pinheads with the lab coats."

He seemed to consider what he was going to say next.

"I did learn something from the pinheads, though ... "

He looked around like he was participating in a conspiracy. Seemingly satisfied he wasn't being overheard, he continued.

"The virus causing all this was made in a lab."

Despite being crushed about losing Victoria, he appreciated this distraction. Having read many books on zombies, he had an immediate retort: "Isn't that kind of obvious? A natural virus doesn't just explode across the world, kill people, and then bring them back to life, does it?"

Hayes looked at him with newfound respect. "You don't seem to be fazed by all this. I'm sorry you lost your friend, by the way. She saved me, too."

"Well, I'm not fazed anymore. Two days ago, when I was attacked by a berserk yoga lady, I was pretty 'fazed.' After the next several zombies attacked me, I started to get used to it. Now I guess I'm immune to the weirdness of it, even if I'm not used to all the blood. Not sure I'll ever get over that." He patted his stomach. "I have issues with the sight of blood."

"So, you call them zombies too? I hear that more and more, but I don't really get it. Aren't zombies things that come out of caskets and walk around slowly, moaning about brains?"

Liam had similar reflections on this very topic, but he was convinced the things he'd seen would be classified as zombies by almost anyone.

"You're talking about old-school zombies. Originally, I think that's what people thought zombies were—the dead who climb out of the ground and chomp brains of those too slow to run away." He scratched his head, then watched as dust fell like rain from his mop. "I think there was an old movie that started people thinking like that. Later, the slowpoke zombies were laughed away as not threatening enough. Today, zombies can be almost any speed, but most are fast."

Hayes seemed hard to convince. "But don't these people seem more like vampires to you? The sick seem to go for a person's blood, not their brains."

His fear of blood was strong, but the more he thought about it, the more it made some sense. Angie especially was a bloody mess, and her apartment was a nightmare of blood. The park ranger up in the Arch was covered in blood, as was the Arch observation deck. Unless he consumed an entire person up there, it meant whatever he attacked had bled profusely, but was still able to get away. Was blood the key?

Still, vampires? He wasn't ready to believe such supernatural nonsense.

"I think these people are dead, but some kind of infection is keeping them from turning off and staying down. But I haven't seen anyone actually die and then come back to life ... " He realized how little he knew about the infected people now causing so many problems for him.

"Last night, you guys knew nothing useful about the sick people. Do you know anything about how the infection spreads?"

"Just what I've heard secondhand. Nothing from official channels. I've not seen any zombies up close yet, so I can't confirm anything for myself. They say the plague infects the victims and makes them crave blood. One consistent data point seems to be the biting by the infected, and their desire to consume as much blood as they can, but no one's sure why. The drained victim then gets up and looks for more blood. Possibly to replace their own."

"Mmm. That doesn't really tell me anything I don't already know. I've seen infected people attacking helpless victims since this all began. You don't know anything useful that could help us fight back or stop the plague?"

Hayes gave a good laugh.

"Look at me, kid. I'm just a driver. I know about as much as you do." Hayes turned to the tunnel opening as a loud explosion echoed from somewhere out there.

Despite feeling bad for the thought, he wished it had been Hayes who had gone up those steps to save them.

No, it should have been me.

2

He and Hayes sat in silence for several more minutes. He thought the whole time about Victoria, unable to solve how to get back and save her. Grandma nodded in the coolness of the tunnel, but he considered waking her up to move her further south, out of the area surrounding the Arch. With so many people fighting, it was no place for an aged grandmother to be hanging about. It wasn't a great place for a kid, either.

Get her to safety, then go back for Victoria.

Liam fumbled for his phone, feeling a sudden urge to text his parents, but there was no signal. He put it back in his pocket, but already thought of when he would check it again.

He noticed a police officer crouching about 100 feet down the railway tunnel, keeping an eye on the southern exit. The northern entrance was a tiny point of light in the opposite direction. There was no way to know who was up there, though he could see lots of people in the tunnel between himself and that pinpoint. The dark tunnel made a great shelter against the gunfire of the larger battle. That much was certain.

He moved Grandma further toward the southern exit, as that was the direction they needed to go. It wasn't easy to push the chair on the rocks, but he got help from Hayes, and they made pretty good time. Grandma woke up but seemed to nod back off fairly quickly with the rocking action of her ride.

The officer held a shotgun and radio as he crouched and kept watch.

He parked the wheelchair about thirty feet from the exit and let Hayes know he'd be right back. He approached the officer from his side, so as not to appear threatening.

"Excuse me. I'm Liam. My friend Victoria and I were the lookouts who went up into the Arch to watch for the gangs."

"Nice to meet you. I guess we both missed the action in the park."

"What do you mean?"

"The captain put me down here to guard this tunnel exit, but nothing has happened. I could do more good up where the action is. What did you see from up top?"

He traded some basic information with the officer, whose name was Jones. He was a large black man with maybe too much gut poking out. Still, he was quite impressive. Liam didn't say anything to offend him, but he suspected he was put down here because he would make such a large target. Not the best attribute to have in a gun battle.

Officer Jones' radio gave him an idea.

"Can you call the captain inside the Arch?"

"Sure, but my orders are to hold here. I don't have anything to report."

"Actually, you do. My friends and I just came from inside the Arch museum. There's a service entrance that comes out inside this railroad tunnel. When we left the captain, he and his people were trapped by a group of looters who came in the north entrance. I think we can help get them out of there."

The officer gave him "the look." He'd seen it many times over the years. It was the look an adult gave him to decide whether a kid could know what he was talking about when something important happened.

"Dad, there's a car flipped over on our street." The look.

"Mom, your phone needs a critical software update." The look.

"Officer, I know how we can save your leader and all those family members." The look.

To his credit, Officer Jones got on the radio.

"Yeah, this kid—What's your name?—this Liam kid said the captain sent him up to the top of the Arch, and now he says he can help our guys get out of the museum."

The officer went over some details with the man on the other end. Liam was grateful to be helping the officers in their sticky situation, but his motives were anything but pure. He was hoping, somehow, he could save Victoria. He was worried his last memory of her would be as a bouncing light going up to the sky.

I'm not going to leave her to die.

3

Officer Jones went back and forth with the person on the other end for many minutes. When he was finished, he shared what he knew with Liam.

"We don't normally liaison with teenagers, but this is a screwed-up day," Jones said with an anxious laugh. The man was sweating profusely through his light blue uniform shirt because the tunnel was sweltering. "Things are pretty bad topside. There are gang members and looters at both of the main entrances to the Arch, as well as at a third entrance on the city-side. Our boys are trapped in the museum. For your plan to work, they would have to cross the waiting area in full view of the armed criminals."

Jones churned on that for a few seconds before continuing.

"But it gets worse. There's a big group of infected really chopping up the remaining citizens on the north side of the park. Our intel says they will be at the Arch sooner rather than later. The gang members aren't very good at killing zombies; apparently, zombies don't die as easily as our guys and gals in blue."

He was visibly angry at what had been done.

"So, our plan is to get any officers still available on this side of the park, sneak through the tunnel you found, and attempt to rescue the remaining officers and families inside the museum."

"But the metal gate-thing is now locked. How are we going to get into the maintenance room?"

Officer Jones smiled. "Leave that to me."

Liam wasn't content to leave anything to chance. He'd seen everything fall apart the past couple of days and trusted nothing to work as it should. But he couldn't exactly tell the police how to do their jobs, so all he could realistically do was tag along and hope they got the job done. And, if he was really lucky, he would emerge from the dark hallway just in time to save Victoria.

It took about fifteen minutes to gather four police officers, including Jones. He was disappointed that was the best they could do, and the hulking black policeman seemed to sense his feeling.

"Don't worry kid, these bad boys are Mobile Reserve," Jones said while patting the combat-looking helmet of one of the new guys. "A super S.W.A.T. team," he said with a little laugh. "This is more than enough firepower to fend off the garbage shooting at our people in there. See these?" He held out his weapon, which Liam thought looked like a sleeker, deadlier version of the rifles his dad let him shoot. "These are highly modified AR-15s. Since the rules of war have been turned off, we're using silencers and fancy bullets today. We should make short work of those bastards. We have some other toys we're bringing to the party, too. It also helps that we'll have the drop on them, thanks to you and your secret entrance."

One of the new guys, who carried a massive shotgun with a drum magazine, gave him a chuck on the shoulder, then handed a battering ram to his larger compatriot. Jones slung the ram over his shoulder next to his shotgun. Apparently, they were going to use that to bash in the metal grate. He didn't doubt they could do it, especially given the large man's bulk. He might be able to punch the thing apart.

While the officers were readying the plan amongst themselves, he stood off to the side, not sure if he should listen in or look busy doing something else. He decided there was one item he definitely wanted to pass on to these guys.

"Um, excuse me. If you happen to see my friend in there, please help her get out. She's about my age. Wearing a black dress. She ran up into the Arch to save me and the rest of our group."

"If we see your girlfriend, we'll grab her."

He didn't correct her designation as his girlfriend, even though it wasn't true. He liked how it sounded, but it made him even more depressed at how things had transpired.

After a few more minutes of preparation, the police officers gathered near the small tunnel entrance and were working the radio. Presumably coordinating with the group inside.

"Liam, do you have any weapons?"

He wasn't sure if he should tell the cops that he was packing a gun but decided now was not the time to be worried about getting himself thrown in jail for concealed carry of a weapon without a permit.

"I have a small pistol, yes."

"OK, listen. Your job is to guard this exit, so when we come back out we find your friendly face and not anyone else. Do you understand?"

"I'd rather go with you guys."

Officer Jones grabbed a radio from one of his mates and tried to give it to him. He pulled the police radio he'd been using earlier out of his backpack, showing he was already plugged into their radio net. "I'm ready to go," he said lamely.

Jones continued, "I understand, son. But trust me. We'll get it done. We need someone here to keep this door open, or we'll be cut down when we come out. Make sense?"

He couldn't argue with the logic, though his heart still envisioned saving Victoria. That wasn't going to happen if he was parked here at this entrance as a glorified greeter.

"Don't use your radio unless absolutely necessary, but you can listen, so you know when we're coming back. We won't sightsee because the Army is going to bake this place, soon."

"Understood." Liam felt a chill run through his spine.

Through it all, Hayes had kept his distance from Liam and the police. He figured the man would want to help protect this exit, but he made no effort to move much past where they had placed Grandma near the end of the railroad tunnel.

He's probably thinking about making a run for it.

The air outside the train tunnel was thick with gunfire, though the odd angles of the sound waves on the interior made it hard to know where it was all coming from.

He also thought he could hear an increase in gunfire coming from the other end of the railroad tunnel. That is, from the spooky and dark section north of where he stood.

Why did I even suggest this?

Hero stuff. Remember?

4

Jones went in first. He had to go in on his knees and elbows since the space was too low for him to crouch and walk. He dragged the battering ram with him. The other three men entered the same way; one of them pulled a large black bag. Liam imagined it was a satchel of weapons.

He checked the pistol on his hip, then stood against the wall next to the opening, holding the radio close to his ear so he could listen in without blaring it to the whole tunnel. There were other people about, but none were anxious to interfere with this operation.

The radio chatter began almost immediately.

"Jones here. We are through the grating and are in the maintenance room. No sign of trouble. Moving to hallway. Out."

A few minutes later a much shorter transmission, in a whisper.

"Jones here. In position. Be ready in five minutes. Out."

He knew the basics of the plan but had no idea of the tactics they would use to extricate those inside the museum. He tried to be patient and wait the five minutes. The radio chatter had completely stopped.

The void gave him time to think of how he could do something stupid, like going up the tunnel himself, then ascending the stairs to try to catch up with Victoria and see if he could help. But he knew that, by now, she was probably down the other leg of the Arch if she kept running once she got to the top. *If* she got to the top.

Ugh. Why did I think that?

Where could she have come down? Was there a room on the north side of the Arch that was a maintenance shed like the one in the south? If so, was there a grate and a tunnel over there too? Did that duct come out on the other end of this same railroad tunnel? He almost started running right then and there, but he looked the other way toward Grandma. She was silhouetted in the evening light of the tunnel exit, now talking to Hayes. Would it be smart to leave her alone and try to force his way into danger?

He couldn't make up his mind.

The radio exploded, "Go! Go! Go!"

The net became unintelligible with all the calls. He listened until there was nothing but a long series of beeps and boops like the frequency just stopped trying.

From inside the duct leading back to the Arch, there was a lot of gunfire, then a lull.

"Infected have overrun both entrances."

What the hell?

The screaming started getting uncomfortably loud in the railway tunnel. The tiny speck of light to the north was nearly extinguished by smoke and haze. He couldn't make out any details, but the sound of gunfire was rolling in waves down the tunnel, as were the screams.

Zombies were already in the railroad tunnel, though not very close as yet. Would he be called to defend this exit from a tide of the undead? It seemed unlikely he could make much difference given the small caliber of his gun. He suddenly felt very inadequate and laughed at the foolishness of thinking he could get Victoria through the other exit—if it existed.

"This is Osborne. We have all our people clear of the museum. We are heading for the train tunnel now. Out." He sounded like a man on the run.

Someone should be coming out soon.

More gunshots up the tunnel. To his dismay, a bullet ricocheted by. He took one step into the smaller tunnel, mainly to shield himself from stray bullets. He worried Grandma had no such shielding.

Someone tapped him on the back, startling him near to death. It was a teenage girl, but not Victoria.

"I was told to come this way. Where do I go now?"

He didn't want to send her out into the railroad tunnel because of the stray bullets, but she was the first of many people who would be coming through this exit, so he had no choice.

"Just come out and sit on the far wall. Keep your head down."

She did as instructed. He vacated the small tunnel, so he wasn't in the way. Soon there was a stream of kids, young adults, and the elderly coming through. Everyone who survived up in the museum was now pouring down. Everyone but the cops. He assumed they'd bring up the rear.

About fifty people eventually made their way into the railroad tunnel, and most took up positions crouched down along the far wall. The screaming and gunfire in the north end had become feverish and was inching closer. He was on the cusp of praying for the appearance of some of the police officers to help stop the tide rolling down the railroad line.

A long ten minutes later, a group of officers poured out, including Jones—now only carrying his shotty. His group did not include any of the three men who had joined him going in. He found Liam and asked for an update on what was happening in the tunnel. The sound of screaming was very close from up north, and many people had run by and were congregating near the south entrance, as if unwilling to expose themselves to the outside—yet.

"There are infected up that way. I've been hearing gunshots and screaming almost this whole time you've been inside. It's too dark to see what's going on for sure."

A few minutes later, several more officers streamed out. This group included at least two of the guys that went in initially with Jones.

There were now about ten officers in the railroad tunnel. They split up to provide a line of defense inside the tunnel as well as a lookout or two near the exit to the south.

More officers trickled out of the small crawlspace, but he had yet to see the captain. Some of them grabbed people who were against the wall—probably family—and made a run for it out the tunnel exit. For some reason, that simple act of desperation chilled him to the bone.

Several female officers emerged, including the one who was hopped up on speed earlier in the day. She didn't even notice him. She immediately headed to the civilians along the wall, apparently searching for someone.

Not long after, some injured officers came out, dragging a couple of other guys who couldn't walk on their own. It looked like they had gunshot wounds.

Then no one came out for a long time. Besides wondering when the bombs would fall, it gave him plenty of time to think about all the grisly ways Victoria could have died at the hands of her pursuers. He also had the time to wonder about the far side of the main tunnel, where he was positive a wave of infected people was coming for him. The gunshots and screams indicated there were still survivors in that direction, though he couldn't tell how close they were.

"We have her. We're coming out." It was Osborne.

Minutes later, a gaggle of officers came out, including one who had no shirt on and looked like he'd just run a marathon. Coming out behind them, was— *Victoria*! Her black dress hugged her body because she was covered in sweat.

He ran to her the second she cleared the roof of the low tunnel and wrapped his arms around her. He couldn't help it. She didn't fight him and even seemed relieved to be in his arms. Or maybe just to have escaped. She looked exhausted. *Well, of course she is, dummy, if she went all the way to the top again.* She had several abrasions on her face and dried blood below her nose—like she'd been punched hard a couple of times.

The captain crawled out with a few soft grunts. He looked terrible, was covered with blood, had a bandage around his bicep, and he seemed to have trouble getting one of his legs out of the tunnel. Once clear, he limped over to Liam.

"We meet again. Thank you for what you did here today. Your plan saved my people from certain death in there. Officer Jones told me of your situation, and that of your friend, so I sent up my best runner here"—he pointed to the guy with no shirt on—"to see if he could find your girlfriend. He found her at the very top. Somehow, she managed to incapacitate one of the bad guys on the steps, but the other one beat her up pretty good, I'm afraid. He was so distracted hitting her; he never saw my man coming. We brought her back down. It was the least we could do to return the favor. You're a real hero, Liam."

Being called a hero by the imposing police leader was nice, but it paled to what they did for him.

Liam walked over to shirtless guy to shake his hand. He wanted to go back and hug Victoria again—*She's alive, thank God*—but gunfire outside was intense and constant, and his survival senses overrode everything else. People outside ran madly toward the water of the river, and the screaming and gunfire inside the north part of the tunnel kept getting closer.

We've run out of time.

As if to prove his point, the park ranger zombie slithered out of the tunnel and bit hard into the back of the captain's ankle.

5

Osborne turned around, yanked out his sidearm, and shot the bloody creature several times in the back and neck. The bullets got the attention of the thing attached to his foot, and when it let go, the captain put a final series of shots into its head. Liam could only stare in horror as the head exploded, the debris plastering the insides of the small tunnel. Then a sudden thought struck him hard.

The captain's been bitten.

Osborne looked down at his leg and yanked up the cuff of his pants to reveal a very tall tactical boot with shallow bite marks on it. He gave a relieved chuckle, then noticed the look of horror on Liam's face.

"Don't worry, son. I've been fighting zombies my whole life."

Fighting zombies—how is that possible?

Before he could ask, Captain Osborne gave him a stern pat on his shoulder and went on to the next crisis, giving orders to his men, shouting above the cacophony of the engulfing disaster. Liam's ears rang from the sound of the captain's point-blank shots, so he simply grabbed Victoria's hand and pulled her up the tunnel to where Grandma sat. She and Hayes looked like they were waiting for the bus, but she clutched Liam's backpack in a way he recognized as fear. Then she saw Victoria standing next to him, swaying unsteadily.

"Nice to see you again, dear." *As if Victoria had just dropped in for tea and cookies.* "Liam, why don't you help Victoria sit down? She looks rather tired."

He did as she suggested, and offered her some water, then looked around. He guessed there were about twenty officers still in the fight. Most of them were facing the dark of the tunnel, pointing their lights toward the clamor coming from that direction. Sometimes people would run by screaming, but more often now it was a zombie that came slinking out of the confusion only to have its head blown off. The far exit had become obscured by darkness, dust and the smoke from multiple weapons. More than a few times, bullets ricocheted to his end of the tunnel, sending citizens flat onto the rocks.

Once the captain had his men where he wanted them in the tunnel, he moved to the opening on the south end. He put two of his female officers in charge of using zip ties to secure the exterior gate of the small service tunnel and told them to shoot anyone attempting to come out.

He saw Liam's group and stopped to ask how they were doing. He also let them know they were going to need to help out when the time came to run—which he said was going to be soon.

"This tunnel is about to get dangerous."

Get dangerous? Liam thought. *As opposed to the quiet Sunday afternoon at the park it is now?*

"We have to move somewhere more secure," the captain continued. "Get ourselves room to breathe. Can you both shoot?" he asked, glancing in turn at Liam and Victoria.

He nodded yes. Victoria was silent, then turned to him. "I'll take that second pistol if you aren't using it. I don't want to ever be unarmed again."

He looked at Osborne. "We'll both be ready, sir."

Osborne gave him a small salute and began walking away. He caught himself when he saw Hayes.

"You have any kind of weapon?"

"I'm not a warrior. I'm a...doctor. I'm too important to fight them with guns."

Osborne responded. "So important you and your friends were willing to spend your time getting drunk in the candy store? I don't think you're as important as you think you are. Neither the zombies nor the gang members will be stopping to ask for your credentials—you can bank on that."

He moved away quickly, meeting up with the remaining officers now guarding the large opening at the head of the tunnel.

Hayes looked back at Liam, but he avoided the man's gaze by pretending to talk to Victoria.

A doctor? Was that the truth? Did he lie to me earlier?

He realized he had just picked up a valuable life lesson. In a world where no one knows your past, anyone can be anyone.

6

The final plan was kept simple. About a quarter of a mile to the south, the train tracks entered another short tunnel before they left the Arch grounds via a long above-ground trestle. The captain figured if they could reach that tunnel, it would put them in good shape to keep moving to the south, out of the worst of the massive scrum taking place all around them. It would also get them clear of the impending military assault. He mentioned that as a casual addendum, as if unconcerned they were nearly out of time.

Some of the officers expressed concern at leaving so many people to their fates up top.

"I know you all took an oath to serve and protect your communities. I did as well. But our communities are gone. What we have now, pretty much everywhere except this little bubble containing our families and us, is anarchy. Our community is now down to our families and the friends we pick up along the way." He nodded in Liam's direction.

"Our only hope of seeing another day is to get out of this fighting so we can take a breath and figure out what comes next." He cinched a bloody rag around his upper arm, gave a grimace in doing so, and continued with his pep talk.

"I want us all to move as fast as we can over to that next tunnel. This one is about to push us out anyway, judging from all the shooting and screaming behind us. I'm sure we can hold them off for a while, but we only have the ammo in our pockets, so if we're going to make a move, we have to do it now."

"Grab your families and line them up here. We leave in five."

Liam checked his weapon, ensured the safety was still on, and practiced thumbing it on and off.

Victoria held her Mark I but was still in a daze.

He leaned over to her.

"Hey, you OK? Have you ever fired a pistol before?"

She fought back a sniffle before speaking. "Yes. My dad took my sister and me to some indoor shooting range back in Colorado several times. We didn't shoot a gun like this one, but we did shoot pistols with magazines."

"That's good. That means you'll have no problem with this. In fact, this is probably much easier to shoot than anything you used with your dad. The trigger is very soft. My dad did something to modify it so "even an old lady could fire it," as he would say. You just point it in the direction you want to shoot and gently squeeze the trigger. I'll warn you though that the ammo we're using is very light duty. It will do fine against any petty criminal, but I don't think the infected will even feel this unless you pop them through the eye or nose. Or, if you're at point blank, it should go through their skull. My dad and I talked about these guns last summer, and he said they were deadly in the proper hands, but you have to know what you're doing. I wish now he had just given me a bigger gun."

"Wow. My parents gave me Bibles for my birthdays. Yours gave you guns. Kinda cool, actually."

He felt a rush of pride, then remembered he was mad at his parents. Sort of.

She continued, "Where do I put it? I don't exactly have pockets in this dress."

He took off his belt and handed it to her.

"I don't need it," he said. "Trust me."

He gave her his holster, which fit the belt and the Mark I perfectly. She wrapped the belt around her waist, so it sat just above her hips, then dropped her gun into the snug holster. A little snap could hold it in place, but he suggested she leave it open as she'd likely need the gun soon.

"It ain't pretty, I'm afraid, but it will keep you in the fight."

She looked up at him with wet eyes.

"I'm so sorry. I just left you guys in there. I thought I knew what I was doing, but I couldn't outrun those two. They caught me at the top. I fought, but... " She gave him a tired smile, but her swollen lip and bruised cheek made it visibly painful for her to do so.

He was about to respond, but she kept going.

"I was so sorry to leave you guys. But I had to save you. I needed to save *someone* after what I'd done in the city."

She leaned into him and rested her head on his shoulder and began to weep. He put his hand on her back to comfort her and further appreciated how soaked with sweat she'd gotten on her escape. It forced him to wonder if he had the same stamina to run those steps again if he'd been asked to save her. It left him in awe at her conditioning, or simply her drive to live.

"I don't want to die in this horrible place. I want to see open sky again. I want to run to the next tunnel. Then never stop. I want to survive. I want you to survive. I want Grandma to survive."

He didn't know what to say. He'd never had a girl cry on his shoulder, and his emotions were in upheaval for so many reasons.

Then the earth rumbled. Everyone looked around like frightened deer in headlights, and they got serious about moving closer to the exit.

The police had nearly gathered everyone.

Osborne yelled at the top of his lungs.

"ONE MINUTE!"

He gently pushed Victoria off his shoulder and held her in front of him. Despite the madness and noise, he looked in her eyes.

"I know this sounds crazy, but I'm not going to let you go. We're going to get through this together. I promise."

Should I kiss her? Would I be taking advantage of her?

His mind was unable to process the flux of emotions swirling around his head and heart at that moment. His face turned to stone.

Victoria gave him a quick kiss on the cheek. Wiping the tears from her eyes with her free hand, she yelled to him over the tumult, "Together?"

Released from his indecision, he echoed, "Together!" and tucked his Mark I in his waistband. His pants were tight enough it would stay there pretty well. With a pretty girl by his side, he felt he could take on the world.

Grandma looked anxious, with her hands on her lap. When she saw him she tapped her ear, a symbol he recognized meant she couldn't hear because there was too much noise. They exchanged a smile as he got her ready.

He and Victoria each took hold of one handle on the back of her wheelchair and pushed her into position along the side of the tracks, facing south out the entrance. The rear guard of officers had closed the distance to be with the bigger group. Children hung on to their parents; the youngest were carried by those with the strength to hold them. Most kids were crying amid all the commotion and noise. Many adults were brushing tears as well. Behind them, a seething mass of plague victims emerged from the dark, smoky tunnel.

Liam took in a deep breath and sucked in the acrid smell from all the gunfire.

The captain and a vanguard of cops with shotguns stood right at the cusp of the portal. With a flourish, Osborne turned around to everyone and gave his most rousing and succinct speech of the day.

"RUN LIKE HELL, BOYS AND GIRLS!"

They all plunged into the chaos.

THE HOLE NIGHTMARES FALL OUT OF

Liam was under the wide-open sky for the first time in nearly a full day and was a little disoriented by the setting sun, heat, and fresh air. The noise of gunfire and panicked screaming came from every direction, accompanied by the angry howls of military aircraft above them. He stumbled a little as he pushed one side of Grandma's wheelchair along the rocky railroad grade while Victoria pushed the other. Grandma did her best to hang on with one hand while she gripped his backpack with the other. They were surrounded by a few dozen men, women, and children making a break from one tunnel to another.

Even while on the run he couldn't help noticing odd details. A couple pulling along a young teen girl, who was, in turn, dragging along a small border collie that wanted nothing to do with her. A nun, black habit and all, easily outpacing almost everyone in her orange running shoes. A young police officer, barely older than him it seemed, pausing to fire at nearby threats with his sidearm—liberally cussing the entire time.

The railroad tracks paralleled the length of the Arch grounds and ran along a shallow trench. He couldn't remember seeing the railroad tracks from the park above, so he figured they were designed to be well camouflaged. A gigantic stone staircase wrapped around and over the tunnel ahead. It helped people get from the park, over the tracks, and down to the nearby riverfront. The tunnel was a couple of football-field lengths ahead.

The remnants of the civilian and military cordon around the Arch, as well as many of the people they were protecting, ran down the hill from up top and either turned into the tunnel ahead or continued forward toward the river. He couldn't see much in the direction of the water. His worry focused on what was behind the survivors as they came off the hill.

Fewer and fewer healthy people exited the park. Some stragglers were caught by the rising tide of blood-drenched infected behind them. The slow. The weak. The injured. Those out of ammo. The overly brave. They fought hand-to-hand with the front edge of the approaching zombies. They either got away quickly or fell to the horde. Most, he was sorry to admit, succumbed.

His heart stuttered as a large vehicle tore through some of the small trees on the hill above. It was the heavy M1A2 Abrams tank he'd seen from up in the Arch—he recognized the make from seeing them in video games—but it had completely morphed into something out of a horror flick. It was belching out great clouds of white smoke, making it impossible to see behind it. Its color had changed from desert tan to Hell's red.

As it plowed over the hill, it crushed several feeding zombies and readjusted its path to avoid the rear of Liam's group. It popped off a small ledge and perched itself directly on the railroad tracks, close enough to him that he could see the sheen of blood covering its entire lower half. The tracks and road wheels were caked solid with—he couldn't even describe the horrors. One detached foot in Angie's car had been enough to terrorize him. The tank's deck was covered with body parts and torn clothing. It was hard to tell, but there appeared to be injured zombies riding along—groping for the living inside the steel beast. He could imagine all the death the tank crew had witnessed—the results were riding with them.

He thought it was just going to continue onward toward the river, along with all the people running in that direction, but instead, it seemed to dig in as it sat on the ruined train tracks. The massive smoke screen wafted along the hillside behind the tank, temporarily providing cover for those—like him—running from the walking plague up there.

He continued to move Grandma down the tracks but looked over his shoulder to see what the tank was going to do. Just as it seemed the billowing smoke would obscure the vehicle completely, the wind shifted slightly, so he could still see most of the action.

The turret swiveled left to face the large tunnel they'd just evacuated. Zombies poured forth from it like filth from a broken sewer pipe.

Shoot them!

The tank's machine gun barked above all the other gunfire in the area and ripped viciously into the mass of lost humanity near and inside the tunnel. The crew had positioned their vehicle perfectly to shoot inside the dark space. He wondered how many sick people each shell would pass through. Would a bullet reach the other end of the long tunnel, passing through zombie after zombie the whole length? The gun pounded in short bursts for maybe thirty seconds.

For its final act, the tank fired one shell from its main gun into the tunnel. The concussion of the shot caused incredible turbulence of smoke and debris around the hull of the tank as if the whole thing was trying to shake off the blood and wreckage coating it. A hundred-yard swath of zombies evaporated in a line drawn from the gun to the tunnel, and he realized the tank had fired a type of shotgun round that inflicted horrible results on flesh. *Who says you don't learn anything from video games?*

The turret turned back to the forward position. He watched as the hatch on top was opened briefly; a tanker poked his head out. He looked in Liam's direction and gave a thumbs-up sign. Then the tank jerked forward, the hatch dropped, and it moved away. It pulled the smoke screen like a curtain behind it. For just a moment, he couldn't see any movement in that direction.

The Abrams tank had bought them a little time, plugging the hole and confusing the pursuit. However, the wave of undead was still there. And it wouldn't be long before the dead would be emerging as the smoke dissipated. He saw what he guessed were the final survivors of the rear guard coming down from above. A rare few were police officers. Most were civilians with weapons. Some appeared to be hunters with long guns or shotguns. Others were dressed in black tactical gear as if trying to be stealthy. And still others were flamboyantly dressed like they might have been going to church—he imagined them as drug dealers, pimps, and the like. But, with zombies not far behind, they were all working together to escape the park, just like everyone left alive.

The captain stopped and turned around as he neared the tunnel, urging his party to run harder. Liam was encouraged by his presence, but the look on Osborne's face as he peered back to where they came from made him once again feel a wobble in the pit of his stomach. He chanced a look back, too; the smokescreen had almost evaporated.

He saw scores of infected pouring out from the railroad tunnel behind them. Even after the terrible damage inflicted by the tank, more took the place of the fallen. The soft tones of the evening light made the blood on their faces, arms, and chests stand out. The confines of the railroad grade ensured they would all funnel in the one direction they could see food—right to him and his fellow survivors.

He pushed the wheelchair faster.

2

Osborne ran into the short tunnel ahead. There were already a good number of people holed up inside, including some with weapons. Liam saw how, after some quick words, the captain arranged those with rifles along the two sides of the opening, so they could protect the flanks of the group running in. It wasn't long before the shooting began. He wasn't willing to turn around to see if anything was hit. He was too close to the goal.

Hayes beat him, Victoria and Grandma to the tunnel entrance by a full minute. Apparently, he wanted nothing to do with the slowpokes.

They wheeled Grandma in among the very rear of the group, just a few women and children behind them. Once inside, he turned to watch and see if his help was needed. At the very back, a few policemen were pulling rear guard duty, preceded by the grievously wounded officers from the museum who were being carried slowly by two of the biggest officers, including Jones.

They moved too slowly.

Any fool could see there would be too many zombies for the group to hold off, but still they kept shooting and reloading. Perhaps if they backed everyone into the tunnel and stood shoulder to shoulder?

He felt for his gun and considered helping but knew he was woefully under-prepared for the battle. He was happy to see the police give the thumbs-up sign to someone above them on the outside of the tunnel. Osborne motioned for them to come down while his men continued to pour lead into the infected crowd closing the distance.

The first guy to come down from just above the tunnel exit looked like a gang member. He hung off the ten-foot wall holding back the soil at the entrance and then dropped down. Dressed in jeans with his underwear showing in a silly fashion, he carried an AK-47 rifle. He took up a position at the front of the tunnel with the remaining police officers and added his firepower to the defense of those inside. In small clumps, other gang members dropped in from above, as well as other civilians, the ones with hunting rifles and other guns that he'd seen moments before, running like hell on the hill above them. The group was gaining fighters like a snowball picks up snow. The tunnel was the only piece of cover in this part of the park. Everyone who saw it ran that way.

The original fight between the rogue gangs and the police was pushed aside as life and death for everyone depended on getting as many guns as possible aiming in the same direction.

Soon there was parity between firepower and incoming zombies inside the channel of the railway culvert. It wouldn't last unless the sick stopped coming. Looking out the tunnel entrance, he saw them swarming like locusts on the hill above. The tunnel was just a place to give the living breathing room while planning their next escape.

He made sure he was close to the captain so that he could listen in. Whatever the plan was, it was important to hear it first, so he could prepare right away. He would give Grandma every chance he could.

One of the gang guys hung by the captain, as did several of the new "good ol' boys" with their camo hunting outfits and long-distance rifles. Like Liam, they all wanted to know what their leader was going to say next.

"Thanks, guys. You saved our asses, but this can't last. We have to keep running to the south. There are too many of these things."

The firing and crowd noise was so loud he couldn't hear many of the details discussed, but he did catch their intention to push further south down the railroad tracks. Several volunteered to stay behind at this rail tunnel to hold off the pack of zombies, while the others got away.

He was impressed that both the gang members and the hunters volunteered to join the police in making that happen. He assumed their families were also heading south, which appeared to be the only real route of escape left to anyone.

He tried to convey what was happening to Grandma, but she tapped her ear again. Her smile told him she was fine. In fact, she seemed almost calm given their grim situation.

"I'm glad you found Victoria again," she mouthed with a wry smile.

"You have no idea," he wanted to say. He flashed a thumbs-up sign and a big grin. He felt as if the weight of the world had fallen off, now that she was back safe with him—with them, he corrected himself.

There were a few minutes left before Osborne was going to push them all out, so he grabbed his backpack, dropped it on the rocks, and checked his gun. He pulled out the magazine from his pistol and ensured it was fully loaded. Victoria stood close by, so he motioned for her gun. He pulled out its magazine to double check it. He knew it was full, but even so—

He was shocked to realize it was *not* full. He had just given it to her and was right next to her while they pushed from tunnel to tunnel. She hadn't had time to fire it.

When did I fire this gun?

He couldn't remember if he switched guns somewhere along the way. In fact, he didn't remember firing *any* gun since they left Grandma's house. He tried to think of what might have happened, though the constant noise of the guns around him made it difficult to process data and think.

I didn't load it correctly in the first place, he decided. He resolved to be better about checking and rechecking his guns.

He slammed in three rounds, seated the magazine back into the frame, and handed it—with the safety on—back to her. He showed her the safety again and had to yell to remind her to toggle it off when she was ready to shoot.

The sound of gunfire reached epic levels in the tunnel. The time to move on was at hand. But all the while, men and women continued trickling in from above, some joining the shooters in the front, and others adding to the pack of civilians in the back.

"We're moving soon!" he shouted to Grandma, hoping she heard him.

3

He happened to be looking directly north out the mouth of the tunnel when he saw a massive fireball inside the park. Not quite on the central staircase directly under the Arch, but a little north of it. The resulting shock wave pushed a warm current through the tunnel. He had no idea what caused the explosion until the captain yelled, "HERE COMES THE AIR FORCE!"

The promised attack by the military had begun. Some of the people cheered, but he noticed not many of the police joined in. They undoubtedly remembered the radio message both telling them to clear out and to forget about getting across the river to safety. He felt excited to see so many of the sick get destroyed, but that was tempered by the vibe coming from the police.

The initial bomb must have been a signal to fire freely at the massive gathering of infected. He dared to move closer to the exit and watched as the hillside above them erupted in all manner of explosions. The captain ordered everyone to retreat as far back into the tunnel as they could. The gunners at the mouth blasted the zombies in the railroad culvert even as they continued their inexorable march forward into the hail of bullets.

"I don't know if the Air Force knows we're here," Captain Osborne shouted, "but if they drop one of those big boys in this area, we're all going to get free haircuts and cough up our lungs. I don't want to be collateral damage, and you don't either. We're moving out!"

He pointed to the back of the tunnel, which opened to a railroad bridge over some streets and then went south into an industrial area along the Mississippi River. From there, Liam guessed they ran along the river practically forever.

The captain organized a spearhead of his men and sent them out the south exit to clear the way. He then had all the women and children, along with Grandma and the wounded, head out and follow those men. This time, there was no speech. He wanted everyone out of the area, pronto.

One last look and he witnessed the flash of another large fireball under the Arch. Liam guessed they were starting up north and working their way down south. Surely, they knew any survivors would be down here, right? Were others up north?

His father's voice popped in his head, giving one of his "life lessons" on government. "Always keep in mind the only thing you can count on in government is that they make things worse."

Confidence is low.

He loved the military because his dad taught him to love it. It was one of the few exceptions to his father's otherwise total mistrust of government. Together they were fond of playing military video games, reading books about military history, and they both celebrated their ancestors who had fought for the United States. However, on this day, the military made it clear they weren't going to let him or his family across the river to find safety from the vile shroud being draped over the city.

Still, he took pride in what the army and air force were doing up the hill right now. As Dad might say, "We paid for those bombs, so they might as well be put to good use."

The volume of sound continued to ebb and flow in the tunnel as he and Victoria pushed the wheelchair southward and out the back. He looked around for Hayes but didn't see him and figured the CDC man was up in the spearhead moving away as fast as he could. The guy wasn't his concern anymore.

As they rolled Grandma out onto the trestle, he got an unobstructed view across the river and above it. He was stunned to a halt. Victoria didn't see him pause, so she continued pushing the chair for a few paces before she also stopped. The wheelchair slowed and shifted to the left, allowing Grandma to see the same thing as Liam. He imagined he was in a movie about a global war. Dozens of aircraft swirled above, like an angry swarm of wasps.

Several huge planes droned by at very low altitude. Each had four propellers and the outer shells were painted dark gray. Two of them flew to the north, one behind the other, while a "crump crump crump" sound came from the guns hanging out their left sides. Liam had read about those big gunships, the Spookys, and recognized the sound was them throwing shell after shell into the horde under the Arch. Two similar planes flew in the other direction just a bit higher.

Far above the jumbos, several formations of sleek fighter planes flew in tight formations. As he watched, a plane would split off and descend toward the Arch grounds and release its payload on the zombies. Those were the big explosions he'd seen from inside the tunnel and they shook the ground whenever they dealt their death blows.

In intervals, a few ugly planes—A10 Warthogs—swooped in low and slow from over on the Illinois side and use their distinctive chain guns mounted in their noses. He couldn't see the zombies behind him, but those planes surely tore apart infected people by the hundreds every time they went by.

The scene was spectacular to observe because so many planes moved in such symmetry. The coordination required to keep them all from colliding was amazing. And they all worked together to kill the infected; that made him very happy, despite the danger to himself.

"Liam, we have to move," Victoria screamed.

He was about to turn until he noticed a formation of M1A2 Abrams tanks at a high point above the riverbank on the Illinois side. While he gawked, they fired in unison over the river into Missouri. The smoke from their guns was the only indication they were adding to the destruction, as the explosions in the park were constant and deafening.

Several little Coast Guard boats were on the water, but they weren't armed as far as he could see. He had no doubt armed soldiers were on board, however. No hope of swimming to safety, even if he had a way to get Grandma across the water.

High up in the sky, above everything, several B-2 Stealth bombers moved in lazy circles. Their black, triangular shapes reminded him of deadly raptors waiting to feast on the dead. He knew nothing good would fall out of those things. That, more than Victoria's sensible pleas, got him moving again.

"Since the zombies can't shoot back, they can put all these planes in one spot, but nightmares are about to fall out of those dark shapes way up there." He finally spoke at an almost reasonable level, though he still felt the urge to yell because his ears rang like crazy, "so we have to move fast!"

"That's what I've been saying," she shouted.

As he straightened Grandma's chair, he looked to his right—back into the city—toward a massive new hotel a couple of hundred yards away. It sat in the front row of buildings lining the western edge of the Gateway Arch grounds, and it caught his eye because it was circular rather than the typical rectangular skyscraper. Its base was thick with zombies, meaning the dead streamed in from both the north and the south now, heading toward the survivors and their loud friends in the sky.

We're drawing them out. Like bait.

He pushed Grandma with renewed enthusiasm.

They were several hundred feet farther down the trestle when a massive bomb blew up close behind their group. Once again, the shockwave hit them, warmer and with much more force than before. He turned around to see what had been hit.

"Oh, crap," he said, not knowing if anyone heard him. "I hope everyone got out of there."

A large plume of smoke churned upward like a black glove reaching out from above the tunnel they'd recently vacated. A few large rocks flew through the air nearby and broke windows in nearby warehouses. As curious as he was about survivors, time was critical in getting Grandma as far away from the action as he could.

He and Victoria did the only sensible thing left. They ran like their lives depended on it.

Behind them, the nightmares kept falling.

4

The explosions never let up, but after several more minutes of escape, he was pretty sure the military wasn't walking their barrage farther to the south. Though safe was a strong word to use, he felt they'd made it away from the bombs. The group they were moving with had become spread out, but all were on the tracks heading in the same direction.

They traveled on a narrow railroad trestle, well above street level. The sick thinned out the further south they walked, coinciding with the increasingly complicated street patterns in the warehouse district below them.

While he walked on the high trestle, he had time to watch zombies catch their human prey below. It pained him to see it, and he was helpless to interfere, but he had to know what they were dealing with. It also gave him something new to focus on, so his shaking arms and legs had a chance to settle down before his companions could see how scared he'd been.

A pair of zombies had caught up to a man walking with a leg injury. He had a pistol, but he unloaded the last few rounds killing the first of his attackers. Liam paid special attention to how that played out, thinking of the pistol in his own waistband. The man tried to parry the second zombie, which he was able to do pretty effectively for several minutes, but with his injury, he could never get away before it was back on him.

The man appeared to look for a weapon to use, but he was on a wide-open street, with only paper and other debris around. He screamed for help from some other survivors running by, but no one stopped. Many had their own pursuit behind them.

The man finally ran out of energy. He was so close to a fence, he might have been able to jump it and get away, but it looked like he just gave up. Death descended upon him and made short work. Unlike most movie zombies, this one wasn't eating brains or pulling out intestines. Instead, blood sprayed profusely, and the man screamed terribly as the thing chomped on his neck. Then, to Liam's shock, the zombie seemed to spend time preening itself, lapping up the fresh blood on the pavement and on its clothes as best it could.

"Don't waste food, there are starving kids in Africa," his mom's voice warned from a dark place in his brain.

A hundred yards more down the trestle he finally looked back at the victim. He expected to see him reanimating, but the man still lay where he fell. His blood-soaked attacker had gotten up and walked quite a way toward the spectacle near the Arch.

After speeding Grandma along the rail line for a few more minutes, the trestle came to an end near a parking lot filled with old trucks and rusted metal debris. Many of the other people had stopped there to rest, giving them a sense of a little security. It was also his last chance to observe any changes.

He asked Victoria to stop. He studied the dead man for several minutes while his companions drank some water. He was about to give up when the dead man shifted and propped himself up to a sitting position.

Liam froze in fascination and also realized his diversion did nothing to stop the shaking of his arm and leg muscles from the fear and adrenaline.

The new zombie looked around, and Liam became like a stone, so he wouldn't attract attention. Something caught the zombie's eye, but Liam didn't see any people near it. Soon it got to its feet and stumbled off in a seemingly random direction. A few moments later, it disappeared in the buildings.

"I just saw a zombie wake up," he said clinically as he continued to grip the chair. "It took him about five minutes to change. They drink blood, I think."

"Blood?" Victoria asked. "You said they were zombies. That means brains, right?"

"It would appear all the books and movies were just fiction, though some zombies do seem to eat parts of the victim." He thought about a certain foot sitting in a certain car. "No one had actually seen a zombie until this plague came along in real life. I think it helps people to think of these sickos as something less than human. 'Zombie' has become synonymous with brainless—hopelessly ruined—humans. It's only natural we would think they would also *eat* brains, as a subconscious way of reinforcing what they already lack. That's why I wanted to see what happened in sequence and how long it took. I think these things are more like vampires than zombies. They are clearly drinking blood while spreading the infection."

"So, they're more like Vombies or Zampires?" Victoria grinned at him despite the morbid topic, then winced from stretching her bruised mouth.

"Hmm, I hadn't thought about it. Vampire-Zombies. VZ's? Like Veee-Zeee's. Does that sound good?"

"Sounds kind of like another word for poop," she said with disgust.

"Yeah, let's forget that. VZ could stand for Venezuela. Maybe we call them ... zuellas?"

Victoria said it, testing it out. "Zuellas. Yeah, I like it."

"Grandma, what do you think of calling these things zuellas?"

"I think you two should have more respect for the dead."

Properly chided, Liam resumed pushing the chair, and Victoria followed his lead. Eventually, she added an addendum to their musings. "Whatever you call it, you should have tried shooting it to save the man. It was the least you could've done."

"Believe me, I would've, but my little pop gun couldn't hit a barn at such a long range. My odds of hitting it and hurting it were effectively zero. Remember I told you only a direct shot to the head at close range will kill a zombie?" He didn't reveal that if he let go of grandma's chair his hand and arm shook like a wet noodle. She didn't need to know that.

"Yeah."

"Besides, Liam has to protect you, my girl," Grandma said while trying to look over her shoulder. "You each must stay focused on what's important now. Don't get distracted by things you can't change. Know when to help your fellow man, but don't do anything that could endanger each other."

She was essentially telling him not to be *that guy* and do something they'd all regret. He knew it was good advice, even if he was prone to such regrettable actions. He held his tongue.

Victoria was similarly silent.

"Why are you two looking at me like that? I know I'm just the old lady along for the ride, but I'm also an observant woman. I see the way you two look at and worry about each other. Even new friends can share strong feelings, especially in times of danger. It's OK. I get it, even if you don't."

Grandma shifted in her chair as if getting ready for a long speech.

"I've been watching things carefully since Liam and I left my house. Sure, I've slept a lot, but I've also seen my share. I listen more than you know, even when my eyes are closed," she chuckled. "But you kids have to be aware of the new reality here. Society is going to break down. It *is* breaking down. The only thing we can do—you, me, Victoria—is go on surviving day after day. We should try to stick with these good men and women, but that won't last unless we all get well outside the city. There are just too many infected people here."

She paused for just a moment. "You two have to care for each other. Avoid distractions. It won't be easy, but it's easier if you can tolerate being around each other. I think you do," she completed her statement with a denture-filled grin.

Liam blushed. Victoria's face was bruised and swollen already, so it was difficult to read her, but he noticed a hint of a smile breaking through her distorted facial muscles.

"Just promise me one thing," Grandma continued. "When my time comes, don't either of you risk yourselves for me. I won't become your distraction! Please promise me."

Victoria only said, "uh huh," without enthusiasm. He also tried to remain vague, only committing to, "I'll try."

Would he leave Grandma to such a horrible fate?

He was ready to tell himself he would never, ever abandon her. But for the first time, his life or death equation was more complicated. *What if* he had to choose between Grandma and Victoria? Sure, she was a girl he'd just met, but he liked her and liked being around her. He figured that was enough of a foundation for mutual survival, and—? He pictured himself having to choose. It hurt even to think of it.

He resolved that he was going to ensure Victoria and Grandma got out of this together, and if possible, himself. He could not pick one life over another.

Yeah, I can live with that equation.

5

The group of survivors who had escaped from the Arch came back together near sunset about a mile or two south of the tunnel. The trestle had gently brought them back to street level, but they were a good distance from any pursuit. Human stragglers kept coming down the trestle, but precious few were from his group.

Liam was dismayed to learn the captain wasn't among the survivors. Repeated radio calls came up empty. Officer Jones was there, as was Hayes. Most of the families and children appeared to have made it, but the number of officers was much reduced. There were a few of the gang members still left, as well as a healthy grouping of regular citizens with firearms.

Left leaderless, the group was suddenly faced with competing interests. Many of the families of the lost officers were understandably distraught. The surviving police were embedded with their loved ones.

The yuppie-looking guy, with his wife and daughter and her spastic border collie, spoke first. "I live pretty close to here and have seen nothing but destruction since I left the house this morning. We should try to swim across to Illinois. There's no way we can escape the number of plague victims we saw back at the Arch. They're going to get through the warehouse district, then swarm this direction and eat us. Even if the Army kills every last one of them at the Arch, there's still a whole city of them to the west of us. We can't outrun them all."

Liam could empathize. He'd thought about swimming every time he looked at the river.

"O fa-show. We ain't getting' wet, yo," said one of the pistol-packing gang men. Liam noticed a couple of young children were attached to him, as well as a woman who appeared to be their mother; an even older woman held her arm, making three generations.

The big police officer, Jones, said Osborne intended for them to keep moving south until they got clear of the city. He was going to uphold that course of action.

Another guy, one of the hunters, seemed anxious to travel *into* the city. If he didn't know better he'd say the man had lost it—he wanted to hunt the zombies to help clean them out of the town. No one seemed anxious to link up with him.

The discussion went on, occasionally punctuated by a snap of a rifle. Infected wandered everywhere now, though not in force. The bombs to the north acted as a zombie-magnet of sorts.

Victoria moved him off to the side. "Well partner, what are you thinking?"

He folded his hands across his Mountain Dew shirt as a way of steadying his shakes, but he was happy to see they were almost gone.

"I'd vote to stay with the largest group going south. It's where we need to go, for one thing, and I trust the captain knew what he was talking about. I can't imagine he'd have wanted us to swim to Illinois or head back into the depths of the city. What do you think, partner?"

"I agree with you. Our best bet is to stick with a group and move south. As much as I want to go back to my dorm and grab my Bible and a fresh pair of clothes, there's no way I'm going back into *that* mess."

He couldn't deny he was secretly happy she had decided to throw her fate in with his, but he also suffered some serious guilt about feeling anything good while the city itself was being consumed by a tenacious disease. He was unsure if that made him a good person for feeling bad or a bad person for having thought it in the first place.

This, Grandma, is why I'm unsure about religion. It makes you feel guilty about everything!

"Sounds like we're in agreement, then," he replied. "Let's see who we're going with. Looks like a decision has been made."

The main group was splintering. The majority, including the core unit of police officers and their families along with a few of the pickup gang members and armed civilians, were heading south as planned.

A few men and women threw in with the local who wanted to swim to Illinois. A couple of families were going, but mostly it was single people, many without weapons. They decided they were going to give the river a shot when it turned dark. They said the only hope was to get out of the city as fast as possible, and the water was the quickest way. None of them believed the Coast Guard would shoot them.

The last little group was with the crazy hunter. He somehow recruited a young family and a second hunter to go with him. They stood clear of the main group already, gathering their things. The husband was a bit on the heavy side like exertion was foreign to him. The wife was very attractive and in much better shape. Their two young kids—one girl and one boy—looked to both be about kindergarten age.

Seems fishy they would want to go back into the city, Liam thought. He couldn't help but get involved, even though he hated having to interact with the hunter guy.

"Are you sure you guys want to go *into* the city? My girl—uh, my friend here—came out of the city and she said she'd never go back because it is so incredibly dangerous. What are you hoping to do in that direction?"

The hunter had his shotgun over his shoulder with his finger on the trigger, like safety was a dirty word to him.

"Easy. We're gonna find a nice warehouse full of food to barricade ourselves in. Then live like kings until help arrives." He looked sideways at the young mother as he said it.

"I thought you said you were going to hunt zombies?" Liam said with skepticism.

The man looked at him like he'd just thrown down a personal challenge.

"What's it matter to you, boy? I changed my mind. Big people can do that." He had a kind of leer to him that exuded ill intent. His facial hair was filthy, as were his teeth.

Liam couldn't let it go, but he looked around to ensure some police were still nearby.

He spoke directly to the couple with their two young kids, "It would be better to stay with the *largest* group. Maximize your odds by sticking together. Stay with people who will *protect* you as long as they can."

The crazy guy laughed and started walking away. Over his shoulder, he said, "Come on my friends, let's go find our fortress. He's just a dumb kid. We'll protect you fine folks."

He didn't know what he said that was so funny, but he noticed the young family drifted back toward the main group. It was a small victory.

The other hunter seemed OK leaving with the crazy man; he started to follow. The mad hunter did stop when he noticed the family wasn't dropping in behind. He pulled his shotgun off his shoulder and held it at a much more dangerous angle. Liam suddenly realized how exposed he'd become. He could get shot by an insane guy just for existing.

The hunter looked at him intently for many seconds, then hocked up a loogie and spit in Liam's direction. To his relief, the man turned around, laughing as he walked away.

"Better hope our paths don't cross again, *boy*." The hunter said it quietly enough not to be heard by the police, but Liam knew exactly what he meant.

Victoria grabbed his elbow and drew him back into the main group.

His mind raced. How many more stupid people were being taken advantage of by opportunists? Did chaos and disorder cloud people's judgment? Were people so far out of their comfort zone now they no longer knew how to function? Even at his age, he knew enough not to pair up with a seedy guy with a powerful gun. Not when the police are in your own stupid group! He realized he was talking about *that guy* again. Only this time it was *that family*, and they were trying desperately to get themselves removed from the script.

He was getting angry, so he tried to temper it.

I saved the lives of that family.

Too bad they don't even know it.

He had very little time to celebrate.

The swimmers started walking away, and the main group resumed its trek south. Officers and gang members alike took point or covered the rear. He and Victoria each grabbed a handle and pushed the wheelchair between them. He saw the metaphor now that he viewed Victoria as his partner. They were all in this together, joined by fate through an elderly woman who, until recently, he couldn't stand to be around.

A massive industrial rail yard lay ahead, draped in the deep shadows of twilight. It had already been three days since the sirens, and they'd escaped the worst of the horde downtown. Now that they were heading south, he hoped they were nearing safety.

Liam was surrounded by predators and there was no time for fear. Friends and family depended on him and that knowledge fortified his spirit. He lifted one of his hands, thankful the shaking had stopped.

INTERMODAL

Marty woke up lying on the bridge, near a lone green sports car parked on the deck with her. As she stood up to gain her bearings, she realized she was in San Francisco. The distinctive Golden Gate Bridge was far out over the bay. She was on another large bridge, braced by metal girders high above, though she had no idea what it was called. It was a bright and sunny day, and the crisp blue water was beautiful.

"I'm dead, and I've gone to...San Francisco?" she said with confusion.

Her husband's avatar was next to her.

"Hello again, Marty. No, not dead, yet. You're on the Bay Bridge, by the way."

"You can read my mind?"

"Read? No, I'm *in* your mind. I'm with you, inside your head. I hear your thoughts as you think them in this place."

"Where are we?"

"That's a very interesting question, my dear. San Francisco, California."

"Al, even I know that. I can see the Golden Gate right there; you know what I meant."

"I suppose I do. You should ask Liam. He knows this place. You and he are developing a special bond which I'm happy to encourage."

She searched her feelings. Of course, she shared a special bond with her great-grandson, though their relationship of the past few days was turning out to be quite different than the previous years of Liam's life all put together. Maybe something *was* changing.

"This is a dream, right?"

With a gleam in his eye, Al gave her a big smile. "Are you sure?"

"I remember going to sleep in the rail yard after the kids wheeled me down the railroad tracks away from that horrible battle at the Arch. Unless I'm mistaken, I'm still sitting in my wheelchair, asleep. That means I've got to be dreaming, or sleepwalking, or something like that, right?"

"You are asleep, but not walking. Let's leave it at that for now—we can't afford to get into the weeds. Some things you have to take on faith, I'm afraid. While we're together, I want to show you this car."

He walked over to the little green sports car, and she followed. The car itself was ancient. It wasn't as old as her, but she remembered seeing the model back in the 1950s and 60s. It was a coupe with a white vinyl top and open windows; the insides were covered with bird droppings and nesting materials. The green paint was well faded on the top, though it was still evident on the sides—bird filth notwithstanding. It appeared to have been on the bridge for decades, maybe much longer.

"This could be the most important car you ever see. Do you know why?"

"I can't think of any reason. I've never seen it."

"I'm sure you haven't. It's OK you don't understand the connection yet. That it's here tells me you are very close to realizing your full potential in this world. I can't say much more than that, or I could upset the delicate balancing act that is leading you down this path. But you should take great comfort at seeing this particular car, in this particular place."

She looked at the car, then at Al.

"You look like Al, and my Lord, how I wish you were Al. But you can't be. Who are you, really?"

"You are very perceptive indeed. No, having conversations with the dearly departed is generally frowned upon by ... the system. In this place, I can look like anyone you have in your memory, put you in any situation you can imagine, and if I'm really lucky, I can guide you on your journey through this troubling time."

She suddenly felt exhausted.

"Mister whoever-you-are, will you please tell me why you've been masquerading as my husband in these dreams?"

"Dearest Martinette, I never intended any harm to you. The closest approximation to my true nature is what you would call an Angel. I serve the Light."

She looked intently at him.

"You're an Angel of God?"

"You won't find me in any Bible, and I make no claim to understand my Creator, though, like you, I hope to see His true face someday. In many ways, I'm just as real and fallible as you."

She crossed herself, knowing she would have to ask the next question.

"I mean no disrespect, but how do I know you aren't lying to me again by saying that? Who you serve."

Al considered and then snapped his fingers. As far as she could see over the bridge row after row of infected stood in lines. An impossible number. Most were missing limbs or had large chunks torn from their bodies. All were ruined in form and substance. Somehow, they were standing there, unmoving, all the way to the other shore.

Al called out to them, "I serve the One True God. You shall bow in His name."

And then ... impossibly ... they all bent to one knee.

And then ... predictably ... she fainted and fell back to the ground.

Falling. Falling. Falling.

2

"OH, MY GOD!"

Grandma woke up with a yell. It must have been a nightmare, because she practically exploded awake, tipping dangerously forward in her wheelchair. Victoria sat the closest and had the good sense to grab her as she leaned over the edge. It was a near-run thing. Would Grandma survive falling flat on her face? After surviving so much, that would be a horrible way to go.

Liam moved closer and spoke softly.

"Grandma, are you OK? You were having a bad dream."

"No. Yes." She looked around and reoriented herself on the rail yard. They'd found it after much walking and just as it became too dark to safely continue.

"No, I wasn't having a bad dream exactly. Yes, I'm fine now that I know where I am."

"Sorry. It's just that you made a lot of noise. We're kind of hiding here from ... them." He didn't know how to say it any more plainly without making her feel bad.

He and Victoria now crouched together next to her, listening to see if any zombies had become alerted by her nightmare. In the vast rail yard, it didn't seem likely, but he took no chances—made no assumptions—anymore.

After several minutes, he breathed out a silent sigh of relief. Nothing seemed to have been attracted to them. The group hid in the narrow corridor between two lines of train cars. The train yard offered many such hidey holes, and most of the police group was in between the same two trains. Hiding and staying quiet. Resting after their run down the railroad from the Arch.

By virtue of their slow movement with the wheelchair, he, Victoria, and Grandma found themselves at the very back of the line, though the biggest cop—Jones—was also there with a shotgun. He was the rear guard.

Liam was near the final car of one of the parallel trains. As things settled back down, a face popped around that last car, looking into the dark corridor between both sets of tracks. Liam could clearly see the black man's eyes—along with his red ball cap. He was a living, breathing person. Jones happened to be facing his way, so Liam made a motion for him to turn around. Jones did and casually moved the shotgun resting against his shoulder to a more actionable position in front of him, though he kept it pointed down.

The visitor paused for a second before walking into the gap between the two lines of cars, with his hands and arms reaching outward to show he was unarmed. He wore a white t-shirt, and even in the low moonlight it was apparent he had a lot of bloodstains on it. He did have a weapon: an ornate gold-plated pistol stuck in the waistband of his jeans.

Liam felt his pocket for his pistol but made no effort to draw until he saw where this was going. Jones would be far more intimidating if weapons were required.

The man looked over his shoulder, back around the train car, before turning his attention once again to Liam and his friends. He appeared to study the situation with great care. Jones stood quietly, making no threatening gestures; just holding his shotgun in a position where he could swing it forward in an instant.

Seemingly satisfied, the man motioned with his arm, signaling someone out of sight to come to him.

Liam unlatched the safety on the gun inside his pocket. If there were more than a couple of men, he knew he'd probably be outgunned in this narrow space, but he was going to help Jones, no matter how futile.

Ten seconds later, a black teenage girl trotted around the corner, toward the group. She was followed quickly by a younger girl holding the hand of a third small girl. Then a couple of very young black boys came around. They were followed by a string of about ten black children of varying ages. A couple of grown women followed the procession. Impossibly, another handful of small kids followed them, including one or two small white children. Finally, another grown black man rounded the corner. The only difference in attire and appearance with his mate was the large number of gold chains draped around his neck. Liam couldn't help but remember a different encounter with a man wearing so many gold chains ...

Jones never raised his gun and waved at the last man as he went by.

The men followed their charges. They ran by Liam with grim smiles, unaware of his internal confusion, and soon disappeared down the line. No words were exchanged.

Liam's hand left his pistol as his blood pressure slowly came back down from the stratosphere. For several minutes, he wondered if anyone else in the large group of survivors would be surprised by this unlikely mix of people running by, but thankfully, no gunfights erupted. Well, not anywhere close. Gunshots were so common as background noise in the distance he didn't even notice it.

He and Victoria were both exhausted beyond words. They settled in next to Grandma, using his backpack as their mutual pillow. Jones hunkered down several paces toward the back of the line.

"Get some sleep, guys," Jones whispered as they tried to get comfortable. "I've got this."

"I'll make sure he stays awake," Grandma said sweetly. "I've been asleep in my chair most of the past few days."

"No arguments here." Looking over at Victoria, her eyes were already shut.

He felt the world owed him a nice night of sleep.

It wasn't long before he was out.

3

Seemingly seconds later, he woke up when Jones gave him a manly chuck on the shoulder as he held a hand over his mouth. Jones was in his face giving the "quiet" symbol. Next, he did the same for Victoria, but she woke with a little squeak.

Jones pointed underneath the last train car and made a motion suggesting they look below to see what was on the far side.

There were lots of undead meandering around an open section of the rail yard, visible because of the low light of the moon. They moved without a unified purpose but more or less faced south. It was impossible to know how many were out there.

Completely exhausted, he didn't feel like he was awake. Probably, this was some kind of nightmare in which he was sitting in a train yard with fifty other people, hoping everyone could be quiet so as not to alert the insatiable, bloodthirsty zombies. Going along with the dream, he calculated the odds of warning everyone.

He soon edged back toward a deeper sleep, his mind aimless. The shambling dead still hadn't noticed anyone. Were they able to see in the dark? Did they have hearing or smell that was better than a live human?

No one really knew the capabilities of these creatures, other than their one apparent skill—finding blood.

He questioned if they did have superpowers, like in any number of books he'd read on zombies. Some were fast. Some were strong. Some couldn't be killed except by complete decapitation. Some were supernatural spirits. Some ...

Zombies aren't real. They're just sick humans, right? Hayes had laughed at that word.

In real life, the sick are just sick. Rather than the archetypical zombie running around shouting, "Brains!" these were just housewives, bankers, and students who got sick with a disease that seemed to cause them to wander around aimlessly. But they had a plague so bad it kept killing even after the host dies. If they knew healthy humans were hiding so close, they'd be swarming to the buffet table.

All we need to make this scene uber-surreal is the idiot priest who tries to reason with them because he believes they are still the children of God and gets eaten, dying with that look of shocked surprise on his face. He looked down the path to see if a priest was coming.

"Hello, Father Cahill!" he called out. Wasn't he the one who had saved them? Why was he doing such a dumb thing, now?

A shove woke him up.

"Stay awake! You're mumbling," Victoria whispered into his ear.

He looked around for the priest and realized he'd been dreaming. Or hallucinating. Either way, he could put everyone in danger if he let his exhaustion get the better of him. He smiled at her and tried to stay focused on the figures moving around on the other side of the tracks.

They seemed to float gently in the cool evening air. The moonlight gave them a ghostly pallor. A dreamy look—

He fought to keep his eyes from closing again. For some reason, he thought of flapjacks.

Minutes went by, and a new stimulus arrived. There, not fifteen feet away, was the most beautiful girl he'd ever seen. She was dressed in a sheer pink nightgown that absorbed the light of the moon and made her seem to glow.

He stood to get a better view, like a Peeping Tom at the girl's summer camp, but felt no embarrassment as he memorized her curves.

"Aw yeah. Victoria, you look amazing tonight."

She smiled broadly at him and slowly removed one of the straps of her gown, letting it fall off her shoulder. It revealed just a little more of her ... He was pleased to see the shimmer of her gown now drifted in his direction.

He panted like a dog. It was wrong to behave like an—an animal—but he reveled in it. He shouted, "Victoria, kiss me!"

"Seriously, Liam?" a girl whispered forcefully in his ear while pinching his upper arm. "Wake up!"

He opened his eyes and turned.

Victoria seemed pretty angry, but she put a finger to her lips to tell him to be quiet.

He glanced around. She wasn't in a revealing pink gown. Instead, to his utter horror, he saw a similarly shaped blood-drenched teenage girl. It appeared as if someone threw buckets of the stuff on her.

Oh, God, no!

The zombie wore a pink nightgown.

"It's not possible." He whispered it to himself. What was he going to tell Victoria—"I was dreaming, and you were wearing a slinky nightgown, but you turned out to be a blood-soaked zombie"?

The blood-covered teenager moved in his direction. Lots of her friends on the far side of the train car followed.

Oh, crap! What have I done?

A train horn blasted, and he covered his ears. An engine turned over somewhere in the yard. A few moments later, a repetitive "bang bang bang" drew closer and closer to them. When the train car behind them banged, he knew what it was. A train was starting to move, and the noise came from each car catching and pulling the one behind it. The final "bang" sounded seconds later, and the whole train was in motion.

The train between them and the zombies remained still, but the dead people could walk right around the last car. The moving train behind him would catch the attention of every zombie in sight.

We have to get out of here.

He looked at the moving train, and a plan occurred to him. He immediately hated it, but a good plan now was better than a perfect plan tomorrow. That was a piece of wisdom his dad taught him about General Patton!

4

Jones was still with them, a few feet away.

"Jones, we need your help." He spoke at a normal volume.

"What are you gonna do, kid? We've got to roll."

He moved over to Jones and hurriedly shared his plan. The big man made a whistling sound as if impressed, then looked at Grandma. Liam figured he was sizing up his idea.

"I don't think I could do a better job. Let's do it."

He and his shotgun moved to block the corridor, so Liam and the girls could get in position.

Liam yelled, "Victoria. Help Grandma out of the chair, please." He ran to his backpack, put it on, then folded the wheelchair down in several fluid motions; he was getting good at it. Then he quickly explained his plan to Victoria and Grandma.

As best he could tell from his position the moving train was about twenty cars long, with at least one engine pulling it. Most of the cars were empty coal tenders, along with a few liquid-haulers and two flatbed cars, both with tractor-trailers on their backs. One of the flatbeds had already passed. The other was the very last car. That was their target. Grandma couldn't very well run and catch the first one. She wasn't going to be climbing ladders to get up on the coal cars, either.

The rest of the group of police and gang members jumped onto whatever cars were closest. He couldn't see the entire group in the black of the night, but he suspected they all had the same idea. To make sure, he yelled, "Everyone jump the train!"

The lead zombies rounded the corner of the parked train. The departing train rolled slowly like it was taking its time feeling through the gloom ahead. He began to wonder if it would be *too* slow, and whether those dead people might also climb on board.

Victoria supported Grandma while he grabbed the big wheelchair. He'd been handling it for a couple of days now and knew it had some heft to it, but he was surprised to find he could barely lift it. As Jones let loose with the first shell, he tried to heft the chair up onto the passing flatcar.

He got it into the air, but it was a horribly placed toss; the chair careened off the side of the car and fell into the rocks next to the tracks. He decided to let it go. With a quick jog, he jumped onto the small ladder near the front of the flatcar and climbed aboard.

Several zombies closed in on Jones, but he shot several of them in quick order. There were *lots* more. He needed Jones more than anyone right now.

"Walk with the train!" he shouted to the women as he ran to the back of the flatcar, which was also the end of the train.

Jones backpedaled rapidly, fired a couple of shots, and then reached into his pants pocket to grab more shells.

Liam pulled out his gun. He threw off the safety and kept the gun low while he looked for easy targets. He could hit just about any of the zombies in his immediate vicinity, but to be effective with the little gun he needed a clean shot to the head. That made things tricky. It was dark. He was moving. The zombies didn't want to be shot ...

"Jones, you have to run; Grandma is walking up the line!"

Jones was in the middle of a reload when one zombie got too close to ignore. In one smooth motion, the big man bashed in the infected woman's face with the butt of his shotgun.

"Stay down!" Jones yelled.

A half a dozen others were close behind her. He finished putting in a last shell, racked it, but then used the sling to throw the gun over his shoulder, and started running back up the line.

Liam was left alone for the moment on the tail of the train. He could have started shooting but held off. Instead, he screamed at them.

"I'm right here, you stupid zombies! *Molon labe*!" He held up his gun knowing it was ridiculous to think of the zombies wanting his weapon.

"Come and take it," the defiant words of the Spartans at Thermopylae; thanks for teaching me that one, Dad!

He screamed and whistled and made as much noise as he could. It had the intended effect. Much of the pursuit moved in his direction, rather than try to follow Jones between the trains. Soon he was a pied piper with fifteen or twenty infected in the wake of the train. He turned around to watch the front of the flatcar.

Victoria and Jones swapped positions, so he could help Grandma walk along. Victoria ran ahead and climbed the moving ladder and sat on the edge of the car, facing Jones. The big man picked up tiny Grandma between both arms and fast-walked until he was a few paces ahead of Victoria.

"Oh dear!" Grandma yelped.

Jones planted his feet and started swinging her backward, then forward, backward again, and then he swung her forward with just enough force to gingerly pass her off onto Victoria's lap.

"No, I can't," Grandma wailed, much too late. Victoria wrapped her arms around her.

It appeared to be as smooth a transfer as anyone could expect at 104 —if they were inclined to hitch rides on random trains in the middle of the night. Jones was tall enough and strong enough to get her up on the flat car, but he had to make sure his feet weren't caught under the train. Once Grandma was safe, he jumped back.

"Oh, mercy me," Grandma continued to complain. Liam hoped she hadn't been hurt but was glad it wasn't him passing her up ... he thought of the wheelchair far behind.

Jones ran ahead again and jumped up on the ladder himself, easily mounting the flat surface. From there, he was able to help a few stragglers who were unable to get on the coal car ahead of them. Several times, he leaned over and grabbed their arms and pulled them up.

As they solidified their position on the back of the train, they rolled by the body of one of the police officers who was injured earlier in the day. As far as Liam could tell, he was the only person from their group who didn't survive this hasty exit.

Looking backward, he had a wave of inexplicable sadness for the sick people behind them. They were normal, healthy humans only a few days ago. Each had a family and many stories to tell about who they were and what they wanted out of life. This disease, plague, whatever it was called, had brought ruin to them and made it necessary for good people to engage in horrific acts of violence. He felt sorry to be a part of that violence, sorry they were dead, but if he was true to himself, he was also very glad to have the tools and the friends to stay alive in this dark time.

He looked at his sports watch. The glow function allowed him to see the time was 4:15 a.m.

We survived for one more night.

Or do I have to see the sunrise for it to count?

SLOW GRIND

Liam only saw a small portion of the rail yard when they arrived from the north. Now, sitting on the train rolling through, he was able to get a sense of how big the place was. He estimated there were hundreds of cars sitting on dozens of rail lines, in a confusing jumble of single cars, strings of cars, and scattered engines.

Many of the stationary train cars had frightened people hiding in them. As his train moved by, people sprang out and tried to jump on the one train that appeared to be going somewhere. It was still moving slowly enough that the jump wasn't excessively dangerous, but with zombies in the wake, you didn't want to blow your chances. Most made it on the first attempt, but a few people tried and failed on cars ahead of Liam and thus ended up on the final one with him. One man —possibly a little tipsy from drugs or alcohol—blew his chance on every ladder he encountered and was only saved because Jones pulled him up at the very end of the last car while arms from the dark reached for him.

By the time they'd left the yard, they had perhaps twenty new people on the last car.

Once the excitement was over, he checked on Grandma. She sat with her back against a tire of one of the tractor-trailers parked with them. Victoria sat next to her. There was just enough light to identify them.

"You two look comfortable," he said with a smile. "I'm sorry I lost your chair. It was a lot heavier than I predicted."

"I'm thankful you thought to get me up here with Jones' help. That was worse than Mr. Toad's Wild Ride." She giggled a bit. "I can't believe I did that! The ladies in my quilting group would think I've gone mad."

Victoria smiled at him, as best she could, given the state of her facial injuries.

"Why are *you* so happy?" Liam inquired.

"Well it isn't because of what you screamed back there," she said with humorous sarcasm. "No, if I'm smiling it's because you got us out of another tough spot. By my count, that makes, ohhh, about 100 times you've saved my life in the past two days. Thank you."

"Well, I got us into the mess, so I had to get us out, too." He tried to laugh it off.

"So where do you think we're going?" she replied, more seriously.

"There are tracks down this bank of the Mississippi River all the way through the suburbs of St. Louis. I think they even go close to my house. Wouldn't that make things simple?"

"But we aren't moving very fast."

"True. It beats walking, though!" There were a couple of disturbing things toward the front of the train. First, something up there was throwing sparks in all directions on the train tracks. Second, whatever caused those sparks also caused a horrific grinding and screeching sound. Taken together, it appeared the train was pushing a rolling lightning-and-thunder show.

Still, they *were* moving. They were safe for the moment. He cautiously imagined things finally looked brighter.

Jones came up next to him. "Thanks for drawing those zombies off me," Jones said. "That was some quick thinking."

"Call it even for your help getting my Grandma to safety. Where do you think this train will take us?"

"Dunno. I live and patrol north of here, so I'm not familiar with the part of town we're in now, or where we might go. I've always heard it was a safer beat down here south of St. Louis, but looking at it now, I'm not so sure."

Liam didn't know the big man well enough to judge if he was joshing him. "I do wish we could communicate with the engineer. We could ask him," he suggested.

Jones smiled in the moonlight, then pulled out his radio. "Jones here. Anyone have any idea where this engine is pulling us? Over."

They waited for a few minutes and only heard one curt response of "No idea."

"Not very talkative tonight," Liam offered.

"No, we got beat up pretty bad. Losing the captain like that. Losing all the others. Rough day."

The conversation died, and Liam had nothing to add, so he excused himself to be alone for a little bit. He took a seat well away from the car's edge and watched the world go by. In the dark, it was difficult to see landmarks or guess where they were, but he had no illusions they had gone very far. In fact, they were going so slow, many of the zombies trailed behind them now. Others came out of the darkness from the city-side of the tracks and often tried to grab for the train only to find themselves bounced along until it went by. A few fell between the train cars, and one or two got sliced in half when they were run over.

They kept coming out of the darkness.

There may have been the faintest hint of the approaching dawn, but it could have been his mind playing tricks on him; he wanted the night to end so badly. The train ride was nice but being surrounded by moaning terrors was enough to drive a person mad. Not knowing where he was going was similarly stressful. He imagined it was safer to the south, but what did he know? Maybe it was way worse.

For a few more minutes, he was lost in thought, wondering how much longer he could stay awake under such conditions. He felt himself nodding and wasn't going to fight it. He vaguely wondered if he'd have another vision of Victoria, but he quickly shut that out. The adrenaline of the jump up to the train had all but worn off.

Without warning, the train lurched to a complete stop. The adrenaline flooded back. It started to overflow as the train reversed—into the horde emerging from the blackness.

It's just not fair.

2

He was awake now.

The rear car backed into a mass of zombies, though not fast enough to do any real damage. A few might have been pushed down and gotten caught under the car, but most bounced harmlessly to one side or the other. They weren't tall enough to grab anyone up on the flat car—the men and women all moved to the middle, underneath the two trailers.

The backward movement didn't go on for too long. The train came to a halt. That's when the shooting started.

Based on the flashes of light reflecting off the glass of the industrial buildings in the area, he was confident the trouble came from up by the engine. Many of the undead headed for the commotion, although the bulk of those surrounding the last car remained at their post because food was right there.

Jones' radio crackled.

"The train started up a dead-end siding. The engineer had to back up, so we can change the track switch by hand. We're also pushing and pulling another engine with its brakes locked. That's the fireworks show. We need time up here. Out."

Jones glanced at him, then at the rest of the people on the last car, and finally on the horde of zombies congregating nearby. "Everyone with a gun start shooting at these things. Especially the ones moving that way!" He pointed toward the engine.

He looked at Liam and said he only had a few more rounds for his shotgun, so he was going to save those. He pulled out his service pistol, a Glock 22, and checked the mag. There was no safety on that model, so he got right to it.

Liam yanked out his Mark I, threw off the safety, and took careful aim at the nearest target.

Bang!

He hit right in the center of the side of the zombie's head. It collapsed on the spot, like a good zombie.

Yippee Kai Yay! You're dead!

Victoria was at his side with her gun. Together, they took aim at the next nearest pair of zombies and shot.

"Yes!" Liam was quite proud of his shooting. It had been a while since he'd last been at the range to practice, but the little pistol was very stable and easy to shoot.

Victoria's didn't go off as planned—she'd forgotten the safety. She quickly disengaged it and got in on the second shot with him.

They both missed.

From there, they fired at will, always at the closest zombies moving forward, which meant they had to avoid shooting some of the others who were still hounding them at the side of the rail car. It was distracting to leave them alive.

Why not kill them?

He took aim at one of the zombies standing in the front row and put a bullet through his eye. He did that for four others in quick succession, amazed at how good he was at shooting. In moments it was reload time.

Victoria hit some but missed many of those on the move.

She was soon out and had to reload, too.

He got his brick-sized box of 1,000 rounds out of the backpack, and together they huddled over it, like kids over their first gross of bottle rockets.

When he was done, he banged out all nine rounds on the zombies level with him as he knelt on the deck. He was nearly finished when Victoria got busy with her next nine rounds. She again aimed for those who were walking.

He reloaded.

Nine hammers slammed.

He reloaded.

Nine more hammers slammed.

It was the first time he got to use his gun the entire trip. He indulged in a kind of bloodlust. He was mad as hell at the zombies for ruining—everything. He couldn't even enjoy a proper time with this girl because they sullied that, too.

A couple of the other men with guns had taken the massive bloodletting—like Liam—as an invitation to shoot any of the bloody targets they wanted. They aimed at the easy pickins' right in front of them, which added to the stack of undead below. Several zombies struggled onto the pile of their mates and could almost shimmy their way onto the deck.

Liam reloaded for the fourth time when Jones tapped him on the shoulder.

"Hey, Liam. What the *hell* are you doing?" He pointed to the dead standing right up against the side.

"I'm killing zombies?" he replied with real innocence.

"Well, for one you're supposed to be aiming at the *walking* ones like your girlfriend over here is doing. But also, you're making a pile of bodies below this side of the car. These freaks are almost up to the deck. They're standing on each other!"

I'm so lethal I made a pile of them?

He snapped himself out of it and saw what he was doing wrong.

"Hey, we have to stop firing at the closest ones!" He tried to order his fellow shooters to halt what they were doing, but it didn't stop the two men right away. The noise was intense. The strobe effect of light from each gun's discharge was mesmerizing. When they paused to reload, he was able to point out what they had done.

"We can't shoot them if they're close to getting up," he shouted, "because that would only make it easier for the next ones."

He was pissed at himself for getting carried away, but he was also inwardly proud he was able to dispatch so many of them. It felt good to deliver some payback.

While he was sorting his feelings, Victoria and Jones went back to work on the forward-moving zombies. There were too many lurking in the dark to effectively target them all, but they still tried.

He was left to tend to the growing problem he had created.

One of the zombies made it partially onto the deck by grabbing one of the chains securing the tractor-trailer. Another then used his friend as a crude stepping-stone. He was just starting to right himself to stand up when Liam shot him in the head. He rolled back off the train car, onto the pile.

If I can't shoot them, what can I do? Yell at them?

The zombie holding the chain seemed—somehow—to know he was providing a service to his fellows. Either by design or by accident, the zombie man shifted while holding the chain but couldn't haul himself up completely. That left him half up and half down—the others used his body to shimmy up like he was a piece of climbing gear.

Liam shot the chain-holder in the face and the man slithered back down, but not very far.

The reports of gunshots remained loud in his ears. One of the men previously shooting the front row was doing it again. Liam looked at him in the flashes of gunfire—and was distraught to see the man's eyes had a glint in them. Was he suicidal? Was he *purposefully* making the pile larger?

"Hey! Stop shooting those standing by the car!"

The man did not stop until he was out of ammo again. He racked his shotgun, pulled the trigger without discharging a round, then gave the weapon a funny look.

Liam walked in front of him as he reloaded. "Hey, remember, you can't shoot the close ones. You're making a pile of bodies for the others to use."

"I don't care. We have to kill them all!"

The man pushed him out of the way and took a step forward. Liam nearly lost his balance as he danced precariously along the edge but grabbed the chain and steadied himself. Hands smacked his shoes. They were too close.

He could have easily pushed me to my death just now.

He flopped on the ground under the trailer to take stock of himself. His panic rose and for a moment the shakes returned.

Two seconds is all it would have taken. Bam! Dead.

Liam inhaled deeply a few times to regain his composure.

The loud, regular banging sound began at the front of the train again, making its way to the back.

He watched the nutter who had almost killed him. The man dodged reaching hands to line up more shots on the nearby zombies, but two hands snagged his legs and he screamed in surprise. Using the legs for leverage, a zombie pulled himself up and took a bloody bite of bare calf. Liam hesitated for a few moments, then realized he had to help, but barely made it to his feet before disaster struck.

The man shot wildly, hitting the one that bit him but not much else. He kicked to shake its teeth off his leg, and he lost his balance just as the banging sound reached the last flatcar. The sudden jerk of the now-moving train was too much. The doomed man tipped sideways and fell directly on top of the unbalanced pile of infected still working their way up. The whole stack crumpled under his weight as the flatcar rolled away. He screamed for many minutes as the train clanked up the tracks.

Each desperate shout reminded Liam, *It could have been me*. Lose yourself for a second and it could get people killed. Just that fast.

I won't forget that lesson, sir.

3

As the train rambled along again, the zombies dropped back into the night. Marty remained at her station, perched near the wheel of the trailer—leaning back to get as comfortable as the situation would allow.

She saw everything that happened with Liam and the pile up of dead, and she saw what happened to the poor man who fell over the side. She grasped her rosary—currently it was around her neck for safekeeping—and said a prayer for the man. His screams had been heartbreaking as they pulled away.

Liam had gone to the back of the train and sat away from everyone else, his head down as if he was lost in thought—or praying.

Victoria used the opportunity to reload and then she sat down next to her.

“I thought we were goners there. Those zombies were almost up here with us.”

“You are right, my dear. I think that surprised us all.”

“I saw Liam go to the back. Do you think he's OK?”

She chewed on that question. How well was Liam taking the end of the world? She'd always seen him as a bright boy, but somewhat socially awkward. Perhaps not unusual for a kid his age and certainly reminiscent of his dad—her grandson. He was also a shy young man, who only blossomed after some time in college. Maybe her progeny needed to get a broader perspective on life before they began to understand their role in it? Or maybe it just took the right woman.

She gave Victoria an approving look.

“Liam will be fine. He just has a lot to process. We all do. So many things have changed, even in this short time. I think his biggest problem is that he feels responsible for me. Not that I blame him, I'm just a frail old lady after all—”

Victoria tried to interrupt and beg her off that line of thinking, but she allowed none of it.

“No, no, it's OK. I can be honest about myself. He feels like he has to take care of me now that his father isn't around, and my nurse was taken by this plague. It's natural that a young man with his character would feel that way.”

Victoria nodded and opened her mouth to speak, but she still wouldn’t allow it.

Marty continued. "I want to share something with you. Woman to woman. I hope this isn't too forward. Liam is the type of young man that would do anything to save someone he loves. He may not be able to distinguish between real love and infatuation as well as an older man, but you've surely seen flashes of his selflessness already. I'm asking you to ensure Liam doesn't do anything *too* heroic if it looks like I'm not going to make it. Again, I'm honest with myself—I don't have that long left, no matter how this whole affair plays out. He does. You do."

Victoria's lips were pressed tight.

"Liam thinks I'm pretty helpless these days, and I guess I can only blame myself. I've come to rely heavily on my nurse for many things I once could do on my own. Maybe I let her do more than I should, merely because I've gotten lazy in my recent years. But I'm going to tell you a little secret that I haven't told anyone."

Victoria leaned in. Marty wore a conspiratorial smile on her face as if she were enjoying the moment.

"The other day, Liam got beat up by a bad man trying to rob us. Liam and his impatience to save me led him to a bad decision. The man pulled Liam out of our car and was getting ready to hurt him. Kill him, I think."

"He told me something about that. He said some good Samaritan must have come along just in time, shot the man who was assaulting the two of you and then left while Liam was still unconscious."

She laughed. "Well, I didn't tell him what really happened. I used his other gun—the one you have now—to shoot that man. I fired three times. The robber never knew what hit him. It was the first time I ever murdered someone—" She knew that wasn't an accurate statement. She smacked her lips as she thought of the right phrase. It wasn't murder to kill in self-defense. "It was the first time I killed someone. It was very disturbing to take a life."

Forgive me Lord. I was happy to save Liam, not happy to kill that man.

Victoria let out a quiet whistle; she was impressed.

"I don't have much strength left in me, but Liam's dad fixed those guns so even a weakling like me could fire them. I just set the barrel on the frame of the car door, aimed, and let 'er rip like I did all those years ago. It wasn't hard at all."

Her voice turned serious. "The crook fell down but crawled behind the car. Even with the gun, I was scared. The hardest part was that I had no strength to get out and tend to Liam. I let him lay there on the ground. Out cold. Time went by and I couldn't hold the gun anymore, and I figured the crook was dead, so I put it back in the backpack, and fell asleep. I have no idea how long we were both out. He came to at some point. Climbed back in. And away we went. Liam was none the wiser about what I'd done."

"Why didn't you tell him? Wouldn't he be proud of you?"

"I go back and forth. I guess I feel, at this point, I'm old enough I don't want him to get ideas about doing crazy things to save me because he sees me as some heroic granny."

"Well, you are pretty heroic!"

"This," she swept her arms to signify she was talking about the world at large, "isn't about heroics. It's about carefully thinking how to survive. Nothing is going to be easy ever again. Security. Food. Shelter. You can't just run around the world shooting guns and being heroic. Eventually, it's going to catch you. They," she pointed off into the distance behind the train, "will catch you."

She waited a long time again before sharing her last piece of advice. "I didn't tell him I shot that man because Liam won't survive this world if he thinks there will always be someone there to take care of him." She said it in a most serious tone but ended on a lighter note. "Even if there is." She turned and gave Victoria her trademark wink.

As the train continued along the tracks, the sun started to make its presence known, though it was still below the horizon. They were able to see the graffiti-covered factories and industrial barge facilities on the right-of-way down the west bank of the Mississippi River.

Both of them saw Liam sitting at the very rear of the platform, looking back toward downtown.

"I hope this isn't too much of an intrusion, but I'm old and don't have time for subtlety anymore." She chuckled at that.

"Liam is quite taken with you. I imagine you've figured that out. You are very pretty, of course, and you have a good heart. I have my reasons for liking you." She reached out and touched Victoria's arm. "Any boy his age would find you quite the catch. Usually, I wouldn't even think of saying this, but times are not normal by any stretch of the imagination."

"Amen," Victoria replied in a soft voice.

"I sincerely hope you and Liam become good friends, and that you'll be in his life a long time. But, while I'm still around, please know that if Liam is ever forced to make a choice between saving you or saving me, I'm going to make sure he picks you. Do you understand what I'm saying, my dear?"

Victoria paused, slowly nodded, then added, "Thank you. Truly. We have been through so much already. Romance isn't really on my mind right now. Maybe if we get somewhere safe where I can think about more than zombies, looters, or the plague, we can talk about the future. We just have to make sure Liam never gets put into that position where he has to choose. I want us all to survive and be happy."

"So do I, dear. So do I."

But Marty had laid it down. And now that she had, she couldn't help but wonder if she had the strength to make good on the implications of her statement. She always came back to suicide. Her religion forbade killing oneself; it was considered a major sin. But if the choice came down to saving herself or saving Liam and Victoria by sacrificing herself, she believed God would understand her motives.

Dear Lord. Please help Liam and Victoria survive this plague.

She studied Liam and wondered what he was thinking. Far behind, shapes shambled in the morning shadows.

Will the zombies follow us?

Sunrise on day four was minutes away.

THE TENTH CIRCLE OF HELL

Liam sat and stared behind the train over the next few miles of track as the sun edged up to the horizon. They departed the warehouse district and moved into a more residential area of apartment buildings and small houses. It was still urban St. Louis, but there were now more trees and less human presence, including zombies, along the rail route next to the river.

Almost without thinking, he slid his phone out to check network status. The soft glow of the screen gave him no comfort because it was still unable to get a signal, so he shoved it away again.

Deep and serious thoughts crowded his mind and he was heavy with worry about what would happen next, but when the first rays of the sunshine hit the train, a female voice cried out in song.

"Oh, say can you see, by the dawn's early light ... "

The woman's voice was beautiful, but Liam wasn't able to see her because she was on a different train car. Her voice resonated over the noisy engine and echoed off a low, rocky cliff on his left, and the sleepy, brown river on his right.

"...bombs bursting in air ... "

A few others joined in, and soon there was a chorus fitting of a baseball game.

The song reached it's crescendo and he joined in for the last line: "... land of the free and home of the brave!"

"Play ball!" someone shouted from nearby.

Almost immediately after his spirits rose with that taste of normalcy, the train lurched in deceleration. He hoped to enjoy the sunrise while riding the train to safety, but they weren't out of the city, yet, so they couldn't be anywhere good.

They'd been moving at ten or fifteen miles per hour, still pushing the dead engine in front, but thankfully it was much too fast for the zombies to keep up. They sometimes came stumbling out of the buildings on his left as they walked for the train, but they fell behind, screaming when they missed the rolling stock of humans rumbling by.

I wonder if they'll follow us, even if they can't see us?

Another mystery of the Zombie Apocalypse.

He stood up and moved around the tractor-trailer to see why the train was stopping. It slowed as it approached the underside of the Jefferson Barracks Bridge, which carried a major interstate across the Mississippi River. It was also the most southern bridge in the St. Louis area and was the last bridge over the river for many miles to the south, as far as he could recall. No cars crossed it now, though some soldiers sat on the span; a few looked over the side down to him. Not too far above the bridge, two small, thin aircraft—drones?—flew in circles.

He walked over to Victoria and Grandma, both still sitting near the wheels of the front trailer.

The early morning ambient light put Victoria in a soft glow that was almost magical. Sure, she was pretty in any light, but right now, covered in lots of dust and dirt from yesterday's ordeals, she made

Liam's heart level up. The light even took the harsh swelling of her lip and cheek and evened them out.

He wondered if she liked him, or merely tolerated being there because she had no better prospects in this catastrophe. The insecure side of his heart said she wouldn't have given him the time of day in any other situation, but the pragmatist said she's had plenty of opportunities to ditch him and Grandma and traipse off with people and groups more prepared than them.

On balance, he accepted that she probably stuck with him because she liked him, at least as a friend. A "fall-of-civilization friend." They made a good team so far, and there was no reason to doubt she was going to stick with him for as long as it took to reach a safe destination—assuming one could ever be found. What would she do if they never found a safe landing spot? What if they had to be together for *much* longer?

All right, Liam. Stay focused on the here and now.

He finished his thought by agreeing with himself that indeed, she was pretty.

"You two look like you're conspiring," he said as he approached Victoria and Grandma.

They had been conversing in low tones, but he was unable to glean any sense of what was said because they clammed up before he was close enough.

"Hey, Liam. Grandma and I were just talking about when you were a little baby. How you'd wear your diapers. That sort of thing." She gave Grandma a smile and turned and flashed Liam a big grin and a wink.

He was near to feigning embarrassment when he saw her face had become black and blue in many spots. She had two black eyes to go with her cheek and swollen lips.

He still thought she was beautiful, but he was serious when he knelt down to look at her. "My god, your face. Are you doing OK?"

"Thanks. Yeah, I'm fine. It still hurts a bunch, but I have both my eyes, and my face will return to normal soon enough. I'll take it if it's the worst that happens to me this trip."

He had a dark vision of that man punching this girl's face, and a wave of violent rage swept over him, a burning desire to track the man down and ... When he realized that man was probably dead, the violence ebbed. A little.

"I don't have any serious meds to help you. Just some ibuprofen. Can't hurt, right?" He dug in his pack, pulled out some rust-colored caplets and passed them to her. She put them in her mouth one at a time and swallowed each one without water.

"Do you know why they're stopping the train?" she asked after downing the last one.

"I think the Army is involved. I can see them up on the bridge. What would they want with a train full of refugees?"

Victoria looked at Grandma and made sure she was comfortable, then stood next to him so she could see, too. She gave him a friendly tap on the shoulder. "Let's go check it out."

"Shouldn't we wait?" he said with surprise.

"You want to know what's happening, right?" Victoria replied.

"Of course."

"The answer is that way," she added as she stepped down the nearest ladder.

Liam passed a bemused look to Grandma and she waved him to go follow the girl in the black dress.

There were no undead in the immediate area. This piece of railroad throughway was mostly muddy riverbank on one side, and a steep escarpment covered in trees on the other. He knew, by the location of the bridge, the area up the hill was the massive Jefferson Barracks National Cemetery. As a fan of zombie books and movies, he noted the irony that the one place you don't find them in real life is the cemetery. Zombies don't rise from the dead, nor do they find living people hanging out there. Maybe that's where they should hide?

There were a few walkers well behind the train, but otherwise, it looked pretty safe to step off. A few men and women ran back to provide security for everyone.

He jumped down to be next to Victoria.

Jones called down to the pair to ask where they were going, but once they told him, he laughed. "I'll stay back here. Someone has to keep your Grandma from running off, too!"

"Nobody's tossing Grandma," she said from behind the tire with a good deal of humor.

People up the line of train cars had the same idea. They took the opportunity to stretch their legs and get out of the cramped cars. Many had climbed into empty coal cars for last night's escape and now tried to trade up to options with more room. A good number found the middle flatcar, while others chose to sit on the highest points of the graffiti-covered boxcars.

Liam noticed a man drift further outside the orbit of the crowd, then continue into the woods. He was apparently going to climb the escarpment to gain access to the bridge above them.

"Is that your friend Hayes?" Victoria asked, pointing to the same loner.

"It kind of looks like him."

They walked up to the front of the train, where the passengers were thickest. Liam pointed to a small trail leading up the fifty-foot hillside. Whoever they'd spotted going up this hill would be easy to follow on such an obvious pathway. The man was already very near the top.

"That's got to be Hayes." He was sure of it now that he could see the man's clothing. The same suit pants and shirt. He couldn't see it from this direction, but he could visualize his ugly tie.

"Do you think he stopped the train?" Victoria asked.

"No idea, but what if he knows how we can get out of the city. Maybe he arranged for us to cross here to safety?"

"I told you answers were this way," she said with assurance before starting up the trail.

2

It wasn't easy for Victoria to scale the steep path in her broken-heeled shoes, but they still made good time. As they reached the top of the hillside, level with the decking of the bridge, they moved cautiously so as not to be seen by the military. Liam didn't think Hayes ever turned around to check if anyone was following, but they couldn't make any assumptions.

"I guess we can't hide from *them*," Liam pointed to the drones above. They shared a nervous laugh.

Hayes had walked about 100 yards onto the northern span of the bridge, into the bright orange rays of the sunrise. This put him about a quarter of the way over the river. The near side of the bridge roadway was completely empty, so there was no possible way to avoid detection if they tried to pursue him.

They crouched at the very end of the decking, partially behind the concrete side railing. Unable to follow Hayes onto the bridge, he examined the highway as it approached the bridge complex. A massive barricade had been set up with tractor-trailers, concrete road barriers, orange construction barrels, and some shipping containers tossed off to the sides of each lane and median to block the approach to the bridge. Cars remained parked on the highway as far as he could see back into this part of St. Louis.

"Odd that there aren't people swarming this bridge."

Victoria looked around before replying. "Maybe the zombies swarmed through here and chased them all off?"

"If the people were run off because of the zombies, where'd they go?"

They both turned their attention back to the man they were following.

Hayes stood in front of a line of Army Humvees in the middle of the span, but they were not letting him get very close. A lone person had come out to meet him, and he or she wore a yellow biohazard suit.

"It doesn't look like they want to get close to him," Liam observed. "Does that mean they think he has the plague? He didn't look sick."

"If he has it, we all have it," Victoria suggested in a reverent tone. "He's been with us for two whole days, now."

Victoria's answer troubled Liam in all sorts of ways. The most tragic was the thought of his friend having the plague. Someone so vibrant and young should never have to suffer from this disease. He remembered his very first encounter with the yoga lady. She also typified the young and the vibrant, and it still took her. That encounter horrified him, but just the idea of Victoria turning into a zombie made him ill. Could he ... kill ... his new friend?

If he turned into a zombie, was Victoria strong enough to put him out of his misery?

He considered all the angles as they watched Hayes talk with the roadblock representative. He was very animated in his gestures and paced back and forth while he spoke. They heard fragments of what he said, even at this distance, because he often yelled in anger, but Liam couldn't make out anything useful.

After about five minutes, Hayes got super agitated. He continued his ranting and arm flailing, but he tried to move around the person with the hazmat suit and walk toward the checkpoint in the middle of the bridge. Immediately, the soldiers leveled their rifles at him. Liam clearly heard the rounds being loaded into the chambers of weapons. He also heard one of the soldiers shout, "STAND DOWN, SIR, OR WE WILL KILL YOU."

Victoria let out a little whistle. "I guess they think he's a *serious* threat."

"Yeah, if they won't let him over, they'll never allow the rest of us."

For a few tense moments, he didn't know if Hayes was going to back down. Any normal person would immediately back off, but Hayes seemed to stand there for a very long time as he apparently thought about it.

"Is he trying to kill himself?" Liam wondered. Everyone handled the stress of the Z-poc differently. His books reinforced that.

Hayes raised his hands and slowly backed away.

Victoria had been leaning forward as if willing herself to see and hear the action, but now she relaxed. Liam also let out a little extra breath he'd been holding. The tension on the bridge returned to normal. Hayes chatted again to the person in the hazmat get-up, but even from 100 yards away, Liam identified Hayes as *crestfallen.*

Ten minutes later Hayes started walking back toward the end of the bridge where he and Victoria were holed up.

"Do we stay here or try to get back to the train?" Victoria asked.

Is everything we do life or death now?

He looked at Hayes walking back, head down with a brisk stride. He glanced to the soldiers at the roadblock. They still hadn't moved from their menacing positions. He surveyed the train down below the bridge and judged whether they could make it back without being seen.

"I don't think we can avoid him at this point," he said. "We might as well force his hand and see what he'll tell us."

"Sounds good. But let's meet up with him over on the hill so that the train passengers can see us. We don't want to meet him by ourselves. Remember ... *dark and scary night*," she said, ending in her spooky voice from her earlier tall tale.

"You win Ms. Scary. Just go!"

They got away from the end of the bridge and sat on a rock out in the open, so Hayes wouldn't be surprised. He felt the best approach was to be friendly, even if he didn't feel friendly toward this man who was clearly lying to them about who he was and what he knew.

It wasn't long before Hayes came around the corner. "You dumb kids almost got me killed," he said without preamble.

Neither he nor Victoria had any response.

"Ah, cat got your tongues?"

He came over and got directly in front of Liam, though he glared back and forth at both of them as he spoke. "I knew you guys followed me, but I thought you'd have better sense than to be seen by the Army up on the bridge. Especially you," he pointed to Victoria, "since you seem to have the brains in this outfit."

"Hey!" Liam tried to interject.

Hayes kept talking. "You guys might not have realized this, but while you were out on your nature walk, you were under the watchful eye of snipers. See the drones up there? These people are deadly serious about not letting anyone, and I mean anyone, cross this river."

"Is that why they threatened to shoot you?" he replied with a bit of attitude.

Hayes looked at him and seemed to rethink his whole approach. He sighed heavily and sat down next to them on the rocks, with the train below partially obscured by the trees on the hillside.

"I can't help but respect you kids. You've done a better job than most in staying alive. But you have to realize this is much bigger than you are. I've done deliveries for government-types like those guys on the bridge for a long time. These Army boys are under orders—very stupid orders if you ask me—but orders nonetheless. You can't just go sneaking around under the watchful eye of those people like you're on some kind of high school field trip. They will shoot you, shoot me, shoot your Grandma, shoot the smallest babe on that train—just on the off chance they can stop the disease from crossing this river."

Victoria jumped in, upset. "First of all," she said, "I'm not in high school anymore. I doubt Liam will ever go back, either. Second of all, with all the zombies walking around and all the infected people, there is no way to prevent the disease from crossing a simple river. Even a couple of *dumb kids* know that."

"You're absolutely right. You share the opinion of most of us roadies at the CDC. But you do not share the opinion of the Joint Chiefs of Staff, and with the president off doing god-knows-what, the military is pretty much in charge of managing the pieces of the nation that are still answering their phones."

"But we saw the military killing zombies downtown," Liam responded. "They helped us escape."

"Well, it may be true they were killing zombies. That's their job. But I was there. Did you see any evidence they were *helping* us escape?"

He thought back to the battle. Except for a few volunteers from the Army and Marines, there were no troops on the St. Louis side of the river during the battle. Only the Abrams tank seemed to help them directly, and that was only for a few minutes. Then the Air Force came in and started the shock and awe. The bombs did drop to the north at first, but later they dropped them further south, including right on top of Captain Osborne. Maybe that was just a mistake in the chaos of war?

"So, it was just a coincidence the bombs, artillery, and tank fire helped us escape?" Liam sniped back.

"You always like to argue, don't you? Why do you think I was running so close to the lead guys trying to get out of there?"

Because you're a coward.

Hayes went on. "Those bombs would have killed us just as sure as the sun rises. We're all collateral now to the primary mission—which is to prevent the spread of the plague."

He reflected on that while Hayes stood back up and brushed himself off.

"Right now, our only avenue of escape is to the south. The Army told me they're patrolling the eastern shore of the river, but they have no presence anymore in the entire state of Missouri. We have to get that train moving and on down the line before the Army changes their mind about letting this unauthorized transport continue out of the hot zone."

"Hot zone?" Victoria asked.

"Yeah," Hayes replied, "the middle of each metro area is now a bright red spot on some general's map. They are letting people escape, for now, but there is going to come a time when they'll try to close the whole thing down. It is pretty standard protocol in viral outbreaks, or so we've been told by our bosses."

He started down the trail, leaving him and Victoria alone with the news.

"Pretty amazing a truck driver can get a meeting with soldiers up on some random bridge, huh?"

Liam thought about that for a second before replying, "Yeah, whatever he does for the CDC, I'll be shocked if it involves driving a truck."

3

He and Victoria hung back on the way down, giving themselves some distance from Hayes so they could talk. This time, he was in front of her.

"Do you think we can trust him?" he asked, already knowing the answer.

"Absolutely not. We know he lied to us about what he does for the CDC. He stopped an escaping train—with a hundred living people on it—so he could talk to his friends on this bridge. At this point, the only thing we know for sure about him is that he has poor taste in clothing."

That gave him a laugh. He hadn't dwelled on the man's fashion sense but had to agree it was pretty bad.

Liam went on. "He told us to head south because the Army was on the Illinois side and wouldn't let us cross, but what if they ordered him to go south? Maybe the only reason he needs us is to help him complete his mission that way?"

"That doesn't make sense, either," Victoria answered. "If he was important, the Army could have tossed him a boat or helicopter, and he could get downriver with no problem. Why would they force him back on this train?"

He considered her question for a few moments as they continued downhill. "You're going to think I'm wearing a tinfoil hat for saying this, but what if Hayes is a big shot at the CDC, trying to get out of town. Maybe he got left behind. Maybe his friends needed to talk to him in person, but they weren't willing to risk infecting themselves by letting him across the bridge? We don't know anything about the disease, the source of the infection, or how the government is responding to this emergency."

Victoria seemed to thrive on the conspiracy. "Yes! That's why he told us the Joint Chiefs are in charge. If the president is AWOL, maybe he's dead? Maybe the CDC—and guys like Hayes—are as confused as the rest of us. He just can't tell us he's trapped because that would mean the government wasn't in control!"

This girl was someone after his own heart. He realized his father's penchant for conspiracy theories had a lot to do with that, but he wasn't going to nitpick.

"If you say anything about a 'shadow government,' I'm going to kiss you on the lips!"

Victoria chuckled behind him.

"Well, right now, I'm fairly certain there is a 'dark-shrouded government' out there. Maybe someday we'll discover the other."

Liam walked in silence as they reached the bottom of the trail. He was unsure of what just transpired between them. Before he could follow up with her, she walked quickly toward the engine at the front.

"I'm going to get some answers from the engineer. At the very least, I want to know where this train is going," she yelled back.

He ran to catch up, impressed at the forthrightness of his lovely partner.

Hayes climbed into the engine compartment, so they figured they'd follow him up the ladder and into the engineer's area as well. As he walked along the side of the engine, he noted it had a name. *Valkyrie.* It was stenciled in large black type, which made it obvious on the orange paint of the engine. He rubbed his hand on the letters as he walked by.

Liam's imagination had drawn the man driving the train as a portly dude with a blue and white striped uniform and a funny little hat that said "engineer" on it. He'd spent too much of his youth watching a TV show about toy trains.

He followed Victoria into the compartment and was shocked to see the engineer was a woman. Her hair had a touch of gray—he had a hard time guessing the age of women—and she wore blue jeans with a filthy white t-shirt. She looked more like a mechanic than an engineer, woman or no.

"Who the hell are you two?" she said with a slightly exotic accent. He guessed she was from Eastern Europe if his dad's war movies were accurate.

"Oh, they're friends of mine," Hayes replied immediately. "They helped me get out of the Arch."

"I see. Well, pardon me for not talking, but I need to get this train going again, and I don't exactly know what I'm doing."

"You did great getting us here," Victoria said. "Thank you sincerely from all of us in the back."

She let her compliment soak in before continuing.

"We're just wondering where you're going? You know, since we're kind of a captive audience."

"Listen. I'm getting this train as far away from those things as I'm able. Going south as far as she'll go. But I have one stop to make—besides this stop for your persuasive friend." She gave a nod to Hayes. "I have to pick up my husband. He's the real engineer. Over the phone, he walked me through some of the basics of getting his engine started, and I was able to get the machine moving, though not very fast. His engine was linked to a mate that has a malfunction, so we all get to watch the light show as we push the wretched thing."

She turned dials and pushed buttons as she spoke.

"Bottom line is I don't know where I'm going besides picking up my family. From there, the track points south. Now go. I'm getting ready to blow the horn, so people know we're moving again."

"Thank you, ma'am. I hope you find your family," Victoria said softly while touching the woman's elbow.

"Yeah, thanks," Liam added.

The engineer stopped what she was doing. "Thank you." Liam thought she looked even more tired and worn down than everyone else. She had the stress of saving lots of folks.

And I thought saving Grandma was stressful.

As he walked out the door, he saw something jammed in a nook where the engine crew kept their gear. He wasn't positive what it was, but he kept it in mind for later reference. It might be the answer to someone's prayers ...

One last look at Hayes—he stayed in the engine—and he and Victoria went out and climbed off the *Valkyrie*. As they did, the engineer—they forgot to get her name—blew two long bursts on the horns to indicate the train was about to start moving.

Liam and Victoria ran together.

Everywhere, people scrambled to get back on their respective freight cars. When he and Victoria finally reached the last car, they were shocked to see a lot more people on it. Many of them were utterly filthy with coal dust. Those citizens smartly opted for the wide-open flatcar rather than the confining filth of the tenders.

The clanging sound of cars grabbing began in the front of the train, signaling departure right as they reached the car with Grandma on it. Liam had a panicked moment that they wouldn't even fit on the crowded car anymore, but Jones stood by the ladder and made space for them to climb aboard.

The police officer gave them a friendly greeting. "Smoking on the left, non- on the right. We have beverages in the front and VIP room in the back. Welcome to the High Rollers Club."

They both laughed.

"And where's the women's powder room?"

"I'm sorry ma'am, but you just walked out of the restroom," Jones said with a broad smile while pointing to the trees on the hillside.

She responded with a horrified "ugh," but Liam found no humor in it. Not because it wasn't funny—he smiled to the big guy to show his appreciation—but because it was true. Nothing was ever going to be the same. Even the most basic things such as plumbing were going to be hard to find unless civilization kept hold somewhere else. St. Louis seemed to be a lost cause.

Right now, the High Rollers Club was the best they had.

Liam stood on the wooden slats of the flat car as it lurched forward. Glad to be moving again. Glad to make it back from his spy mission. But mostly he was glad to have his feet out of the toilet.

4

They moved with no time to spare. A crowd of zombies approached from the trackway behind them. The answer to an earlier thought of Liam's was that yes, the plague victims *were* going to follow the train regardless if they could see it or not. It seemed impossible, but zombies themselves were "impossible" a week ago, too. Who knew what they were capable of? Then again, maybe they just kept walking in the direction they were already pointed?

The train reached speed once more. Now that he knew the engineer wasn't a professional, he understood why they weren't breaking any speed records. With the crowd packed tightly on the flatcar, it was probably a good thing they weren't going too fast. Falling off the final car would be terminal.

He and Victoria snaked through the crowd and made their way to where Grandma sat against the truck tire. They squeezed in next to her and spoke of what they saw up on the bridge. She took it in with her usual calm demeanor, which agitated him.

"Grandma, why aren't you more concerned about him? We think he's trouble."

"Ah, Liam, when you get to be my age, it takes a lot to concern yourself with every detail of what's going on. It doesn't matter who he is to me, as long as this train keeps moving south and gets you and Victoria out of harm's way. That's where we'll find your house, your parents, and hopefully some law enforcement to control these sick people. You two should stay away from him, though, if you think he's dangerous."

"Well, that's easy enough. We just avoid the train engine because that's where he is."

"Yeah," Victoria added, "he likes to be closest to escape."

Victoria laughed, but he wasn't sure how to take that. If the CDC guy knew more than they did, perhaps being in the front of the train was the smart play.

Unsure of himself, Liam sat back to think. He immediately drifted off as the car rattled along, but it wasn't sixty seconds before lots of gunfire from up in the front jerked him awake. People who stood near the edges of the car began screaming and almost as one they recoiled from the edges. Several tried to wedge themselves under the big trailer into the space where Grandma sat and forced him and Victoria to move Grandma almost directly underneath the axle of the big trailer.

"We have to see this," Liam said before he was trapped by everyone. "Let's go," he said to Victoria.

"Quick! Go. I'll be fine." Grandma would say that if she were falling over Niagara Falls in a wooden barrel, but he had to leave her.

The pair managed to get out from under the tractor-trailer.

Oh, crap.

The train entered some kind of quarry complex. On their left, next to the muddy brown river, were huge conveyor belts and machines that dumped the white rock onto barges and trucks. On the right was a maze of roadways where oversized dump trucks—had they been operating—hauled rocks from the deep tunnels of the mine.

Hundreds of parked civilian cars and trucks created a line of traffic along the rock path around and down into the big hole in the ground, to some point below his field of vision. It seemed suicidal to drive a car into a hole in the earth with everything else going on. Sort of like driving into your own grave.

Zombies by the thousands surrounded most of the top edge of the pit quarry. He noted this facility was next door to the bridge they were just on, and the mystery of the big blockade with no people was now solved. The cars had been diverted off the highway, away from the closed bridges, and seemingly directed here.

"Why would they drive down *into* a quarry?" Victoria asked. "Couldn't they figure out the zombies would follow them in?"

"I think you can read my mind," he said weakly.

He could only imagine what drove them on. When zombies are crawling all over your car, and the interstate is permanently closed, maybe the quarry looked like somewhere they could hole up—literally—and defend themselves. The train continued ahead, running over some of the wandering zombies. People in the forward cars fired guns at the infected orienting on the train. Many of the zombies, at least on the topmost level, were willing to turn away from their quarry inside the quarry and focus on the much closer blood factories rolling up to them on the train.

As he got closer, he got a better impression of what was going on inside the pit. The cars were parked around a spiral road, which descended until it reached the bottom. He still couldn't see that bottom, but he could guess people were down there trying to hold off the zombies who were following the spiral behind them. The jam went back toward the highway. It seemed everyone mistook this for a road to safety. Once inside the gravity well of the pit, they had no choice but to continue down because the rim was already awash in zombies and there was no backing up. How far could they drive into the rocky tunnels?

So many mysteries here.

The second-level loop around the mine had a second access ramp that allowed some people to escape on foot back to ground level before they got too far down the hole. He saw people using that ramp, running out both directions around the rim of the mine. Some were coming toward the train. Others were heading into the woods or back toward the highway.

The largest group headed for the train—toward rescue. They were up against an area thick with zombies waiting on the edge. Some members of their group were using weapons to try to clear a path. He judged there was *no way* those people could get through so many undead without help from this side.

The engineer gave a long blast on the air horn. The train slowed down to an even slower crawl, but not a full stop.

"What the hell? Is she going to try to save those people?" Victoria wondered.

"It sure looks like it. But who is going to save us?"

As they watched, the right side of the train was engulfed front to back by plague victims, each trying to gain purchase on a car. He looked back—and wasn't surprised to see a large group of zombies coming from the direction of the train tracks behind them. The followers had never stopped following ...

They only had a few minutes before zombies would be surrounding them from almost every angle. There was essentially nothing he could do to change the outcome of this battle against so many attackers.

That didn't mean he wasn't going to try.

5

Liam looked at his options, briefly hoping someone else would suggest a plan.

"I think we should do something," he told her. "No one else is helping."

"If you've got a plan, let's hear it," she countered.

He could try to organize some kind of rescue mission with police and gang members forging out into the crowd of zombies to try to meet up with the incoming group of people—but he was pretty sure that would fail based on the sheer size of the rising horde. And they'd waste a lot of ammo; ammo had to be running low for most of the police.

He looked over his shoulder to the river side of the complex. Several big dump trucks sat there. His first thought upon seeing them came from one of his zombie books. He couldn't remember the name, but in it, huge dump trucks were used by evil men to deposit large buckets of zombies on the good guys. He doubted that could happen here in real life. No evil men were lurking by the trucks.

"I think if we get into one of those dump trucks, we can use it to push through the thickest part of this crowd of zombies and help those people cross over to the train."

She looked at where the trucks were parked, how fast the train was crawling along, and the status of the people in the group moving in their direction.

"It's going to be close."

"Good enough for me."

Though the quarry side was clogged with infected, the other side of the train was almost free of them. The massive crowd behind was uncomfortably close, but still a few minutes back. Once they caught up to the train, all sides would be consumed. There was little time.

He felt stupid saying it, but he yelled to Jones and Victoria as he went down the short ladder.

"Cover me!"

Jones said something he couldn't hear, but Victoria yelled, "Go for it!" as if he were part of a sporting event.

He dodged around a couple of walkers who happened to be in his way as he ran the fifty yards to the trucks. He had his pistol, but speed was more important than killing any one or two random z's.

It was large, but he was glad to see it wasn't the truly enormous dump truck he'd seen on National Geographic specials. It was just a normal-sized dump truck.

He had no trouble scaling the side but was stymied at the door. It was locked. He hadn't even considered what he'd do once he got into the cab. Now he wasn't even going to make it inside.

He took out his pistol and readied it to shoot out the glass. At the last second, he realized he was about to do something stupid. He engaged the safety and then used the gun as a hammer to break the window. In seconds he was inside. He found a lone key in the ignition. He figured these trucks never left the premises and thus never needed their keys removed. If someone got in at night they could joyride around the quarry—the teen boy in him imagined what a fun night that would be—, but the big gates in the front would keep anyone from leaving the property.

With a turn of the key, the big rig started to turn over, then sputtered to a stop. He steadied himself as he looked out the window, ready to try again.

This is going to be a piece of cake!

The train was moving slowly down the track from his right to his left. The engine was now coming in line with the southernmost part of the open pit and was at a point closest to the people trying to get out of the mine. The back of the train was starting to be enveloped by those infected already lurking at the mine, while the group of trailing zombies was still a couple of hundred yards behind but closing quickly.

It's now or never.

A second turn of the key did no better. The truck started for a moment, then died. Only then did he look down and realize it was a stick shift.

Are you kidding me?

He looked down at the extra foot pedal on the floor. Purpose unknown. He had never learned to drive a stick. His parents had two cars with automatic transmissions.

On an ordinary day with plenty of time, he knew he could figure it out. When zombies were pushing in from multiple directions and people's lives depended on the results—he decided not to risk it.

He kicked open the door, scampered down the side, and ran back toward the train. On his right, the zombies were uncomfortably close. Again he dodged the few random infected between the trucks and the train. He would only have time to return to the truck one more time before the larger group was upon him. It all depended on finding someone who could drive a stick.

Fortunately, he had a large fan base watching him, including Victoria and Jones—both had moved to the front ladder of the flatcar.

"Can anyone drive a stick?" he yelled, out of breath.

He looked at Victoria—it just seemed like that was how it would go—but he was surprised when Jones jumped down.

"Let's go, man."

He gave Victoria a smile, then turned around with his big friend and started back.

The man was big indeed, but fit for his size. After all, he was a police officer. But even with their combined speed, they made it to the truck just ahead of the leading zombies in the rear. Jones had to push one of them over to give himself room to climb.

Once in the cab, Jones started the truck like a pro and pulled forward.

"Look, kid, I got this. When we get up to the train, I'm going to pull up next to the rear car, and you're going to jump back on."

"I can help you!"

"No doubt. But those people are going to need all the firepower they can get on the train. You have to hold *them* off," he said while pointing to the arriving crowd of undead. "Once you do that, maybe you can clear as many of the zombies as possible between the survivors and the train. Wow, I can see the whole thing now that I'm in this seat."

Liam shared his perspective. It was obvious what had to be done. It involved running over a lot of sick, bloody, ruined people to save the healthy ones beyond.

He wanted to stay with Jones because he felt it was his idea to use the truck, but he quashed his ego and acquiesced to the request to return to the train.

Jones pulled out his radio as they neared the train.

"This is Jonesy. I need you guys to coordinate some shooters to help clear a path for those people—and kill any zombies I miss when I drive through. Good luck. Out.

"Good luck, kid. Get ready to jump." Jones expertly maneuvered the truck alongside the flatcar, and he was able to step out of the cab while holding the door, and jump the couple feet over to the crowded platform. Many hands helped pull him in.

Once he was safe, Jones slowed so the train would pass him on his right, then he turned to cross the tracks and accelerated along the right side of the train. It was all physics from that point.

The train was about halfway off the property of the pit mine. The engineer stopped the train just as Jones turned toward the mine. She sounded the horn over and over for extra emphasis, drawing in friend and foe.

Jones also laid into his horn as he started crushing zombies. The dump bed was empty, but the vehicle was so massive it had no problem handling the ever-greater number of infected it was pushing aside—and under. It was making a path as Liam had intended.

The big dump truck started turning along the outermost ring of the spiral around the top of the mine. It moved almost directly away from the rail line and directly toward the mass of people pushing for the salvation of the train.

He couldn't see exactly what was happening with the truck once it started moving away, but the bloody trail of downed zombies behind it told him enough.

"Aw, man. We should have gotten several of those dump trucks working, and we could have cleaned up this mess!" Victoria said, as if realizing something important.

He looked at the remaining bank of trucks with longing, but the trailing zombies were catching up to his car.

He and Victoria moved as best they could through all the people huddled in the middle. Grandma was safely ensconced under the truck's axle, so they didn't have to worry about her. That was the only good news.

Did they all follow us?

With so many zombies converging on the back of the train, they would have to shoot to stay alive, no doubt about that. But all that shooting would lead to the dead stacking up under foot—which was how they almost climbed onto the flatcar the last time.

What they needed was for the train to start moving again. That would have to wait until the people were rescued. In the meantime, everyone was in danger.

The zombies arrived like the pull of a blanket over their heads.

The shooting arrived with them.

6

As he suspected, there were a lot of new guns on the back of the train. Many of the people who came out of the coal cars had weapons, and they were anxious to get in on the action. As soon as the zombies shambled up to the back of the train, they plugged away at them. Before he could shout any warnings, it became impossibly noisy.

He and Victoria tried to use their weapons from where they stood, but they were dismayed to realize there were too many bodies standing in front of them to even consider using a gun. The outside row recoiled inward from the tide of plague-driven zombies washing up at their feet. It was mere moments before the first victims were snatched off the car and into the sea of hands, inciting panic among the remaining passengers as they pushed, pulled, punched, and clawed their way into the middle of the train car. Some tossed strangers off the edge to stay alive—it was a stampede smothered inside a murder-suicide.

What was once going to be a heroic defense of the rear car, turned swiftly into a debacle of fratricide. Fearing they'd be tossed out, he grabbed Victoria's hand and pulled her back on top of him as he fell beneath the tractor-trailer near Grandma. She was packed in like a sardine in her section. He wondered if she was being hurt by all the struggling people.

The most effective shooters, the ones inflicting the most damage, were at the rear. They had the most room, and because they grouped together in anticipation of the trailing zombies, they had plenty of time to prepare.

In under a minute—much faster than his smaller group had done earlier—they had created enough carnage to stack the dead directly behind them. Like before, the zombies used their fallen comrades as a biological ramp to crawl up to the survivors. Hands grabbed at passengers' legs. One shooter fell, then another. Then more.

Within minutes, and despite the withering gunfire, the zombies were up on the flatcar, tearing through the rear contingent and moving forward. He looked at Victoria and saw the fear in her eyes.

The tractor-trailer was parked so the legs holding it up were near the back of the rail car. That put about 80 feet, and 50 or so adults—only some with weapons—between them and the incoming wave.

He caught sight of Grandma who was watching the whole thing unfold. She gave him a weak smile as she huddled with everyone else under the truck. Escape was impossible for her.

"Liam," Victoria shouted over the gunshots and screams, "can you call the engineer? We have to move this train, or we're going to be swamped."

"I don't know if she has a police radio up there. But I'll try." He repeatedly tried to raise someone up in the front of the train. No one answered.

He tried to get a look over to Jones and his effort with the dump truck, but there were too many faces staring back at him, blocking most of his view.

"Liam, we have to do it ourselves. We can jump on the car in front of us and keep going until we reach the engine."

He thought it sounded crazy, but he couldn't think of a better plan. Grandma was in some serious trouble if they didn't make something happen for her. He could stay and fire round after round from his gun, but more zombies were surrounding the train than he could realistically dispatch, even if he used all 1,000 rounds from his backpack.

He trusted Victoria.

"Grandma, Victoria and I—"

"Yes, dear. Please hurry!"

He did something he had never done in his entire life. He gave Grandma a kiss on the cheek.

"I'll save you. I promise," he shouted, hoping her hearing aid would pick it up.

He and Victoria slithered through the mass of people and made their way to the front of the rear car so they could jump the small gap to the next car—an open-topped coal hopper. A couple of zombies milled about in the gap, but it was an easy jump for both. A quick climb and then over the lip of the car.

There were several people in that coal car, but only a pair of men were hanging over the edges to shoot at the zombies. The walls of the hopper were too high to effectively wield a weapon. The high, metal walls made the people inside very secure—unless there was an impossibly large pile of zombies outside—but it took them out of the fight as well.

They ran along the interior, avoiding women and children sitting inside. With a quick jump and pull to the top of the far wall, he was able to straddle it. He planted his foot on the ladder up the outside of the car and extended his hand to help Victoria up and out. He could tell she wanted to do it on her own, but she was still wearing a black dress and flats with broken heels. Not exactly the best outfit for running, jumping, and climbing.

The next car was a big, enclosed, freight car. They hurriedly clambered on top and ran forward among a few of the people who sat up there. The engine was about twenty cars ahead.

From the high vantage point, he turned to his right and was able to take in the action playing out as Jones reached the group of survivors next to the mine. He had forced the truck through to the cheering men and women. The number of zombies had been reduced, perhaps by as much as half along the roadway. It might be enough.

It looked like Jones was going to turn the truck around and push more dead out of the way on his way back, but Liam had to keep moving and wasn't able to watch any more.

They worked their way up the train cars. Some were simple up-and-overs like the freight car. Many were challenging, such as dropping into and climbing out of the coal cars. One unique coal car was particularly difficult because it had sloped panels in the front and rear, making it slippery as grease to get out. Victoria's shoes were incredibly slick on the coal dust, and when she finally dragged herself high enough where he could grab her, it looked like she had black stockings on her legs. Her arms and face weren't much better, but he did enjoy holding her hands, however briefly.

They passed many of the remaining cops and gang members, both frantically firing into the core of the zombies swarming between them and the arriving survivors. He hoped they wouldn't accidentally hit anyone that wasn't already infected.

They were only a few cars from the front when they heard desperate wailing coming from the group of survivors out in the action. He didn't see the dump truck anywhere. There was nowhere it could have gone in that short of time. Except—

"Oh, no." He could guess what had happened. Jones had driven off the edge of the pit mine. How far down was the next level? He couldn't see below the lip of the mine.

Victoria was speechless. She gave him a slight nudge in the back as if to say they had to keep moving.

There was no time for mourning. The group from the pit seemed enraged at the loss. They kept coming, killing zombies as they got in their way.

A few minutes later, and he and Victoria boarded the walking platform surrounding the engine. They ran inside the side door and found the engineer on the right side of the compartment, watching the action unfold from her window.

"You have to move the train! Even a hundred feet will help," he shouted at her.

The engineer jumped, obviously startled. "Good god, you scared me!"

"Oh, sorry," he said in a less frightening voice.

She pointed outside. "Shouldn't we wait for them to get here? They aren't far now. I stopped so we could save those poor people."

"They can still reach the train even if we move a few feet. The rear car is piled high with infected. That pile will fall if we move the train. We have to do it now!"

She looked at him, then at Victoria, who was vigorously nodding.

"OK, just give me a second, and I'll push us a few feet."

He looked out the window as the train started to move and could see the panic in the faces of those running toward him, so he moved out onto the walkway of the engine and starting waving them in. He noticed Hayes was already out on the platform, toward the back, watching the action. Still without a gun.

Liam had no intention of doing nothing. He started carefully aiming at the zombies down below, each hit making a little more room for those who were so close to sanctuary. He ran through his nine rounds and was left with an empty gun in his hands. He hoped he helped. There seemed to be large gaps in the crowd of dead closest to the side of the train. Enough space for the runners to make it through.

Thank you, Jones. I won't forget you. Maybe I'll write a book about you.

Soon the panting survivors arrived and scrambled up to whatever car they happened to reach first. Several children were being dragged on the ground by older children, probably their siblings. He tried not to dwell on what had happened to their parents. There were many fewer survivors than when he first saw them on the far rim of the mine. They had suffered horrible casualties.

Once they were safely on board, the train began to roll faster. The survivors at the bottom of the mine were left to their own version of Dante's Inferno. But then, so were hundreds of thousands of others behind them, back in the city. Each a potential vector for the deadly plague.

And there's one less hero in this crappy world.

VALKYRIE

Liam only had a few minutes to think about what just happened while he rode on the outer railing of the engine. They had saved a lot of people—maybe forty or fifty by his estimate. But he had lost his new friend, and he was unsure of the status of Grandma, or how many had died defending the rear car. They had to put some room between themselves and the frenzy of zombies behind them, but—

He went back inside.

"I need to check on my Grandma. She's on the last car."

"Not to worry. We have one more stop ahead. There's a road and a little park a mile ahead where I'm meeting my family. You can run back when I stop for them."

"Won't that give the zombies a chance to catch us again?" Victoria asked. "They seem to be able to follow us pretty well."

"I'm not just going to drive the train right by my family, am I? We're stopping for as long as it takes to pick them up."

He and Victoria moved out onto the platform around the engine. He gave her a devilish smile. "You know, you did pretty good coming over the train. We could run back on top of all the cars while we're still moving."

"Are you nuts? One fall and you'd be dead. The zombies would catch you before you could climb back on. Assuming you don't get yourself cut in half by the wheels."

"Well, it works in the movies, but I guess you're right. We'll wait until the train stops and then run back on the ground."

"'Bout time you listened to me," Victoria said cheerfully.

They had a few moments to wait while the train ground its way through the beginnings of the wooded park. A high cliff rose above the right side of the tracks, so they watched out over the river on the left side.

Things happened so fast today; he tried to process it. Speaking loudly over the dragging created by the disabled engine, he asked: "Do you think Jones made it?" He didn't know what answer he wanted to hear. That he was still alive but surrounded by endless zombies or that he died quickly and heroically.

"I don't know. But I worry we're all gonna die out here. Maybe not on this train, but out in this new horrible world. We joke about calling them zombies, but we ignore the truth. They are Death. I know I shouldn't say it. I don't want to say it. But it's how I feel after everything we've seen. Even my prayers feel hopeless."

She took a deep breath. "A few days ago, before the plague, before we met, I almost wanted to die. Now I've found I want to live, but we may all die anyway. Funny, huh?"

He didn't know how to answer because his head was foggy. The exhaustion caught up with him in the lull.

The pitch of the motor changed. The engineer had begun to throttle back.

With great effort he focused on what needed to be done in the moment. "Well, I think we're going to make it. And I'll tell you something else; Grandma is going to make it, too. You and I will make sure of that!"

"Amen!"

He turned to her and got serious again. "I want you to stay here because I'm coming right back as soon as I know Grandma is still OK. You and I have to stay up here, so we know what's going on."

"Liam," she said with a bit of rejection.

"I promise I'll be right back. Make sure no one moves the train before I return." Liam secretly nodded to Hayes, still standing toward the back of the railing.

"I guess that makes sense, but I bet I'm faster than you," she said. A moment later she looked at her dirty dress shoes. "But not in these."

"I'll be fast enough, but I want to race you someday," he said, knowing it was a bit awkward to suggest. That did, however, end the conversation.

He didn't mention part of his request was so he wouldn't have to worry about her *and* Grandma in the dangerous rear car. He wanted Victoria to stay in the engine where she'd at least have some protection. In a perfect world, he'd get Grandma up into the engine as well, but without her wheelchair or walker to move her, he didn't want to risk having her on the ground if the train started moving again.

Liam prepared himself to jump. When the train had nearly stopped, he was off and running.

"I'll be right back!"

Victoria, watching behind him, shouted, "Give her my best!"

2

He approached the rear car to the sound of guns. A few shooters were still alive on the flatcar, and they shot up the remaining zombies as best they could. Many of the other survivors climbed off that last car, making for the safety of the high gondola cars, or the tops of boxcars.

"Grandma," he shouted when he spotted her, still under the truck axle.

"Hi, Liam," she replied, pointing up at the sky. "What a beautiful morning."

"Yeah, sure. Glad you're in such good spirits. I was worried sick!"

"You left me in good hands. Though we lost a lot of good people."

He climbed up, then shimmied under the trailer so he could be next to her. He gave her a hug. Despite saying she was on a pleasant morning train excursion, her hands trembled just like his had done after he was almost shot by that fake policeman. It scared him to see her in such a state. He grabbed some water and small grain bars from his backpack and shared them with her. He also reloaded his gun and dumped a ton of the small shells into his pockets, so he'd have some with him.

They watched as the last of the injured zombies got cleared from their rail car by the few remaining gun handlers. Everyone that hadn't moved to other cars stood or sat in a small area near the front of the flatcar. The back half was now tainted with lots of blood, though the bodies themselves had been pushed off.

"They're picking someone up, and then the train will be moving again."

He looked over his shoulder to see if they were followed. The front of the zombie wave from their engagement at the quarry was slowly coming around the corner. They were still several minutes behind but closing the distance with the inevitability of a sunrise.

Liam lifted the radio from his backpack, knowing it didn't work the last time.

"This is Liam. We have to move the train. The horde will be here in minutes. Over."

There was no reply.

Is this thing on?

He tried a few more times and still got no response. The train hadn't moved, either. He thought angrily of every movie he'd ever seen where the radio goes out at the most inopportune time. He couldn't fathom how his radio would similarly fail at his most desperate hour.

"Grandma, will you be OK back here? I have to run up front and tell them what's coming."

"I'm not going anywhere. I'm a little sore from that big man throwing me. Did he save those people, dear?"

"He saved 'em, yep." He avoided his eventual fate.

"Oh, that's wonderful," she replied, appearing satisfied.

"I'll be back for you!" He grabbed his backpack this time, slid out from under the trailer, then off the flat deck. She appeared tiny under the huge trailer. He gave her one last wave and dashed away.

The zombie pursuit slowly approached.

At least they can't run.

He wondered how far *he'd* run today because he was doing it again. Briefly, he tried to guess how long the 20-car train was, so he could figure out the distance, but that only lasted a few paces because he spotted his friend.

She stood on the edge of the engine and his first impression was that she was a mess. Bruised face. Hair as wild as a cave girl. Black evening dress torn in several places. Legs and arms coal-covered and sweat-soaked from exertion. But she was also striking in her poise and strength, though that illusion was ruined when she spoke.

"Get your buns up here!" she cried out.

He ran the rest of the way, and she gave him a warm hug as he climbed aboard.

"I thought you'd been taken," she said with emotion.

"I've only been gone a couple of minutes."

"Seemed like you were gone for a half hour. I'm sorry, I have a horrible sense of time."

"Let's get inside. The train has to move, now." Together they entered the engine cab, but the driver wasn't there.

They found her unloading an SUV on the other side of the train along with several kids, a man who must have been her husband, and an older woman. They carried flats of bottled water, pillows and things for the kids, and several guns. They piled everything on the end of the platform where he stood to watch. He and Victoria helped put the gear inside the engine where it would be protected.

"We have to hurry! There are zombies near the back of the train again," he called down, unsure who might be listening.

He didn't hear the guns yet, which would be the telltale sign trouble had arrived.

To his relief, the man climbed onto the engine and ran past him into the compartment. To no one in particular, the guy yelled out, "I snapped the brake lines on the dead engine. We can open her up now." His accent was similar to the woman engineer, if not a little stronger.

Once inside the compartment, the man went to work spinning up the engine. Liam assumed he must be the engineer husband of the woman who had been driving. The horn rang out multiple times, each one a long three-second blast. No mistaking it was time to leave, though he only passed a couple of people loitering off the train itself.

The kids came up next. Two young boys, about nine or ten years old, both dressed in jeans and sweatshirts—like they were trying to wear some protection from the biters. Liam thought it might backfire given the heat of the days of June, but he commended them for thinking ahead.

Last up was the woman engineer and her older friend. Once aboard, she ran into the compartment and shouted, "Aboard!"

Shooting started in the rear of the train as it lurched forward.

The man was, indeed, the actual engineer of this train. The engine hummed at fever pitch as he tried to get them up to a fast cruising speed. After many hours of running along at a near-to-walking pace, it seemed like they were on a bullet train. They still pushed the dead engine, but it was no longer sparking and thundering. They were free of that problem, and the powerful engine hit its stride quickly.

"This is amazing!" he shouted to Victoria. He pulled her out to the walkway where his wild hair started blowing around. The breeze caught her hair, too, and she stood like a puppy dog in the car window as they cruised along. They shared a smile and he once again noted how bruised and banged up her face was, even under such wonderful circumstances.

"We're going to make it," he mouthed to her.

He had just enough time to celebrate feeling kinship with Victoria when the train came around a bend and screeched in deceleration.

She lost her balance and bumped into him. He was happy to be on the receiving end of that impact, but it didn't soften what he saw ahead.

They were so close to freedom now. The bridge over the Meramec River, and to the suburbs, was a quarter-mile in front of them.

But there was one more roadblock.

3

The engineer eased off the brakes and let the engine continue the last quarter of a mile toward the end of the line. Some kind of factory or building was on their right—it had four large smokestacks and a huge pile of coal next to it. They went under another conveyor belt that seemed to feed coal from a depot near the river. The train finally went under a large metal pipe of some kind and then skidded to a stop about fifty feet from a bridge.

Several emergency services vehicles—including a green fire engine—were parked on the other side. A number of police cars and highway department trucks also flanked the far edge of the bridge. All of them had their blue and red lights flashing, giving the whole thing a nervous energy. But the real showstopper—a large construction crane—dangled a massive wrecking ball over the middle of the tracks.

The superhero part of his brain tried to run the numbers on whether the train could plow through all that stuff and survive, but it came up with bad news. The engineer seemed to find the same answer as well because he applied more brake, rather than gas.

Several men stood in the middle of the bridge, near the wrecking ball, guns in hand. The message was clear: this was the end of the line.

The engineer spoke up. "These guys again! The City of Arnold is on the other side of that river. They closed all the road bridges into their jurisdiction, including Interstate 55, which is where we tried to cross two days ago. That's when I called Tatia and told her to try to reach my train and bring it south, so I could meet her. I was hopeful they hadn't blocked this route, though I should have known better."

A few handfuls of people huddled in the bushes and trees on the approach to the bridge. Other survivors emerged from near the big pile of coal. No one came out to greet the train. He figured they were watching this new development at the blockade. If those people weren't being allowed to cross, what hope did the passengers on the train have?

The engineer paced around a bit, then spoke to his wife. "Is there any way we can back up the train and cross downtown? Is it still open?"

She shook her head no.

"We came from downtown," Liam interjected. "The military bombed it to a pulp."

The engineer continued. "There are some routes through the city we might be able to use, but I bet they all end just like this one. No one wants to let any of us city folk come into their turf."

Minutes went by as the engineers deliberated other routes through St. Louis. They found an ancient railroad map tucked under a seat, but none of the routes offered a path to safety. Nothing was as sure as the safety one river away from them.

He looked at Victoria, sensing he needed to do something to help. "While you guys think about other routes, Victoria and I will go talk to the people guarding the bridge. We'll see if they're letting anyone across. Maybe they just don't want the train to go through, but the people are fine?"

It was a lame excuse, but he wasn't running on much sleep. He very much wanted to talk to the authorities on the bridge, so he could figure out what he should do next to protect Grandma and Victoria. He thought of finding a boat or swimming across. Maybe he could find something floaty to put Grandma on. Maybe the little river was shallow enough to wade across at some point. There had to be a solution.

Hayes, who had been in the background during most of the recent action and discussions, jumped in. "As a CDC employee, maybe they'll talk to me." Without waiting for approval, he stepped out of the cab and started down.

Liam and Victoria ran out to follow him.

The engineers and their family were content to wait in the safety of the engine. He suspected they were delaying a decision on backing out until they saw what would happen next.

A couple of the St. Louis police officers dismounted from the train and wanted to meet on the bridge as well, but Hayes was very persuasive, arguing he was their most senior government official and could get them across. Too many in the group approaching the bridge would constitute a threat to those on the far side of the river. Better to take it slow ...

Liam said nothing to that. It could very well be true.

The trio walked out onto the bridge, careful to not put a foot through the open railroad ties.

"We meet again," Hayes said. "I guess you two never leave each other's sides, huh?"

"So what. What's it to you?" Victoria snapped, as she raised her hands high in the face of the police ahead.

"No need to get defensive. Just making small talk." His bemused tone suggested he knew he pushed her buttons.

"That's far enough!" an officer in a black uniform shouted from ahead. "By order of the Mayor of Arnold, Missouri, you are ordered to turn around and return to the safety of your homes."

"Safety of our homes?" Victoria muttered.

Liam softly spoke to Hayes. "I'm from Imperial. It's just south of Arnold. They might let a local through."

"It's OK, kid. I got this."

"I'm Doctor Hayes, and I work for the CDC. I'm under the direct command of the President of the United States. He orders you to allow me to proceed on foot to complete my duties relating to this pandemic!"

The officers laughed.

"Congratulations! You just won me fifty bucks. I bet Billy here one of you would pull that 'I'm with the government' bull."

"I can prove it. I have ID!" Hayes pulled out his wallet and waved it in the air.

"No, thanks. We aren't taking any chances with that Ebola-crap flying around."

"Don't you idiots know the plague is everywhere?" Hayes shouted. "It's already on your side of the river. I guarantee it."

Liam gave him a nudge. "Be nice!"

"Our orders are to stop *everyone*. We have family here and aren't taking any chances."

Hayes thought for a moment. "What about locals? My friend here lives in Imperious, to the south of here."

"Imperial!" Liam shouted to correct him.

"Ha, ha, nice try! Look, I don't care who you are. I had to send a sweet little group of nuns packing, so my sympathy meter is in the crapper. You people aren't getting across this bridge."

"Just allow me to come over. I'm perfectly healthy. These others aren't important. I'll make sure you're rewarded by the Federal Government." Hayes took a step to be away from Liam and Victoria.

The lead officer also stepped forward. He was in the black uniform of the local constabulary. Liam respected his AR-style tactical rifle. The big scope was impressive. He seemed to take it personally. "Are you bribing us?" His rifle pointed to the rail ties below, though there was a warning, too.

Hayes huffed as if he wasn't used to being turned away from anywhere he wanted to go. He spun around and started walking back.

Maybe he is a nobody. That's the second time today he's been turned back on a bridge.

Inwardly, he snickered at how Hayes talked himself up but wondered if he was laughing at his own misfortune. If the guy was the important dude he claimed, they might all be getting to safety right now.

Victoria asked the lead cop, “Is there any hope? We have a whole train of families, kids, old seniors. Can you at least give us an idea how to survive? Their homes aren't safe. Nothing back that way is,” she said while pointing over her shoulder.

Victoria's plea, and Hayes' retreat, seemed to temper the lead man. He slung his rifle back over his shoulder and took several steps in their direction. Still a good distance away.

“Look. There's nothing we can do. Our orders are very clear to hold this bridge and prevent the plague from reaching our neighborhoods. Reach our families. I feel for you. I really do. But if I let you across, and the plague kills my best friend's baby girl, I'd never forgive myself.”

He took another couple of steps.

“You guys can hole up in that power plant. It has strong doors. Lots of room. Good for defending yourselves. It has a chance. We might even be able to get some food to you.”

It sounded like the most reasonable thing he'd heard all day.

Not ten seconds later, shots echoed from the back of the train. Fate always seemed to catch up to him.

“Thank you for your offer,” Liam said. “But that noise means the walking plague has caught up with us. My Grandma is on the train and we're going back to fight. We have to do something.”

He took Victoria's hand and together they jogged off the bridge.

4

After they got off the railroad ties of the bridge, he let go of her hand and sprinted ahead of Victoria.

“I'm going ahead to get her ready!” he said as he let go.

She may have been a runner, but her shoes slowed her down. He ran full speed to rescue Grandma and wasn't stopping or slowing for anything.

"I'll be right behind you," she replied.

He ran past Hayes, who looked lost near the front of the dead train.

Liam ran past the two engineers and their family, standing at the door of the *Valkyrie*'s engine room. One of the little ones waved down and he gave a sideways wave while on the run.

He yelled to the other passengers as he went by, "Zombies are here! The train is blocked ahead."

As he ran by all the cars of the train, he repeated his message. He saw the confusion of those left alive. Stay on the train and fight until overwhelmed or get off the train and hope to escape. He didn't look back to learn which choices they made, nor did he offer his teenaged gamer advice, which would have been to fight it out. His only concern was Grandma.

The tracks were bullet-straight here, so he could already see the last car. The zombies were widely spread out behind the train, but they were coming in great numbers a bit further down the right-of-way. Some of them *were* faster than the others. Those advance zombies were picked off by the remaining shooters, but guns would be useless in a matter of minutes.

This is it.

He had never really appreciated the concept of death. Not even in any of the many situations he'd survived the past several days. He knew he'd been in a bad spot with that robber, but he didn't have time to think about death until *after* it happened. Now he was staring at Death as it walked toward him. It felt like walking along the edge of a high cliff over a bottomless pit. The anxiety tried to blossom in his midsection and he sensed his arms were in danger of getting the shakes again. Would it force him to cower in a clump of flowers like he did on that first day?

Man up, Liam! Think and plan.

His father's voice was stern, and he tried to think ahead, but Grandma was his only concern at that moment.

He scrambled up onto the flatcar in one fluid jump. Unlike his fiasco hopping the fence in Grandma's yard, he wasn't doing it to look cool. He was doing it to save lives. He pulled her out from under the trailer and apologized profusely for being rough. She didn't complain at all; he was glad of that.

She was the only living person left on the trailing car. She'd been aware of that, too, because she held her rosary, and she had a speech of sorts worked up.

"I've been very proud of you, Liam. You've certainly grown into a man the last few days. Now you have to let me go. We can't both survive this. You need to protect Victoria. I told her you two would look out for each other when the time came."

She pointed behind them. "This is that time."

Liam didn't even acknowledge the statement. He slid off the side and pulled her over the deck and into his arms. He was surprised how light she was. Light, yes, but still too heavy to carry her all the way back to the bridge as the hero part of his mind suggested.

He set her down, put his arm around her waist, and walked her away from the encroaching horde. Something in him solidified. He was adamant he was not going to abandon her and run. He couldn't explain the sentiment. It certainly wasn't logical, but it wasn't baseless emotionalism either. He was *compelled* to save her. Like everything would be OK if he could get her to safety.

In seconds, Victoria arrived. She grabbed Grandma on the other side, and they made even better time. Not quite a jog, but a decent-paced walk.

Don't look back.

As they passed each car, he realized some people chose to stay and fight. Others ran like mad to all points on the map. Some headed to the nearby Mississippi river—perhaps hoping to swim to safety. The fastest ran the open ground over to the coal plant. Some scrambled up the steep wooded slope nearest the back of the train. Trying to outclimb the pursuit. None of those was realistic for Grandma. Her only option was the bridge ahead.

The surviving shooters made short work of the isolated lead zombies, but the rest of the tide started enveloping the train.

As Liam, Grandma, and Victoria walk-ran along the tracks, so did the noise. Screams of people who got caught. Curses of men and women. The frantic cries of children. The excited drone of a surging pack of angry, feral, zombies. The shooting also intensified, staying very close behind them.

Some who jumped off the train to escape jumped right back on as they realized what headed their way, but many people who had abandoned the train had the same idea as Liam. They gambled their lives on being able to cross the smaller river to their front. They were all much faster than he was with Grandma, even the children.

Don't look back.

He was shocked to realize there were fewer and fewer shooters behind them. *They finally ran out of ammo. They'd been in a shooting gallery all morning.*

Several officers and a few of the remaining gang members and their families stayed in a tight group and ran for the bridge. The engineers and their family also ran forward. Everyone left alive from the train made for the only direction suitable for the very young, the very old, or the slow.

Most of the train cars were empty, save the scattered few who chose to stay put. For the most part, those people ducked out of sight when he saw them as if they were unwilling to call attention to themselves.

They walked as fast as Grandma could go with two people to help her along. A half-carry, half-drag arrangement. Even so, as he approached the *Valkyrie*, Liam dropped Grandma's weight onto Victoria and told them to continue without him for a minute, and he climbed the side of the diesel. He was happy neither asked questions. Victoria kept the pace, moving Grandma toward the bridge.

He rushed to where the engineers and crew stowed their gear. The item he spotted earlier was still there, so he grabbed it, tucked it into his waistband, and ran back outside and along the railing. He ran forward to the nose of the *Valkyrie*, then hopped to the dead train engine at the very front. He ran the railing again until he reached the absolute front of the entire train. He barely slowed as he flew over the handrail, hanging on just long enough so he could deftly drop the last few feet to the ground. He willed himself to ignore the noise of the infected wave approaching.

He pumped hard as he ran to catch up to the two women. Victoria and Grandma entered the group standing on the near side of the bridge. He knew what he did was reckless, but it felt right and necessary. It helped that it didn't endanger anyone but himself.

Liam closed the final distance. A good number of the surviving police officers and gang members from the train fanned out with guns at the ready. One man stood out from the whole group: a shirtless guy with a pair of bandoliers filled with vibrant red shotgun shells slung over both his shoulders, forming a distinctive "X" on his chest. He cradled the shotgun against his shoulder, and he waved Liam in while puffing on a fat cigar.

Never look back!

He sped across the last fifty feet of track leading up to the bridge.

When he entered the group, a thunderous boom almost made him lose his bowels because it was so shockingly loud. As if on cue, the group unleashed an explosion of gunfire into whatever was right behind him. Some of the zombies were *much* closer than he thought possible, given his speed.

The fusillade bought some breathing room, but the end was already written unless they could all get over to the other side. He wasn't about to suggest both sides start shooting each other, but that would be one scenario for sure if they were in a video game.

He caught up with Victoria and Grandma and they dragged her over the bridge, passing by all the survivors left from the train. There were several he recognized as the "new people" from the pit mine. Kids saved from the Arch grounds and elsewhere along the way were now universally in tears. A few older people had made it, but no one was even close to Grandma's age. A group of nuns was also mixed in. Where did they come from?

The trio neared the midpoint before the Arnold Police screamed over the noise and waved their guns in warning. He and Victoria had started carrying Grandma without realizing it. They set her on her feet, but her body had gone slack, so he eased her down to lie on the wooden bridge.

"Grandma ... " he began. Her eyes were closed. A light seemed to have gone out of her face.

"Grandma! Wake up!" He flopped down next to her, completely at a loss what to do.

Victoria knelt on her other side, reaching for her wrist and neck—searching for a pulse.

"I can't tell if she's breathing," she announced in a steady voice.

Liam sat useless as she tried CPR under the press of the nearby battle. He held Grandma's hand, willing her to come back. Time seemed to fizzle as his vision clouded with tears.

Finally, when he found his focus, Victoria sat next to him covered in sweat from exertion and tears from crying. She gave him a sad, stunned look. "I'm so sorry. I think she's gone."

"What? No! No! No!" He didn't know who to blame. The police blocking them? The zombies? Himself? He was a fool to take her into the Zombie Apocalypse ...

Victoria's demeanor changed like the Missouri weather. She wiped the tears, cleared her forehead of sweat and grime, and got a serious look in her eyes. Her sadness turned to anger, and unlike him, she had a target already picked out.

"They. Are going. To pay!" she said tersely to him as she got to her feet.

She shouted above all the other noise, surprising and encouraging him at the same time.

"You stupid bastards! She's dead because of *you*! You could have saved her! Can't you see that? We're all going to die for your worthless rules. The plague can't be stopped. Look!" She swept her arm back toward the train and the advancing undead. "It's here right now, and you're standing there with your hands in your pockets! D—" She paused for an awkward moment as if thinking if she should say something more.

"Damn you all!" she finally blurted out.

Tears rolled down her cheeks and she collapsed beside Grandma. Obviously spent.

He had tears in his eyes, too, but inside Liam felt ... empty. Much like after his first encounter with Angie. At that moment all he could do was hold Grandma's hand one last time and appreciate everything she'd done for him. The screams of men, the concussion of guns, and the deathly buzz of the zombie horde were all distant background noises.

"Liam, don't fuss over me. Save Victoria," is what Grandma would say to him.

He looked up and saw the lead police officer walking a few steps closer toward where he and Victoria comforted Grandma. His men called out to him, warning him not to get too close. Liam found that ironic. Grandma would have laughed at that too.

"I'm so sorry I couldn't save you, Grandma. We were so close." Still holding her hand, he experienced a million memories of his time with her like a fast-forwarding movie. Some were from when he was a child playing at her home. Many were more recent, including a nice home-cooked dinner the two of them shared in her kitchen. At the time, he tried to pretend he didn't enjoy it, but afterward he admitted he did. He couldn't remember why he'd been so scared of being with her back then.

"Thank you for all you did for me," was all he could say. His emotions shifted like the autumn wind and his apathy turned to a deep sadness. It all made sense why he'd started crying and once he realized what he'd lost, his tears were impossible to control. Like his wobbly legs and arms so long ago, his insides were now hopelessly out of sorts.

Grandma was gone forever.

What do I do now?

For the first time in a long while, even his gamer's brain was out of creative ideas.

SHADOW GOVERNMENT

Marty woke up in soft green grass while lying on her back next to a large frozen waterfall. Not frozen in ice. Frozen without motion. Several trees and bushes grew in the vicinity, but the waterfall tumbling into a crystal clear natural pool was the attention-getter. A strange, inky darkness surrounded the scene.

Her amazement multiplied when she looked up. A nearly infinite number of stars beamed down from the heavens. To her eyes, they had to be part of an elaborate illusion because each one seemed to have planets spinning around them. The number of visible points of light was beyond reckoning.

Her husband or angel—she wasn't sure which—sat cross-legged, not far from her. "Hello, Marty. You've made it to the end of the line."

"I'm dead?"

"Why do you always think you're dead? No. I'm pleased to say you *still* aren't dead. I meant you made it to the end of the rail line." He chuckled a little and continued. "You passed out while you ran with your two young friends. I don't think they realized you had surpassed your limits. They now believe you're gone."

"I get mistaken for dead a lot these days," she said, recalling the incidents with the priests back at the Arch. "I'd hate for poor Liam to get that impression."

"It's no wonder you're so loved. You never think of yourself."

She couldn't help but think of her deceptions of not telling Liam about Angie or about shooting the robber. She was feeling guilty for her sins of omission.

"Don't trouble yourself with minor things like that. You made legitimate decisions to protect your great-grandson. Though, looking at how hard he tried to save you just now, I think your plan backfired."

"I think he wants to prove to Victoria he can protect me."

"Perhaps. But maybe he wants to prove to *you* that he can protect you."

"I guess we all lose. We're all going to die, aren't we?"

"You mean eventually? Yes, I'm afraid you're all going to die. But are you going to die today? That's less clear."

He stood up, offering a hand. Her body was strong in this place, so she was able to take it and be on her feet in a flash. He guided her to the clear pond.

"What is this place? Is this Liam's memory from a book, too?" she asked as the shock faded a bit.

He walked slightly ahead of her and answered while looking up at the majestic waterfall. "Do you know what makes you so important?"

"No, I've been kinda busy lately to be introspective." She gave a tired laugh. Her body might be refreshed in this place, but her mind was still saddled with the death and destruction of the last four days.

"Ha! I love your sense of humor." He pointed to a section of froth on the frozen waterfall, very near the bottom. The area didn't light up, but she had no trouble focusing on the one tiny dot he indicated. "You see that drop there? Right there! That's Earth."

"I think I'm hallucinating. Planet Earth is in a waterfall?"

"Actually, it would be most accurate to say you're looking at a type of chart of all the planets in the universe. Not to scale, of course."

"Now, let's get a little closer." As he said it, the "waterfall" seemed to magnify, so the Earth was about the size of a marble among an untold number of similar marbles. She watched him move his fingers over a very faint ghost keypad, manipulating the waterfall. "Ah, there we go. Now, do you notice anything unusual about your planet?"

She looked at the multitude of worlds, distracted by the beauty and wonder of it all. Some looked very much like Earth, verdant and cloud-filled. Others were desert worlds. Some appeared to be gas worlds, shown with slightly larger marbles. Looking up, the planets seemed to stretch to infinity. But most of the orbs had a bright light around them; an artificial background glow which seemed to make them pop out from the waterfall itself.

"The Earth doesn't have that white glow behind it. Many of the others do."

"Most excellent! Yes. Yes. That cosmic glow represents many wonderful things. The underpinning science would take me a human lifetime to explain with mathematics—and perhaps some philosophy."

"Oh dear. I don't have that much time left in my life."

"*Au contraire,* my Martinette. You are just now reaching an age where you can appreciate what I'm about to tell you. A younger person doesn't have the maturity to reach this place unassisted. That maturity is what makes you so special."

"Is that a polite way of saying I'm an old and worn-out woman? That's what I feel like when I come here."

"No! Not at all. I wish I had more time with you, but demands have been placed on both of us. Your attention is needed out on the bridge. I have a whole universe to manage." He pointed to the waterfall as if that explained everything.

Seeming satisfied, he touched his floating keypad and swiped the waterfall away and replaced it with an overhead view of herself lying on the bridge, surrounded by a stunned Liam and a distraught Victoria as she "spoke in tongues" with foul language. An officer in black moved a bit closer as his men yelled at him. Panning out, the scene showed the police on one side of the bridge, armed but not shooting, and the infected attacking mercilessly toward the survivors of the train on the other end.

"You have much to do. The first baby step you must take is to carry a tool with you out into the world. That aid will help you get off this bridge. Your next steps must be to establish a connection with the two most important people in your life. I'm impressed how fast you developed the link with Liam—the green car on the bridge was *his* memory, probably from one of his books, if I had to guess. And the last cosmic leap you will take is establishing the light behind your planet on the waterfall I showed you."

"I want to believe I'm important to whatever," she looked around her, "this incredible place is, but you can see what's going to happen just as I can. There's no way, short of a miracle, I'm going to survive the day."

Al smiled. "My dearest Martinette, have I got a surprise for you. I'm not only going to get you across that bridge, but I'm going to change the course of your entire life in the process."

"You're talking in riddles. What *exactly* is the tool you're going to give me?"

"It's something, my gregarious friend, for which you are well-suited," he said in a friendly voice. "A message."

He whispered something in her ear. Then he whispered it again. "Your planet's future depends on your ability to recall this information." He gave her a tooth-filled smile and winked exactly as she would have done.

No pressure.

2

Grandma started to cough.

He and Victoria screamed in unison. "She's alive!"

"We're so glad! We—" Liam said through his tears before Grandma cut him off with a wave of her hand.

Grandma tried to speak, so they sat her up and leaned in close.

"Call out for Beth Ramos," she instructed.

"Beth Ramos? Who's?" he started to ask, but didn't finish the question. He would have done anything she asked of him just then.

"Beth Ramos!" Liam shouted. "I'm looking for Beth Ramos!"

She whispered again, "Louder."

"Where's Beth Ramos! We need her over here!" He yelled as loud as he was able into the din of the chaos. He faced the group from the train, assuming Beth was one of the women she'd been talking to back on the flatcar.

The lead officer of the police blocking the bridge, who looked to be about forty, well-tanned and muscular, walked the remaining distance to where Grandma was lying. Another officer from the vanguard ran up to be by his side, asking, "What are you doing, Sarge? You can't mingle with them. You might get sick."

Liam spun around to face them. Victoria angled that way as well.

"She's calling out for Beth Ramos." Sarge said to his officer.

"You're kidding me," the second officer said with surprise.

The leader went down on one knee beside Grandma. "Why do you want Beth Ramos?"

He leaned closer to hear her weak voice over the volume of gunfire in the battle nearby.

"I don't know what this means, sir, but I was told to ask for Beth Ramos, and then give a message to the person who answered the call. I guess that's you?"

The officer nodded.

"Well, the message I'm supposed to give you makes no sense to me, but maybe it will to you. 'Darcy and Jokie Bunny want you to save these people'."

"WHAT? How—" he choked up. "What's going on here?"

Liam, bewilderment on his face, looked from Grandma to the confused sergeant and then to the other officer, who put his hand on the sergeant's shoulder.

"Beth was Phil's wife. Darcy was his daughter. Jokie Bunny—I don't know."

"Jokie—" The sergeant struggled to control his voice while a lone tear hugged the side of his nose. "Jokie Bunny was Darcy's lovey, a stuffed toy rabbit. No one could possibly know about that rabbit. Darcy slept with it every night. We figured she couldn't live without it and made her keep it in her bed because we didn't want it to get lost. But we did let her take it out *one* time. She went with Darcy when my wife took her to stay overnight at a friend's house. It was going to be the first time we let her sleep away from home."

A deep breath as the sounds of battle continued to ride high.

"My girls never made it." He fought the tears, but without much success.

The other officer jumped in. "Phil's wife and daughter were in a terrible traffic accident this past winter. We all went to the funeral in support. Is that how you knew their names?"

"I was told by," she took a deep breath, "what I believe was an angel."

Phil lifted his tear-stained face and stared at Grandma for several long moments. Perhaps deciding if she was crazy.

"No one could have known about Jokie Bunny. No one. I believe you, ma'am."

"Billy, bring up the men. We're going to fight at the front of this group. Let's help them across. To hell with orders. Those sick things won't be stopped by a little water. We can't let these people die while we watch and do nothing."

"You got it, Sarge."

Billy ran back to his mates to round them up.

Phil used his radio to instruct those on the far shore. He called out certain leaders, requested certain weapons, and finished with "—and enact our plan Badrovik as soon as we're all across. Out."

Phil stood up, brushed the tears from his eyes and said, "Get your grandma across the bridge. I'd like to talk to her when we're all safe on the other side. If my wife and daughter—however it's possible—want me to let you guys across, by God, you're going to own this bridge."

Billy's group arrived, ready for the evacuation effort. As they reached Phil, he yelled, "OK, guys, let's spray those sickos with a lead shower—Go! Go! Go!"

They all took off into the crowd of people clumped on the dangerous side of the bridge. Cheers went up with the survivors when they realized what was happening. The zombies had made it into the front edge of the train passengers. The burn line between the living and dead hovered at the bridge's edge.

He and Victoria lifted Grandma to her feet one more time. “Glad to see you are OK,” he said.

“Me, too,” Victoria added without hesitation.

“That makes three,” Grandma said, barely loud enough to be heard over the battle.

With the deck clear, they walked toward the safe side of the span.

The Arnold Police funneled the survivors back, putting themselves nearest the fighting to fend off the blood-slick attackers as they continued to swarm toward the officers and remaining armed men from the train.

When the fresh officers made it to the tip of the spear, they began retreating as a unit back across the bridge, expending ammo at a horrible rate. They were experts at the head shot—the only shot that seemed to down the infection instantly. Of course, any good student of zombie literature knows that. These guys didn't disappoint. Only a precious few officers got snatched during the murderous onslaught. Some accidentally fell through the railway ties, or off the side, to the water below. Zombies often followed them down.

He and Victoria got Grandma to the safe side, then stood behind a police car to watch the approaching storm. The organized police line fell back in good order, ensuring nearly all of the train survivors made it. As each rank of officers crossed to the near side, they fanned out to cover their brothers and sisters still out on the span. It was a rare thing of beauty in the chaotic escape.

The last of the men filed onto the near shore, but now the bridge itself was crammed solid with plague victims. Some slipped off the sides as their numbers swelled. The constricting crush of infected funneling onto the narrow railway bridge insured bullets couldn’t miss. He again thought of the Greeks at Thermopylae, wondering if he accidentally paid too much attention in Social Studies class. The horde advancing on them were not flesh-and-blood Persians, however, and the infected continued to swarm, undeterred at any losses, willing to climb over piles of their peers collecting on the near end of the bridge. An endless procession of zombies arrived on the far side and there wasn't enough ammo here to kill them all.

"I have to help," he said as if realizing his fate.

Victoria grabbed his arm, and he was prepared to argue with her, but she merely said, "Wait up."

She needed a moment to pull out her gun and get it ready. He used the time to grab his box of shells. "We'll keep this with us."

He looked at Grandma as she stood leaning against the car. For a moment he wondered if leaving her was the right thing to do, but if the zombies made it across because he stood by and did nothing, there would barely be time to say goodbye to each other. Better to play it safe and make sure that didn't come to pass.

"We'll be right over here," he shouted to Grandma.

The couple got right up to the edge of the upper part of the river bank, a little to the right of the main force of the police.

"We're kind of far, but we'll hit them in the side of the head. That will give us the best chance of downing them."

"I trust you, Liam. Let's give them hell."

The range was about thirty or forty feet, he guessed. Not close enough to guarantee a hit with each shot, but it was the best he could do without interfering with the bigger and more effective guns closer to the bridge.

Together, he and Victoria aimed and fired at the swelling mass creeping along the railway decking toward the untainted southern shore. It was an incredible kill box, and the dead fell in waves, but the overhead trusses of the bridge served as brackets that kept many of the zombies from tumbling over the sides. As more bodies fell, the rest of the zombies climbed the steel girders to get over their friends.

And they kept coming.

Liam rattled off nine shots and dipped into the box to reload. He focused completely on shoving them into the little metal magazine as fast as possible. When finished, he held his hand flat in mid-air to ensure it wasn't shaking. His insides were wobbly with fear, but it wasn't affecting his exterior.

"Be scared later," he said to himself.

Victoria finished her shots and began her reload, too.

"I got one, I think," she said.

"Yeah, hard to tell with all the bullets flying," he admitted. His main concern was contributing however he could. If they put enough lead on the bridge, he was certain they'd kill something. So many of his books reinforced the idea that even one less zombie could make the difference.

While he was on his third trip to the ammo box, the large crane came to life and moved the giant wrecking ball first backward a considerable distance, and then forward, then backward again. It reminded him of Jones preparing to hand off Grandma. It appeared to be the final piece of Officer Phil's plan. The crane had huge black letters with the name of the construction company: Badrovik.

The wrecking ball slammed into the side of the bridge, directly over the concrete support pier jutting up from the muddy water below, knocking many of the zombies over the side while ripping up a good portion of the decking and rails.

"Run!" Liam shouted.

Pieces of the bridge shattered from the impact and flew all over the place. Many of the police had to run, too.

From behind a police car, he watched as the second hit sheared off the rest of the top deck and left a gaping hole where scores of the mindless horde tumbled in. The final few blows hit the pier on the near shore, and the middle of the bridge sagged into the water. The monsters could walk onto the span, but it was now a crude ramp guiding them down into the water. It was ugly, but it worked.

"Let's go back," he said as he tapped Victoria's arm.

A few zombies remained on the shortened near piece of the bridge but were quickly eliminated by the guys returning to the middle.

The remaining zombies on the far shore were visibly agitated at being denied the most direct route to their victims. Liam silently gave them all the finger as he returned to the river bank. Victoria copied him. That small act of mutual defiance made him feel much better. Tons better than when he did the same thing to that sports car driver back on Grandma's street.

Some of the zombies that tumbled down into the mud tried to climb the bank right below Liam and Victoria. Each of them managed to down a mud-covered man, but Liam had to dispatch the final woman because Victoria had to go reload. The young woman scampered up the steep riverbank and looked almost normal because the blood and gore was momentarily washed clean. His final thought was that she looked familiar—he'd seen her chasing the train somewhere along the way.

Or she reminded him of Victoria.

Whatever her origin, he lined up a shot and put one into her face. The zombie fell over backward and slid into the murky water.

"Last one is gone," he said when Victoria got back on the line.

"Thank God," she replied as she keyed the safety and then holstered her weapon.

He picked up the ammo and headed over to Grandma. She greeted them with a weak smile as they approached.

Zombies kept coming over the broken bridge for a bit, and some fell off the end and got swept downstream or sank to the bottom. Eventually, they seemed to know the battle had ended and that food was now far away, and they stopped trying to cross. Perhaps they sensed easier pickings at the power plant.

Dust and debris floated everywhere, and the remains of the bridge jutted out of the rushing water below. The current danced through the wreckage and made a metallic howl through the hollow girders wrapped around the pier. It almost drowned out the sounds of moaning—and screams—coming from the far side of the river.

He took the opportunity to speak to his two lady friends in a normal voice.

"I say we take a five-minute break before we try to move on to my house."

"That sounds heavenly," Grandma said. "I need to sit down again. Maybe a little longer than five minutes, I'm afraid." She motioned away from the police car.

After a short walk, they placed her on the ground up against the trunk of a large sycamore tree, then each took a seat flanking her. She held her rosary tightly to her chest, much as she had when he first saw her in bed several days ago.

Phil came up to join them.

Liam stood right back up. "Officer Phil, this is Mrs. Martinette Peters, my great-grandmother."

"Oh Liam, my mother was 'Mrs. Peters.' Please call me Marty," she said to Phil with returning good humor.

"Do you mind if I sit down and talk to your great-grandma alone for a few minutes?"

"Grandma, you OK with that?"

She gave him a silent thumbs-up sign.

Victoria got up to join him, and they walked off.

Liam looked back in the direction they'd come for a few minutes. Small groups of living people ran down the far bank and tried to swim across the river, sometimes trailed by zombies. Many swimmers made it into the arms of the waiting police rescuers, but some were unlucky and got snatched from below. Shooters on the police side picked off the zombies as best they could.

"I can't watch this," Victoria said with sadness.

"Me, either," he admitted. "And just to be clear, I'm never going to St. Louis again."

"Deal," she said as they walked away.

3

He strolled side by side with Victoria further down the railroad tracks, out of the immediate vicinity of all the police still around the bridge. It gave them some time to talk in peace. As they walked in the open, they each noticed the other with their hands on their guns.

"I guess we're veteran survivors now," she said. "We're tending our weapons like our lives depend on them, huh?"

Liam knew she was right, although he still didn't feel like a survivor. More like a lottery winner after seeing all the people who didn't make it. Where did that huge crowd at the Arch end up? He couldn't even imagine.

"So, what's next, partner?" She had a broad smile as she said it.

He gave her an exaggerated inspection from her feet up to her head. "Nope. You aren't the same girl I found lying on the grass. You've gotten over your guilt and have gone out of your way repeatedly to save me, Grandma, and who knows how many others. I think you've made up for any shortcomings you may have imagined for yourself when this whole plague-thing started."

Victoria winced at the word guilt but was quick to respond, "And you aren't the awkward boy who ran me over and practically hid behind your grandma. I've seen you do some amazing things the last couple of days that would have made most guys wet their pants in fear."

"Well, it may surprise you to know one thing that still makes me whiz in my drawers is asking a pretty girl out on a date."

She gave him a sideways glance but hid her reaction and kept walking and talking. "What are we planning to do next? Do we stay with the police we met at the Arch or strike out on our own with Grandma?"

He slowed down as he formulated a response. "I have to get to my parents' house. They don't live far from here. My dad is kind of an expert at survival and stuff, so finding him will help us a lot. Besides, I can show you all my dorky rock n' roll posters, my retainer, and my pocket protector."

They both laughed.

"My parents are in Denver. I don't know that I'll ever see them again." She said wistfully. "Maybe someday I'll try to get out there if things ever get back to normal. I don't think they ever will, though. I'm going to be stuck in your home state of Mizzer-y. No offense."

Her body language conveyed a sense of deep despair. Not that he blamed her, because she obviously missed her family. That would be a blow to just about anyone. He admitted to himself he would follow her to Denver if she asked him to go. He found himself suddenly unwilling to part from her, so he figured now was the time to cheer her up.

"I got you a present," he said with renewed energy.

It immediately brightened her face, bruises and all. "Really? When did you have time to go shopping? The stores are all closed." She gave him a painful-looking grin, but her smile didn't diminish.

"Well, I didn't buy it, but I didn't steal it. I think it was abandoned when I acquired it."

"I'm intrigued."

"Close your eyes and hold out your hands and I'll give it to you."

Her green eyes peered into his for a long moment, but she did as he asked, smiling happily. He pulled the item from under his untucked shirt on the non-gun side of his waistband. He gently put it in her hands and invited her to look at it.

It was a small, travel-size Bible.

"You were looking for one when we met, so naturally, I've been trying to find one every minute of the day since then." He smiled to be funny but admitted it was pretty near the truth.

Victoria was tongue-tied for several moments. He knew that was not an easy thing to do.

"Thank you, Liam." She said it in an almost reverent tone.

"It's only the New Testament. I'm working on getting you an Old Testament. I've got scouts roving the countryside as we speak." Again, he laughed at his joke to make himself feel less self-conscious that he was trying to do something nice for a girl. He also did his best to keep it casual and avoid any hint he wanted something from her in return. He just wanted to do a good deed for her that didn't involve shooting sick people in the head.

"Liam, it's absolutely perfect. Truly, this is the most thoughtful gift anyone has ever given me."

Whoa!

"Where did you get it?"

He hesitated for a moment, wondering if it would get him in trouble.

"I saw it in the train engine when we were up in there the first time, and I ran up there—"

Here comes full disclosure.

"—I ran up there that last time we were running from the zombies with Grandma. I figured it was the final chance I'd have to get it for you. I didn't know we'd live past the bridge. I felt it was worth the risk."

"Well, your feelings on this matter were completely wrong. Nothing is worth risking your life like that. Consider this a slap on the wrist." She took his hand and tapped it playfully. "But I do 100% appreciate this, and I'll treasure it." Her smile was infectious.

They strolled on the gravel road for another couple of minutes then turned around and walked back. They both agreed was unsafe to be so far from Grandma or lots of people with guns.

On the return trip, Victoria surprised him by holding his hand.

Totally worth it.

4

When they reached Grandma, she was done talking to Phil. He was giving her a big hug and let go as they got close. His face was flushed red; he'd been crying some more.

"I don't know how your grandma did it, but she answered my prayers. She really did. Thank you both. I, uh, need some time alone to process this. Please excuse me." He walked off, avoiding eye contact as he went away.

"Grandma, what did you tell Phil about his wife?"

"I don't know if I understand myself. Somehow, I knew to call out her name and the name of his daughter and share their desire to get us across. I had one more message, but that was just for Phil. I'm having trouble remembering how I knew it, though. *I'm old*, you understand," she said with an expression that conveyed "And that's all I'll say about it."

"Grandma, I think we just witnessed a miracle. There's no other way to explain how that happened."

"The Lord works in mysterious ways."

She said it with a big sigh, then settled herself against the tree as best she could.

He had to admit it was nearly providential the way he found Victoria from out of the tens of thousands of people in the Arch grounds. That she would turn out to be such a critical person in helping him and Grandma get out of the city. And the one big favor he did in return was helping her find a Bible, and that a Bible turned up where it did, when it did. Was it all a divine mystery, or just a lot of amazing coincidences?

He still had trouble believing in God, but he desperately wanted to believe in something. He craved the same fearless faith as these two women, though it struck him that even if he chose to go back to church, there might not be any churches left.

Maybe Victoria was put here to help me find my way spiritually?

His anger at being "dumped" at Grandma's house by his father had long since dissipated. If anything, his parents had done him a favor by putting the two of them together at precisely the same time the world fell apart. It almost seemed his dad anticipated what was going to happen. Almost like he knew.

Wait. What?

He dismissed it as absolute rubbish. His father was always spouting off—he would claim he was "discussing intelligently"—things like government conspiracies, media collusion, and military-industrial scheming. But those were just silly theories.

Right?

He was 99% sure it was all bunk. But the last 1% was elusive. His whole worldview fell apart if that rounding error couldn't be sorted. But his dad saw the government as the bad guy. Always. That mindset might be believable if he were reading one of his books on zombies, but in the real world it seemed completely insane. All his book learnin' did nothing to help him recognize real zombies until they got up in his face and tried to bite him—so he couldn't necessarily trust those books as his guide anymore. He looked over to the police back at the bridge—the people who just saved them—and realized *they* were the government. He wanted to believe they represented help, not some massive internet-fueled conspiracy. He resolved to keep his eyes open; to prove his father wrong. He wanted to toss out that last percent of doubt.

For now, he was 100% sure he had to come up with a plan for their next move. He still had a deep fear he'd end up being *that guy* and step on a rake at the worst possible time, but after all he'd just seen and done—and survived—that irrational fear was receding. He had to be smart in looking ahead.

He'd been guiding Grandma the past four days, and he admitted it would be nice to hand her off to Mom and Dad—the "professional" caretakers. But even if they arrived at his home this afternoon, he wanted to spend as much time as he could with her. After all, she wouldn't be around for much longer. Would she? He recalled a phrase she'd once said in her sleep. Something about living to be 120. Rather than fear of spending more time with her, he found anticipation. If things got back to normal and she lived that long, he'd celebrate each birthday with real zest. If things got back to normal ...

Thinking of his parents, he checked his phone for the millionth time to see if it had a signal. He tried not to get too bummed when he confirmed it was still offline. It appeared as if he'd have to physically walk to his house to talk to them.

Victoria bumped him with her hip to get his attention.

"Do you see our friend Hayes anywhere?"

He looked around. "I can't say that I have. I don't remember him being in the group crossing the bridge either, though I wasn't taking a head count. He could have made it across and then run off. Maybe he swam across. Or he could have made a run for it when we were on the other side. He seemed pissed these police officers wouldn't let him pass."

"If he made it, he'd probably still be yelling at the cops," she said with sarcasm.

"Hayes was an idiot trying to be something he wasn't. He would have been pretty stupid to run off alone just because he felt slighted. No one can survive this thing alone. Look at us. We just barely made it with a whole army helping us."

They let that percolate for a while. Grandma was fast asleep again, up against the tree. She had one arm over Liam's backpack, always protecting it.

Victoria reached for his hand and pulled him gently from the orbit of Grandma. She set down her new Bible next to Liam's pack, where it would be safe.

"Grandma's sleeping against a tree, just like you were when we met."

Victoria laughed, "Does that mean I have to smash her fingers, or are you the expert?"

"I still feel horrible I did that to you. I don't think she would like me if I let that happen to her."

Victoria smiled broadly; a lovely look, even if she wore too much coal dust and bruises for makeup. "I think she would forgive you, just like I did." She kept pulling him around the bulk of the massive tree trunk. "There's a question I want to ask you, now that it looks like we might live beyond this conversation."

The police and survivors near the bridge were blocked from their view. She let herself lean back against the bark, arms at her sides, and put her right foot partway up the trunk, so her leg was bent at an angle, pointing directly at him. Her dress hiked up a little, revealing her knee, and he saw it was jet black with coal residue. A testament to all they'd survived. Her posture, positioning, and proximity had him thoroughly confused.

Victoria compounded his confusion by asking, "I was wondering if you could tell me more about the shadow government?" Her effusive smile was contradictory to the serious question.

What in the hell does she mean?

Liam remembered their discussion earlier—it seemed like weeks ago—thousands of zombies ago—dozens of departed acquaintances ago—a train ride from hell ago. He told her if she said the code phrase, "shadow government," he would kiss her on the lips.

Clueless Liam from four days ago would never have figured it out.

Survivor Liam of today returned the wide smile and kissed the girl.

Maybe the Zombie Apocalypse won't be so bad.

In the moment, he felt alive. Energized. Steady in mind and body. Unafraid of going into the suburbs.

What's to fear, when you're traveling with two bad-ass heroines?

###

EPILOGUE

14 hours before the sirens.

Angie Jacobi was Marty Peters' live-in nurse. She finished her chores for her 104-year-old friend tonight so she could go pick up her granddaughter, Mary Beth, from work. The girl's mom had called and begged Angie for this favor. She knew better than to even think about arguing with her daughter-in-law.

"Thanks for picking me up, Grandma. There were some creepy people coming into the store today."

"I don't know why Cheryl kept the place open. Everyone should be staying home, now."

"Well, they sold out of shovels, hoes, machetes and all kinds of other yard junk. You should have seen how many chainsaws we moved. It would be great if they weren't using them for the wrong purpose. People said they needed them for fighting. How crazy is that?"

Angie took a moment to consider. "I'm sure they're just scared. We all are."

"You're scared? I've never seen you scared—about anything."

"This isn't *anything*. This is *something*."

"You believe all that internet stuff about zombies and the undead? I've seen videos from overseas on my phone, but it looks fake to me. Not half as real as those zombie TV shows."

Angie steered the car through the evening traffic. Mary Beth lived in the county with her family, but worked in a small corner hardware store near the double flat she shared with Marty. She spoke with her mother and they agreed to let the young woman stay in the city for the night. Tomorrow, Mary Beth would get a ride back home—and Angie resolved to put her foot down about her still working in the dangerous metropolis. She couldn't imagine why her mom insisted she go to work, and normally knew better than to question her about it, but this was different.

The young girl had access to the internet and what was happening overseas, but Angie had spent time volunteering in a local clinic. She held her tongue about the things she'd seen "disposed of" by social services, but she was sure the sickness wasn't just overseas...

"Once we get to Marty's, I want you to stay inside, do ya' hear? I have a bad feeling about the direction things are heading. There are even fewer cars than normal out tonight. Something is wrong."

Emergency vehicles skittered back and forth the entire journey, giving added weight to her belief something wasn't right. Several times during their trip through the city blocks, she had to pull over to allow the howling cars and trucks to get by. They came and went like angry bees.

"We're almost home, thank God." Angie was back to familiar territory. She drove in front of Marty's house on her way to park the car around back. "Do you want to get out here, dear? You can run in the front."

"Nah, I'll go around back, walk you in," Mary Beth said without looking up from her phone. "We have to stick together, ya' know?"

Angie nodded and continued down the block, turned right at the corner, and was just about to turn right into the alleyway when her car was bumped from behind.

"Oh dear!"

The collision was just a strong nudge, but it frightened her and she put on the gas rather than the brake, sending the car past the alley. She finally stomped the brakes and parked in the middle of the street, but then a black van pulled around her, so it blocked the front of her car. She put the car in park a few feet from the side of the van, bemused that they probably thought she was going to run from the scene. Next she wondered if she even had her registration and insurance information where she could get it.

With a tired sigh, she said, "Of all the things happening in this world. Now this. Can you check the glove box? My car registration should be—"

The accident caused Mary Beth to drop her phone next to the seat, and she spent a moment trying to retrieve it before turning her attention to the glove box.

"They are getting out," Angie said.

Mary Beth stopped her search to check it out.

The door of the van slid open in front of them. It was near-dark outside, so it was difficult to see the other party. The van parked so she had a view of the driver's seat through the opening created by the sliding door, but she couldn't make out the driver. Her headlights shone into the van but revealed nothing.

Angie reached for her glove box to help Mary Beth but got goosebumps for a reason she couldn't explain. The van wasn't just a normal van. There was a partition behind the front seat. It was a lattice of metalwork, like a dog catcher would use. No one got out of the van to exchange paperwork and the longer she waited, the more uneasy she felt.

"Grandma? Everything OK?" There was just a touch of heightened concern in the girl's voice. "Should we maybe leave?"

"Yeah, maybe—"

Before she could finish her thought, the front window of the van descended. A few seconds later, the passenger threw something at them. The heavy object banged against the glass of the windshield, though it didn't break.

"What the? Is that..."

"OH MY GOD!" Mary Beth shrieked.. "That's a person's foot!"

Something pushed the car from behind. Another van had come up to block them in.

Time stood still for Angie. A shape emerged from the emptiness of the cargo van. An arm appeared first. Then a head. The creature was large. The size of a very big man. In fact, as it emerged, she could see it *was* a very large man. He came out on all fours. Sniffing the air.

He jumped onto the hood of the car, apparently attracted to the bloody foot. He was a hulking thing, wearing nothing but bloody cargo pants and boots. His upper body was lacerated in many places, though the blood had long since dried. He was gaunt, but the muscles stuck out like some kind of sick medical dummy. The side of his neck was a festering explosion of veins and arteries, as if he had been assaulted by a ravaging wolf. His head was skeletal, with very little hair.

And the eyes...

Her granddaughter screamed.

Angie reached over to Mary Beth and covered the girl's mouth. "Shush. He's probably on drugs, or something. He looks crazy."

Mary Beth nodded, but had to put her own hands over her mouth to control her involuntary sobs.

"Listen. I need you to run to Marty's. I'm going to run the opposite direction and draw it away."

"It's looking—at me," Mary Beth whimpered.

"No, it's looking at the foot. You have to do as I say."

The girl shook her head vigorously in the negative. "I ... I don't know where she lives. These houses all look the same from the back."

"Run that way," Angie said while pointing backward. "Find her house from the front."

It was the best plan she could summon. She'd been in other confrontations with belligerent patients over the years, and distraction was the order of the day until help could arrive. All she had to do was keep it away from Mary Beth, so she could call the cops. With a final look at her granddaughter, she pulled her keys from the ignition.

The man on the hood slid a bit but didn't fall off.

"I love you," she said with despair. "You'll be fine, OK? Just run when the man leaves."

"I-I love you, too," the girl replied.

Angie opened her door and ran like hell. As fast as a woman of 58 years in decent shape could run in a pair of cheap tennis shoes. She left her car door open, assuming the thing would follow her. It did jump to the street as if to pursue, but it stood up and turned to Mary Beth instead. Angie realized her plan was doomed.

"RUN!" Angie screamed.

The guy turned back to her, unleashed an open-mouthed howl, but then jumped in the car. Mary Beth opened her door but didn't get out, so the sick guy crawled in next to her. Not knowing what to do, Angie ran around the rear van, and up to Mary Beth's open door. The girl screamed in mortal terror the entire time.

Angie had heard stories of exotic drugs making people do crazy things like cutting off their own noses or hands, but this was beyond her imagination.

So much blood.

Angie tried to pull the girl from the blood-splashed face of the man, but her seat belt was still hooked.

"Mary Beth, your seatbelt!"

"Grandma, help," Mary Beth wheezed, like she was out of breath.

Angie moved to get a better look at the man. He was now in full sight, tearing into the soft flesh of the teen's side with a bloody mouth. To get to the seatbelt release she'd have to reach between the man and her granddaughter's body. It was impossible.

"Oh God, please help me," Angie cried out.

She needed a weapon and checked the backseat for anything useful, but it was empty. She turned forward and saw the severed foot on her windshield, nearest the passenger side. She reached for it and brought it back to the gap of the door, ignoring the disgusting feel in her hands. Angie swung it as an awkward club against the man's head. He looked up and snapped several times at her. She tried to swing the foot again, but it was too slippery. It fell uselessly to the floorboard in front of her dying granddaughter.

The girl stopped moving.

This drugged out monster of a man had just killed her lovely Mary Beth. Angie looked at her through the tears in her eyes as the man continued to press his face into her bloody side. Angie took a step back and saw the big picture. The person or persons in the van were making no effort to help. *They* had done this intentionally.

When she looked back inside, the unnatural man was already facing her. She took a few more steps backward and tried to close the door. The man more or less slithered over Mary Beth and fell out of the doorway so he could crouch on the pavement. He looked at her with empty eye sockets. Angie felt a wave of despair envelope her. She stumbled and fell to her backside. She had to resort to crawling backward with her elbows ...

The sicko jumped on top of her, covering her with Mary Beth's blood.

"Oh God, no! HELP!" She screamed as loud as she could—as if finally realizing there was a need for it—willing someone in the neighborhood to rescue her.

Pinned to the ground, her last thought was of the girl in the front seat. How she failed her so completely. How quickly this all happened.

She felt the teeth go into her neck. She struggled as best she could, but the fear was absolute. She went from panicked resistance to abject surrender in moments. Her vision floundered, and her breathing became labored. She closed her eyes, asking God for forgiveness.

An eternity later, a man with a red baseball cap came into her field of vision. He shot something at the drugged-out man on top of her, and he ran away.

"Are you OK?" the rescuer said in slow motion.

"I don't know," she tried to respond. "Where is Mary Beth?" Her voice was just a whisper because she couldn't catch her breath.

"She went to your house," red hat said. "Run to her!"

Then he was gone.

Angie got up, teetering on the edge of awareness. Mary Beth wasn't in her front seat.

She's at my house?

Angie walked up the alley; compelled to reach the safety of her home. She looked down at her feet, but the sight of those shoes plodding ahead, one after the other, made her stomach churn. She tried to keep her head up, but that was painful. Her neck burned on the left side, so she pressed her hand to stop potential bleeding like a good nurse.

Angie went through the rear gate, and stumbled up the walkway through her backyard, and into the narrow channel between her home and the next. She held her arms out and could almost touch both brick walls, which for some reason made her giggle uncontrollably.

She rounded the corner of the house and moved up the ramp to the pair of front doors. Marty's entry was on the right. She looked at it for a long time. Marty could call for help. Marty could—

The cloudiness in her brain wouldn't allow her to complete the thought.

"I must get home to Mary Beth." Returning home was *important*. She desired it the most.

She shuffled over to her own front door, to the left of Marty's. It was unlocked but was stuck—as usual. She gave it a good shove and it pivoted inward for her. She swung it shut. The steep wooden stairway loomed above. The bright lights in the entryway and on the stairwell hardly registered.

"I'm coming, Mary Beth."

She held on to the banister as she took each step one at a time. She pulled herself with her hands as much as she used her legs. Several times, she became so dizzy she nearly let herself go. She giggled again, this time at the irony of surviving a grievous neck wound, only to die falling down some lousy steps. A pause was necessary at the top. She fell to her knees, depositing blood on the floor.

"I'll clean that up later, don't worry, Marty."

Angie dragged herself to her door a few feet from the steps. The handle was a convenience to help her regain her feet. It was unlocked, and she tumbled through.

"I'm home, Mary Beth. I'm just going to lie down for a bit, OK?" She wobbled in the direction of her bedroom.

I'll just put myself to bed. I'll feel better in the morning.

###

ACKNOWLEDGMENTS

First and foremost, I want to recognize my own 104-year-old grandmother for being the inspiration for the character of Marty. Her passing was also the driving force behind my desire to write this book. I had over 40 years to benefit from her presence in my life, and she became my archetype for the strengths and weaknesses of someone so advanced in age. I regret to say she passed away in 2014 after living an incredibly long and healthy life. I give my real grandma a single mention in this book, when Al tells Marty that in a parallel universe she "passed away peacefully in her sleep today." That is my homage to her. The rest of the book is written in the character of Marty, who only shares broad strokes with my late grandmother. I couldn't hope to write faithfully in the voice of a real person.

However, I tried to write Marty with my grandmother's physical abilities as I remember them, because I didn't want a superhero character that didn't ring true. Could she have walked a couple miles in the June heat, with a young man helping her? Could she have survived stumbling away from Angie? Could she endure lying on the bed of a flatcar for several hours? On a normal day, the answer might be no. No woman of 104 goes out and tries these things. Yet, if the world was ending, and she had to do those things to protect her family—absolutely she would have tried. In that light, Marty shares many of the best qualities of my real grandma, though I'm pretty certain mine never lassoed anything.

Because of who she was and how she influenced the character of Marty—and my own upbringing—the trajectory of the entire *Sirens of the Zombie Apocalypse* series has a more positive and uplifting direction than it might have otherwise. Liam must remain guarded with so much evil in the zombie world, but he learns to search for the positive in mankind, and in himself. In that sense, I can relate to his character, having existed in a world containing such an upbeat person as my own "Grandma Marty." His spiritual growth throughout these books would have made my real grandma very happy.

On reflection, it seems almost sacrilegious to put the idea of my sweet grandma into what is essentially a piece of horror fiction, but I would find it hard to write her into any other genre. If she had her druthers, she'd probably say I shouldn't use her as the basis for anything at all, and instead write about someone more interesting. Others in our family might suggest a grandmotherly character should only exist in a friendly story akin to Ray Bradbury's *Dandelion Wine*, in which the grandparents are presented in a much more mundane setting. But that wouldn't be me. I think people become extraordinary when faced with great challenges. Perhaps it means I just don't have a developed sense of drama, as it appears I need the entire world to collapse and zombies to pour forth before I can take a snapshot of a person and characterize them inside that world. I'm okay with that. I think she would be as well.

Most of my research for this book consisted of me walking around St. Louis city and county, where I live. I spent some of my youth pounding pavement through the red brick flats of South City. I've spent countless hours on the highways of this metropolis. I've visited the Gateway Arch numerous times, though I've never been invited to walk the steps to the top. However, if you take the trams up and down the Arch there are windows inside those cars so you can see the metal staircase from time-to-time. Other locations throughout my books are places I've been, though some of the details were edited to keep the story moving along. The area underneath the Arch is surprisingly complex in real life, so I had to simplify. There are air vents for the underground museum up on the surface, though I admit I have no idea if any go into the railroad tunnels. I'd like to think they do. You never know when one might come in handy.

General Patton is one of my personal heroes. You may see his influence in several of my novels. In this book Liam loosely quotes him. "A good plan, violently executed now, is better than a perfect plan next week." This is very apropos for writing a novel. I started writing this story in the summer of 2014. The first draft was done in December 2014. And the edits...oh my. To let my beta readers off the hook, any errors remaining in the manuscript are completely and utterly my own.

Finally, I want to thank my family for believing in this project. It took just over a year to turn this glimmer of an idea into a nice-sized novel, and it wouldn't have been possible without a supportive family.

E.E. Isherwood

ABOUT THE AUTHOR

E.E. Isherwood is the New York Times and USA Today bestselling author of the *Sirens of the Zombie Apocalypse* series. His long-time fascination with the end of the world blossomed decades ago after reading the 1949 classic *Earth Abides.* Zombies allow him to observe how society breaks down in the face of such withering calamity.

Isherwood lives in St. Louis, Missouri with his wife and family. He stays deep in a bunker with steepled fingers, always awaiting the arrival of the first wave of zombies.

Find him online at www.zombiebooks.net.

BOOKS BY E.E. ISHERWOOD

E.E. Isherwood currently has six books in the *Sirens of the Zombie Apocalypse* universe. Visit his website at www.zombiebooks.net to be informed when future titles are launched.

The *Sirens of the Zombie Apocalypse* series

Since the Sirens

Siren Songs

Stop the Sirens

Last Fight of the Valkyries

Zombies vs. Polar Bears

Zombies Ever After

Book 1: *Since the Sirens*

When fifteen-year-old Liam goes to stay with his ancient great-grandmother for the summer, he immediately becomes bored around the frail and elderly woman. He spends most of his time at the library texting friends or reading dark novels. But one morning stroll changes everything as the Zombie Apocalypse unloads itself directly into his life. Now he and his 104-year-old guardian must survive the journey out of the collapsing city of St. Louis while zombies, plague, and desperate survivors swirl around them.

Book 2: *Siren Songs*

After escaping the chaos of the collapsing city, teens Liam and Victoria are faced with a difficult choice. Do they try to find Liam's parents or defend their suburban home from refugees and the infected? They find new allies to hold things together, even as the government appears increasingly impotent in the face of a mutating virus. And why is a representative of the CDC trying to enlist Liam's 104-year-old grandma to his cause?